THE FINAL SHOT

Charles Holborne Legal Thrillers

Book Seven

Simon Michael

Also in the Charles Holborne Series

The Brief

An Honest Man

The Lighterman

Corrupted

The Waxwork Corpse

Force of Evil

Nothing But The Truth

THE FINAL SHOT

Published by Sapere Books.

20 Windermere Drive, Leeds, England, LS17 7UZ,
United Kingdom

saperebooks.com

ISBN: 978-1-80055-491-7

To Elaine, my Sally.

ACKNOWLEDGEMENTS

I owe a great debt to John Pearson for his two books, *The Profession of Violence: The Rise and Fall of the Kray Twins* and *Notorious: The Immortal Legend of the Kray Twins.* I recommend both to readers keen to learn the Krays' true story, and I thank Mr Pearson for his painstaking research, from which I have shamelessly borrowed.

Similarly, I have relied on *Nipper Read: The Man Who Nicked the Krays,* written by Leonard "Nipper" Read himself, with James Morton. Very sadly Mr Read died in April 2020 of Covid-19. He was truly a police legend and, if it is possible to know a man by what he writes, a very decent bloke.

As always I have to thank my beta readers for their thoughts, corrections and eagle-eyed attention to detail, including Neil Cameron, Debbie Jacobs, Carly Jordan, Steve Witt and Karen Crawford. The opinion of these last two, both Americans, on the very English matters related herein, was particularly useful.

I remain very grateful to Amy Durant, Caoimhe O'Brien, Richard Simpson and the rest of the Sapere Books team for their patient support.

Last, and never least, my thanks go to Elaine for everything else. A lovely reviewer recently expressed the hope that I had "found my Sally". I have.

PROLOGUE

THEY THINK IT'S ALL OVER…

It takes six bullets to finish off Frank Marshall.

Even then the shooters, two of his best friends, aren't sure it's enough.

He'd kissed Louise goodbye, passionately, just inside the front door. The clinch went on so long that Gerry and Vince, sharing a glance, became worried he'd take her back to the bedroom for another session. Vince glanced at his watch and raised his eyebrows. Although the van had arrived later than planned, it was still only just after 6 a.m., so Gerry, in charge, shook his head.

Eventually Marshall let the girl go. She must have been nervous, but she continued to play her part well. She looked up into the giant's soft brown eyes, reached up with one hand to stroke his face and gave him one last soft kiss on the mouth.

'Bye-bye, lover,' she said. 'It's been fun.'

Gerry nodded to Vince, who opened the front door and looked out onto the quiet street. Horn Lane, Acton, in west London, was usually a busy thoroughfare, a bus route passing a mixture of shops, small blocks of flats and semi-detached houses, but at that time of the day it was deserted, still asleep. The bedroom windows on the opposite side of the road were curtained, many with flags. Union Jacks were well represented but the majority were the flag of England, St George's red cross on its white background. Several of the cars parked silently on the street displayed football pennants and scarves in the same colours. People would soon start waking up to the biggest day English football had ever known.

Vince turned and beckoned.

Before stepping out, Marshall checked his inside jacket pocket, for the twentieth time that morning. He pulled out a ticket, holding it delicately between his huge fingers so as not to mark it, and read it yet again: *Empire Stadium Wembley, East Standing Enclosure, Entrance 10, World Championship, Final Tie, 1966.* Satisfied, he slid it carefully back into his pocket, tapping his chest twice to make sure he could feel it through his jacket.

Only then did Marshall allow Gerry, waiting patiently beside him with Marshall's bag in hand, to escort him across the pavement to the back of the nondescript van idling by the kerb. The rear door opened from inside, causing a slight hitch in Marshall's stride, as if he hadn't expected someone to be inside the rear compartment, but he nonetheless permitted himself to be guided in, bending low and crawling forward on his knees. He cast a glance behind him, hoping to wave farewell to Louise, but the door had already closed behind her.

Marshall turned and shuffled on his backside towards the front of the van, positioning himself with his back to the wooden bulkhead separating him from the driver and front passenger. He was too big for this form of conveyance, but he understood the need. The thought went through his head that he was going to be pretty stiff by the time it was safe to let him out at Wembley Stadium, but he was so excited he pushed the concern away. His old friend, Ronnie Kray, had finally come through, and his new life was about to begin. He was also looking forward to seeing Gracie and the boys, although, in truth, they featured rather lower in his priorities than either the football or Ronnie Kray. Nonetheless, he was assured they'd be there, waiting for him.

Gerry threw Marshall's bag into the back and shuffled up as well, sitting on the wheel casing behind the driver, and the third man, the one who had opened the door to them, positioned himself on the wheel casing opposite. Only then did Marshall realise that it was his old friend from HM Prison Wakefield, Cliff Stewart.

'Hello, Cliff,' he said, surprised and pleased. 'Long time, no see.'

'All right, Frank?' replied the other.

Marshall felt a wave of gratitude to Ronnie for laying on good mates to accompany him. Most of the day was going to be spent in the van, and the three of them would be able to chat, maybe even play some cards if there was enough light.

Marshall heard the front passenger door open and close as Vince got in. Gerry knocked on the panelling and the van pulled away.

They had travelled no more than fifty yards or so when Gerry reached inside his coat, pulling out a silenced automatic. Marshall saw it and reacted immediately. He launched himself across the van towards Gerry but simultaneously felt a thunderous blow to his right shoulder and knew he'd been shot by Cliff. The impact affected his trajectory and he missed Gerry, landing on his side on the floor of the van. Gerry's automatic fired twice further, the bullets entering Marshall's abdomen. An awful smell filled the small space. Marshall grunted and flopped onto his back. Cliff fired a second and more precise shot into Marshall's exposed chest.

Marshall lay still, his eyes closed and his freshly ironed shirt blossoming dark red. Gerry flipped Marshall's jacket open and retrieved the football ticket from the breast pocket. Perfectly positioned, right at its centre, was a bullet hole. Cliff frowned at Gerry in puzzlement.

'Souvenir,' explained Gerry, wiping blood off the ticket onto the shoulder of Marshall's jacket.

Perhaps it was that movement or perhaps it was a coincidence, but then, to the astonishment of his friends, Marshall lifted his head, so Gerry shot him twice more in quick succession, behind his ear. Marshall flopped back to the floor.

It was over.

CHAPTER ONE

Six months earlier

Charles Holborne and Sally Fisher are finishing their evening meal in the kitchen of Charles's freshly renovated house on Wren Street. They've been back together since Christmas and are beginning to get used to their new routine. It's both familiar and different.

The house, located between Gray's Inn and King's Cross, enables them to walk in twenty minutes to the centre of legal London, the Temple, where they both work. If Charles jogs, as he likes to when he and Sally go in at different times, it takes ten minutes. That proximity has added two valuable hours to Sally's working day, freeing her from the commute to and from her mother's cramped two-up two-down terraced house in Romford, where she grew up and to which she returned when she walked out on Charles the previous year.

Sally loves the house, its four floors, high-ceilinged rooms and ornate plasterwork, and the street, all faded Georgian elegance. She has spent the last couple of months finishing off the decorating and diplomatically re-doing some of Charles's less successful handiwork. This room, the kitchen, is her favourite. She had feared that, situated in a half-basement, it would be too dark, but the new extension is mostly glass, which makes the space bright and airy. Before she moved in, Charles ripped out all the fetid carpets, stripped and varnished the beautiful oak floorboards, replaced the tall wooden shutters — which were so rotten they fell off the hinges — with salvaged replacements and replaced the 1930s kitchen. It now looks modern but still feels welcoming, the heart of a family home. Sally's been imagining happy family meals at the long table; maybe even a house-warming party, although the problems surrounding the potential guest list have put her off raising the idea with Charles.

The new living arrangements have transformed Charles's life too. Before the move, this was his pattern: work late, often until midnight, in the Temple; walk across Fleet Street to his apartment less than a hundred yards away; and slump at the kitchen table with a bottle of scotch and whatever food could be thrown together. One or two evenings a week: jog to the sweaty boxing gym in Kennington to thrash a heavy punchbag or, if anyone was willing, a sparring partner. Weekends: usually more work, but if the weather was inviting, a walk into the East End to meet old faces at old watering holes, maybe Blooms in Aldgate or the Bagel Bakery in Brick Lane; occasionally a late night at Ronnie Scott's or another Soho venue for jazz or other excitement.

All that has changed. Aided by a fortuitous month-long run of cases in London, he has managed to return home every evening by seven o'clock. Tonight he got in before Sally and had a meal on the table for them within five minutes of her unloading her bags and taking off her coat.

No midnight oil burned in Chambers.

No solo jaunts up West.

No late-night drinking.

Charles Holborne is a reformed man.

To an outsider, Charles and Sally seem like any young couple embarking on life's romantic dream, decorating, shopping and cooking together, and sharing a lot of time in bed.

But that's only half the story. Both are acutely aware that their last ill-fated attempt at cohabitation ended after only six months, due to Charles's failure to commit to a lifestyle that involved Sally and then, as they drifted apart and stopped communicating, his short-lived and murderous affair with a young American starlet.

This half of the story has been told and retold. Everything that could be said about it, every charge on Sally's indictment and every scintilla of mitigation available to Charles, have been rehearsed and re-rehearsed. After several months apart; several months of Charles's entreaties and, finally, a softening of Sally's heart, she pronounced her verdict: she would give him another chance. His last.

Now they both wait to see if he's capable of taking it. Despite early promising signs, she is not yet convinced and, in common with many of his clients, Charles remains on probation.

In summary, while physically and practically they have returned to living together, emotionally Sally still occupies the spare room.

Charles collects the plates and stands.

'Well, when's the fashion show?' he asks, nodding towards the new shopping bags at the end of the table, which Sally has yet to mention.

'It's only a coupla things,' says Sally, defensively.

'Doesn't bother me,' he says, running the water until it gets hot. 'You can spend your money how you like. But do I get to see them, or is it a surprise? What is "Foale and Tuffin" anyway?' he asks, nodding towards the bags. 'Sounds like a racehorse.'

Sally laughs and shakes her head. 'Are you serious? You've not heard of 'em?'

'New shop chain?' he hazards.

'They're famous! They're the two fashion designers who opened a shop off Carnaby Street. Both English and both *women*. It's a first.'

'Oh, right. Come on, then, let's see.'

Sally rises, swings the two bags over her shoulder and Charles listens to her running upstairs. A couple of minutes later she returns. She's changed out of her work suit and wears a simple sleeveless mini-dress in lemon with orange hip pockets in the shape of a large capital "D".

'Well?' she asks, executing a pirouette.

Charles looks over from the sink, his hands immersed in soapy water. His eyes travel up her slim stockinged legs, appraising. 'It's very pretty. But isn't it a bit … well, short?'

'No,' she says firmly, 'not at all. Do you like it? For spring, that is?'

'I do,' he says.

'Wait there. I'll show you the other one.'

She races back upstairs and reappears after another few minutes. This time she is wearing a polo-necked jersey mini-dress, black and very close-fitting.

'Wow,' exclaims Charles softly. 'But can you wear that in public? It's … you can see everything.'

'I was a bit unsure about it. The models are all flat-chested, straight up and down, and I'm a bit bigger —' she cups her breasts — 'on top.'

'For God's sake, don't wear that to my parents'. Dad'll have a stroke. But you do look amazing. Like Diana Rigg in *The Avengers*.'

'Ooh, that's an idea!' she says, and she skips out of the room. She reappears a few seconds later wearing Charles's old flying jacket. 'Emma Peel!' she announces.

'It's too big for you, and it's falling apart,' he points out.

Her nose wrinkles and she sniffs the collar. 'Plus it smells like a dead sheep,' she adds. 'But in principle? If I could find something like it? Does it work?'

'It works.'

She sees his frown. 'But?' she prompts.

'Nothing.'

She comes over to him. 'What?'

He shrugs. 'You'll be fighting them off,' he says miserably.

She pulls him towards her and he realises from the movement that she's taken off her bra.

'The only person conscious of the age difference is you,' she says, divining, again, what is worrying Charles. Charles will be forty at the end of the year; Sally is only twenty-five. 'You look young for your age, you know you do. Although it wouldn't hurt to freshen up *your* wardrobe a bit. You've been wearing the same slacks and tweed jackets since I met you and…'

'What?'

'Well, your clothes are a bit … middle-aged —' she sees his horrified face and realises she's pressed the tender spot again — 'which you aren't, of course —'

'Thirty-nine isn't middle-aged!' he protests, genuinely stung.

'No, no, you're right,' she backtracks swiftly. 'But … well, you've seen what people are wearing now. There's some great stuff down Carnaby Street, and you'd look so good in it! Anyway,' she finishes hurriedly, forestalling any further response from Charles, 'I'll get out of this and dry up.' She points to the washed pots and pans. 'Leave them for me.'

'No, it's fine. I'll do it.'

'Is your plea ready?'

'More or less,' he prevaricates, not looking up.

She pauses and shakes her head. 'Look, Mr 'Olborne, sir,' she says, rather unsubtly recalling their former work relationship, 'I geddit, okay? There ain't a barrister in England who don't have to work some evenings. If you've got work to do, go and do it!'

Sally is an East End girl who left school at sixteen. Although she has considerably smartened up her act since then, when under stress or alone with Charles — with whom she can be herself — her native Cockney still shows through the veneer.

'It's fine,' he insists. 'I can go in early.'

She approaches him and reaches up to turn his face to hers. 'Charlie, listen to me. I won't have you regularly creeping in at midnight, but this —' she indicates with a sweep of her hand the oak trestle table bearing the residue of their meal — 'it's completely different. You're home early, we're eating together … this is what I wanted.'

'Good.'

'And,' she persists, 'that's what makes it okay if you *do* have to work in the evenings every now and then.'

'I promised, Sal, and I meant it.'

She examines his olive complexion and curly black hair. His expression is open, tentative; he reminds her of a little boy who's been punished and is anxious to be good. He pulls the sink plug.

'You've still gotta do your job,' she says. 'You can't afford to fuck up some case to prove how much you love me.'

'It won't take a sec to do these.'

She shoves him away from the sink, both hands on his chest, no easy feat for a five-foot woman of barely half his weight. Charles, a former heavyweight, is ten inches taller and six stones heavier than she.

'Go and work!' she orders. 'The sooner you start, the sooner we'll be in bed. Bed? Remember?' She does a little shimmy, all moving parts, and gets the response for which she hoped.

He grins and concedes. 'Fair enough,' he says, drying his hands. 'What're you going to do?'

'When I'm finished here I want to call Sonia.'

Sonia, Charles's sister-in-law, and his brother, David, produced the Horowitzes' first grandchild a week earlier, a boy named Jonathan. His circumcision, due in two days' time, is causing Sonia to lose sleep. Sally, who isn't Jewish, thinks the practice barbaric, but she likes Sonia and is being supportive.

'She'll appreciate that,' says Charles.

'So go and finish your prep, and maybe we'll have some of the evening left.'

CHAPTER TWO

Miss Barbara McIntyre, Chambers' senior clerk, shakes her head and tuts as thunderous footsteps approach the clerk's room. She knows exactly who is about to burst in. Of her forty or so guvnors it is only Mr Holborne who always takes the stairs at a run, two or even three at a time, and his fifteen stones landing heavily on the ancient timbers of the Dickensian staircase generate thuds that can be heard throughout Chambers.

'One of these days,' she mutters, 'he's going to go straight through the floor to the basement.'

The junior clerks, Jennie and Jeremy, known throughout the Temple compendiously as "JJ", share a private smile.

Sure enough, the door swings open and Charles breezes in. 'Morning everyone,' he says cheerfully, striding directly to the pigeonholes. He flicks through the post awaiting him, humming.

The staff have all noticed the improvement in Mr Holborne's mood since Christmas. Chrissie, the cleaner, reported confidentially to Barbara that she's no longer having to dispose of an empty bottle of scotch from his desk every second or third night.

Charles and Sally's relationship is supposed to be a secret. Accordingly, courtesy of the dark arts of the clerks' rumour mill, it is common knowledge and everyone in the Temple is talking about it.

Relationships between clerks and guvnors, even from separate chambers, are considered improper. For a clerk and a barrister actually to live together is akin to the son of a peer of the realm eloping with a below-stairs maid. Many of Charles's gossipy colleagues are scandalised, but then, as they love to mutter to one another over afternoon tea, what can you expect? He's a working-class thug with a past, whose acquaintances include thieves, con artists and murderers. Everyone's heard about his relationship with the Kray twins. It's no surprise that a man like that is shacked up with his ex-clerk. Frankly, they say, he has no place in their honourable profession, and "something should be done about it". To date, nothing has been done about it because, for all their outraged disapproval, Charles Holborne is a top-notch advocate and a rainmaker; very few in Chambers have not benefited from the work he personally generates.

By contrast, the junior clerks are pleased. They all know Sally, who is little older than they, and they like and admire her. She is the youngest senior clerk in the Temple. Where she has gone they hope to follow, and so far as they're concerned, Mr Holborne's a decent bloke, almost one of them; so why not?

Barbara's attitude is more nuanced and proceeds from a different starting point. Brought up in a strict Presbyterian Kirk in Edinburgh, it is the morality of the situation which most disturbs her. She disapproves of sex before marriage; she disapproves even more of people living "in sin"; she disapproves most particularly when the sinners concerned are one of her guvnors and his former clerk. She fears it will give Chambers a sleazy reputation.

On the other hand, her Christian compassion provides the jumping off point for her dispensation. She saw at first-hand how utterly miserable Charles was following his breakup with Sally, and her heart went out to him. Always the odd man out in Chambers, he had few friends there on whom to rely, and she was dimly aware of some sort of family rift, so little succour was to be had there either. He was lonely and not looking after himself, missing meals and smoking and drinking far too much. It was a shock to see a man built like a brick barn, someone who normally exuded such rude vitality, looking so peely-wally.

Furthermore, she reminded herself, it was unfair to judge Mr Holborne by the same standards as her other guvnors. Despite the accent and polished manners acquired in the RAF and as a scholarship student at Cambridge, above stairs/below stairs distinctions were probably meaningless to him; the poorer classes just didn't live by the same standards.

Finally, and despite the fact that clerks are not supposed to have favourites, she nurtured something of a soft spot for Mr Holborne, which couldn't be said of many of her more privileged, entitled guvnors. Charles Holborne, né Horowitz, pulled himself up by his bootstraps from the most unpromising of beginnings, and for a Scot brought up to value hard work and self-reliance, that counted for a lot. Furthermore, he was a team player, always prepared to help out the clerks with a late return or to take time to explain a difficult point of law to a pupil. He was also one of the few barristers in Chambers who regularly took pro bono work. He had first-hand experience of being at the bottom of the pile, and he'd never forgotten it.

So Barbara has put aside her personal distaste for Mr Holborne's unsuitable living arrangements and tries to ignore the persistent sniping of some of her other guvnors. As Charles's mental state improved she increased his workflow and now, several weeks later, she can see one of her star performers returning to the top of his game.

'You've been asked to do an urgent conference at two this afternoon, sir,' she says to Charles. 'Do you want me to accept?'

'What is it?'

Barbara indicates an open set of papers on her desk, including a newspaper. Charles goes to her desk and looks at the headline to which she is pointing.

'The Sharpe trial? Didn't it finish last week?'

'It did. They want you to advise on appeal.'

'Me? What happened to Firth and Robinson from 7 KBW?'

'Sacked. The Instructions say you only have three days left to file Notice, if you advise in favour, hence the hurry. Will you finish at the Bailey in time?'

'If I get on promptly. I'll see if I can schmooze the clerk.'

'Good. The papers'll be on your desk when you get back.'

Charles turns to leave.

'Also, if you have a minute before you go, sir, I need a quiet word,' says Barbara, pushing back her chair from her desk. 'Upstairs?'

'Sure,' replies Charles.

Charles follows Barbara's swishing tweed skirts and lavender water up to the second floor. She opens the door to the corridor on the other side of the landing and leads the way to Charles's own room. She knocks and, receiving no reply, enters. Charles follows. The desk opposite his, belonging to his former pupil Peter Bateman, is loaded with briefs awaiting attention but Bateman is absent.

Charles drops his court robes onto the frayed leather inlay of his desk. As always, he glances at the Thames, judging the tide and the wind.

'What's up?' he asks, transferring his attention to the tall Scotswoman.

Barbara closes the door carefully behind her. When she speaks, it is with a lowered voice.

'The pupillage committee decided we'd enough work to warrant two first-six pupillages this year.'

'I know. Good news, isn't it?'

'Aye, it is. But we have a problem. One of the new pupils was allocated to Mr Bradley.'

Charles frowns. 'Oh dear. Whose idea was that?'

'His.'

'Really?'

Marcus Bradley, a sneering, supercilious snob of a barrister, delights in taunting others. He gets away with it because, as Charles is forced to admit, he has a brilliant mind and is widely tipped for silk followed shortly by the High Court bench. Nonetheless, Bradley is so unpleasant that he is the most reviled barrister in London. He and Charles have squared up in court, in Temple committees and on one occasion, remembered fondly by Charles, physically.

'Completely confidential, sir?' says Barbara. Charles nods. 'Mr Bradley applied for silk.'

'Really? I'd say that was a tad early, even for someone of Mr Bradley's skills. But I'm ahead of you. Queen's Counsel can't have pupils —'

Barbara interrupts him. 'He didn't get it.'

'What? The brilliant Marcus Bradley, knocked back? Oh, the poor chap,' grins Charles, the *schadenfreude* so heavy it seems to drop him into his seat. 'So he's not going to be Marcus Bradley QC after all. At least, not this year. How dreadful for him.'

'Now, now, sir,' chides Barbara, but she permits herself a small smile.

Everyone in Chambers knows how Bradley used to torment Charles incessantly about his working-class background, his Jewish heritage and his supposed criminal connections.

Barbara wonders again why suddenly, and without explanation, it all stopped.

'Turns out he gave Mr Justice Hodgson as a referee. I'd have warned him not to, but he applied without telling anyone.'

'Why?'

Barbara does something Charles has never seen before, which is to draw up a chair from the side of the room and sit at his desk, not in front of him, as a client might, but to the side. It feels oddly intimate, as if she were about to confide some gossip to a friend.

'It appears he was unaware of the extent to which he offended the judge during last year's libel trial. There were several high points,' she continues, her voice lowered even further, 'but one of the best was: *"If your Lordship would perhaps address what he is, no doubt, pleased to call his mind, to Section 2…"*' For her impersonation she drops her Edinburgh accent and does a passable upper-class English.

Charles laughs loudly. 'Ha! Great career move. But, if he didn't get silk, he can still be a pupilmaster.'

'Well … yes and no. The pupil started with him three weeks ago. It's no' gone well.'

'Is the pupil too dim for his elevated intellect?'

'Just the contrary, actually. She's a Rhodes scholar with a law degree from Harvard. And before you suggest other reasons, such as class, her father's a US diplomat with a family tree in New England dating from the Pilgrim Fathers. So it's not snobbery either.'

'What, then? Ah, the clue's in "she", I take it?'

'Correct. Having now met her, he doesnae want a female pupil and he doesnae want … someone of her colour.'

'She's Black?'

'I'm not sure of the proper categorisation. Her father's white and her mother's Black. Brazilian, apparently. They met when he was posted to Rio de Janeiro.'

'I've never heard Bradley express colour prejudice before,' muses Charles. 'He's usually equally vile to everyone.'

'Perhaps it's something to do with the fact that he was convinced he'd get silk, and looking at the back of this girl's head is a constant reminder of his failure,' suggests Barbara.

'And hubris.'

Barbara lowers her eyes momentarily, attempting unsuccessfully to disguise her agreement. 'Anyway, he's been making her life a complete misery. He has her sitting facing a corner of the room and won't let her leave her desk or even speak. Last week she waited two hours to ask permission to go to the library.'

'Poor girl.'

'I know your name's not on the approved list, but your Inn would certainly add it, if you asked. I respect your wish not to have a pupil, and of course it's entirely your decision —'

Charles interrupts. 'I'll take her. She can start tomorrow. In fact, she can start right now.'

Barbara smiles. 'She's in court with Mr Bradley until this afternoon, but I'll give her the good news when she returns. Thank you.' She stands and replaces the chair.

'What's this young lady's name?' asks Charles, picking up his things.

'Miss Hudson. Maria Hudson.'

CHAPTER THREE

There is no sign of Miss Hudson that afternoon, and Charles suspects that Bradley's case must have run on. It's just as well, because the papers in *R versus Sharpe* are two inches thick. He barely has time to skim them before Jeremy is knocking on his door and showing the clients in. Charles stands.

'Your con, sir,' says the young clerk and he shuts the door behind him.

Charles is faintly irritated and makes a mental note to have a word with Barbara. When a barrister has never met either his instructing solicitor or clients before, the clerks are supposed to make introductions.

Facing Charles is a young man carrying a briefcase. He wears drainpipe trousers, winklepicker shoes, a short, tightfitting jacket and a mophead haircut à la Beatles. Standing behind the young man is a matronly middle-aged woman in a fur stole and a rather odd fur hat that resembles an upside-down egg cup. Beside her is a thin-faced man wearing a leather jacket. He's in his early twenties and has deep-set blue eyes and fair hair.

Charles's gaze moves from one to the other, momentarily unsure which is his instructing solicitor. He decides that of the three, the Beatle lookalike is the most likely candidate.

'Mr Tindall?' he asks.

The other steps forward to shake Charles's hand. 'Yes.'

A mod solicitor, notes Charles silently. *Maybe I am getting middle-aged.*

'And may I introduce you to our clients, Mrs Eileen Sharpe and her son, Robin?' says the trendy young man.

Charles shakes hands with Mrs Sharpe, noting that she is wearing an engagement ring with a diamond the size of a broad bean.

I wonder what crime paid for that.

The son stays back and studies his shoes. Charles invites them all to sit.

'We appreciate that your Instructions only arrived this morning,' says Tindall, getting out his papers, 'but as you know, time to appeal to the Court of Criminal Appeal is only ten days, and unfortunately seven of those have already gone.'

'Yes. I'm afraid I haven't had time to absorb the detail, but of course I've been aware of the case.'

No one in England is unaware of the trial of the Reverend Stanley Sharpe. Like Charles, Sharpe was born in the East End of London and embarked on a life of crime. Unlike Charles, he pursued it vigorously and successfully. For the decade spanning the war years, Stanley "The Knife" Sharpe was feared and respected throughout the underworld. He came from the generation before Charles and the Krays, and the twins learned much from him. He had interests in, or took protection money from, several racetracks, clubs and pubs. He also ran a couple of successful car showrooms.

These were the bread-and-butter of Sharpe's business empire. The jam, and the income-stream he enjoyed most, came through the bevy of extremely high class escorts he supplied to rich Arabs, wealthy businessmen and members of the aristocracy, and the lucrative blackmail opportunities that followed. These Sharpe pursued with a ruthless rigour. It was said that at one time over fifty prominent Londoners, including several women, bore the long buttock scars inflicted personally by Stanley's knife. One was even rumoured to have sat (delicately) in the War Cabinet.

Then, within a very short time, his life came tumbling down around his ears. Charles doesn't know the whole story, but he remembers something about a mental breakdown. Sharpe was pronounced fit to plead but, in no condition properly to instruct his legal team, he was imprisoned for eight years for conspiracy to rob. He was sent to Long Grove Mental Hospital, a high-security psychiatric hospital that housed certified and dangerous criminals "at Her Majesty's pleasure".

The rest of the story was covered extensively in the newspapers and on television. Sharpe got religion. As he recovered from his mental illness, under the tutelage of a charismatic prison chaplain, he became a Christian and used the rest of his incarceration to study for a theology degree. On his early release he applied to join the Church. Within a decade of his conviction, he had acquired a pulpit in an Essex parish and a book deal for his memoir, entitled, rather unimaginatively, *Redemption.* He was frequently heard and seen on panel discussions on the BBC. For many Christians he was the poster boy for the transformational change that occurs when one accepts Jesus into one's heart.

It was again front-page news when, at the back end of 1965, he was arrested for the murder of Frank Marshall, one of Ronnie and Reggie Kray's oldest friends. As quickly as Sharpe had been accepted as a reformed man of peace and virtue, he was now condemned as a hypocrite and murderer.

'Let me give you a quick summary of the Crown's case, if you wouldn't mind,' says Tindall. 'In October of last year Reverend Sharpe, Mrs Sharpe's husband and Robin's father, was arrested for the murder of Frank Marshall, a member of the Krays' gang. As you probably read, he was convicted last week.'

'I did read about it. There was no body, was there?'

'That's right. There was plenty of evidence about a public confrontation with Marshall and little doubt that Reverend Sharpe went to Marshall's home the day afterwards. But thereafter the evidence was largely circumstantial; very little physical evidence and no body.'

'I understand that the initial confrontation occurred at a youth club, is that right?'

Mrs Sharpe answers, speaking in a soft Irish accent. 'Stanley was opening a youth club in Canning Town when that man arrived and started trouble. I was there.'

'What sort of trouble?'

'They told all the children to … leave … although they used foul language, you understand, and started threatening Stanley.'

'Threatening him with what, and to what purpose?'

'The big man, Marshall, said he was bringing a message. This was the twins' patch, and they didn't want Stanley on it.'

'But it was just a youth club, wasn't it?' asks Charles, puzzled. 'There was no suggestion that your husband was interfering with the Krays' … business arrangements, was there?'

Tindall answers. 'No, but there was apparently some bad blood between Reverend Sharpe and Ronnie Kray from their time at Long Grove. Their sentences overlapped.'

'Do we know what caused the bad blood?'

Tindall shakes his head. 'Reverend Sharpe refused to say and, of course, Ronnie Kray was not part of the Crown's case.'

'Do you have any idea, Mrs Sharpe?'

'No. I asked Stanley, but he said it was in the past and he'd rather not dwell on it.'

'Mr Sharpe?' asks Charles, turning to the son.

This is the first time Charles has focused on Robin Sharpe. He is a striking young man with white-blond hair and a pale bloodless face. In contrast his eyes seem unnaturally blue, like the glass eyes of a doll. He shakes his head.

'No. I would have been very young, still at school.'

He looks away from Charles and stares out of the window. Charles frowns. Robin Sharpe looks disengaged, as if he'd rather be somewhere else.

'Do we know why Reverend Sharpe went to Marshall's home the day afterwards?' Charles asks Tindall.

Mrs Sharpe answers. 'He went to remonstrate with Marshall, to ask him to persuade the Krays to let the club continue. He was passionate about it. He said that if such clubs had existed when he was a boy, he would never have got into trouble.'

'And that was the last time Marshall was seen alive?'

'Yes,' replies Tindall.

'Forgive me if I haven't quite mastered the detail yet, but am I right in thinking there were signs of a struggle at Marshall's home?'

'Yes,' confirms Tindall. 'And there was blood on the front doorpost and a clump of hair and skin attached, which the Crown claimed came from Marshall. So they proved that there'd been some sort of fight at about the time Mr Sharpe was there, which was the last time Marshall was ever seen.'

'Not much for a conviction of murder,' comments Charles.

'I agree,' says Tindall. 'Until we get to the confession.'

'Which Mr Sharpe disputes giving.'

'Exactly.'

Charles shakes his head.

This is the daily diet of every defence barrister working in London. The Met's practice of fabricating false confessions to stop gaps in a prosecution case or sometimes to settle scores with criminals is now so ubiquitous it has its own term of art. To "verbal" a suspect — to manufacture a confession the suspect never gave — is now an expression gaining currency even outside the profession. But to verbal a vicar? A high-risk strategy. The policeman or men concerned would have to have been very confident indeed.

'You attacked the confession at trial?' asks Charles.

'Of course. But the officer concerned didn't budge. The jury believed him.'

'Who was it?'

'A DCI called Wheatley.'

Charles looks up sharply.

'Do you know him?' asks Tindall.

'Oh, yes.'

Charles knows Detective Chief Inspector Wheatley only too well. When based in Buckinghamshire, Wheatley was the officer in charge of the investigation into the death of Henrietta, Charles's late wife. An upright military man with a pencil moustache perched on a strangely long top lip, and a clipped and brazen delivery of outright lies, juries seem to like him. He nonetheless has a long-standing reputation in legal circles for corruption — not the financial corruption endemic in the Met, such as taking bribes or selling information — but the twisting and falsifying of evidence when it suits him. As a result he has a sparkling clear-up rate and is tipped for very senior rank.

'He was a horrible man, Mr Holborne,' says Mrs Sharpe. 'Arrogant. Not at all like Mr Read.'

Tindall explains. 'As you'll see when you've a chance to read the papers properly, the case was initially investigated by an Inspector Read, but when it became a murder investigation Wheatley stepped in.'

'That Mr Wheatley destroyed half my home when he and his men searched it. All for nothing,' says an indignant Mrs Sharpe.

'But that's beside the point,' says her son with evident irritation. 'The jury believed him and the Court of Criminal Appeal won't interfere with that. We've been through all this.'

Charles turns to the young man in surprise. 'Do you have any experience in the law?' he asks.

'No,' replies Robin Sharpe. 'Neither a criminal record nor any qualifications in law. But I've done my homework. I'm right, aren't I?'

'Yes, you are exactly right. The question of who was telling the truth about the confession, your father or DCI Wheatley, is classically a question for the jury. If they decided to believe Wheatley, as they must have done, the appeal court won't go against that.'

'What about the summing up?' asks Tindall.

'That's what I've directed most of my attention to since I opened the papers,' replies Charles, 'but I'm sorry to say it was impeccable. A scrupulously fair summary of the evidence on both sides, and unimpeachable so far as the law is concerned.'

Robin Sharpe turns to his mother. 'I told you. This is a waste of time. And money.'

'I can't believe he did it,' she says simply.

Robin Sharpe snorts scornfully.

'You're not convinced?' asks Charles of him.

The young man doesn't answer.

'Ever since he was arrested,' says Tindall, 'the newspapers have been digging. You know what they're like, especially when they smell hypocrisy. They claim to have unearthed a lot of other criminality too.'

‘They’ve all turned against him,’ says Mrs Sharpe. ‘Even Robin,’ she adds sadly.

Robin Sharpe speaks angrily through compressed lips, still staring over the Thames. ‘I don’t know how you can forgive him, after the way he treated you. I haven’t.’

She shakes her head. ‘You don’t understand, darling.’

‘What is there to understand?’ Robin demands, his voice rising.

Charles speaks softly. ‘I don’t want to pry, Mrs Sharpe,’ he says, ‘but is this relevant to your husband’s appeal?’

‘No, not at all —’ she says, but Robin interrupts.

‘I disagree.’ He turns to Charles. ‘My father’s a fucking hypocrite,’ he says, ‘and a bully. His so-called conversion was completely fake, put on to pull the wool over the parole board’s eyes. He hasn’t changed at all. It wouldn’t surprise me if he *did* kill Frank Marshall!’

‘No, Robin,’ says Mrs Sharpe, ‘you’re wrong.’

The room falls silent for a while.

‘Do you think you can help us, Mr Holborne?’ asks Mrs Sharpe in a quiet voice.

Charles turns to Tindall. ‘I assume that, because you had to attack Wheatley’s integrity regarding the confession, Mr Sharpe’s previous convictions all came out.’

‘Yes,’ replies Tindall. ‘The jury heard all of it.’

Charles sighs. ‘On what I’ve seen so far, Mrs Sharpe, I’m really sorry to tell you that, no, there is no realistic chance of an appeal. I agree with Mr Tindall that the evidence of motive is very weak, and most of the Crown’s case was based on circumstantial evidence. But then there’s the alleged confession. That, taken with your husband’s former criminal record … I’m sorry to be blunt, but while his … conversion … is admirable, for most of his life he *was* a career criminal. He has convictions for serious violence. So the jury were faced with an apparently respectable policeman claiming your husband confessed to him, and the denials of a former criminal with convictions for dishonesty and violence. It can't be said that the jury was unreasonable in preferring the evidence of the police officer. In those circumstances, the Court of Criminal Appeal won't interfere. I promise I will read the papers through in more detail and if anything occurs to me, I'll be on the phone to Mr Tindall immediately. But short of finding new evidence which wasn't available before…'

'Can't we look for further evidence?' asks Mrs Sharpe desperately. 'I promise you, Mr Holborne, he was a changed man. Genuinely, a man of God.'

'Theoretically. If we found something strong enough, the court has power to extend time for an appeal. But there wouldn't be legal aid for such investigations and it would be expensive.'

'How expensive?' asks Mrs Sharpe, unconsciously fiddling with her engagement ring.

Charles turns to Tindall. 'Do you have a reliable private investigator?'

'Yes, we use a couple. But I agree it wouldn't be cheap. I'd need, say, one hundred and fifty pounds in the first instance. That should cover a couple of weeks' preliminary work. In all I'd expect something closer to five hundred.'

Mrs Sharpe's eyes open wide. 'Really? That much? I don't have anything like that. I've got no means, and, well, you probably know how little vicars earn. I've had to leave the vicarage and I'm lodging with my sister.'

'Mr Sharpe?' asks Charles, turning to the young man. 'My papers indicate that you have a business?'

'It's a small second-hand car showroom in south London.'

'Would you be able to put Mr Tindall in funds for further investigations?'

'No. In the first case, the business isn't doing that well. And secondly, I'm not sure I'd want to, even if I had the money.'

Mrs Sharpe puts a gentle hand over her son's. 'Please, Robin. For me?'

'No, Mum, I'm sorry, but I wouldn't spend a penny to get that man out of prison.'

'Please —'

'No. Absolutely not. And I can't understand why you'd want me to. Aren't you happier now? Haven't you had enough?'

'But —'

'No, I said!' The young man stands, pushes his chair back suddenly, whirls round and strides to the door. 'You have a good look at my father's criminal record, Mr Holborne!' he shouts, and he opens the door, goes through it and slams it shut behind him.

His shout and the noise of the door reverberate around the second-floor corridor. The three people remaining in Charles's room listen to Sharpe's angry footsteps recede and then the outer door also bangs shut.

'I'm so sorry about that, Mr Holborne,' says Mrs Sharpe eventually.

'Do you mind explaining why he's so angry about this?' asks Charles.

She shakes her head. 'I don't want to discuss it and, frankly, it's not relevant. Let's just say that Robin and his father did not enjoy a close relationship.' She stands suddenly, muttering 'Excuse me,' and also hastens from the room.

Charles turns to Tindall. 'I'm very sorry, Mr Tindall. But I guess you knew the score.'

'I did. But as you can see, Mrs Sharpe is having difficulty accepting it. I thought she might take it better from you. You'll need to go and see Sharpe, though.'

'Do you have funds for me to make a trip to … where is he?'

'HM Prison Durham, I'm afraid. But, yes, Mrs Sharpe gave me enough for this conference and for you to meet her husband. Not enough for me to come with you, though. Would you mind going on your own?'

'No, that's fine. Let's go and find Mrs Sharpe. We'll get a date in the diary on the way down. But it's not going to be before time expires, I'm afraid. Not that it would make any difference. Do you know what the son was referring to, concerning his father's convictions?'

'No,' answers Tindall. 'The fact that Sharpe senior was a career criminal, no doubt.'

'Maybe, but I sense there was more to it than that.'

'Are Reg or Ronnie there?'

'Hold on a tick,' says a male voice.

A hand half-covers the mouthpiece at the other end. A man shouts. 'Can you call Ron or Reg?'

There's a pause. Muffled bar noises can be heard, voices rising and falling in conversation and the click of billiard balls.

'This is Reggie.'

'I'm sorry to trouble you, Mr Kray. It's Trevor. Ronnie sent me up to Weston 'cos Big Frank was getting a bit twitchy. But he ain't here.'

'What do you mean, he ain't there?'

'The girlfriend says she ain't seen him for a coupla days.'

'But we gave them another ton only last week!'

'I know, but she says the money's all gone and they had another row. They made up, but then he started crying. Said he missed his boys.'

There is no response except a gale of laughter from somewhere in the bar.

'All right. Leave it with me.'

'You want me to stay here or come back?'

'Stay till tomorrow and see if he shows up. After that, come back.'

'Whatever you say, Mr Kray.'

CHAPTER FOUR

The following Monday Charles sets the alarm for half past five in the morning, rises silently, showers and dresses in the dark.

The train for which he is aiming, leaving King's Cross just before seven o'clock, will take over four hours, but with luck and no delays he should have time to interview Stanley Sharpe and be back on a southbound train to London by early afternoon. Although his fees won't cover the expense, he decided to book first-class tickets for himself and Maria. They can have breakfast on the train and use the travel time to do some paperwork.

Charles has only met his new pupil once, briefly, on the previous Friday. She had started work on some of Marcus Bradley's Instructions and asked to remain with him long enough to complete her draft pleadings. There was no need for her to do so, and she earned additional credit in Charles's eyes for her professionalism; it must have cost her several further days of torture.

She turned out to be a slim bespectacled young woman with light brown skin and an impressive halo of hair, a style recently popularised by The Three Degrees. She seemed shy, although when she had something to say she expressed herself concisely in a soft Bostonian accent.

Having packed his briefcase, Charles puts his head back into the bedroom, not intending to wake Sally if she's still asleep. She turns over.

'Charlie?' she asks, her voice croaky.

'Sorry I woke you,' he whispers.

'You didn't. Listen.'

'What is it? I've got to run if I'm going to get this train.'

'You haven't said much about your new pupil.'

'What's to say?'

She sighs audibly and there is a moment's silence. 'Do I need to spell it out?'

It takes Charles a moment to realise what Sally means. 'Oh, I see.' He shakes his head in puzzlement. 'I can't believe you think I'd even consider something like that. It would never occur to me. Leaving all else aside, she's a pupil! Just a kid.'

Sally sits up further in bed and flicks on the bedside light. Her Mary Quant hairdo is on end and a pink line crosses her cheek and forehead from where her face was pressed into a fold in her pillowcase. She looks sweet and inviting, but her voice is sharp. 'She's my age,' corrects Sally. 'And she's very pretty.'

'Is that so?'

'So I hear.'

He approaches the bed and bends to kiss her forehead. 'You've no need to worry, I promise,' he says softly.

'Just be careful, okay?' says Sally shortly, and she turns off the light and slides back down the bed.

Maria is waiting for him on the platform at King's Cross, his Instructions, tied in pink ribbon, under her arm. As warned, she wears a heavy overcoat and scarf. Despite some snow flurries over the last couple of days, the weather in London is relatively mild for February, but Charles has been to Durham before.

'Read it?' asks Charles.

'Yes, thank you,' she replies, handing the brief back to him.

'Excellent. Let's find our seats.'

Once on the train and having ordered breakfast, he gives the pupil two further briefs to read. Without mentioning Bradley, he orders her to interrupt him at any time should she have any questions. She smiles and nods.

Charles has brought plenty of paperwork to occupy him for the journey, but before he starts work on a new set of Instructions he takes the papers in the Sharpe case and reopens them. He leafs through Sharpe's CRO docket, the dated list of his previous convictions compiled by the Criminal Records Office.

It is several pages long. Like many from impoverished and broken homes, Sharpe's history is familiar: by the age of eleven he had moved from petty thieving to street robbery; as a teenager it was stealing cars and breaking and entering; then a significant step up: after learning his trade from more experienced criminals during his first significant period of imprisonment, he graduated to armed robbery.

At first nothing about the extensive record strikes Charles's eye, but then he notes that, interspersed with the major crimes, there are two or three convictions for breach of the peace and one for common assault. All are listed as an adjunct to other, more serious, criminality, with Sharpe's defence team asking for them to be TIC, "taken into consideration", when their client was sentenced for much more serious offences. This minor violence appears to have stopped after Sharpe's release from prison following his conversion, except for one case which occurred more recently and for which Sharpe received the very minor penalty of a conditional discharge.

The CRO document gives no details beyond the date of the offences, the courts of conviction and the sentences, but these minor offences seem at odds with the general pattern of Sharpe's offending. Charles has known or represented many criminals, and Stanley Sharpe is different to most. The Krays, for example, could burst into foolhardy, unpredictable violence without considering the implications. Ronnie in particular can't control his temper, and is forever punching, cutting or shooting those unfortunate enough to have offended him. In one well-known instance he shot one of his own men in the foot for a perceived slight.

Before reforming, Stanley Sharpe was the polar opposite: a clever, methodical criminal who planned meticulously, took no unnecessary risks and kept his head down. Drawing attention to himself by the shouting, pushing and shoving characteristic of breaching the peace strikes Charles as out of character.

Charles packs away the Sharpe file and unties the white ribbon of an Obscene Publications prosecution, surreptitiously burying the offending, and imaginatively explicit, photographs at the bottom of his briefcase to prevent accidental offence to passing fellow travellers.

The train pulls into Durham station on time. Charles and Maria step onto the windswept platform and she understands immediately why it was necessary to wrap up. The area around the station is covered in deep snow and the temperature is markedly below that which they left behind in London, but the skies are blue and cloudless.

'We can take a cab, or we can walk and I'll show you some of the sights. It's about twenty-five minutes to the prison,' says Charles. 'It's worth it; Durham's very pretty.'

Maria shivers. 'And very cold.' Her glasses steamed up on descending from the warm train carriage and she peers at him from over the rims.

'It's the wind blowing off the North Sea. But I'm told you get used to it,' explains Charles.

He nods at a pair of passing students wearing university-branded jumpers and no coats.

'Okay,' she says, a little reluctantly. 'Let's walk.'

Charles leads her down North Road towards Framwellgate Bridge, where they cross the River Wear for the first time. The snow-covered roads and pavements are clearing with the passage of traffic, but every few yards they pass dirty piles of snow from the previous falls. As they pass, Charles points out the castle and the cathedral looking down on the city. They cross the river for the second time at Elvet Bridge and head towards the prison.

'Wow!' exclaims Maria when she first sees it.

'Impressive, isn't it?'

'It looks more like a museum than a prison,' she says.

The main building is indeed impressive. Constructed of yellow sandstone, it has three sets of double doors reached by wide stone steps and, above, a pediment supported by four two-storey Doric columns. Towering over all is a white clock tower surmounted by a dome. Maria moves towards the central doors.

'No,' says Charles. 'We mere lawyers go in over there.' He points to a much less grand side door. 'Damn,' he mutters quietly to himself.

'What?'

'I forgot to tell you to leave your handbag at home. I've not had a female pupil before. I'm afraid they're going to go through it, and prison guards can be quite…'

'Salacious?' she offers.

'I was going to say laddish, but childish might be more accurate.'

She shrugs. 'I guess I'll survive. There's not much in there to interest them.'

'You'd be surprised. It doesn't take much.'

At reception, Charles announces that they are present for a legal visit and he gives Sharpe's full name and prison number. They are shown into a side room alone and told to take seats.

Minutes tick by. Charles looks at his watch and wanders back into the main reception area. Two gaolers in uniform have their heads together, laughing. He has the feeling that he and Maria are the subject of their conversation. One of the gaolers senses Charles's presence behind him and looks round.

'Go back into the waiting area please, sir,' he says.

'We've been here fifteen minutes. What's the hold-up?'

'Just go back where you were, please, sir. Someone will be with you soon.'

Charles rejoins Maria. A few minutes later they hear barred doors being opened and locked again with a clang. Footsteps go past their door and a further conversation begins at the desk. Charles gets up again and approaches the group of three uniformed men.

'Okay, here's another,' says one, a fat man with a glistening shaved head. 'A Jew, a Black and a Paddy walk into a prison —'

He catches sight of Charles over the shoulder of one of the others. He grins and looks away. The others look round. The newcomer, a heavy-set man with a network of fine burst blood vessels on his cheeks and additional pips on his epaulette insignia spins round and points at the room in which Charles and Maria were installed.

'You should be waiting in there, sir. I'll be right with you.'

Charles locks eyes with him for a moment but then returns to the room. Moments later he hears footsteps and the senior officer stands in the doorway.

'I'm Senior Prison Officer Potts. I'm sorry, but we can't let her in,' he says, nodding at Maria.

'Why? She's a barrister here to see her client, just like me,' says Charles.

'We weren't warned she'd be here, and we've got no women on duty. This is a Category A prison for men only, so there are no women gaolers. We can't search her.'

The other two officers have approached and are lurking behind their superior. The fat one is smirking.

This is a wind-up.

'I don't believe you,' replies Charles calmly.

Potts's eyes widen slightly. 'Are you suggesting I don't know the regulations?' he says, his chin set in a defiant challenge.

'I'm saying I don't believe there are no women officers on site. I saw the legal visits list on your desk and it includes women. Who's Mrs Charlesworth, for example? So your rota must include female officers.'

Potts grins unpleasantly. 'I'm not having some poncy London brief telling me my job. I say there're no women officers available, and that means there are no fucking women officers available! Now you can leave this … person … outside and we'll process you and let you get on with your legal. Or…'

'Or what?'

'She can sign a disclaimer —' and he indicates with a hitched thumb the fat man standing behind him with a clipboard in his hand — 'and let *us* strip-search her.'

Charles hears a sharp intake of breath from Maria to his left.

'Do you think I was born yesterday?' he asks. 'Let me suggest a third possibility. By this time tomorrow, the governor of the prison will receive formal requests from the Bar Council and the Lord Chancellor's Department for the shift rotas for today. And, when they show at least one woman on duty, as regulations demand, the governor will have no choice but to follow it up with a disciplinary against you *personally*. The

Prison Rules 1964 prohibit even a *prisoner* being searched by an officer of the opposite sex, let alone their legal adviser. And what started out as a bit of fun will end with your face all over the newspapers, you out of a job, and your cushy final salary pension gone. Now, is this really the way you want to go?'

Potts's face colours. He takes a step into the room and half-raises one hand.

Charles frowns.

Really? Physical violence?

One does hear occasional stories — gaolers are a law unto themselves — but still. Even with two others to back him up Charles can't quite believe the man would be so stupid as to cause a ruckus with a barrister, and with Maria as a witness.

Charles decides to call Potts's bluff. He grins, slips off his jacket and throws it across the room to Maria, who catches it neatly. He parodies the pose he would use in the boxing ring.

'All right, let's try that,' he says equably. 'Then you can add a bloody nose and a charge of assault to the list.'

Potts becomes suddenly still, sizing Charles up.

'You arrogant fucking Jew-boy,' he whispers. 'Are you threatening me?' He turns to the others. 'See this? This man is threatening me.'

'Not at all. You raised your hand to me, so I'm adopting a defensive posture for reasonable fear of imminent assault. Now, what's it to be?'

The gaoler hesitates.

Charles can read his mind. This is Potts's domain, of which he is the absolute ruler, and he isn't about to allow an unknown barrister to face him down, especially in front of subordinates. On the other hand, he's imagining the consequences of letting his temper get the better of him. Even if they were to teach Charles a lesson, he imagines Charles going back to London bloodied and bruised at their hands. How much political clout does the barrister have? They'd have to call the police, make up some charge. Could they make it stick?

Charles watches Potts reach the conclusion that he doesn't need a public and career-damaging dispute with a member of the Bar, especially when his pension is only a couple of years out of reach. His fists unclench and his shoulders drop.

Charles extends his arm towards Maria for his jacket.

'Good,' he says with a smile. 'We'll play nice. Now, you get one of the women officers on duty, your colleagues here can search me while you're gone, and we can all get on with our day.'

Ten minutes later, having been searched sullenly but correctly by gaolers of the appropriate sex, Charles and Maria are shown into a conference room where their client awaits them. The third of the trio of gaolers shuts the door and stands outside in the corridor. Maria has not mentioned the incident at all.

The Reverend Stanley Sharpe sits at a small table in the middle of the room. His shoulders are hunched, his forehead almost touching the table. His thinning grey hair and mottled scalp make him look vulnerable and old. He wears the regulation uniform of a convicted prisoner, blue shirt and dark serge trousers, but both seem a size too large. The sharp angles of his bony shoulders are visible through the prison issue, as if the man inside had disappeared to be replaced by a wooden coat hanger.

'Mr Sharpe? I'm Charles Holborne of counsel, and this is my pupil, Miss Hudson. I think Mr Tindall told you we'd be coming? He apologises that he can't attend but, as you know, funds are tight.'

Sharpe looks up slowly, as if his head were too heavy for his neck. Charles sees a long pale face, the planes of which are so sharply defined they seem to have been hewn from a block of ice. Sharpe's eyes, a pale light blue, add to the effect of coldness.

'Yes,' he replies.

Charles's first question is usually to ask how his convicted client is getting on in prison, but Sharpe's appearance speaks for itself. He has deep hollows under his eyes, which glisten as if on the verge of tears. His lips are chapped and cracked and there is a livid bruise on his chin. Rarely has Charles seen such a picture of misery. Sharpe's head drops again and he stares at the table.

The barristers take seats and Charles opens his papers.

'Mr Sharpe, did Mr Tindall report our discussion in Chambers?'

Sharpe nods but doesn't reply.

'Good. I'm afraid my conclusions haven't changed since then,' continues Charles, 'but I would like to understand some of the evidence a little better.'

Sharpe nods again.

'So I have a couple of questions, if you don't mind. As I understand it, you don't dispute there was an argument at the youth club, or that you went to Bethnal Green to speak to Marshall the following day.'

'Yes,' he repeats, his voice a mere exhalation.

Maria looks at Charles with a frown, and he shakes his head slightly as he records Sharpe's reply.

He's depressed. But then who wouldn't be?

'Why did you go to his home? Particularly after the threats and argument the previous day?'

There is a long pause before Sharpe answers, but he eventually takes a deep breath and speaks without looking up.

'To remonstrate with him; appeal to his better nature.'

Like an engine coughing reluctantly to life after several refusals, Sharpe's thin voice now rustles on, directed at a spot on the scored and stained table beneath his forearms.

'We both grew up on the streets of east London. He knows as well as I the risk to young men, of drifting into crime.'

'And he wasn't receptive?'

'He listened, but he had his orders. He does what Ronnie and Reggie tell him.'

'Do you have any idea why the Krays would be so opposed to a youth club?'

'No.'

'Your wife mentioned some sort of grudge from when you were at Long Grove with Ronnie.'

'Long time ago.'

'Nonetheless.'

They have to wait for Sharpe to respond.

Has he run out of steam?

'I broke the code.'

'Meaning?'

'From his perspective, I grassed him.'

'Do you want to explain?' probes Charles.

'Really? Very well. He was … how would you put it? Forcing his attentions on a very disturbed young lad, and I reported it.'

'I see. Crossing Ronnie Kray is a dangerous thing to do.'

'Yes, but, as I said, a long time ago. If Kray wanted revenge, he could have taken it any time over the previous decade. I can't believe that's anything to do with sending Marshall to close my youth club.'

Charles is less sure — Ronnie Kray has a long memory and a broad vindictive streak — but he makes a note and changes tack.

'Very well. Let's go back to the day Marshall disappeared. How long was your discussion with him?'

'Ten minutes.'

'Was there an argument, any violence?'

'No.'

'If you don't mind me pointing out the obvious, Mr Sharpe,' says Charles cautiously, 'you and Marshall both have form for using violence to settle disputes. Given your history, it wouldn't be surprising if violence erupted.'

'I don't believe in it anymore. I tried to appeal to him and I failed. So I left.'

The room falls silent as Charles and Maria both make notes.

'And he was alive and well at that stage?' asks Charles.

Sharpe nods.

'Can you explain the blood and hair found by the police outside Marshall's home?'

'No.'

'Are you saying there was a fight with someone else, after you left?'

'How do I know? But he's an enforcer for the Krays. Violence is his job description.'

'But your former legal team found no evidence of that,' points out Charles. 'Mr Tindall interviewed the neighbours. No one else went to the house until Mrs Marshall returned from picking up the boys from school, when she found the door open and her husband gone. You seem to have been the last person to see him alive.'

'He's still alive,' says Sharpe simply.

'What makes you say that?' asks Charles.

‘Because I’ve been set up.’

‘That doesn’t really follow, Mr Sharpe, does it? But in any case, by whom, and why? Because you opened a youth club?’ Charles spreads his hands, indicating how unlikely that would be.

‘I don’t know.’

The room again falls silent. Sharpe’s eyes lose their focus. It’s as if he has left the lawyers behind. Then he wakes.

‘You told Tindall that if we could prove Marshall’s still alive, that would be conclusive.’

‘Well, obviously. You can’t be kept in prison for killing a man who’s still alive.’

‘And for that we need a private investigator? Not the police?’

‘They’re not going to be interested. They’re happy; they got their conviction. In any case, as I know from painful personal experience, DCI Wheatley is the last Met police officer alive to start digging if it might undermine his own case.’

‘So it’s hopeless.’

‘I’m very sorry, but as I explained to Mrs Sharpe, I can’t certify reasonable prospects of success on the present evidence, so there won’t be any legal aid. And your wife’s financial situation is, as I understand it, rather difficult.’

‘And Robin?’

‘I did ask him, but he got angry. He won’t contribute.’

Sharpe nods.

‘Not surprised?’ asks Charles.

‘No. I did my best with him, but…’ Sharpe’s voice tails off and he shrugs.

Charles allows the silence to lengthen before speaking again.

‘I noticed that interspersed with the major offences on your record there were a few instances of breaching the peace and one common assault,' says Charles. 'They seem a little … inconsistent perhaps, with the others.'

He leaves the comment hanging. Charles thinks he sees Sharpe's face colouring slightly, but the prisoner doesn't answer.

'Might they explain your son's attitude?' probes Charles.

'I never lifted a hand to Robin,' sighs Sharpe. 'Not once.'

'But —'

'Do you mind, Mr Holborne, if we move on? If Robin won't help, he won't.'

Sharpe remains with his elbows on the table, his gaunt face staring at the surface. Charles can hear his slow breathing and faintly, in the background, the usual sounds of prison life: metal doors being opened and closed; buzzers sounding, laughter, barked orders, and the regular squeak of a trolley wheel as it passes down the corridor outside where they sit. Charles waits.

'How is she?' asks Sharpe eventually. His voice is so quiet that Charles can barely hear him.

'Mrs Sharpe? She seemed well enough. Anxious, obviously. She had to leave the vicarage and she's worried about how she's going to support herself now.'

'I suppose she's gone to her sister's.'

'Yes.'

'It didn't take them long,' he whispers.

'Who?'

'The diocese. To move her out.' He pauses. 'I've been praying about this.'

'Sorry, Mr Sharpe, I don't understand. You've been praying about your wife's accommodation?'

Sharpe suddenly looks up into Charles's face, showing the first faint signs of animation. 'Are you a religious man, Mr Horowitz?'

Charles frowns, unable to follow Sharpe's train of thought. 'No,' he says, 'I was brought up Jewish, but it didn't stick.'

'I was brought up C of E. It didn't stick either. It's strange how I came to God. Or God came to me. I keep asking myself why, having revealed Himself to me and shown me the path He wants me to take, He should tear it away from me like this. Of course, it's a test. I see that. But I can't see the purpose. And I feel abandoned.'

'I'm afraid I don't know how to console you, Reverend. But this isn't forever. You've been sentenced to mandatory life, but with good behaviour you could be out in ten or twelve years.'

'Ah,' says Sharpe, the ghost of a smile on his thin lips, 'that assumes I pass the test. And I'm not sure I shall.'

'Sorry?'

'Before I was a Christian, I viewed imprisonment like … what do you call it? You can insure against it … yes, business interruption. I took precautions, of course, but I knew that every now and then I'd make a mistake and probably end up in prison for a while. I was able to keep things ticking over outside, and be patient.'

'And now?'

'I don't know if you can understand this or if I can explain it properly, but this injustice is so … so *wasteful*. I have a calling, I saw my path clearly, and now I am full of rage for being … thwarted. In here I am useless. Useless.' His voice disappears into a whisper. 'God tests us, and He doesn't test us beyond our ability to endure it. But what if I *can't* endure it? Does that mean God is wrong? How can God be wrong?'

'What do you mean you can't endure it?'

Sharpe hangs his head.

'What are you saying?' persists Charles.

When he answers, Sharpe's voice is so soft it is almost inaudible. 'I have … terrible … sinful thoughts.'

'Are you saying you're considering suicide?' Sharpe doesn't answer. 'Look, Mr Sharpe, I'm the wrong person to guide you in this. I lost my faith years ago, if I had any in the first place, but maybe … you should speak to the prison chaplain. I understand you derived much comfort from it at Long Grove. Your feeling of helplessness, not understanding God's purpose for you, surely that must be very common inside a prison?' Sharpe looks up slightly. 'The chaplain must have experience of this; I can't believe he wouldn't be able to help you.'

'Yes, I do have an appointment to see him.'

'Good. Now,' says Charles, anxious to move to a subject on which he has some expertise, 'is there anything we need to discuss about the case itself?'

Sharpe shakes his head. 'Well, maybe just one thing. Would you be prepared to go and interview Marshall's wife?'

Charles is about to refuse when Sharpe's eyes lift and meet his. Charles sees the desperate plea in the man's eyes.

'I *know* Marshall's alive,' he insists. 'He might've been in touch with her. I know I'm asking a lot — it's not your job, I know that — but, I beg you!' he implores. 'Last throw of the dice?'

Charles nods. 'I won't promise … but I'll see what I can do,' he says.

Charles and Maria are back on the train, nursing cups of coffee in first-class. They have said very little to one another since leaving the prison.

'So,' says Charles, leaning back in his seat and smiling, 'questions?'

Maria takes off her glasses to clean them, and Charles notices that she has unusually large eyes. Very pretty eyes.

'What was the point of the conference? I read the notes from your meeting in the Temple. You said nothing new to what you told the solicitor and the wife.'

'Yes, but he wanted to see me in person. If you're telling someone he has to spend the rest of his life in prison, or most of it, especially for something he says he didn't do, it's only fair to do it face to face. Also, you never know what might come out of these meetings. So often I've thought it'd be a waste of time, only to be given a nugget of essential information.'

'And were you?'

'Not this time, no.'

'What was all that about the minor offences? How were they relevant to this appeal?'

'They weren't, but I was curious. Robin Sharpe was adamant that he wouldn't help pay for his father's appeal, even though I think he probably could, and he was angry at his mother even pursuing it.'

'You thought Sharpe was beating up his son?'

'No, his wife, and Robin witnessed it.'

She considers Charles's response. 'I think I like the Reverend Sharpe even less than I did before the conference.'

'Yes, well, fortunately, it isn't necessary for us to like our clients.'

'What about the search by the prison officers?' asks Maria.

'What of it?'

'Well ... why? What caused that confrontation? Was that due to me being there? Or do you usually excite that sort of response?'

'No. My problems normally come higher up the food chain. But the racial thing … yes, every now and then.'

'So, that kicked off because I'm Black? Or because I'm a woman? Or because you're … Jewish?'

'You missed one. I'm a "*poncy London brief*", remember? That's often enough in the provinces. In any case, between the two of us we ticked pretty much every box.'

She considers his response, and then nods to herself. 'I see.'

'What else?'

'Well … this hasn't got anything to do with Mr Sharpe's case, and I don't want to pry into your personal matters … but he called you "Horowitz". And what was your "painful personal experience" with DCI Wheatley?'

'Ah. Yes.'

Charles turns to stare out of the window and for a few minutes he merely watches the countryside trundling past. By the time he turns back to her, Maria has opened the papers on which she was working on the way up. He reaches a decision.

'I guess you'll hear the gossip anyway,' he says, 'so you might as well get it from the horse's mouth. A lot of people from the East End knew me by my former name, which was Horowitz. I changed it to Holborne to try and avoid exactly the sort of thing that happened this morning. And as far as Wheatley is concerned, as you've probably already learned, I was framed for the murder of my wife a few years back. Wheatley was a superintendent in the Buckinghamshire Constabulary then. He got demoted for a while, and then reinvented himself in the Met where his particular … skill set … is more valued. He didn't plant evidence on me but he ignored — actually, no, he *buried* — the evidence which eventually proved my innocence.' Charles watches her face as she assimilates what he's said. 'Anything else?' he asks.

Maria shakes her head. 'No, not for the moment. Thank you.' She returns to the papers she was studying, finding the relevant page and making a note in the margin, as if the events and the discussion were interesting, but something that happened to someone else.

Is that it? What's she thinking?

That it wasn't going to be like this in the land of cricket and fair play? Or that she's bitten off more than she can chew, and should reconsider her career choices?

Or maybe just her pupil master.

She pauses and looks up again. 'I can see why Miss McIntyre chose you to replace Mr Bradley.'

'Yes?'

'Apart from the obvious reasons, you're what my dad would call a scrapper.'

'Is that good or bad?'

The young woman doesn't answer but returns to her papers.

'By the way,' adds Charles, 'barristers, even pupils, address their clerks by their first name. So it's not "Miss McIntyre" but "Barbara".'

'Okay. Thank you,' she says.

They fall silent and eventually Charles takes out another set of Instructions to prepare. Maria continues to read her papers. It is half an hour before she speaks again.

'Actually, I do have one more question. Why did you agree to go and see Marshall's wife?'

'Did I agree?'

'Pretty much.'

'No idea. Just felt sorry for the man, I suppose.'

Before she turns away, Maria's expression betrays surprise, perhaps even revulsion, but she makes no comment and focuses again on her papers.

CHAPTER FIVE

'How would you feel about having Maria round for dinner one evening?'

Charles and Sally are hanging the last of the curtains in the first-floor dining room. It's not a room much used; they have yet to entertain anyone and they have all their meals in the kitchen. Charles would have been happy to continue using it for storage, together with the ladders, tins of paint and tools still in daily use. Sally would not. Shortly after moving in she measured up, ordered material and got to work on her pre-war sewing machine.

'Why?'

'Well, she's alone in the country, for a start.'

Sally gets down from the stepladder, moves it a few feet, and climbs up again. 'Where are her family, then?'

'Her father's a diplomat in Brussels. He's got a flat here, which is where she's staying, but he doesn't come over much.'

'And the mother?'

'She doesn't talk about her, but I think she's a professor of art or something in the States.'

'No brothers or sisters?'

'She hasn't mentioned any. That's one of the reasons I'd like to ask her. She seems quite shy, and I'm not sure she has any friends.'

'And you want to be her friend?'

Sally's tone is neutral, but she gets down from the ladder again having fastened the last hook and keeps her back to Charles. He can't decide if she's angry. He circles round to face her and takes her hands in his. She avoids his gaze.

'Sal, this isn't like you. She's alone in a foreign country, in a profession where she's not wanted. It's even worse for her than it is for me! I feel sorry for her, that's all. And…'

Finally, she looks up. 'And?'

'Well … being totally honest, if you meet her you can't say I'm keeping her somewhere in the shadows.'

'And inviting her here means you can't be having a … *thing* with her.'

'Maybe not, but you'll be able to see for yourself if our relationship is professional or … something else.'

She doesn't answer.

'What more can I do for you to trust me again?' he asks.

'Avoiding young, female and attractive pupils would be a start.'

'I didn't want a pupil at all, but Barbara specifically asked me. Are you telling me that none of our junior clerks gossiped with yours? I don't believe it. You can't keep Jeremy's mouth shut with metal plates and rivets!' He sees her answer from her expression. 'So you *know* what happened, and what a horrid time she was having with Bradley.'

She nods reluctantly. 'Yes.'

'I wasn't going to say no to Barbara just because you'd be suspicious, was I?'

'Don't bullshit me, Charlie. You didn't give me a thought before agreeing.'

'That's not true,' he says, stung. 'But Bradley was making her life hell, and someone had to do something. She'd either have had a nervous breakdown or left the Bar altogether. Or both.'

'So, as always, Sir Galahad just jumped in with both feet. You can't help yourself, can you?'

'What?'

'Saving everyone. Did it occur to you that sometimes it's not your responsibility? If our circumstances were different I'd have been the first to say you should take her. It was a nice thing to do but … timing, Charlie, timing!'

She pauses and looks down. Finally she sighs and nods.

'Okay then. Not a week night, though. One of us has to be at home to cook something.'

'Thank you.'

Charles knocks on the door of 12 Brierley Gardens, Bethnal Green. He located the address of Mrs Gracie Marshall from the prosecution papers in Sharpe's original trial. His intention is to speak to Mrs Marshall as briefly as possible and be back home shortly after seven to eat with Sally, whose turn it is to cook. It is quarter past six, and it has been dark for almost two hours. The evening is bitterly cold. A silvery sheen of frost is already forming on the pavements and tops of parked cars.

Charles is not really sure what he's doing here, on a busy east London pavement with muffled commuters hurrying past him to get into warm homes. Sharpe's retainer, such as it was, has certainly expired, but Charles feels an obligation, of a sort, to a desperate man for whom he felt some pity.

He knocks for a second time, without much optimism. He can see through the open curtains that the house is in complete darkness. Slightly disappointed, but conscious of a duty done, Charles turns to retrace his steps to Bethnal Green underground station and the few short stops to Chancery Lane. As he steps onto the pavement, he finds himself face to face with a young couple intending to walk up to the front door.

'Can we help you?' says the man.

'I was looking for Gracie Marshall.'

'She doesn't live here anymore,' says the woman. 'We just moved in.'

'You don't know where she's gone, do you?' asks Charles.

'Yes,' replies the woman. 'I've been posting her letters to her. Hang on a sec…'

She starts rummaging in her handbag. She comes up with a postcard. On it, handwritten in big childish capitals, is an address.

'Here,' says the woman, showing Charles the card, but the street is so dark that he has difficulty reading it. The young man uses his cigarette lighter to illuminate the card. Charles inclines his head to study the address. William Street, Stratford; he knows it well.

'Thanks,' he says, and makes to move off.

'If you hang on a tick,' calls the woman, moving to the front door with her key in hand, 'I'll see if anything else's arrived for her. I don't think she had much time to arrange her move.' She opens the front door and bends, leafing through a small handful of envelopes. 'Yes, here you are.'

She turns and holds out a brown, official-looking envelope. Charles hesitates.

'Looks important,' says the woman.

Charles takes it with some reluctance and tucks it into an overcoat pocket. 'Thanks,' he says.

'Good evening,' says the young man, and he follows the woman into the property. The door closes.

Charles moves off, but when he reaches the main road he pauses to check his watch: already six thirty. There are only two further stops on the Central line to Stratford, so with luck he could be there in ten minutes, but it's heading out of the City and away from home. He hesitates for another moment, undecided. He could simply re-address the letter and pop it in a post box at Bethnal Green, abandon his mission and get home to Sally in time. But, then, he's come this far… He reaches a decision and jogs towards the underground station.

He finds a telephone box by the ticket office but it's occupied. In any case, Sally's likely to be en route from the Temple to Wren Street. He'll call her on the way back.

A train is pulling onto the platform as Charles arrives at a run and, seven minutes later, he is stepping out of Stratford station. It takes less than two minutes to walk to William Street.

The last time Charles was here, in 1940, William Street was being cleared by bulldozers, the houses having been destroyed early in the Blitz. He's surprised to find that it hasn't been rebuilt. Instead, he finds himself walking along a long row of wartime Nissen huts. Erection of these single-storey prefabricated buildings began after the Blitz to house bombed-out families. Half-cylindrical structures with curved corrugated iron roofs, they have a poor reputation: draughty, damp, and prone to rusting. They were certainly not intended to last more than twenty years.

The street lighting has still to be replaced, and Charles is unable to see if numbers identify the huts. Several are empty and derelict, their doors and windows boarded up or gaping open into the darkness within. He has walked almost to the far end of the row before he spots one with a number attached to its wooden railings. He turns around and retraces his steps, pointing at each D-shaped building as he passes and counting back in twos.

He stops outside one of the huts with light coming from behind the curtains, and knocks on the flimsy wooden door. It opens almost immediately.

With the light behind her, he cannot make out the features of the woman who greets him.

'Sorry to disturb you,' he says, 'but I'm looking for Mrs Gracie Marshall.'

The silhouetted woman opens her mouth to reply and then stops abruptly. She leans forward slightly, examining Charles's face.

'Charlie?' she asks. 'Charlie Horowitz?'

'Yes?' says Charles uncertainly.

'It's me,' she says. 'Gracie, Williamson, as was.'

Charles frowns, still not recognising the woman.

'Leonora?' she prompts. 'From the Windmill?'

Recognition dawns. 'Good God!' exclaims Charles. '*You're* Gracie Marshall? Of course I remember you. You broke my heart.'

Charles last laid eyes on Gracie Williamson, stage name "Leonora Bonney", two decades earlier; before he became Charles Holborne, and before he turned twenty.

It was a similarly freezing night in early 1945. He and other junior officers based at RAF Hornchurch had weekend passes and took the train up West. On arrival at Leicester Square, one of the pilot officers announced that he was going to the famous Windmill Theatre; he'd taken a fancy to one of the dancers, he said, and wanted to see her perform again. What he actually meant was that he'd taken a fancy to one of the dancers and wanted to see her naked again. By 1945 the Windmill was infamous for its "nude tableaux". Dancers were permitted to take up exotic poses on stage, completely naked, as long as they complied with the Lord Chamberlain's injunction, imposed on the grounds of public decency, that they remain completely immobile. Any movement, even of an eyebrow, could be construed as lascivious behaviour tending to corrupt public morality, and might cost the theatre its licence.

The pilot officer's proposal receiving enthusiastic support, the group of airmen walked up Shaftesbury Lane and joined the long queue of servicemen on the streets of blacked-out Soho. The queue snaked out of the theatre and was so long that it extended well past the Lyric Theatre Gallery entrance. They spent an uncomfortable forty minutes stamping their feet and blowing on their fingers while they waited to get in.

By the time they were admitted and joined the jostling mass of young men in uniform crowded at the back of the auditorium, the show was finishing and they just caught the curtain calls. Charlie, the old hand, suggested they take part in the "Windmill Steeplechase" and remain for the next show. As the aisles filled with a solid mass of departing theatre-goers heading for the street, a boisterous race would begin from the back of the auditorium to the front over the backs of the stalls seats — hence the "steeplechase". Charlie led the charge and they managed to claim four of the best seats in the house, front row stalls, centre stage.

Shortly before the finale of the last show, the audience was enthusiastically clapping in time with an act in which the young women of the chorus were playing the parts of servicemen, marching up and down the stage with rifles as they sang. One of Charlie's mates elbowed him in the ribs and shouted.

'See the one on the end?' Charlie looked where he was pointing. 'She's giving you the eye.'

At the end of a line of high-kicking soldiers danced a tall young woman in an army helmet. She had blonde hair and very long legs. Her "uniform" consisted of high heels, extremely short tight pants and a cut-off blouse that descended to just below her breasts. From his position, close-up and below her,

Charlie was able to see that she wore no underwear. He looked up again in time to see the dancer wink at him.

The final number was the climax of the show and featured a young couple meeting for the first time in an art gallery, dancing and singing of their unrequited love. As the song progressed, curved bays at the back of the stage were in turn illuminated by a spotlight and in each one, framed as if she were a statue, was a naked woman in a classical pose.

As each spotlight bloomed to life, Charlie looked to see if the tall blonde would be featured. It was not until the end of the song when the couple fell into a clinch and the applause started that the last bay was revealed. The woman was perched on the stump of a classical pillar, a Greek drinking vessel on her shoulder. She wore some form of diaphanous tunic which fell off her shoulders behind her and which hid nothing. She was entirely still but her lips were pursed in a half-kiss. She was staring directly at Charlie.

'You jammy bastard,' said his colleague. 'If that isn't an offer, I don't know what is. You've made a new friend.'

Deciding to play his luck, at the end of the show Charlie bade farewell to his colleagues and waited at the stage door. Sure enough, a few minutes later it opened outwards and a man in a cloth cap, open-necked shirt and waistcoat looked him up and down.

'You're the one,' he concluded. 'Well? Coming in?'

The man had a roll-up cigarette clamped between his lips, and it bobbed up and down like a tiny conductor's baton as he spoke. He stood back, holding the door open.

'Yes, please.'

'They're still getting changed,' said the man as Charlie passed him. 'She says to wait in the canteen. Go right to the top of the stairs.'

Charlie climbed the stairs as they snaked from one floor to the next. He passed rooms marked "Accounts", "Rehearsal Room", and "Costume" and then an arrow pointing somewhere below him that said "Stage". He found the canteen at the top of the building. It was deserted but the lights were still on. He sat at one of the tables by the door, lit a cigarette and waited, turning his RAF cap around in his hands. His heart was beating hard, not only from climbing five storeys.

A few minutes later the tall woman arrived and strode confidently towards him. Without a word she sat at his table, heat and perfume emanating from her, and took a cigarette from his open pack on the table. Charlie, remembering his manners, leaned forward and lit it for her. She drew a deep lungful of smoke and sat back, evaluating him. She was older than he'd thought, late twenties or early thirties, but she was even more beautiful than she'd appeared on stage.

Eventually she nodded and smiled.

'Okay, Flyboy. I'm Gracie,' she said in a surprisingly cultured accent. 'Are you buying me a drink or what?'

She guided him to a Soho club where Charlie spent all his ready cash on two meals and a lot of expensive drinks. He didn't notice. He was mesmerised.

Charlie had no experience of women. "Leonora" seemed to him the apogee of sophistication. She was magnetic, dangerous, and as out of bounds for him as it was possible for a woman to be. Firstly, and obviously, she wasn't Jewish. Furthermore, Charlie's Victorian-era parents were of the opinion that there was only a cigarette-paper morality gap between actresses and prostitutes. Finally, nice Jewish boys like Charlie were not supposed to have sex before marriage, and sex with Gracie was, frankly, the only thing that horny, nineteen-year-old Flight Lieutenant Charles Horowitz could think of right then.

They ate, talked, laughed and danced. She was easy to talk to and seemed to find him funny. He learned that she shared a flat with a girlfriend who worked in the Ministry of Information and that it was only a short walk from there. They left at 4 a.m. when the club closed.

As Charlie helped Gracie into her coat on the freezing dark pavement, he thought the night had gone well. He expected her to take him by the arm and walk him back to her flat. He was at fever-pitch of anticipation. Instead, she leaned forward, dizzying him with her perfume, kissed him on the mouth for a glorious thirty seconds, disengaged, said goodnight and walked off.

Charlie was so stunned it took him a moment to realise that the night wasn't, after all, going to end in this amazing woman's bed but on the cold night bus back to Hornchurch. Her high heels *clip-clopped* round the corner and she was gone.

The pattern was established. Whenever Charlie had a pass, he would go to the show and wait for her outside the stage door. She would appear and they would walk arm-in-arm to a nearby club. She would be charming, flirtatious and inviting, and Charlie would empty his wallet paying for her food and drink. He never got beyond the goodbye kiss.

One night, a month or so later, Charlie waited for over an hour at the stage door but Gracie didn't show. Giving up, he was on his disconsolate way back to the underground station when he saw her leaving via the front doors, laughing, arm in arm with an extremely tall American army officer who outranked him.

Not to be deterred, Charlie continued to go to the show, sitting in the front centre stalls, staring desperately up at the lithe dancer. She ignored him.

Eventually his mates at the base persuaded him that he was wasting his time and money and he stopped going. He never expected to see "Leonora" again. He never forgot her.

Twenty years later, here he is, standing at her door.

'Oh, my goodness!' she exclaims. 'Talk about a blast from the past! What on earth are you doing here?'

'Can I come in?'

She blocks his path. 'I'd rather not. The boys are inside and…' Her head drops and she looks at the pavement.

'It's about Frank,' explains Charles.

She reconsiders. 'All right,' she says reluctantly. 'But please don't look at the place. We've only been here a few days and it's really…' Her voice tails off.

She stands back. As Charles passes he thinks he detects the smell of spirits.

He enters a room with a semi-circular roof lit by a single bare lightbulb hanging from the apex of the ceiling. Unpainted wooden boards partition off an area at the back from which Charles can hear the sound of young children squabbling.

Because the walls curve to the ground, most of Gracie's furniture will not fit the room. It's all been left in the centre, and the place resembles a second-hand furniture store. Indeed it looks as if someone has taken the entire contents of a house, furniture, clothing, children's toys and kitchen utensils, and chucked them into a pile.

'Sorry about … this. Here,' she says, and she removes some clothing from an upturned tea chest, 'take a seat. I'd offer you tea, but I've got no change for the gas meter.'

Charles reaches into his waistcoat pocket. 'Here's a shilling,' he says.

'No, no, thank you,' she replies. 'Though I do have a bit of brandy. It's only cooking brandy, but it might be okay...'

Charles guesses that Gracie has already sampled the cooking brandy and found it to be "okay".

'No, I'm fine, thanks.'

She sits heavily on a stool next to him and Charles has an opportunity to evaluate her. The harsh light from above her head does her no favours. He realises for the first time that the blonde hair he found so compelling during the war must have come from a bottle, because her colouring now is dark brown threaded with grey. She wears a cardigan with a tear in the sleeve over a grubby blouse and her skin has an unhealthy grey pallor. She's gained a lot of weight since he last saw her and is developing jowls and a double chin. Were it not for her voice, he wouldn't have recognised her at all.

She sees his gaze. 'Don't, Charlie.'

'Don't?'

'Don't look at me like that. I can't bear it.'

'Oh, no, Gracie —'

'I know I look terrible. I've gained a few pounds recently. Dancers often do when they stop dancing. It keeps you slim, all those cigarettes, no meals and lots of exercise. And I've not been myself since Frank...'

She looks towards a photograph in a frame on a sideboard. It seems to be the only ornament or piece of decoration to have been unpacked.

'Is that him?' She nods. 'May I?'

He stands and picks it up.

The photograph shows Gracie in a floor-length white wedding dress, her veil pulled back, standing outside a London church. She looks exactly as Charles remembers her. Behind her is a family group, parents, aunts, uncles and children. By her side, and towering over her, is the groom, Frank Marshall.

Charles is built big, but Marshall is a giant, at least six foot six by Charles's evaluation and with the physique of a bodybuilder. It is possible to see biceps, quadriceps and trapezius muscles bulging through the material of the enormous wedding suit. Marshall was handsome, with wavy light brown hair, a wide brow and a big grin. There's a friendly placidity, an innocence, about the open face, which is in stark contrast to the stories told of Marshall within the East End criminal fraternity. Many thought him a psychopath, capable of extreme violence, especially against authority figures. Whenever the Krays needed a police officer taught a lesson, Marshall was their go-to enforcer. He would inflict pain on their orders without qualm, sometimes without restraint.

'He was a lovely man,' says Gracie sadly. 'People didn't understand him.'

'Yes?'

'All that stuff about his violence, but he was never like that with me or the boys. He was gentle as a lamb, if you knew how to handle him.'

Charles replaces the photograph and sits again.

'So, what are you doing here, Charlie?'

'I'm a lawyer now, a barrister —'

'A barrister, eh?' she interrupts, and Charles detects the ghost of the mocking smile he knew so well. 'Yes, I knew you were a clever one. And now I think about it, you had plenty of brass neck. Being a barrister would suit you.'

'I do okay. Anyway, my client is convinced that Frank isn't dead.'

'If he isn't dead, where is he?'

'I don't know, Gracie. Could he have just, you know, left?'

She shakes her head firmly. 'No, never. We were happy and he adored the boys. He'd never walk out, especially without his wallet and keys. And there was blood on the door where he was decorating — he had the day off to do the spare room — and a clump of his hair and skin on the doorpost. There was definitely a fight. Wait … you said "client"?'

'Yes.'

'Who's your client?'

'Well, that's the thing. It's Stanley Sharpe.'

'You're acting for *him*?'

Charles nods. 'Sort of. He says he's innocent and knows nothing about Frank's disappearance.'

'That's not what the jury said, though, is it?'

'No. But I know the police officer who conducted the enquiry. Once he had a confession, by whatever means, he had all he needed. He wouldn't have looked hard for Frank. In fact, not at all.'

'Are you saying you think Frank's still alive?' she asks, childlike hope in her expression.

Charles is finding it difficult to reconcile the vivacious, imperious dancer he knew with the woman before him. The intervening decades have been cruel to her. Charles is uncomfortably aware that their roles have reversed. She is no longer the older, more sophisticated woman and he the naïve teenager. She seems lost and vulnerable, while he's now the confident, worldly professional man. He feels a wave of pity, but his compassion embarrasses him. Is he judging Gracie, merely because life didn't turn out as she hoped?

'No, at least not yet. But he was never found, and I don't trust Sharpe's alleged confession.'

'So you're looking for him?'

'I can't. I'm not a private detective, and it's against my professional rules. But there's nothing to stop you instructing someone to do some digging,' he says, realising as the words leave his lips how foolish a suggestion it is.

'I'm behind on the rent and the fridge is mostly empty,' she says without shame. 'How could I pay for a private detective?'

'No, silly idea.'

'What, then?'

'Has anything else occurred to you since your police interview? I don't need you to go through what you told them. I've seen the witness statements, including yours.'

She shakes her head. 'Nothing. It was just a normal day. Are you aware of his … work?'

'Yes. He worked for the Krays.'

She nods, bowing to the further humiliation.

'Well, things were quiet, and he had the day off. One minute he was there, the next he was gone. The only odd thing was what Reggie Kray said.'

Charles frowns. 'What was that? There's nothing about the Krays in the prosecution papers.'

'No, why would there be? It's just that I rang Reggie as soon as I found Frank had disappeared. I thought maybe he'd know if there'd been some trouble. And he told me to phone the police. I just thought it was odd.'

It is indeed odd. In their manor the Krays, not the Metropolitan Police, are the law. The twins would *never* encourage anyone to go to the police, less still the wife of a missing lieutenant.

'Yes, that is strange,' says Charles quietly to himself, pondering.

Two boys aged about eight and ten appear behind Gracie, both in school clothes. The older child has outgrown his uniform while the younger one's is too big for him. Both jackets and shorts show signs of having been mended more than once.

'Mum?' says the elder, cautiously.

'Give me a minute, Johnny. I'm just talking to my friend.'

'We're hungry,' says the smaller child.

'I gave you a sandwich a minute ago.'

'But we're still hungry,' complains Johnny.

'If the gas was working, do you have anything for them?' asks Charles.

'Really, Charlie, I don't want to ask you.'

Charles stands and walks towards the kitchen area. There's a gas stove next to a couple of feet of peeling counter. Under the counter, hidden by a filthy curtain, is a metal pail containing a scrubbing brush and, behind it, the black box of the gas meter. He crouches, slots a shilling into the meter and turns the butterfly-shaped lever.

'There you go,' he says, standing up. 'One thing puzzles me. Haven't the Krays sent anyone round with Away Money?'

The Krays operate an informal charity for members of the Firm who are "away", namely, in prison. One of the gang comes round with a wodge of cash, perhaps food, to make sure the family is looked after, and sometimes to make sure the prisoner doesn't start talking to people on the inside to whom he shouldn't. In some cases, when a Firm member is sufficiently valued, the twins have been known to pay off (or beat up) impatient landlords.

'No. They have in the past, but not this time. Maybe they don't if one of them is … missing, rather than inside.'

'Right.'

Charles takes out his wallet and leafs through some bank notes. Gracie approaches him and puts a firm restraining hand on his.

'Absolutely not, Charlie.'

'Just to tide you over.'

'I said no.'

'But —'

'I've been down that route before,' she says, her tired eyes locked onto his, trying to convey a subtext she will not or cannot articulate. 'Before Frank and I got together. And I promised myself; never again. So I won't take money from any man, except him. I'm very grateful, Charlie, honestly I am, and I know you'd not expect anything in return. You're not like that. But it's simpler if I just say no. And I'll pay you back that shilling, soon as I can.'

Charles hesitates, a couple of notes still between his thumb and forefinger.

'I mean it, Charlie,' says Gracie with a glimmer of her former assertiveness. 'Now put your money away before I get cross.'

'If you're sure,' he says, putting his wallet away. 'Didn't your parents have a large farm, Wiltshire, maybe?'

He has a faint recollection of a wealthy family somewhere in the West Country.

'I haven't been in touch with my family for years.'

'Then what are you going to do?'

'You needn't worry about me. I've got people I can turn to.'

There is a clank behind them as the older boy lifts a heavy kettle onto the gas ring. He reaches for a book of matches on the counter.

'Just a sec,' says Charles, and he strides over. 'Can I see that, please?'

'What, these?' replies the boy, holding out the matches.

Charles takes them and turns them over in his hand. On the front is what caught his eye: the design of a windmill. In tiny lettering across the body of the building is the famous slogan: *We never closed.*

'Do you know about these?' he asks Gracie.

She comes over and looks in his hand. 'They're just matches. That's where I met Frank.'

'Yes, but how long ago was that?'

'Well, Johnny'll be ten in July so ... about eleven years. Why?'

'When did you give up working there?'

'The same, maybe a few months less.'

'So,' persists Charles, 'you've had this book of matches knocking about for over ten years? Really?'

'I'm not sure where it came from. We had to leave Brierley Gardens in such a hurry, stuff was just thrown into bags and boxes. I found it when I unpacked here.'

Charles turns the book over in his hand again and returns it to Johnny. 'Can you light the gas yourself?' he asks.

'Course I can, mister,' says the boy scornfully, and he proceeds to do so.

Charles holds out his hand for the matches. 'All right if I hang onto these?' he asks Gracie.

She nods. 'Yes. But what're you going to do?'

'I'm not sure yet. But I'll do what I can. If I have any news, may I pop by?'

'Of course, but I'm hoping we won't be here for long. How do I contact you? If I hear anything?'

'I'm in the phone book. Look for the address in the Temple. But my name's Holborne now, with an "e" on the end. Oh, and the new people at Brierley Gardens gave me this for you.'

He hands her the envelope and turns to depart, but she grabs his sleeve. She leans forward and kisses him on the cheek, her eyes filling with tears.

'You always were a lovely boy, Charlie Horowitz. Whoever's got you now is a lucky girl.'

'That's what I keep telling her,' he replies with a grin. 'Be well, Gracie.'

CHAPTER SIX

Ronnie Kray walks down the steps from Weston-super-Mare station into the forecourt, his two young minders flanking him. The seaside town throngs with holidaymakers in the summer months but is much quieter in winter, and Kray and his associates are among only a small handful of people arriving off the train. They wear tailored suits, leather Italian shoes and cashmere overcoats, and are about as inconspicuous as if dressed as Christmas elves.

Kray doesn't like trains. They always make him irritable. He was already exasperated at having to leave London with so much going on, and the journey has enraged him further. The two boys with him — they are, indeed, little more than well-dressed boys, neither more than nineteen or twenty — gradually fell silent as the train travelled westwards, fearful that the slightest word might set him off.

A little man is waiting for them at the foot of the stairs. He wears a duffle coat and a very long scarf wrapped around his neck so many times that the bottom half of his face is invisible.

'Trevor,' says Kray, nodding.

'I'm really sorry you've had to come down, Mr Kray.'

'Yeah, so'm I.'

'Honest, he'll only take it from you. He goes on about you all the time, constantly.'

'Yeah? What's he saying?'

'Oh, Ronnie's this, Ronnie's that. He's my best friend. He's my hero. I'd do anything for that man. That sort of thing.'

'Let's get this over with, then. Where's the car?'

'Follow me.'

The little man leads them to a dusty Morris 1000 parked around the corner and they all pile in.

'Are they still in that flat?' asks Kray.

'No, they moved to a new place, above the decorating supply shop. But he wants to meet us outside the Lido.'

'Why?'

'Didn't say. But it's just as well, 'cos the girl was hanging around.'

Frank Marshall is unmistakable when they arrive. It's a bitterly cold day and the few pedestrians abroad scurry from shop to shop, heads down into the spiteful wind. Marshall stands on the pavement, his hands resting on the railings, the only stationary person, towering above all around him. He seems indifferent to the freezing conditions.

'Right,' says Kray once the car has come to a halt. 'You can fuck off, all of you. I need to talk to Frank in private.'

The two pretty boys look at one another in dismay. Mods with a taste for shiny suits and sly violence are ten a penny in London; here they'll attract attention. Furthermore, neither fancies freezing his balls off on a windswept seafront with nothing more interesting to look at than boarded-up amusement arcades.

'Come on,' says Trevor cheerfully. 'I know where we can get a cuppa.'

The three of them decamp, leaving the door open for Frank Marshall to get in. He closes the door behind him.

Marshall leans over the back seat to Kray in the front passenger seat, offering his hand. Ronnie hesitates — he has a dislike of touching others — but he reciprocates, his hand disappearing as it's enveloped in Marshall's huge fist. It is shaken with great enthusiasm.

'It's so good of you to come, Ronnie!' For a big man, Marshall has a surprisingly soft voice. 'I'm honoured, truly honoured, that you'd come all this way to see me.'

'Yeah, well, we need a word, don't we? You can't go on as you have been.'

Marshall holds up his hands in submission. 'I know, I know, I know, it was wrong of me. But Judy and I've been rowing something rotten, and she's getting right on me tits.'

'I warned you, Frank, didn't I? You never want to take a woman along. They're nothing but trouble.'

Marshall hangs his head, and nods. 'Yeah, yeah, yeah, I know. But I ain't like you, Ron. I need a bird, you know that.'

Kray does know. Frank Marshall has been part of his and Reg's lives since they were schoolboys, and even then the giant's voracious sexual appetite was legendary. Trevor has been phoning reports back to London on a daily basis, and by his account Marshall needs sex half a dozen times a day, and that's just with Judy; God knows how many others he's been picking up when Judy's back's been turned. In addition to being built like a bodybuilder, Marshall has a handsome face, and as long as he's not riled, he is also naïvely charming. In all the time the Krays have known him, he has never been without at least one woman in his life, usually several.

When not having sex, according to Trevor, he spends most of his time doing press-ups and other calisthenics, showering and repeatedly combing his hair in front of the mirror. He is inordinately vain.

'So what's the score with Judy?' asks Kray.

Marshall shakes his head. 'It's all right most the time, but ever since the money ran out she's always wandering off. Sometimes she stays out overnight. And she won't tell me where she's been.'

'I don't understand how you got through all that cash so fast. It should've lasted you a year at least.'

'But, Ronnie, she likes to go out dancin' 'n' that.'

'Is there anywhere to dance in this shithole?'

'Yeah, a coupla places, if you look for 'em. And she wants me to buy 'er dresses, and shoes 'n' stuff. And she may look skinny but, I'll tell you, she eats like a bleedin' 'orse! Please, please, can I come back? I'll keep me 'ead down, I promise. And I bought this false beard, like, so no one's gonna recognise me.'

'No, Frank. We agreed. At least a year, and then maybe abroad. You can't come back now.'

'But the bloke's been convicted!'

'So?' replies Kray, losing his temper. 'I've explained this to you a dozen times! You're supposed to be dead, you fuckin' dimwit! You can't come back just 'cos he's inside!'

'Now, Ronnie,' says Marshall in a reproving tone of voice, 'don't talk to me like that. It ain't nice.'

Kray makes an effort to remain calm. He can't imagine Marshall actually using violence against him, but he can't be sure. Ronnie Kray is an experienced and vicious fighter, but he knows he'd be no match for Marshall, especially in the close confines of a car. He packed a Smith & Wesson Chief Special in his coat pocket just in case.

'I'm sorry, Frank. I'm just worried for you,' he says in a placatory tone.

'I can look after meself, you know I can.'

'But if you're seen, it'll mean prison. Perverting the course of justice 'n' that? Honest, Frank, you're better off here.'

'But there's fuck all to do here! And I miss me boys.'

'I understand. Look.'

Kray digs into his jacket pocket and brings out a roll of notes in a rubber band. 'There's fifty quid there. That should keep you going for a bit longer while we work something out.'

Marshall takes the money and considers it in his palm.

'Well … that's generous, so thank you. But … you couldn't make it a ton, could you? I'd like to get out the flat, maybe rent one of them bungalows up the coast a bit.'

'Bungalows?'

'Yeah, I'd like the view. I like looking at the sea.'

'And you'd stay put there, would you?'

'Yeah, I could do,' says Marshall, but Kray isn't convinced.

'What about Judy? You want me to take her back to London?'

Marshall shakes his head. 'Nah, she'll be fine. She don't wanna go 'ome anyway. She fell out with her parents.'

Kray digs into his pocket and hands over a few more notes. 'That's all I can do for the minute, okay?'

Marshall nods. 'Thanks, Ron.'

'But don't let me hear you're back in the Smoke, got it?'

'Got it.'

CHAPTER SEVEN

The church of St Mary the Virgin, Ingatestone, Essex, dates from the early eleventh century. At least, so reads Charles from the card pinned to the noticeboard in the south porch. It is a peaceful place on a winter's Wednesday afternoon, and Charles enjoyed exploring its interior. He is always amazed at the atmosphere shared by houses of religion, no matter what denomination. He has often suspected that the universal sense of peacefulness (he would resist the word "spirituality") is in fact carried into the buildings by its believers, rather than inhabiting the building itself but, he has to admit, some of it seems to remain even when the buildings are empty.

The church is small and Charles's exploration took little time. For the last ten minutes he has been standing in the porch, from where he can observe the car park and warm his face in the winter sun.

Eventually a small car arrives and a thin young man wearing flares and a rather surprising green velvet jacket emerges from it.

'Mr Holborne?' he calls as he hurries across. 'I'm so sorry I'm late.'

He arrives at Charles's side and shakes his hand.

'I'm afraid something came up at the last moment. I'm still struggling, to be honest. Shall we go in?'

He leads Charles back inside the echoing place of worship.

'I apologise for my ignorance,' explains Charles to the man's back, 'but I'm not sure how to address a deacon.'

'Oh, Mr Smith will do. No one really bothers with the formal title. In fact, Julian is better still.'

There is a small table at the back of the church bearing a charity collection box, a pile of hymn books and some leaflets. By the side of the table is a small stack of plastic chairs from which the deacon extracts two.

'Will here be okay?' he asks. 'I assume you don't want to pray?'

'No, thank you,' replies Charles. 'This is fine.'

'Well, then,' says Smith, snatching a glance at his watch, 'how can I help you?'

'As I explained on the phone,' says Charles, 'I came to ask about Reverend Sharpe. I'm not officially representing him, but he has asked me to make some informal enquiries.'

'What do you want to know?'

'Did you know him well?' starts Charles.

'Not very. I finished training at the beginning of last year, so I met him for the first time about ten months before he was arrested.'

'And you worked together for that period?'

'Yes.'

'You'll be aware of what's been in the press. That he is accused of being a hypocrite, still involved in crime…' Charles stops as he sees the deacon shaking his head vigorously.

'Everyone here thinks there's been a terrible miscarriage of justice,' says Smith firmly.

'Why is that?'

'Well, this parish has never had such a successful priest. You couldn't miss it. He devoted his entire life to his ministry. The man never stopped. No matter what time of day or night, if one of his parishioners needed help, he'd be there. You should have heard the Bishop — "If only we had a dozen more like him" — things like that. He tired *me* out, and I'm thirty years younger!'

'It must have been a shock when he was arrested for murder.'

'It was. None of us believed it. That's why so many of us wanted to give evidence to support him.'

'But I have the original trial papers. No character witnesses were called,' points out Charles.

The deacon looks uncomfortable. 'Yes. We were told not to.'

'Who by?' asks Charles, sensing corruption.

'By the bishop. He came to speak to us, right here, in the church. It was thought that it was all too … political. He didn't want the church involved. I think he also felt that he might be criticised for offering Stanley a pulpit.'

'I see. The parish doesn't extend into the East End of London, does it?' asks Charles.

'No, of course not.'

'Then do you understand why Reverend Sharpe was opening a youth club in the East End?'

'Well, ours is quite a comfortable community here, and Stanley thought we should be doing something to assist those less fortunate than us. He thought it would be a good idea for some of the boys in Canning Town to have a different experience, you know, fresh air, countryside and so on? So we formed a partnership with the local church there, a sort of "twinning" scheme, you see? We invited a group of them to come to our youth club here, make friends and so on, until such time as a similar club could be organised in Canning Town. The night of the … trouble … with those men, was the opening night of the new club in the East End.'

'Were you there?'

'Yes, I was, although I didn't see the confrontation as I was in the kitchen.'

'Was Reverend Smith angry or upset afterwards?'

'I wouldn't call it that, no. He was sad.'

'Had you ever seen him angry, perhaps violent?'

'Good heavens, no! We were all aware of his previous history — he made no secret of it — but there was never anything of that sort. He came across as completely dedicated, determined to do what he could to support everyone in the community, but particularly young men who might fall into crime. In fact, he used to talk about his past to the youngsters. He was completely open about it. He used his life as an example of what could go wrong. And what could go right.'

'I see.'

Charles pauses and watches the thin man snatch another glance at his watch.

'I'm so sorry, but I really am terribly busy,' explains Smith. 'The new vicar isn't starting until next week, and I'm doing what I can to fill in, but I'm very inexperienced. I really have to go.'

'Yes, of course.'

Smith stands and Charles follows suit.

'Do you think you can help him?' asks the deacon, re-stacking the chairs.

'To be honest, no, I don't.'

'That's a great shame. We'll be praying for him, and your endeavours on his behalf.'

For the next few weeks, Charles is too busy to address his mind to Stanley Sharpe or Frank Marshall. He is fully occupied prosecuting a serial rapist at the Old Bailey, and that trial is followed immediately by one of his increasingly frequent civil claims, a claim for life-changing personal injury, in which he acts for the plaintiff. Towards the end of the rape trial, he finds himself working every night until midnight to prepare the civil claim in time. He hates it when two difficult cases, particularly in different fields, are listed back to back; more so when his opponents are too clever by half and he has to be on his toes.

Sally is supportive and uncomplaining. Instead of working in Chambers, Charles now brings his papers home, which at least has the advantage that Sally can spend time with him while he works. She brings her sewing basket up to the fourth bedroom, presently his study, and works in the corner, or she stretches out on the little couch and reads.

Charles's Instruction on behalf of Sharpe has ended, and his papers have been returned to Tindall, the young solicitor. The case, insofar as there ever was one, is done, but the little book of matches with the windmill design remains propped on his desk. Charles sees it every day, and it admonishes him. It represents unfinished business. Now he knows how difficult Gracie's life has been, including, if he understood her hint correctly, a period on the game, he would like to help her, even if he is no longer involved in the Sharpe case. So he will make one last effort; if that fails, he will close the chapter and consign her to his back story.

The following week, Charles unexpectedly finds himself at a loose end when the defence team in the personal injury claim offer to settle for a very acceptable figure. The case ends after only two days' evidence. The day after he rises late, eats a leisurely breakfast alone in the kitchen and dresses in casual clothes. He collects the matchbook from his desk and sets off to walk into Soho.

It is very cold, below freezing, but the sky is clear and the packed snow from the previous month has disappeared. Charles decides to avoid the main roads. He has been ducking and diving the narrow byways and cobbled alleys of London since he was a child, and they feel as familiar to him as his childhood home, but he still enjoys the sense of discovery. You never know what lies around the next corner, what nefarious business transaction upon which one might stumble, what new corner café or club looks worthy of a visit, or what eighteenth-century building has been demolished to make way for a new office block or shop. The city is changing fast, and there's a new colourful vibrancy to it which he finds exciting. The fact that he knows London as well as any cab driver gives him a sense of belonging and invulnerability. This is Charles's "patch"; he's untouchable here.

He jogs across Gray's Inn Road and heads west along Guilford Street. Then, instead of continuing straight on towards Russell Square, he turns left onto Lambs Conduit Street and zigzags through the narrow streets west, south, west and south again until he reaches Shorts Gardens and the start of Soho. There used to be a family restaurant here, run by a Jewish Italian couple who managed to escape to England shortly before the war. They were acquainted with the Horowitz family through Charles's mother, and Millie and Harry Horowitz used to bring Charles and his younger brother David here on Sunday afternoons for kosher ice cream. It is years since Charles has been to the restaurant, but he is dismayed to find that it's gone. In its place are blacked-out windows and a heavy curtain in front of the door, above which in lurid red paint are the words "Sex Shop".

Charles continues westwards into the heart of Soho, noting that there is a new "Private Shop", a strip club and an art gallery, all of which must have opened in the last few months. A young woman at considerable risk of hypothermia stands in the strip club's doorway. Bump and grind music crackles from a speaker hung above the door. Charles admires the girl's attempt to look inviting, but her absence of clothing is fatally at odds with the climatic conditions. Her goosebumped skin reminds him of one of his mother's plucked chickens before going into the pot, and her red nose and blueish lips owe nothing to make-up.

'Give it up, girl, and get a hot drink,' he says sympathetically as he passes.

She laughs. 'I'd rather have a pair of bloomers!' she cackles behind him.

From Cambridge Circus onwards he is in Soho proper, and here he starts encountering the working girls. It's still not quite noon, but he remembers being told by one of his very first clients that if you haven't been working too late the night before, there's good lunchtime business to be done with the office workers. He avoids Shaftesbury Avenue and continues down Old Compton Street, during the course of which he is accosted, twice, by girls with "large chest for sale" cards pinned to the doors behind them. A third, rather better dressed, offers him "French lessons" in an odd accent that's more Peckham than Paris. He declines, to her puzzlement, in French.

Great Windmill Street, when he reaches it, is packed. The pavements on both sides are double-parked with contractors' lorries and there are builders and scaffolders everywhere. Two shopfronts are being renovated, and it looks as if a third has just been finished. What for a generation used to be an old-fashioned electrical retailers is now a record shop, and a man wearing a mod suit and a purple shirt is setting out boxes of second-hand LPs on the pavement. *A Hard Day's Night* blares from inside. Next door is a new espresso bar.

Charles turns in a full circle, scanning his surroundings. The grey monotones of the war years, which continued for a decade through rationing and rebuilding, are finally disappearing. Soho is changing fast.

He looks up at the Windmill's frontage. Its famous sign, *We Never Closed*, usually picked out in brilliant white lightbulbs, is dark, but the foyer doors are open and Charles enters. He approaches a young man in the box office.

'We're not open yet,' says the man. 'The next showing's at two-thirty.'

He points to a board above him showing the programme times for a film.

Charles looks more carefully at the advertising poster. It portrays several naked and half-naked girls under the strapline *See the orgies they dared to film!* followed by the title: *Sextet — Six women for every man!*

'Is the Windmill a cinema now?' he asks.

'Yes, mate. That's why we advertise films.'

'But when did it stop being a theatre?'

'Last October. But there's just as much juice now, I promise. Wanna ticket?'

'No, thank you. I'm looking for one of the girls in the chorus.'

'Ain't we all?'

Charles retraces his steps onto the pavement. After a moment's consideration, he heads for Haymarket and, thence, Chambers.

The place is bustling by the time he arrives. The courts have just risen for the short adjournment and several members have popped back to check their post and make a few calls while eating a sandwich before rushing back. Charles's informal attire attracts a few glances and, as he enters the clerks' room, Barbara tuts loudly.

'What?' says Charles innocently.

'You know the rules, sir. Suit and tie, even if you're not in court or seeing clients.'

'I'm perfectly smartly dressed,' he protests, indicating his slacks and jacket.

'Other members will have clients in, even if you don't, sir.'

At that moment Peter Bateman, Charles's roommate, enters at a rush. 'Off on holiday, Charles?' he says, digging through his pigeonhole.

'Very funny. I only came in for a phone number, Barbara. Tindall and Co.?'

'Then you don't need to be in here, do you, sir?' says Barbara. 'If you go up to your room, I'll put you through.'

Charles runs upstairs to his corridor, two stairs at a time. Bateman sees Barbara's scowl and laughs. 'You'll never change him, you know?'

Maria is working at Charles's desk as he bursts in. 'Oh, I'm sorry —' she says, leaping up.

'It's fine. Stay where you are.'

'It's just that these papers are so —'

'It's fine. I'm just here to make a call. I can do it from Peter's desk.' He sits opposite her. 'Have you met him yet?'

'Yes, he was just here.'

'He's nice, isn't he?'

'I don't know. I'm sure he is. I … I didn't know what to say to him.'

'Why on earth not?'

'He's just so … English. And so posh.'

'He is, but don't let that bother you. Anyway, you're posh too, aren't you? Diplomat father, famous sculptor and professor for a mother and all that?'

'It's not the same.'

'Well, we've been thinking of having some people round, for lunch. Or dinner, maybe. You can meet him properly then —'

He is interrupted by the phone ringing on his own desk. Maria picks it up.

'No, sorry, Miss … Barbara, he's at Mr Bateman's desk.' She hangs up and the phone rings again in front of Charles.

'Thanks, Barbara. Put him through.' Pause. 'Hello, Mr Tindall.'

'Hello, Mr Holborne,' says the young solicitor. 'How are you?'

'Fine, thanks.'

'So, you heard about Mr Sharpe?'

'No, what's happened?'

'Oh, well, I'm sorry to report that he's been assaulted by a group of other prisoners. He's still alive, in the hospital wing, but apparently it was a close call.'

Charles leans on the desk, his free hand running through his curly hair. 'I'm so sorry to hear that,' he says softly. 'Do we know why?'

'Not really. It was well organised, and the governor thinks it might've been ordered from outside the prison.'

'What makes him think that?'

'The weapons used. Four coshes were smuggled in and the four attackers used one each. As if they were sending a message; a deliberate attempt to beat him to death.'

A departure from the conventional method of dispatch, a quick shiv to the aorta in the shower block. Quite novel.

'You don't have any news, do you?' asks Tindall.

Charles sighs. 'Only bad news, I'm afraid. I did go and see Gracie Marshall, but she's heard nothing. She was resigned to the fact that her husband's dead, and I may have raised her hopes unnecessarily. I also thought I might've stumbled across something, and I checked it out this morning, but it's a dead end. I don't know what else can be done, unless you instruct a private detective.'

'You know the problem with that. In fact, the only reason I'm still in touch with the Sharpe family is because I'm selling the lease to their showroom in Dulwich. It was the last of Stanley's business operations, and Robin's been running it since his father became a vicar.'

'Do you think he would've had the money for his father's appeal?'

'Probably not. I've seen the accounts and it's barely made a profit for years. Apparently all the old stock's going for a song.'

'Really? Perhaps I should pop down,' replies Charles, thinking of Vera, his rusting and unreliable Austin Healey sportscar, so named due to its registration number, VER 525. Sally hates the car, not unreasonably, considering she regularly has to sit on a towel to avoid the puddle of rainwater that gathers on the passenger seat.

'Do you have a buyer for the site?' asks Charles.

'We did, but the deal fell apart.'

Charles remains silent for a while. 'There doesn't seem to be anything more I can do.'

'No, I don't think so. But thanks for trying.'

'Okay. And thank you for letting me know.'

'Goodbye.'

Charles hangs up, and leans back thoughtfully in Peter's chair. He sees Maria's questioning look.

'That chap we went to see in Durham. He was beaten almost to death. Apparently they only just got to him in time.'

'Really? I find it difficult to be sorry.' Charles frowns at her. 'Well,' she continues, 'he's got a very long criminal record, even if it is a few years back, he's a wife-beater, and now a jury's found him guilty of murder. Not much of a loss to society. I'm not sure I could even defend someone like him.'

'Someone like him?'

'Yes. People who've done terrible things, people who I know are guilty.'

'But until the jury reaches a verdict, you never "know" they're guilty, not unless they tell you. And if they do, you're not allowed to put a lie before the court.'

Charles finds Maria's attitude surprising. She may have only recently started pupillage, but she's an intelligent and well-qualified lawyer.

'What's more, if we start refusing to represent people accused of terrible crimes,' Charles continues, 'there could never be a fair trial. We'd be pre-judging the evidence and usurping the jury's function. Especially when we know that evidence is routinely bent and tampered with by corrupt police officers, wouldn't that be immoral?'

Charles searches Maria's face to see if she has understood him, but her expression is unreadable.

'If you're going to do criminal work,' he says, 'especially for the defence, you're going to have to put your own opinions to one side.'

She bends her head to her papers without answering.

'What made you want to be a lawyer?' asks Charles. 'In fact, come to that, why practise as a barrister in England when presumably you could practise in the States?'

'I've always been interested in the legal system,' she replies, looking up and smiling briefly. Something about the way the smile slides off her face the instant she returns her attention to the papers on the desk bothers Charles.

'I bet that wasn't the answer you gave at interview,' he says, trying to find a jocular tone. 'You'd never have made it to the second round.'

'I can't remember what I said, to be honest. I was very nervous. Mr Hamilton and I spoke about lots of things.'

'Robert did the interview himself?' asks Charles, surprised.

'Mr Hamilton? Yes.'

'Hmm. He must have been impressed by your application. He usually convenes a panel to make pupillage decisions.'

She shrugs slightly but doesn't look up, and it's obvious she wants the conversation to end. He decides not to persist. He also decides that it's time to firm up the proposed dinner date and get Sally fully on board. He may be the professional interrogator living at Wren Street, but he senses that in this instance he should, as his American counterparts would put it, give first seat to Sally. She has a genius for befriending people and putting them at their ease; she'll discover more. He also makes a mental note to speak to Robert Hamilton QC next time they pass in Chambers; perhaps he can fill in for Charles some of his reticent pupil's background. Charles knows one thing with certainty: his antennae are tingling. In just the same way as he can tell when a witness is only giving half an answer under cross-examination, there is more to Maria Hudson's story than she is revealing.

CHAPTER EIGHT

Charles storms up the steps and pushes open the front door with his elbow. The door bangs heavily against the recently repainted dado rail in the hall and summons Sally, who was putting on her coat.

'Fuck! Fuck!' he shouts. He is holding his hands up in front of him like a surgeon waiting to be gloved by his theatre nurse.

'What the hell's going on?' says Sally. 'Look what you've done to the paint!'

'The bloody car won't start, and I've got oil all over my shirt cuffs!' He runs past her and down the stairs into the kitchen.

She hears the water running in the sink and follows him down. 'What is it?'

'I've no idea. I thought maybe the points, again, but they look fine. It's not firing, so maybe the petrol pump? Or the carburettor? Can you give me a hand?' He holds out his hands again, wet and soapy, for her to pull his suit cuffs up towards his elbows and undo his cufflinks.

'You should've taken your jacket off first,' she says.

'I didn't want to touch it.'

'Your shirt's not too bad. And I'm not going to say "I told you so". But I told you so. How much more money are you going to pour into that old rust-bucket?'

'I know, I know.' He rinses his hands and Sally passes him a kitchen towel.

'I know you love Vera,' she says sympathetically. 'But don't you think it's time to get something a bit more reliable?'

'Yes, yes, yes,' he replies, impatiently.

He's not cross with Sally. He knows she's right. She's warned him several times that one day the Austin Healey would let him down just when he needed it. Today's the day. He has to be at Aylesbury Assizes by ten o'clock, and he was already cutting it fine. He looks at his watch.

'What're you going to do?' she asks.

'It's too late to get a train.' He shakes his head. 'Well, this is going to teach me a lesson. I'll have to find a cabbie who'll take me all the way, and this afternoon I'll look into buying something new and boring. Maybe they'll tow Vera as part of the deal.'

She puts a consoling hand on his arm. 'Why not see if we can rent space in a lock-up garage somewhere within walking distance? There are loads under the arches at King's Cross. Then you could get her fixed up and use her for fun, you know, during the summer. If you get the hood mended, I'll even come out with you.'

He pauses, considering. 'That's a good idea. I'll make enquiries. Thank you.'

Charles checks both hands and, satisfied they're clean, takes Sally's face in his great paws. He bends and kisses her tenderly on the lips, marvelling as always at the softness of her skin and how good she smells.

I'm so lucky to get a second chance at this.

'Sorry I can't give you a lift,' he says into her hair. 'Will you be okay?'

'I'll be fine. Let's head up to Gray's Inn Road. I'll put you in a cab and walk from there.'

Charles's day continues downhill. The taxi fare from central London to Aylesbury costs significantly more than the sum marked on his brief; his case is listed before His Honour Judge Machin, a very experienced but thoroughly unpleasant judge; it is called on last of the ten-thirty list; his client's character witness, who was coming to tell the court that he had a job lined up for the client, fails to attend; and, despite what Charles considers to be a brilliant plea in mitigation, the client goes down for two years when Charles advised no more than eighteen months at worst.

He descends the steep stone steps to the cells to see his client with a heavy heart, wondering if he might be able to draft grounds of appeal in the taxi on his return journey.

To Charles's surprise, the client is philosophical.

'I always thought you was a bit optimistic, Mr 'Olborne, sir,' he says, shaking Charles's hand. 'With my record I expected two, maybe even two and a half. Really good plea, though, I thought. I enjoyed listening to you.'

Charles finds himself in the unusual position of being consoled by his own client, who is about to start two years' imprisonment.

'Really? Didn't do much good, did it?'

'Well, it's that bastard Machin, ain't it? No, you was very good. Don't you worry about it.'

'I was thinking that maybe we should appeal.'

The man screws up his face and shakes his head. 'Nah. Let's leave it. I've got nine months under me belt on remand, so as long as I keep me nose clean, I'm almost halfway. It could take longer'n that to get the appeal on, and I'd rather know where I stand, see? But thanks anyway.'

So Charles shakes his cheerful client's hand again and returns to the court foyer to look for a call box. There are two on the wall, but one has been vandalised by a disappointed litigant and there is a queue for the other. Charles waits patiently and eventually gets to the front. He dials and when he hears an answer at the other end, presses a coin into the slot.

'Is Sergeant Sloane on duty?' he asks. 'No, it's a private call. Charles Holborne.' He waits until his friend is put through. 'Hi Sean.'

'Charles. Good to hear from you, but I'm a bit busy, I'm afraid…'

'That's fine. I just need a quick favour. You know Reverend Stanley Sharpe, convicted of murdering Frank Marshall a couple of months back? He's got a son called Robin. Early twenties. Anything known?'

'Jesus, Charlie, you've got some cheek! I'm not your personal CRO!' Sloane's tone is light, but Charles detects definite irritation.

'I don't need criminal records, Sean, just a quick steer. I'm thinking of buying a car from the son, and just want to know if he's straight.'

Charles hears the long-suffering policeman sigh. 'As far as I know, he's straight. Or as straight as a second-hand car salesman ever is. But that's off the record, and I'm not responsible if he sells you a ringer. Okay if I get back to work now?'

'That wasn't difficult now, was it? Thank you. Still up for Wednesday?'

'All things being equal, yes.'

'Good. First round's on me.'

'And the rest. That'll cost you dinner.'

'Happy to. Thanks, mate. I do appreciate it.'

Charles hangs up.

The court building is now half-empty, most of the barristers, solicitors and police officers having drifted off for lunch. He looks at his watch; quarter past one. He curses. He's missed the next train from Aylesbury and now faces a long wait on a cold platform.

Then, at last, his luck begins to change.

'Charles?' says a posh voice behind him.

Charles turns to see a barrister walking towards him. James McPhee has a mixed practice and still works from Charles's former chambers, where Sally is the clerk.

'I didn't know you were here today,' he says. 'Have you finished?'

'Yes. I was before Machin,' confirms Charles.

'Commiserations. He doesn't get better, does he?'

'Nope.'

'Are you on the train? I'm not going all the way in, but if you fancy a catch-up, I can give you a lift to London.'

'Ah, that would be excellent! My car wouldn't start this morning and I had to take a cab here from King's Cross. Thank you.'

'You're not still driving Vera, are you? That old girl should've been scrapped years ago.'

'Don't you start. I'm getting it in the neck from Sally, too.'

The two men descend the steps of the beautiful old building where the Great Train Robbers were sentenced eighteen months before. They walk towards McPhee's car.

'You live somewhere in south London, don't you?' asks Charles as he slides into his colleague's dry, well-upholstered Jaguar which, he notes wryly, smells of leather and walnut and not burnt oil and rotting carpet.

'Blackheath, why?'

'Well, if you're going home, that would suit me rather well. I'm told there's a garage in Dulwich Village which is closing down and where I might, possibly, acquire a reliable vehicle at a bargain price. Could you drop me there?'

'No problem at all, old chap.'

"Sharpe's Luxury Motors", when Charles finds it, is not at all what he expected. He feared finding a forecourt with chained gates and a "For Sale" sign on the fencing. Indeed, he was sufficiently uncertain that he would find the place open that he asked McPhee to wait while he scouted out the premises.

The garage, however, is bustling. Lines of luxury cars front the lot, with a good selection of less ostentatious vehicles towards the back. There are even a few clean-looking vans with prices in their windscreens. The combined showroom and office building at the far end of the forecourt matches the company's stock: clean, tidy and well-appointed. Charles thanks McPhee and lets him go. He doesn't expect to buy a vehicle that instant, but North Dulwich station is only fifteen minutes into London.

Charles walks up and down the rows of shiny vehicles. If he has to buy a boring car, there are plenty here from which to choose.

Charles is looking inside the driver's window of a Jaguar XKE coupe with a fixed head which he rather fancies — but which he knows Sally would veto — when he is approached by a salesman.

'Good afternoon, sir,' he says. 'Can I help you, or are you just browsing?'

'No, I am looking to buy a car. Is Robin Sharpe here today, by any chance?'

'Do you know Mr Sharpe?'

'Yes, or rather, we've met recently in connection with a legal matter.'

'Police?' asks the young man guardedly.

It would not be unusual in this business for a car salesman to be nervous. Even honest car dealers sometimes find themselves inadvertently selling "ringed" or "cut and shut" vehicles. Ringed vehicles have been stolen to order, their vehicle identification numbers ground off and replaced, and given the identity of a vehicle previously scrapped after an accident. Cut and shut vehicles are made up of the undamaged front and rear ends of two identical luxury vehicles which have been written off and joined to create a new car; they're expensive, shiny death-traps. Nonetheless, there is something more about the salesman's demeanour, perhaps the way his professional smile freezes, that makes Charles wonder if there may be more to it than that.

'No. I'm a barrister. I was instructed by Mr Sharpe. Is he in?'

'I'll go and see. Do you want to sit inside?' He nods towards the Jaguar. 'I can get the key.'

'No thanks. I'll keep looking, though.'

A few minutes later, Charles sees Robin Sharpe's white-blond head weaving its way between the lines of cars towards him.

'Mr Holborne,' he says, shaking Charles by the hand. 'This is a pleasure,' he adds, but his face is creased into a frown and anxiety lines his eyes. 'Is this a professional visit or about Dad?'

'I need to buy a car,' says Charles simply, 'and I remembered your line of work. My Austin Healey died this morning.'

Sharpe's face relaxes. 'Oh dear! Well, I'm sure we've got something suitable. And, in all the circumstances, I'm sure we can give you a good price. I understand from Mum that you carried on making enquiries without being paid. I meant to telephone and thank you.'

Charles waves away the thanks. 'No need. Your father asked me to go and see a potential witness, but there was nothing in it, I'm afraid.'

'Well, Mum was very grateful. Come into the office and I'll show you some options. This lot is only half of what we have.'

Sharpe leads Charles across the forecourt.

'I understood that the lease of the garage was being sold,' says Charles. 'I wasn't even sure you'd be here.'

'It *has* been sold,' says Sharpe, 'but I'm delighted to say we found a buyer to take the lease *and* the business as a going concern.'

'That must be a relief.'

'Yes and no,' replies Sharpe. 'The new owners have put in a lot of capital, which is why we're able to restock, redecorate and so on, but it's no longer a Sharpe business. I'm an employee now.'

He guides Charles across the showroom and through a door into an office suite. Charles follows him down a short corridor.

'Are you looking for a replacement for the Healey, another sports car?' asks Sharpe over his shoulder.

Charles replies to the young man's back. 'No, I got outvoted on that. I think I need something a bit more suitable for a young woman who likes to wear miniskirts.'

Sharpe laughs. 'I get you. Do you want new?'

'Not necessarily brand-new, but certainly no more than a couple of years old.'

'We've a good selection matching that description. Sorry about the mess. The new owners are redecorating.'

Charles is passing a room opening to his left covered in dust sheets.

'Mind that,' says Sharpe as he enters his office, pointing to some stacked chairs and other odds and ends half-filling the corridor. 'Come in. Coffee?'

'Yes, I think I will, thank you. Black, no sugar.'

Sharpe presses a button on his desk. 'Gloria? Two coffees please, both black.' He points at a chair opposite his desk. 'Take a seat.'

'Now the business is on safer foundations, might you reconsider your decision?'

'Decision?'

'Not to contribute to your father's appeal.'

Sharpe looks up and glares at Charles. 'If this is the reason you've come here, you can bloody well leave straightaway!'

Charles raises his hands in submission, taken aback by the other's vehemence.

'No, I assure you, I need to buy a car. In fact, I'm on Shanks's Pony.'

Sharpe stares at him, his body unnaturally still. A full five seconds elapse before he relaxes.

'Fine. But I'm quite serious. My mother may be deluded, but I'm not. My father is exactly where he belongs. I thought I made my views clear when we met.'

'Fair enough,' replies Charles.

Sharpe takes a pad out of his desk drawer. 'So, have you a budget in mind?'

The next few minutes are prickly, but Sharpe gradually calms down as they talk prices, insurance costs and hire purchase. Finally, Sharpe stands and takes a file from a filing cabinet, skimming it briefly.

'Follow me,' he says coolly. 'I think I can show you something that meets all your requirements.'

An hour and one phone call to Charles's insurers later, and Charles is driving cautiously off the forecourt in his "new" two-year-old Rover 2000 P6 in an attractive dark blue, the winner, Robin Sharpe assures him, of last year's European Car of the Year award.

'It's the perfect family car for a young professional,' Sharpe told him, 'but it has a sense of style as well. I'm sure you'll be happy with it. We're supplying them new all over Europe, even a few to the States.'

Charles sees Sharpe in the rear-view mirror, watching him drive away. The salesman who first approached Charles is standing very close to Sharpe, inclining his head as he says something in the other's ear. Both have their eyes fixed on the Rover as it turns around a corner and out of sight.

As he drives through south London traffic, Charles has to concede that Sharpe was right. He loves the car. Its sleek looks and quiet handling, its leather seats, thick, clean carpet and working radio; all a great improvement on his draughty, rattling and smelly sports car. Now he is in a modern comfortable vehicle, he wonders why he put off the purchase for so long. He so enjoys driving back to Wren Street, despite the rush-hour traffic, that his conversation with Robin Sharpe slips completely from his mind. In later years, he will wonder if that forgetfulness eventually cost a man his life.

CHAPTER NINE

'For Christ's sake, Charlie, get out the bleeding way!' Sally shoves Charles away with her elbow, a hot roasting tin between her gloved hands.

'I'm just trying to reach the cutlery,' he protests.

'We won't need cutlery if I ruin this roast!'

Charles steps back to let his lovely but stressed girlfriend open the oven and slide the tray back in.

It is not the first time Sally has cooked beef Wellington, and Charles knows she is perfectly up to the task, but he did wonder out loud if it wasn't a bit ambitious for their first Sunday lunch — new oven, new house and the first time they've entertained. He didn't want Sally putting herself under unnecessary pressure, particularly with guests who don't know one another and some of whom she has never entertained before.

'What's the time?' she asks, yet again.

There are red spots high on her cheeks and she is perspiring slightly. Her hair, which she tied back in a hurried ponytail to check on the meat, has escaped and she tucks it behind an ear.

'One thirty-five. We've twenty-five minutes.'

She yanks off her chef's apron. 'Okay. I'm going to get changed.'

'Why? You look lovely.'

'I'm hot and sweaty and I need to get out of this blouse. That has to come out and rest in twenty minutes,' she says, pointing at the oven. 'Don't put the vegetables on yet.'

'No, chef.'

'Can you finish laying the table?'

'Yes, chef.'

'Don't forget to wash the new wine glasses.'

'No, chef.'

'And stop taking the piss.'

'Definitely, chef.'

'Charlie, I'm not in the mood.'

She makes to walk past him but he grabs one of her hands and turns her towards him.

'It's going to be fine, sweetheart,' he says softly. 'The meal is fine. The house looks great. *You* look great. We're going to have a lovely afternoon. You've known Peter for years, since he was a baby pupil. And his girlfriend is charming. Stop fretting.'

She takes a deep breath and manages to calm herself slightly.

'I know,' she replies. She doesn't sound convinced.

Sally wishes she'd resisted Charles's charm offensive and refused to host this lunch. The problem is, he doesn't understand.

Peter Bateman, Charles's former pupil, has never been anything other than perfectly friendly to Sally, but when he worked with Charles at Chancery Court she was the junior clerk. Although only a pupil, Peter was her senior professionally, in social status and age, and though she is no longer his clerk, she remains very conscious that he comes from money, the landed gentry. There are Cabinet ministers and High Court judges in his family. He has never been to her home, he has never seen her socially and she's terrified she will be judged and found wanting. As for his girlfriend, Amanda, she is apparently some sort of cello prodigy and now plays in a famous orchestra, the name of which Sally has been told but has already forgotten.

Sally is terrified, and Charles will never understand.

Sally has watched him breeze with equal confidence into cocktail parties hosted by peers of the realm and Benchers of his Inn, and drunken knees-ups in the roughest of London's pubs. The man's a chameleon. In the East End he's the cockney tough guy made good; in the West End he's the cultured barrister with interests in the arts and jazz and a slightly exotic past. She marvels at the way his speech changes, even the way he walks, according to the company he is keeping. He seems completely unconscious of his protean nature.

At one time she imagined he was the most socially confident man alive, and that was part of the attraction, but their time as a couple has taught her that this amazing dexterity is an act. Fundamentally, Charles is just as unsure and shy as she, but the performance is so slick that no one sees through it.

'I mean it,' he reassures. 'And you'll have Sean and Irenna if things get sticky. Which they won't,' he adds quickly.

'Yes, I know.'

Charles's policeman friend, Detective Sergeant Sean Sloane, had a rural upbringing as far removed from Sally's as possible, but his parents were dirt-poor Irish tenant farmers and he has no tolerance of airs or graces. Neither has Irenna, his South African doctor girlfriend. Sally has got to know them well over the last few months and feels very comfortable in their company. She'd go so far as to say that they're becoming part of her extended ad hoc family.

Maria Hudson, on the other hand, remains a complete unknown. She has twice agreed and then cried off proposed dates, and Charles isn't even sure she'll attend today. Sally has told him that this is the last time she tries, and Charles has agreed.

'Okay. But I'm still going to get out of this blouse. I can't greet your posh friends with sweaty armpits.'

She tips her head back in invitation and he bends to kiss her.

'Do you know how much I love you, Sally Fisher,' he murmurs, 'you and your sweaty armpits?'

'I think so.'

'Good. Well, what are you waiting for? If they're early, they could be here in ten minutes,' he teases.

'Do the glasses,' she orders, running from the room.

Sally needn't have worried. Peter and Amanda and Sean and Irenna all arrive at the front door at the same moment, bottles and flowers in hand. Charles opens the door to find them giggling at something Sean has said.

Once Charles has served drinks, Irenna goes directly down to the kitchen to help Sally put the final touches to the meal, Sean and Peter launch into talking shop, and Charles acquiesces in Amanda's request to see round the house and starts the guided tour. Finally, twenty-five minutes after the other guests arrive, the doorbell rings again and Charles finds Maria on the doorstep. Under her coat Charles sees a miniskirt and white knee-length boots.

'Hello there,' he says. 'You look very trendy.'

'Oh, no, too informal?' she replies, suddenly worried. 'I haven't done English Sunday lunch before.'

'Absolutely not. You look lovely. It's just the first time I've seen you not wearing court dress,' he reassures her. 'Come in.'

That makes Charles think about the others' clothes. He tries to recall Peter and Sean's attire. He can't remember exactly, but they're both in flared blue jeans and one of them — Peter, perhaps? — sports a turtleneck sweater. For the first time, Charles is conscious of being the oldest in the group, by almost twenty years in some cases. It's a discomfiting thought. As he takes Maria's coat and directs her into the lounge, he pauses long enough to examine himself in the hall mirror. What he previously thought were perfectly appropriate shirt and slacks now seem a bit dated.

Maybe it is *time for a makeover.*

The afternoon goes well. The beef is perfect and conversation flows. By the time Sally serves her signature "afters", poached pears, and Charles opens a bottle of dessert wine, Sally's concerns have entirely evaporated. Like most of her guests, she is slightly tipsy. Even Maria seems to have relaxed somewhat, although she's declined all but a half-glass of red wine, and she has less to contribute to the conversation than the others, even though they spend some time talking about President Johnson's enthusiasm for the war in Vietnam.

Late afternoon becomes early evening, and no one seems keen to break up the party. Charles had planned on a walk but the weather is against him, cold with periodic showers of sleet, so Sally removes his beloved jazz from the record player, replaces it discreetly with a selection of her 45s, and they play charades to a background of The Yardbirds, The Beach Boys and The Monkees.

It is Irenna who first notices that Maria is no longer in the room.

'Didn't she go to the toilet?' asks Sally.

'That was a while ago,' replies Irenna.

Charles gets up and steps into the hall. He finds Maria by the front door, coat, gloves and scarf on, her hand reaching for the doorknob to let herself out.

'Leaving?' he asks, surprised.

'Yes … sorry … I've got to go. I didn't want to disturb you all.'

'Oh. That's a shame.'

Sally joins Charles in the doorway from the lounge, her hand around his waist. 'Are you off, Maria?' she asks.

'Yes. I've had a lovely afternoon. Thank you so much for inviting me.'

'It's been good to meet you. Are you … has anyone said anything that's … upset you?'

Maria shakes her head vigorously. 'No, no, not at all! I was just explaining to Charles that I didn't want to disturb your game.'

She takes a couple of steps forward and grips Sally's free hand with one of hers. It's an odd gesture.

'Thank you so much,' she says again.

With that, she turns and scurries out of the front door, closing it behind her. Charles and Sally listen to her feet clattering down the steps to the pavement and look at each other.

'That was weird,' says Charles.

'Do you think somebody said something?' asks Sally.

He shrugs. 'I didn't hear anything. We were all just mucking about and then, suddenly, she wasn't in the room.'

Peter pops his head into the corridor. 'Has she gone?'

'Yes,' replies Charles. 'If I hadn't gone out at that moment, she would've left without a word.'

They return to the others.

'I know she's American,' says Peter, flopping into a chair, 'but that was very odd even for a Yank. You'd have thought she'd have learned to thank her host and hostess and not just disappear.'

'I wonder where she was going?' muses Charles.

'Home, I expect,' says Irenna.

Charles shakes his head. 'No. I don't know if you saw, Sal, but she'd got changed. She was wearing some sort of evening dress and her make-up was different. Plus, she had a leather pouch thing with a sort of metal bar that flipped over the handles.'

'Like a music case? For carrying sheet music?' asks Amanda. 'I've got one of those.'

'Is she a musician?' asks Peter.

'She's never said anything about it,' says Charles.

'She didn't say very much about herself at all,' comments Sean, lighting a cigarette. He looks around the room. 'Does anyone remember anything concrete that she revealed?'

Everyone shakes their heads.

'One thing I do know,' says Sally. 'She's not keen on law.'

'How do you know that?' asks Charles.

'A couple of things she said, but more particularly the way she said them. We were chatting, about nothing much in particular, and I asked how it was going in Chambers, was she enjoying the work? She didn't answer for a bit, and I watched her winding herself up to look enthusiastic.'

'Her written work's very good. Very sharp,' says Charles. 'Have you seen any of it?' he asks Peter.

'She drafted something for me a couple of weeks ago and it was pretty good. I went through it with her and she understood where she'd made a few mistakes. So I think she's bright enough. Though I have noticed that when you're not in Chambers, she leaves very promptly. Sometimes before the clerks. Barbara's noticed as well.'

'That won't do her any good,' comments Charles.

‘I think there’s a family tragedy, there,’ says Irenna.

Everyone turns to her.

‘What makes you say that?’ asks Sally.

‘We were sharing expatriate stories, you know, how we came to be in England? She was very evasive. And I got the impression that things weren’t great between her parents.’

‘Well,’ concludes Charles, ‘she’s a mystery. And if she doesn’t like the law, I don’t know why she’s bothering with it.’ He stands. ‘Coffee, anyone?’

CHAPTER TEN

Charles and Sally wait at the corner of Chancery Lane and Fleet Street for the traffic lights to change. It's a miserable day, very cold, with low grey cloud and persistent rain, that sort of very fine, very wet rain that penetrates clothing and chills to the bone. Sally clings to Charles's arm and leans into him. The umbrella he holds is just a bit too small to cover them both, and her left shoulder and his right are getting drenched. When the traffic relents, they jog across the road and shelter briefly under the arch leading to Inner Temple Lane.

'Have a good day,' says Sally.

'You too.'

They kiss briefly, and Sally takes the umbrella and runs off. Charles is about to continue walking along Fleet Street to enter the Temple through Mitre Court when he hears Sally call back to him.

'Don't forget the manual!'

He waves in reply and strides off.

The entrance to Chambers is crowded when he reaches it, several clerks and barristers having arrived at the same moment. Hats and coats are being shaken and umbrellas opened and closed vigorously. Charles excuses himself through the crowd and runs upstairs to the clerks' room.

The only member of staff already there is Clive, the spotty and insouciant teenager employed as Chambers' dogsbody. He is crouched over the gas fire with a twist of old newspaper, trying to get it to light.

'Morning, sir,' he says, looking up.

'Morning. Has anything arrived from that garage?' he asks.

'I've not looked at the post yet,' says Clive. 'I did phone them as you asked.'

'Thank you.'

Charles and Sally had planned to take the Rover out for a drive the previous weekend, but the front tyres looked slightly deflated to Charles's eye, and on looking for the manual in the glove compartment to check the appropriate pressures, he couldn't find it. Having searched the car from back to front, he concluded that he drove off without the manual or service record, both of which he's sure he examined at the garage.

Clive is busily leafing through the tall pile of unopened envelopes on his desk. He reaches a fat one addressed to Charles personally, and not "The Clerk to Mr Holborne".

'Is this it?' He hands it over.

Charles tears open the envelope and takes out a shiny new manual for the Rover. 'Yes. Thank you. Do me a favour and put it on my desk with everything else, will you? I'll see you this afternoon.'

'All right, guv,' says the youngster.

Charles is back in Chambers at his desk. He has endured a frustrating day. The principal prosecution witness telephoned the court to say her car had broken down and that she would be late. The case was put back until not before noon, and the trial following it ran on for longer than expected. By quarter past four, when the judge rose for the day, Charles's case had still not been recalled. After a complete day at a court building with one broken coffee machine and no canteen, everyone, the prosecution and defence witnesses, barristers and solicitors, was fractious. A wasted day, and unless Charles can persuade the Legal Aid Board to treat it as the start of the trial, which he thinks unlikely, he'll be paid the rate for an adjournment, the princely sum of five pounds.

He picks up the phone. 'Can I have an outside line, please, Jennie?'

When he hears the purr of the dialling tone, he dials Chancery Court.

Sally picks up. 'Chancery Court?'

'Hi Sal.'

'Hi. How's your day going?'

'Crap. We didn't get on at all. I was wondering how long you're going to be, as I'd like to go home and snuggle up in front of the TV with my favourite girl.'

'You'd better give her a call then, 'cos I'm going to be late.'

'Oh, really? Why?'

'Mr Stanwyck's wife went into early labour this morning. She lost the baby. Mr Stanwyck's been at the hospital all day. He's supposed to be starting a three-month intellectual property trial tomorrow, but he's returned it. I need to find an IP silk at quarter to six ready to start tomorrow. And there are four boxes of papers.'

'Oh. I see. Okay. Shall I wait?'

'Up to you. I might find someone on the next call, or I might be here for a couple of hours. I've got your former senior clerk—'

'Stanley Wigglesworth?'

'The very same — working the Old Pals Act from home. If you've anything to do that needs your urgent attention you could get on with that, and maybe call me back in an hour? If you decide to go home, there's some soup left in the fridge or you can pick something up on your way.'

'Okay, love. I'll see how I feel. Good luck.'

Charles hangs up. He looks askance at the pile of new Instructions awaiting his attention in the circle of light cast by his desk lamp, but can't summon the energy to open any of them.

Idly, he picks up the Rover manual and starts browsing. He makes a note of the appropriate tyre pressures and the service intervals and flicks through the booklet to its end. On the inside of the back cover he notes some handwriting. It's in light blue ink, and the characters are tiny, running round the margins of two sides of the cardboard cover. Charles pulls his desk lamp towards him and peers at the faint pen marks. They are largely illegible, but they definitely include figures and some form of calculation, ending with something that he *can* read: "£6000".

Then Charles's attention is drawn to the page immediately next to the back cover. It looks like graph paper, with faint vertical and horizontal lines across its surface, and has a different texture to the other pages in the booklet. The hundred or more other pages, covered in all the usual technical diagrams, advice and instructions, are glossy and flat, but this page is rougher and textured, almost like blotting paper that has got wet and dried out.

Suddenly uninterested, Charles throws the booklet on his desk. An idea strikes him. He will see if Dai Griffiths, who is now a professor at King's College and therefore only a short walk from the Temple, is available for a pint.

Charles likes to introduce Dai as his "prop friend". He met Dai in a scrum, each propping up one side of a hooker and, when not on the rugby field, Dai spent his time propping up the local bars, usually, and to the annoyance or entertainment of the other drunks, reciting Dylan Thomas at the top of his beautiful baritone voice. It astonished everyone, including Dai himself, when at the end of their three years, he was finally awarded a degree, not, as Charles predicted, in "propping" but in his subsidiary subject of philosophy. If Dai ever found himself in a lecture hall or seminar, it would have been by accident; he spent by far the greater part of his time at Cambridge on the rugby field or in pubs.

As Charles reaches for the telephone, it rings, startling him. He picks up.

'Mr Holborne?' says Barbara.

'I thought you'd gone.'

'I'm on my way out. There's a call for you. She wouldn't give her name but said it was to do with the murder appeal, the one you did for Tindall's. Would you like me to put her through?'

Mrs Sharpe? No, she'd have given her name. Gracie Marshall?

'Yes, please.'

'Very well. I'm locking up down here. You're the last one on your side.'

'Thank you.' Charles waits.

'Is that you, Charlie? It's Gracie.'

'Hello. Is anything wrong?'

'No. It's Frank. He's been seen.'

Gracie's Nissen hut home looks much tidier this time. The main space now resembles a strangely shaped bedsit with a double bed in the centre of the room and a small table at its end, where the boys are eating a pork chop and mashed potatoes. The hut is steamy from cooking and smells of burnt fat.

Gracie makes Charles and herself some tea and beckons for him to follow her into the partitioned area at the back. In the centre of the room, pushed back against the rear wall, are the boys' bunkbeds. To one side is a small couch. Gracie kicks toys and clothes out of the way as she picks her way across the bare boards to the couch and indicates that Charles should sit next to her. She keeps her voice low.

'Last Friday, I arrived to pick up the boys from school and two of the other mums approached me, said they were sure they'd seen Frank hanging about the day before. They reckoned he had a beard and was wearing a hat pulled down over his eyes. At first I didn't put much store on it.'

'Why not?'

'Well, all they could really say was that the man was very big and wearing a disguise. It's not much is it?'

'No.'

'But then I bumped into Deala as I came out of the labour exchange, and he said he'd seen Frank too.'

Frederick Wheeler, known to everyone as "Wheeler Deala" or just "Deala", is a "face"; everyone in the East End knows him.

'And Deala knows Frank well?'

'Yes, of course.'

'So you put more weight on that.'

'Exactly.'

'Where and when did he see Frank?'

'At a pub on the Old Kent Road called the *Frog and Nightgown*. Know it?'

'Yes. That's Richardson territory, though, isn't it? I can't see anyone in the Krays' Firm going near it, not unless they were looking for trouble.'

Gracie shrugs. 'I wouldn't know about that. But Deala was sure. He actually spoke to him.'

'What, he spoke to Frank? And Frank admitted it was him?'

'No. He pretended he was someone else, but Deala was certain. Thought it was funny. Frank got up and left. Didn't even finish his pint, supposedly.'

'When was this?' asks Charles.

'Two nights ago.'

'All right,' says Charles, knocking back the last of his tea. 'I'll check it out.' He pauses. 'I don't suppose you've still got any of Frank's clothes here, have you?'

'Yes, of course. Why?'

'If I walk into the *Frog* looking like this —' he indicates his three-piece suit, cotton shirt and starched collar — 'I won't even make it to the bar. It's a rough place, and I'd rather not draw attention to myself.'

'You're a big bloke, Charlie, but not a giant like Frank. You'll be swimming in any of his stuff.'

'Even a coat and hat might do.'

'Okay. Let's see what we've got.'

An hour later, Charles pushes open the door of the *Frog and Nightgown.* He wears an old raincoat, probably a three-quarter length on Frank Marshall but full length on him and ample to cover his own clothes, and a tweed cap pulled low over his eyes. His tie and stiff collar are shoved into one of the pockets, leaving an open-necked tunic shirt. There is nothing he can do to hide his polished black shoes.

The *Frog* is a low, single-storey modern building forming part of the estate of new council homes lining the busy A2, the Old Kent Road. It is charmless. Its glazed frontage looks out onto pavement, railings and the constant passage and repassage of vehicles. Nonetheless, within a short time of its opening, it swiftly became the go-to watering hole of some of south London's nastiest villains. Only a month earlier a man was stabbed to death here, his body remaining upright at a corner table until a barman discovered him at closing time. Here

Charles is well off familiar territory; if trouble were to start, he won't be able to trade here on his East End connections.

He orders a large scotch and scans the room. No sign of either Frank or Deala. Charles takes his drink to a seat from which he can observe the front door, and settles down with a newspaper to look as inconspicuous as possible. The news coverage is all about the forthcoming snap election called by Harold Wilson.

An hour later, the pub is filling up and there's still no sign of either man. Charles has gone largely unnoticed, but as empty tables become scarcer he has watched other drinkers glancing over at him more frequently. It's only a matter of time before someone asks to share his table. He looks at his watch; it's approaching nine o'clock. He decides to abandon his mission.

He pushes back from the table and slips outside. Even at this hour the road is busy, buses and trucks thundering into and out of central London. There is a bus stop immediately outside the pub windows, and for a moment Charles considers waiting there for the next northbound bus. As he is deliberating, he feels a tug on his sleeve. He turns swiftly. An elderly couple stand before him.

'Deala?' says Charles in surprise.

'We've been waiting for you to come out,' says the man.

Charles frowns, puzzled. 'You weren't in the pub, were you?'

'Nah, we was having our tea there, next door.'

Deala points to the building immediately next door to the pub. It's the "OK Café", a greasy spoon, just closing for the night.

'They do a lovely liver 'n' onions. Anyway, we saw you go in. Come on,' says Deala, looking over his shoulder at the brightly lit pub windows, 'walk with us a bit. We can't talk 'ere.'

Deala takes the woman's arm and heads southbound. Charles falls into step with them.

'Charles Holborne,' says Deala, 'meet Mrs Renée Brathwaite. Renée, this is Charles Holborne, or as I knew him before he got posh, Charlie Horowitz.'

Charles leans across Deala to address the woman on his arm.

'Pleased to meet you, Mrs Brathwaite,' he says.

'Likewise,' she says.

Deala's friend is, by Charles's estimation, probably a decade younger than Deala, in her late sixties. She's taller than Deala and well turned out, sporting a twin set with pearls under a short fur jacket. Her platinum-coloured hair is well-coiffed and she wears enormously long false eyelashes and startling pink lipstick.

'So, what you doing south of the river?' asks Deala.

He pronounces "south" like "sarf".

'I could ask you the same.'

'Oh, I'm down 'ere quite a bit nowadays, since I started walking out with Renée,' says the old man, patting the woman's hand fondly as it rests on his arm.

Charles smiles.

Frederick Wheeler is one of life's gentlemen. Soft-spoken and surprisingly un-pushy for a car salesman, he'd chat to you for half an hour or more on one of his forecourts, whether or not he thought a sale might come of it, and if he sold you a car that broke down within a short time, he'd do his best to put it right. His reputation for honesty and straight dealing made him a success in an otherwise dodgy business in an even more dodgy town, and Charles has never heard a bad word said of him. Charles's thoughts are drawn to Stanley Sharpe, another man with an interest in the car trade, but as different to Deala in his attitude to life and his fellow man as it is possible to be.

Deala is now pushing eighty and was married to his childhood sweetheart, Iris, before the Great War. Iris died in the late 1950s and, with her, the light in Deala's eyes. He gave up the day-to-day running of his business to his two sons and semi-retired. Charles would still bump into him in some of his old haunts and always stopped to chat, but the old boy wasn't the same. So sad, said everyone.

'That's good to hear,' says Charles. 'The boys must be happy you've got … a new friend.'

'Oh, I ain't told them yet, and make sure you keep *shtum* if you see 'em. They're good boys, but I know 'em; they'll be accusing Renée of gold-digging soon as you can say "knife".'

He turns to the woman on his arm and smiles up at her. 'Are you digging for my gold?' he asks her.

'Could be,' she replies chirpily.

'Well, you dig away, girl!' he laughs, and pats her bottom.

She giggles like a teenager and Charles smiles. It seems that Deala might have rediscovered some of his former jauntiness.

The old man turns his attention to Charles. 'So, what's the score? I'm guessing you want the gen on Frank Marshall, yeah?'

'Yes. How do you know?'

'Well, for one thing, I ain't never seen you around 'ere. A bit coincidental, only a coupla days after seeing Frank. And secondly, that's Frank's 'at, ain't it? I'd recognise that manky ol' thing anywhere.'

Deala chuckles to himself.

'All right if I speak openly?' asks Charles.

'Don't you worry about Renée.'

'In one ear, out the next,' chirrups Renée happily.

'Okay. I went up to Durham to see Stan Sharpe. He's convinced Frank's still alive, so I tracked Gracie down and promised I'd poke around a bit and see what came up. How sure are you that you spoke to Frank?'

'Hundred per cent. Despite the daft disguise.'

'Gracie mentioned a beard?'

Deala laughs. 'I swear, he looked like an old goat! You could see the glue. I recognised 'im the second me eyes landed on 'im. And it was definitely 'is voice.'

'And you saw him, what, just the once?'

'Yeah.'

Charles pauses, considering the information. 'Now he's been clocked, I guess he won't be back here in a hurry,' he muses.

'No. But you could try 'is girlfriend.'

Charles brings Deala to a halt. 'There's a girlfriend?'

'I don't know if there is now, but there definitely was.'

'Well, well. Gracie knows nothing about *that*. Got a name?'

Deala shakes his head. 'Not her first name, but her parents are called Bishop, Doris and Gregory Bishop. They were quite well-to-do Ilford people and I knew 'em, especially him, before the war. Sold him a few cars over the years. They moved to Haringey a while back, and I delivered the last car there.'

'I don't suppose you remember the address?' asks Charles hopefully.

'No, somewhere on the Ladder, I think. It'll be in the filing cabinet, unless the boys've cleared out the old records. I'll have a look. If I find anything, I'll drop it into chambers over the next coupla days, if that's okay.'

'You're a diamond, Deala. Thanks.'

Forty minutes later, Charles is on Gray's Inn Road, a hundred yards short of Wren Street, when he recognises a familiar figure ahead of him.

'Sally!' he calls.

Sally turns round and waits for Charles to catch her up.

'Have you been in Chambers all this time?' he asks.

'Yup,' she says. 'And you?'

'No. I got a lead on Frank Marshall and went to check it out.'

'And?'

'And it looks as if he might still be alive, after all. I'll tell you all about it when we get inside. Did you find a replacement silk?'

'No. The junior is going to apply for an adjournment first thing and, if unsuccessful, do it himself.'

'Lucky sod!'

She laughs. 'He doesn't think so. He's bricking it.'

'Really? That's how careers are made! Remember my first murder, after Mike Rhodes Thomas fell down the Old Bailey steps?'

'Course I do. But he's more junior than you were. Plus, he doesn't have your overweening confidence.'

'"Overweening"? That's a big word. Did you learn that at senior clerks' school?'

'You know what I mean, Charlie. You've never gone in for self-doubt, at least, not professionally.'

They turn into Wren Street and both catch sight of the Rover parked in front of the house at the same moment.

'Did you —' starts Sally.

'Yes. It's on my desk. I'll sort out the tyres tomorrow.'

'Good. Then we can drive to Romford on Sunday, see Mum, and take her out for tea somewhere.'

'Lovely idea,' replies Charles, perhaps a tad too enthusiastically.

Fortunately, Sally is getting her keys out of her bag and doesn't see the grimace on his face which would not have passed muster as a smile.

Sally is the first to hear the telephone ringing inside.

'Is that ours?' asks Charles.

'Yes,' says Sally, running up the front steps.

She manages to get the door open but is too encumbered to move quickly. Charles slips past her and runs down into the kitchen, just catching the telephone before it rings off.

'Terminus one-five-two-five?' he says breathlessly.

'Charles?' comes the voice of Charles's younger brother, a single syllable of urgency.

'Yes, David, what's up?'

'Mum's wandered off somewhere. Dad and I are going out to look for her. Can you lend a hand?'

'Of course. Have you called the police?'

'Yes, but they won't be here for a while. Dad doesn't think she's been gone long, so we're going to search the surrounding streets.'

'It could take me half an hour to get there.'

'Yes, I know, but start looking from Golders Green station, along Golders Green Road, up Brent Street as far as the park? The route's very familiar to her.'

Sally enters the kitchen quietly, puts her bags down and leans against Charles, trying to hear David's end of the conversation.

'Why would she go out at this time of night?' asks Charles.

'Apparently it wouldn't be the first time,' says David. 'She seems to have lost track of time. I didn't realise it but, according to dad, she's sleeping more and more during the day and rattling around the house at night.'

'All right.'

Charles can hear his father's voice at the far end of the line, urging David off the phone.

'Thank you. You might try the *shul* after that,' says David.

'Okay. See you later,' finishes Charles, hanging up.

He turns to Sally.

'I heard,' she says, starting to pull on her coat again.

'Are you coming?' he asks.

'Of course I am.'

They lock up again, get in the car, and head north. Sally looks across at Charles in the driving seat but he is concentrating furiously on the road and remains silent. She puts a sympathetic hand on his thigh, but says nothing.

She finds it hard to understand Charles's relationship with his mother. Millie has bullied and taunted Charles all his life for making choices of which she disapproved, most particularly his disinterest in Judaism, of which she, Sally, is the latest demonstration. Sally has never seen the fierce, upright little woman give her elder son anything but grudging affection. Millie Horowitz is, or until recently, was, clever, articulate, funny, sarcastic and, to Charles himself, cruel. Many a son in Charles's situation would have distanced himself from, or even broken off contact with, a mother who treated him thus, and yet Charles keeps coming back for more. He is trapped between hating her and her inflexibility and, as he is demonstrating now, profound love and protectiveness.

That internal conflict has been exacerbated since Millie's diagnosis with dementia. Sally thinks that, deep down, her partner still clings to the hope that his mother will forgive him and accept him for who he is. The two of them are so similar, in so many respects; Charles's fondest wish, perhaps unrecognised by him, is that he and Millie may still make peace and be kind to each other. In short, he wants her to love him, consistently, which is all he's wanted since he was a child. Millie's diagnosis is now forcing him to accept that repairing their relationship may never be possible. Time is running out.

Sally looks again at her partner's worried face.

They reach Golders Green station in just over twenty minutes, Charles having broken most of the speed limits en route. This is a comfortable Jewish suburb and the shops lining Golders Green Road are principally owned by Jews. Dress shops, bakers, greengrocers, delicatessens — even opticians and travel agents — all will be familiar to Millie. However at ten o'clock at night the wide pavements are almost deserted and the shop windows unlit. The only establishment still illuminated is Lindy's Patisserie by the station, but it is deserted and its chairs are piled on the tables ready for the cleaners.

Charles and Sally cruise slowly along the main road, slowing further every now and then to crane round at the few pedestrians they pass, but there is no sign of Millie. They travel all the way up Brent Street and turn left into Queens Road. At Hendon Park Charles pulls into the kerb.

'You're going to search the park?' asks Sally, doubtfully.

Charles takes a deep breath and shrugs. 'I don't know what else to try.'

Sally looks at the clock on the dashboard. 'It's an hour since David rang. They might already have found her. And the two of us can't possibly comb a large park like this in darkness.'

Charles nods. 'You're right.'

He starts the car again. 'I'm going back via Hendon Central.'

'She can't possibly have walked that far. Can she?' asks Sally.

Charles shrugs again. 'Depends how long ago she left home. If Dad was sleeping in front of the television she could've been gone a couple of hours before he realised. She's a very determined walker. David and I could never keep up with her when we were little. It's not impossible, and there are one or two late-night shops there.'

Charles pulls up outside the underground station. The shops he remembered being here have gone, replaced by an office block, which is in darkness. He is about to re-start the ignition when Sally touches his arm.

'Look,' she says, nodding towards the brightly-lit underground entrance foyer.

There are several figures in the space. One is his mother.

'Thank God!' he says, leaping from the car. Sally follows him.

Charles runs between the tall Doric columns supporting the entrance and across the tiled floor.

Millie Horowitz is at the barrier, looking up at two men wearing London Underground uniforms. Once of them has her gripped by the elbow and she is struggling to free herself. Charles cannot yet hear the words being spoken, but it is plain that an argument is in progress.

'Get off me, you bastard!' she shouts loudly.

'Mum!' calls Charles as he approaches.

Charles is astounded — Millie *never* uses profanity — and although her wild eyes land on Charles's, she doesn't seem to recognise him.

The two men look over to him.

'Do you know this lady?' asks one in a West Indian accent.

'Yes, she's my mother.'

'She tried to get on a train without paying,' says the other, 'and when my colleague stopped her, she hit him.'

Millie is wearing an overcoat and a scarf, but on her feet are her bed slippers and underneath her open coat Charles can see a cardigan over a nightdress. She is still struggling, trying to swing at the official's head with her free hand. She is so tiny and frail by comparison that he is able to hold her off easily, but Charles is having difficulty believing what his eyes are telling him.

'Mum!' repeats Charles. 'This isn't like her, I promise,' he says to the hapless official.

'Charles?' says Millie, apparently noticing him for the first time.

'Yes, it's me.'

'What're you doing here?'

'Looking for you. Dad's frantic with worry.'

'I don't know why he should be. I told him I was going to Cohen's.'

'Cohen's?'

'In the market. We need herring for tonight.'

'That's Petticoat Lane, Mum!'

'Of course. You think I don't know? I've been going there since I was a girl.'

'But … Mum … the Lane's closed now. It's gone ten.'

'Don't be ridiculous!'

With surprising strength she pulls her arm out of Charles's grip and makes to head through the ticket barrier again.

'I've told you, madam,' says the other London Underground official, barring her way again, 'you can't travel without a ticket and you've no money for a ticket. Listen to your son.'

Millie comes to a sudden halt. She stands with her overcoated back to Charles and Sally; a tiny, upright, elderly woman wearing slippers. Charles feels as if his heart might break.

She turns slowly. There is something new in her expression. She draws herself up to her full height.

'Take me home, please, Charles,' she says with quiet dignity. 'I can't be dealing with these people.'

'Of course.' He turns to the two officials. 'Is that all right?'

'Yes,' says the West Indian. 'Take her home. I see she's not herself.'

'Thank you,' says Charles. 'I'm sorry if … I'm sorry. This isn't her.'

He and Sally each take one of Millie's arms and start walking her back towards the car. Millie notices Sally for the first time.

'Look, Charles, it's little Sally.'

'Yes, Mum, I know.'

'How are you, Sally?' asks Millie. 'You've not changed, you know? Bright as a button, you were. And so pretty. Isn't she pretty, Charles?'

'Yes, she is.'

'It's lovely to see you again,' says Millie to Sally, 'after all this time.'

'It's lovely to see you again too, Mrs H.'

'Would you like a hot chocolate, dear?' asks Millie. She turns to Charles. 'She loved hot chocolate when she was little. I used to make her one whenever Nell came up from Romford with her finished work. You always left the shop with a little brown moustache.'

'I'd love a hot chocolate, thank you,' says Sally. 'When we get home.'

They install her in the back seat of the car and Charles moves off.

He regards his mother in the rear-view mirror. Her face is turned away, and she stares out of the side window of the car, watching the traffic passing on the other side of the dark road.

CHAPTER ELEVEN

A week has elapsed.

What is now being referred to by Charles and David as the "The Great Herring Run" brings home to them the degree to which Harry is struggling. He is exhausted. Millie's sleep pattern is so disrupted that they're both awake for much of the night. It was because Harry fell asleep in his armchair shortly after their evening meal that Millie was able to leave without being heard and get so far from home before being found.

There is a carer in place already but she only comes in two or three times a week, and her task is principally to prepare meals, do some basic tidying and make shopping lists. For the rest of the time Harry, himself in poor health, is doing everything, shopping, making lunches, cleaning the house and helping Millie to bathe and dress. It's not that she can't undertake such tasks, he insists; she simply forgets what she's doing halfway through them.

Charles raises for the first time the possibility of finding Millie a place in a Jewish care home. Harry becomes furious, refuses to discuss it, and the subject is not raised again. With the assistance of their parents' synagogue, the brothers engage another carer, a woman to come to the house for a couple of hours every day, and Harry is persuaded to put in place some basic security measures, such as keeping the keys in his dressing gown pocket once he's locked up for the night.

The brothers know that these are not adequate solutions, but it's all Harry will tolerate.

Charles and Maria sit in Charles's room in Chambers, working quietly. The rain blows, almost horizontally, off the Thames and hammers onto the tall sash windows.

Charles is preparing an opening speech for the grievous bodily harm prosecution he is starting the following day, and he's asked Maria to prepare a parallel speech which he will go through with her. He feels his stomach growling and looks up at the clock on the wall.

'Fancy lunch in Hall?' he asks.

Maria looks up. 'That's very kind, but no thank you. I don't really enjoy it.'

'Are you struggling with your dinners?'

All pupils have to eat a certain number of dinners in Hall before they can be called to the Bar. They sit on the long benches in "messes" of four, ideally made up of a couple of pupils, a practising barrister and a judge. Strictly one is not supposed to speak to anyone outside one's own mess. The purpose is to enable young barristers to familiarise themselves with the etiquette of the Bar and meet future colleagues. Charles supports the ancient tradition in principle, but he agrees that the quality of the catering at Middle Temple leaves much to be desired.

'It's not just the food. Didn't you find it alien, a bit intimidating?' asks Maria.

'Yes, a bit. But it's a lot worse at Gray's Inn. A breach of etiquette or procedure in Hall there requires you to pay a penalty.'

'Penalty?'

'They get you to stand on the table and sing a silly song, recite a poem, or make a speech, that sort of thing.'

'And how's that supposed to contribute towards one's education in the law?'

He shrugs. 'It's … tradition, I suppose. Most of our colleagues have been to public schools where that sort of thing happens all the time. It was foreign to me until I went to Cambridge, but I adapted to it.'

'Maybe you wanted to. Maybe it was more important to you to fit in.'

Charles looks at her with some surprise. That is a remarkably perceptive comment from a young woman who knows him so little. He *did* want to fit in, fiercely, even before he met the Hon. Henrietta Lloyd-Williams, eldest daughter of Viscount Brandreth, whom he was desperate to impress. He'd shed his Cockney accent and was copying his peers' languid speech patterns within days of starting.

'But it makes me feel even *more* different,' says Maria. 'It seems to me the rules are designed deliberately to identify outsiders. If you don't know them, you reveal you're not one of "them". Over here I'm Black, I'm a woman, and on top of that I'm required to draw attention to myself because I don't know these ridiculous traditions!'

This is the first time Maria has ever spoken to Charles about what it's like to be a Black woman at the English Bar; indeed, it's the first time he can remember her expressing *any* strong opinion in his presence.

'You know, you'd have got on rather well with my late wife,' he comments. He sees Maria's expression. 'No, I'm serious. She constantly berated me for joining a tribe that was never, ever going to accept me, whatever I did.'

'She was right.'

'To a point, yes. I'll never be one of "them" but I am making my way okay. Maybe I should ask you the same question she asked me: why are you doing it?'

Maria smiles, and there are so many layers to her expression that Charles is unable to decipher it completely. 'It's a long story. Let's say, it seemed a good idea at the time.'

'And now?'

There is a long pause before Maria answers. 'My father still thinks it's a good idea.'

She stands, effectively ending the conversation.

'You've bought me lunch most days,' she says. 'Yes, I know, it's a *tradition*, but today I'm going to buy you lunch. I know how much you love Mick's,' she says, referring to the famous café on Fleet Street, 'although God knows why. So how does a bacon sandwich with that revolting brown sauce sound to you?'

'It sounds great. And a packet of crisps, please. Will you get yourself something?'

'If I can find anything on their menu that doesn't involve incinerated meat,' she says, pulling on her coat. 'Honestly, Charles, when will you guys realise just how terrible your English cooking is?'

'I realise, thank you very much. You think I've never travelled outside England? But what can I do 'cept embrace it?'

After finishing their lunch, which in Maria's case consists of an apple, a banana and a chocolate bar, Charles sits her down next to him and compares her proposed opening for the Crown to his. She has done a pretty good job and it only takes Charles half an hour to point up the differences.

The telephone on Charles's desk rings. He picks it up. 'Yes?'

'A gentleman named Wheeler has just popped in,' says Barbara, 'and left you a note with an address. Do you need it urgently?'

'No, thank you. If you leave it in my pigeonhole I'll collect it on my way out.'

He hangs up and checks his watch.

'I have to go out for a bit. On top of that pile is a case called *R versus Burnham*. It's a prosecution under the Offences against the Persons Act. Look at the evidence and have a go at drafting the indictment. I should be back before you leave.'

Charles departs, collecting the address left by Deala as he goes.

Charles has to get to Duckett Road, part of "the Ladder" in Haringey. The Ladder is so-called because the twenty or so residential streets running east-west between the parallel Green Lanes and Wightman Road resemble the rungs of a ladder when viewed on a map. It's a fiddly journey from the Temple: District line to Victoria, Victoria line to Finsbury Park, Piccadilly line back south to Manor House and then a twenty-minute walk, but Charles is glad of the opportunity to lose himself in the mass of flowing London humanity, and think.

He's asking himself why he's doing this. He's no private detective and he has no wish to be one. He knows too many to be fooled into believing their lives romantic or exciting. The bulk of their work is grubby and boring; not to mention very badly paid compared to the average barrister. No, trudging up Green Lanes on a freezing winter's afternoon to poke his nose into other people's business bears no comparison to the rewards of Charles's actual job.

Part of his motivation, he knows, is the prospect of demonstrating that DCI Wheatley is corrupt. If Charles can prove that Frank Marshall is alive, the "confession" recorded by Wheatley must be false. With luck, Charles might even end the bent copper's career.

So, it is personal, but that's only part of the reason. The events surrounding Henrietta's death occurred years ago and, insofar as corrupt police officers go, Wheatley is far from the worst. Unlike many in the Sweeney, he's not skimming off the top of recovered money, bullion or drugs. In contrast to most of the Dirty Squad, the Obscene Publications Squad to give its proper title, he's not taking envelopes stuffed full of fivers to run interference for Humphreys and Silver, Soho's most notorious pornographers.

No; he doesn't believe his brush with Wheatley wholly explains it, despite the policeman's anti-Semitism and his refusal to consider the evidence that pointed to Charles's innocence.

As for the people concerned, it's not as if Charles has any real connection with them. His romance with "Leonora" was short-lived and seems a lifetime ago, and he's only met Mrs Sharpe once. But the thought of those two middle-aged women does make him pause. They are the innocents in all this, and both have lost husbands. True, one husband might be a murderer and the other a philanderer who took to his heels, but that's not the point. Despite being unceremoniously dumped by Gracie, he liked her at the time and treasured her memory thereafter. She was kind and gentle to a naïve young man, and she could have made him look ridiculous. Then there's the estimable Mrs Sharpe, that middle-aged matron grieving the incarceration of a husband whom she believes to be the victim of a miscarriage of justice.

Perhaps that's it.

Two women, oddly united in their loss by this case, tugging at his conscience. If he can help, he will.

He gets out of the tube at Manor Park and heads north on Green Lanes.

There's not much green in existence. This is the old drovers' route, used for centuries to take cattle from the pastures to the north of the city into the meat markets at Smithfield. It acquired its then name, "Lane of Greens", from the patches of common land used by the drovers for their cattle all the way down the route. Indeed Charles's destination, Duckett Road, is named after one of them. Now, however, it's full of traffic, both vehicular and pedestrian, and it's noisy, dirty and heavily built-up. It's also multicultural; Charles passes, in quick succession, the premises of a Cypriot supermarket with boxes of brightly coloured vegetables spilling onto the pavement, a Greek tailor, a Turkish photo studio and a kosher butcher with the Star of David above its door.

He turns left into Duckett Road and climbs the hill, looking for number 30. It's part of a terrace, small but well-maintained. If Mr and Mrs Bishop were, as Deala said, "well-to-do Ilford people", they've apparently come down in the world.

Charles unlatches and pushes open the wooden gate and rings the doorbell.

The door is opened by a harassed-looking man in his sixties. He is mostly bald and wears thick-rimmed glasses and a woman's pinafore with frills around its edges. He has a spoon in his hand.

He looks Charles up and down. 'Yes?'

'I'm sorry to interrupt you, Mr Bishop. My name's Charles Holborne. I need to speak to you about your daughter.'

'Have you found her?'

'No. I'm trying to —'

'You'd better come in,' says the man and, with that, he turns on his heel and walks swiftly to the end of a short corridor and down some steps towards the back of the house, leaving Charles on the doorstep.

Charles enters the house and closes the door behind him. Hesitantly, he follows.

'Down here,' calls the man.

Charles descends half a dozen steps and finds himself in a kitchen facing the rear of the house and its garden. Mr Bishop, if it is he, crouches with his back to Charles, feeding a woman in a wheelchair. She wears a tabard covered in food stains and her hands fall loosely in her lap. Mr Bishop is touching the spoon gently to the woman's lower lip. He makes eating motions with his mouth to encourage the woman to open hers, but she doesn't appear interested. Her head is half-turned to look over her shoulder at a blank wall and her eyes are unfocused.

'Doris dear, this is a policeman, come about Judy,' says Bishop. 'Well, Mr Holden, do you have any news?'

He speaks facing away from Charles, persisting with his efforts to persuade the woman to open her mouth. Charles decides not to correct the mistake as to his identity or the misheard name.

'No, I'm afraid not. Has she been in contact?'

'No, we've heard nothing. Come on, Doris, open up.'

'Is there any possibility she might have somewhere else to stay? A boyfriend's, for example?'

'I've told all this to your colleagues. She worked long hours, but she always used to come home to sleep.'

'So, you reported her missing?'

'At Hornsey.'

'Do you remember the date?'

Now Bishop turns towards Charles, a puzzled and irritated expression on his face. Charles watches the spoon drifting away from Mrs Bishop's mouth towards her ear.

'I can't decide if you lot are incompetent, or you just don't care,' he says despondently. 'I used to work for the tax office, you know, 'til Doris got worse, and I tell you, if I did my job half as badly as you people do yours, this country would've gone bust. You're a disgrace.'

'The date, please, Mr Bishop?'

'Twenty-ninth October last year. We left it two days before reporting it.'

A cog slips into place. Judy Bishop disappeared on exactly the same day as Frank Marshall went "missing".

The loaded spoon suddenly flies across the room and Charles realises that Mrs Bishop has knocked it out of her husband's hand. It's difficult to tell if it was deliberate or some sort of spasm, but she is now staring at Charles, her eyes wide and her mouth gaping. Purée trickles from her open mouth and down her chin.

'For Christ's sake, Doris,' mutters Bishop. 'Look, just leave, would you? You can see this isn't a good time.'

'Yes. I'm sorry.'

Charles turns and climbs the stairs to the upper hall, Bishop following right behind him. Charles opens the door.

'If you find her, you will tell her to come home, won't you?' asks Bishop over Charles's shoulder. 'We don't care what she's done. We just want her home safely.'

'Of course.'

Charles steps outside, but then turns. 'Did she have a boyfriend, do you think?'

There is a minute hesitation before Bishop answers.

'She never used to tell us anything, but I think there was someone. Someone she met at ... her workplace.'

'The Windmill.'

'Windmill? Never heard of it,' says Bishop, but Charles detects the lie instantly.

'Thank you Mr Bishop,' says Charles.

The door closes behind him.

CHAPTER TWELVE

The underground stations and interchanges are much busier on the return journey as rush hour builds, but the trains less so; Charles is heading back into town while the main flow is in the opposite direction. He runs up the steps to Chambers shortly before five o'clock and pokes his head into the clerks' room.

The room is hot, steamy and a cacophony of noise. All three clerks are on the telephones and Clive, the junior, is at his desk, a telephone in his hand and a finger on the button ready to put the next call through to the first available clerk to become free. Those actually speaking are having to raise their voices above the incessant clatter of typewriter keys as the secretaries, Wendy and Margaret, race to get completed work typed in time for the last post.

Jennie looks up, her hand over her mouthpiece. 'You know where you are tomorrow, don't you, sir?'

Jennie's job includes the task of checking every barrister out at the end of the day; making sure he or she knows where they're supposed to be in the morning, and that they've all their papers.

'Yes, thank you.'

'And that is?' asks Jennie, colouring slightly.

The youngster has been given strict instructions to hear her guvnors repeat where they're going and when, but she is painfully, pathologically shy. Even quizzing Charles, the friendliest of the barristers in Chambers, is difficult for her.

'Old Bailey, court ten, not before ten thirty,' says Charles, winking at her. 'And the papers are on my desk.'

'Thank you, sir.'

'Is Miss Hudson still in?' he asks.

'She was five minutes ago, but she looked to be getting ready to leave,' answers Barbara from the other side of the room, making eye contact with Charles. She has a phone to her ear but is apparently waiting on the line for someone.

'Is this a regular occurrence?' asks Charles. 'Leaving this early?'

'Yes,' says Barbara.

Her disapproving tone is eloquent and, in her, implies significant annoyance.

'Her work seems okay,' says Charles, sticking up for his pupil.

'But the lass is almost invisible,' replies Barbara. 'We need a chat about it, but not now. If she continues like this, when the committee comes to decide if she should be offered a tenancy, none of the other members of Chambers will know who she is.'

'I'll have a word,' offers Charles, 'but it's a difficult balancing act, isn't it? Pupils must appear industrious and keen, but they can't come across as pushy or demanding.'

'Aye, it *is* a balancing act,' confirms Barbara, 'which she is presently getting quite wrong. Now, sir, if you don't mind leaving us to it...'

As if to prove her point, two new phones start ringing simultaneously.

As Charles steps back out of the clerks' room, he catches a glimpse of Maria's distinctive hair as the young woman steps out of the building and turns to her left. On impulse, he follows.

She heads west, along Fleet Street and then the Strand towards Charing Cross. The pavements throng with people puffing vapour trails in the icy air as they hurry for buses and trains, but Charles has no difficulty following her bobbing Afro. She cuts across Leicester Square and heads into Soho.

By the time she reaches Gerrard Street, Charles has a growing suspicion as to her destination. Below her winter coat he can see the flashes of a hem of an evening dress and gripped in her gloved hand is the music case.

Maria stops at number 39 and pushes open the door.

'Ronnie Scott's,' breathes Charles. 'I'll be damned.'

Charles, a lifelong jazz fan, knows the dingy, electrifying club very well. He missed the now-famous venue's opening in October 1959, but he's been there every couple of months since early 1960, particularly after the ban on American jazzmen was lifted. He's enough of a regular to be recognised and greeted by most of the staff. Indeed, one of the bouncers owes his job there to Charles. A former client, he was looking for work on release from prison, and Charles vouched for him. Four years later the man is now an indispensable part of the team.

Charles pauses on the pavement. The club doesn't open for almost two hours and, despite being known, he won't be welcomed this early. He is also wary of being seen by Maria; he doesn't want her to know he followed her. He waits a few minutes on the cold pavement in case she comes out again, shuffling from one foot to another and rubbing his hands. Then, simultaneously reaching a decision and critical hypothermia, he follows her inside.

The door's unattended. Charles quietly descends the steps to the basement. The cloakroom and bar are also deserted. Then he hears the first notes of a piano and he follows the sound of music.

Maria sits at a piano on the low stage. Two other musicians accompany her, a drummer and a bassist. All but one of the spotlights hanging from the lighting pipes are dark. Undetected by the others in the room, Charles lowers himself into a chair near the back to listen.

The three musicians seem to be rehearsing something new, or at least new to some of them. Maria starts, plays a few bars, stops to ask about a key change, and then starts again. Then the bassist falters, checking the tempo, but after a few moments they settle down. Charles frowns. Through Maria's improvisation he can't place the melody at first, but then it strikes him, and he smiles broadly. Maria is playing one of his mother's favourites, something she used to hum when he was a child, Jerome Kern's "All The Things You Are". And she's good; very good. Charles is no musician, but he knows his jazz and has listened to enough jazz pianists to know when he hears something special.

The trio reaches the end of the song and hash back and forth a few more details between them. Then Maria suggests a Bill Evans tune which Charles also knows, and she launches into "Waltz for Debbie". This is even better than the first. Her improvisation is varied, at times moody and reflective and at others fast and complex. Charles can't believe he is eavesdropping on a private concert of such quality, and one given by his pupil. He is particularly impressed by Maria's unselfishness. He has heard many gifted but less experienced solo artists "hog the tune", not allowing other members of the band their solo moment in the limelight, but Maria gracefully retreats into the shadow to allow each of the other musicians their moments to shine.

“Waltz for Debbie” ends and Maria stands unexpectedly. Charles, fearing discovery, also rises hurriedly, scraping his chair on the floor as he does so. He spins and slips back out of the room, but not before Maria calls, ‘Hello?’

He runs lightly up the steps to the street, praying she didn’t identify him.

Striding back down Gerrard Street, Charles is still smiling to himself. That, he thinks, answers a lot of questions.

CHAPTER THIRTEEN

'Fancy a pint? Maybe *The Clachan*? Or, better still, *The Prospect*?'

Charles is speaking on the phone to DS Sean Sloane.

'Love to,' replies Sloane, 'but as you'd say, it's a real schlep now I'm not in the City. It's hardly convenient for you, either. I could get there Sunday, as I've got the weekend off but —'

'No, it won't wait that long. I've something to tell you, and it's quite urgent.'

'Now what've you been up to?' says Sloane, only half-joking.

'Nothing,' protests Charles, feigning outrage. 'I've just got some information you might like.'

'Doesn't sound like you've been doing "nothing" to me.' He pauses. 'I guess I could manage a swift half this evening, somewhere in north London.'

'Can I suggest that it's away from your nick, then? Do you know Maximilian's in Hampstead?'

'The new burger place? Just round the corner from the tube?'

'That's the one.'

'What's happened to your curfew? Doesn't Sally require you to be home by seven?'

'That is a gross calumny. Sally has explained to me that we like to spend the evenings together,' corrects Charles patiently, 'and I'm sure she's right.'

'You poor sod. You're really under the thumb, aren't you?'

'If so, I love it. And her. But it so happens that she's got a committee meeting tonight, so I've an evening pass. Come on, Maximilian's is very trendy, lots of young things, and it could save your life.'

'How's that?'

'Well, it'll save you having to cook for one thing.'

Sloane considers. 'All right. It'll have to be early. I can be there for half six.'

'See you then.'

Charles hangs up and looks across at Maria. She's deep into a set of papers for Peter Bateman.

He has said nothing to her about her moonlighting. He hopes she'll trust him sufficiently to tell him about it at some point. At the same time he has been trying to persuade other members of Chambers to give her some work so she can get to know them and demonstrate her competence.

Bateman alone has been willing. The reluctance of other members of Chambers is puzzling. Charles can't believe it's caused by racism in every case, although there are several for whom that is obviously an issue. The attitude of a couple seems to be that Maria is battling inevitable failure, so where's the point? Even if *they* aren't bothered about her colour or her sex, she'll never achieve a majority within Chambers to vote her in. Furthermore, she's up against a young Cambridge graduate whose own father was in the set until his death a few years back. White, public school-educated and with a still-strong familial connection to Chambers, he'll garner the necessary votes without even trying, if only out of sentiment. Charles, however, has seen the young man's work and is not impressed. Maria's heart might not be in it, but her intuitive understanding of the concepts involved is far stronger than his. So Charles is trying hard on her behalf, if only to keep her options open.

'I'm going to leave a little early this evening,' says Charles.

'Okay.'

'But can I suggest that, if possible, you stay at least until six?'

'Why? Is there a problem?'

'No, not a "problem", but it won't do any harm if you're seen to be working hard. In fact, if you have no other commitments, perhaps you could work later still, say seven or eight even, every now and then. Not every night, you understand; just enough to be noticed.'

Maria studies Charles for quite a while before answering. 'Okay.'

'Don't forget, you are in a competition. And whether you choose to apply for a tenancy here or not, it does no harm to keep your options open.'

'Okay,' she repeats, and bends her head to her work again.

Charles opens the door to Maximilian's to be assailed by a wall of ear-splitting pop music and fried food smells. A young woman in a miniskirt and Harlequin-patterned tights bounces towards Charles in time with the music, a clutch of huge menus held out before her as if they were her dance partner. Before she reaches him, she executes a little move followed by a wiggle in time to "Yeh, Yeh" by Georgie Fame. It is so joyous that Charles laughs.

'I'm meeting someone,' he says when she settles, scanning the dark room for Sloane.

Charles is amazed at how crowded the place is, despite the early hour. There are very few available tables and half the restaurant appears to be occupied by young people, some, including a large group of rowdy female teenagers, still in school uniform.

'Him?' says the young woman, pointing across a sunken level to a line of banquettes on the far side of the restaurant.

Charles follows her arm and sees Sean waving at him from the shadows, a huge poster of a pouting Jean Shrimpton behind him.

'Yes,' replies Charles. 'How did you know?'

'He's your age, more or less. And cute, so I noticed him,' replies the girl, executing a sort of impromptu curtsy.

She leads Charles down some steps, across the floor and up to the banquette where Sean waits. She leaves them with two menus and another curtsy.

'This is some place,' shouts Sean.

Charles slides into the seat opposite. 'It makes me feel old,' he complains.

'What's that?'

'I said, it makes me feel old!'

'Right! And too loud for us to talk!'

Charles attracts the attention of the waitress. 'Any chance you can turn the music down a little?'

'It gets quieter soon,' she replies. 'We turn it down a bit after the kids have gone.'

Charles and Sean order burgers and fries ('When did they stop being chips?' asks Sean grumpily) and wait for their drinks to arrive. Sure enough, a lot of the teenagers are donning coats to leave and the volume of the music does reduce.

'So? What's so urgent?'

Charles takes a swig of his vanilla and peach milkshake and wipes his mouth with the back of his hand. 'Remember I called to ask you about Robin Sharpe, son of the Reverend Stanley?'

'Yes.'

'Do you remember the case against the father?'

'Some. Not much evidence, as I recall.'

'Except the confession. Do you recall the identity of the senior investigating officer who obtained that confession?'

'My old boss, DCI Wheatley.'

'Correct.'

'With whom you have history.'

'That's the fella.'

Charles pauses to allow a different waitress to deliver their food, recite the extensive list of sauces and mustards available and for Sean to make his choice. Charles declines.

'What if I were to tell you,' Charles continues eventually, 'that I might be able to prove that Marshall's still alive?'

'I'd ask for proof.'

'But if you were satisfied with it? What would you do next?'

'How do you come by this information?' asks Sean suspiciously.

'Forget that for the moment. I've done nothing dodgy, I promise. But I'm serious, Sean, what would you do?'

'I'd take it upstairs. Very, *very* carefully.'

'You mean you'd have to find someone you could trust.' Sean nods, his mouth full. 'Someone senior to a detective chief inspector? Is that possible?'

Sean shakes his head. 'Not for me, it isn't. Too far above my pay grade. I'd try to find someone honest, and senior enough that they'd have the ear of someone higher still.'

'Like Nipper Read, for example?'

'Just like Nipper Read.'

CHAPTER FOURTEEN

Charles and Sean walk together towards Hampstead underground station, Charles filling the policeman in on the remaining details of his investigations. They board a southbound tube together.

Sean is planning to travel to Finchley Central to meet Irenna at the end of her shift and needs the other branch of the Northern line. Charles accompanies him as far as Camden Town, where Sean jumps out. Charles checks his watch: only eight thirty. He hesitates. He too could get out here and return to Wren Street but, if his experience is anything to go by, Sally will still be in her chambers committee meeting at Chancery Court. He lets the doors close. He'll go into the Temple, finish off what he was doing when he left early to see Sean and, with luck, meet up with Sally. She'll have organised sandwiches for their meeting, but he guesses she'll probably need a drink. Frustrating affairs, chambers meetings.

The Temple, when he gets there, is quiet and still. Mist from the river crawls up the steps at Queen Elizabeth Building, hugging the stone flags of Garden Court and blurring the yellow light of the gas lamps. At this time of night the traffic noise from Fleet Street has all but gone; Charles hears the sounds of the river and the wind stirring the bushes in Temple Gardens. Shrouded in darkness and muffled by the thick night air, the Temple looks and sounds much as it would have in the eighteenth century.

Charles arrives outside Chambers. The blurred lamp of the moon is low in the sky and almost full. Its light strikes the top halves of the tall plane trees lining the courtyard. Devoid of their leaves, their shiny branches remind Charles of upward-pointing skeletal fingers.

He looks up to his room on the second floor. The light is still on. It's too late for the cleaners; perhaps Maria heeded his advice and is working late?

He pushes open the street door. The outer doors on the first landing leading to the clerks' room and waiting-room are locked and Charles climbs to the second floor. The outer door to his corridor is still wide open as it usually is throughout the day, flat against the wall, but the inner door, normally closed by a fierce self-closing mechanism, is also half-open. Charles looks down, wondering if perhaps some books have been left at the foot of the door to prevent it from closing, but there is nothing there. Then he looks up.

The mechanism has been detached and hangs like a V-shaped arm at an odd angle. From his position on the threshold he can see into the first room on the corridor, to his right, where a chair lies on its back. Papers are scattered over the floor. Charles suddenly feels the hairs on the back of his neck rise.

His first instinct is to call out for Maria, but he thinks twice about that and instead creeps along the corridor towards his own room. He has learned over the years where the creakiest floorboards are situated, but the timbers of the building are hundreds of years old and he cannot avoid them all. Realising that he has lost any element of surprise, he leaps forward and sprints the remaining few yards to his door.

His room is empty, but it has been ransacked. Every drawer has been opened and its contents tipped; all the law books on the shelves have been thrown onto the floor where they lie, like piles of discarded leather bricks.

Charles turns and looks into the room behind him, used by two of the junior members of Chambers. Their room is usually a total shambles in any case, but to Charles's unfamiliar eye it looks as if it too has been searched. As he scans that room, reflected flashing blue light shines onto the darkened wall and Charles realises that an emergency vehicle of some sort has arrived down in the courtyard. A few seconds later he hears footsteps on the staircase and whispered voices. He goes to investigate.

Two police officers in the dark uniform of the City of London police are on the landing, as is an elderly man in what appears to be a smoking jacket. Charles's sudden appearance startles them, and one of the police officers makes a grab for his arm.

'No!' says the elderly man. 'I know this person. He's a member of these Chambers. I'm sorry, young man, but I don't know your name.'

'I'm Charles Holborne. My room is off this corridor. I've only just walked in, but it looks as if we've been burgled.'

'Stay there, please,' orders the other officer, and the two of them enter the corridor cautiously.

'I live in the top flat,' explains the old man in a soft voice. 'Hugh McAllister.'

'Ah, yes, Judge, I've seen your name on the board downstairs. Pleased to meet you. What happened?'

'My wife and I heard noises from underneath, over there.' He points towards Charles's room. 'We do hear you occasionally when you're working late, the jazz and so on, but it's no disturbance. Nice to know the place is occupied, actually, as it can be a bit desolate in the Temple at night. But this time it was banging and scraping, as if somebody was throwing things around, so we called the police.'

The two policemen return.

'There's no one there now,' one of them says. 'Is it possible they're anywhere else on the premises?'

'I don't think so,' replies Charles. 'All the other corridors are locked.'

'Come with me and have a quick look in the room,' one of the officers says to Charles. 'Don't touch anything. Just tell me if you think anything's been stolen.'

Charles follows the officer back to the door of his room. He looks in, careful not to touch any part of the doorframe.

'It's difficult to tell with this much mess, and I'll need to check all my papers —' he points to the legal documents and Instructions scattered over the desks and floor — 'but nothing stands out. There's not much worth stealing, to be honest. About the only thing worth even a few quid is that decanter.'

Charles points to the decanter lying on its side, its last dregs of whisky forming a pool underneath it.

'Okay. We'll call it in. A Scenes of Crime chap will need to have a look at it before you go in.'

'When's that likely to be?'

'Tomorrow maybe, or Thursday.'

'This corridor houses nine barristers, most of whom are going to turn up tomorrow morning to collect briefs for court. If they can't enter, it's going to cause a lot of cases to collapse.'

'We don't control the SOCOs' diaries, sir, but I'll explain the situation to the station.'

He conducts Charles back to the landing.

'Now, gentlemen,' he says, 'I'm PC Collingwood and this is PC Metcalfe, and we need to take your details, please.'

Collingwood is in the process of taking out his pocketbook when they hear shouting and scuffling from the floor below. A third officer in uniform comes into view. He has someone in custody who is resisting, and is struggling to haul them up the stairs.

'I've got her! She was running off towards the Embankment.'

'Get off me, you idiot!' shouts his prisoner.

It's Maria.

She manages to wrench an arm out of the officer's control, and swings it round. It hits the policeman's helmet. The helmet is still fastened under his chin, and is knocked forward over his eyes.

'You bloody little bitch!' he shouts.

Collingwood and Metcalfe race down to assist their colleague.

'Stop!' shouts Charles. 'I know that woman! She's a pupil in these Chambers!'

The three officers, all now with a hand on a different part of Maria, turn simultaneously to look back up the stairs at Charles.

'What? She's a barrister?' says the officer most recent to arrive. 'I don't believe it. Why was she running off?'

'Let go of me!' demands Maria.

'No fucking way! You just assaulted me, and I'm arresting you for assaulting a police officer. You don't have to say anything —'

'Officer,' interrupts Charles.

'— unless you wish to do so —'

'Officer! You've made a mistake! Don't compound it by making another. You're about to arrest a barrister working from these chambers. I'm a senior barrister here and the gentleman behind me is Judge McAllister, a former judge of the Court of Appeal. We're both witnesses to what you're doing.'

The arresting officer looks from Charles to the judge standing behind him and then to his two colleagues.

Metcalfe raises an eyebrow.

'Eamon,' he says gently to the third policeman, still gripping Maria's arm. Maria is released.

'Why were you running away, miss?' asks Collingwood more calmly.

'I saw the burglar, or at least I caught a glimpse of him. I was just making myself a cup of tea — look, you can see on the floor where I dropped it.'

She points back up to the landing and, sure enough, in the doorway, to the left of the door jamb where no one had seen it, is an empty mug lying in the centre of a darker patch on the carpet. Metcalfe climbs the stairs to it and bends down. He places the back of his hand close to the mug to gauge its temperature without putting fingerprints on it.

'Still warm,' he announces.

'The man was throwing things around in our room. I was going to call the police from here, the room nearest the door, but I was afraid he'd hear me, and in any case I realised I didn't know how to get an outside line. So I snuck back downstairs and was running to the call box just outside the Temple when this ... *idiot* ... tackled me. Look!' She points to her knees, which are grazed and bleeding, and holds up a hand. The heel of one palm is scraped raw.

'It was an honest mistake,' mutters the officer.

'Yeah, right,' spits Maria scornfully. 'A Black woman running somewhere — got to be guilty of something!'

An hour later Charles and Maria sit in the clerks' room while Sally crouches in front of the pupil and bathes her damaged knees. Sally was leaving Chancery Court when she saw the police cars and went to investigate. Charles, the judge and Maria have all given brief accounts to the police. Full statements will only be required if the fingerprinting turns anything up.

One officer remains upstairs on the landing, awaiting the arrival of a Scenes of Crime Officer who, they have been assured, will be there before midnight.

Maria is still shaking.

'You look like you need a drink,' says Charles.

'Yes,' she replies, her voice quivering slightly. 'Is there anything?'

'I doubt it. Not down here. Barbara's strictly teetotal and I can't see her permitting the juniors alcohol.'

'I'll just have to manage, then.'

Charles lifts her hand to examine the cuts on her palm.

'I tried to break my fall,' she explains. 'Now I know what it's like to play rugby. That guy hit me like a steam train.' She pauses, and her eyes film with tears. 'He just wouldn't believe me. I kept trying to explain, and he just wouldn't listen. It's no better here than at home!' Her chest heaves and tears start running down her cheeks.

'They enter a mindset of "You're the criminal, I'm the policeman, and you're going to be arrested" and it's impossible to stop them,' says Charles. 'But I don't think it's as bad as in the States.'

'What do you know about it?' she asks bitterly.

He holds onto Maria's hand, trying to console her, but her sobs become deeper, her chest heaving with great jagged breaths.

'I'm sor-sorry,' she manages. 'It was such a shock. I didn't see him at all before he hit me.'

'It's fine. Let it out,' soothes Charles, hearing himself and hating the useless trite phrases. 'It must have been very frightening.'

Sally makes eye contact with Charles, trying to convey something, but he frowns, uncomprehending.

'Maria,' she says softly. 'Would you like to come back to ours tonight? You're very welcome, if you'd prefer not to be in that apartment alone.'

Maria is still crying hard, but she shakes her head. 'No. I want to go home,' she sobs.

'Are you sure? It's no trouble.'

'Thank you,' she manages, 'but no. I'll be fine.'

Charles stands. 'I'll go find a taxi.'

CHAPTER FIFTEEN

The following morning Charles goes directly to the Old Bailey to start his GBH prosecution. He waits until the last possible minute to go into court, but Maria doesn't appear. At lunchtime he slips out of his wig and gown and, still wearing the rest of his court robes, walks swiftly back to the Temple and directly up to his room.

He opens the door apprehensively. The Scenes of Crime Officer has obviously been and gone. There are patches of silver powder residue everywhere, on the doorframe, around the door handles and light switches, on the back of his chair and at various points on his desk, particularly around the telephone.

As for last night's chaos, it isn't quite as bad as he feared. The clerks have done their best. The law books are back on the shelves, although they remain out of date order, and an attempt has also been made to sort out the scores of documents lying randomly on every surface. The papers on which he was actively working are now back on his desk and the rest on the shelf to await attention, but he doubts all the documents have been put back in the relevant briefs. He sighs at the thought of the amount of time it's going to take to sort everything out.

It is only then that Charles realises he is not alone. Although Peter Bateman's desk is available, as is Charles's own, Maria sits on a lone chair in the corner. She looks small and vulnerable. Her hands are folded in her lap — Charles sees a bandage on one — and she stares, unfocused, into space.

'Hi,' says Charles gently. 'I was worried about you when you didn't show up.'

She starts and looks up. 'I'm sorry. I just couldn't manage it.'

'Have you seen a doctor?'

She shakes her head. Charles goes over to her. Her eyes are red and her mascara smudged.

'Why don't you go home? If you're not feeling up to it. Take a day or two; come back when you feel better.'

She looks up. 'Would you mind?'

'Not at all.'

'I don't want to let you down. But I am feeling a bit shaky.'

'I promise you, it's absolutely no problem.'

So she leaves, without a further word.

Charles goes downstairs to check his messages. There is only one, requesting him to call Sean Sloane at the police station. The clerks' room is relatively quiet and he asks to use Jennie's phone to save him going back upstairs. He gets through almost immediately.

'Hi, Sean.'

'Hello. Thanks for calling back. Would you like an outing to *The Prospect*?'

'Always. Why the change of mind?'

'No change of mind. I'll be on duty. I shan't be alone.'

Charles pauses, assimilating what Sloane's just said. 'That was quick.'

'The buyer expressed unusually keen interest. What about this afternoon, straight after court? It's not too far for you, if you're at the Bailey.'

'Yes, that'll work. Is five o'clock okay?'

'Perfect. See you then.'

Charles thanks Jennie and leaves Chambers at a jog. If he's quick there'll be time to stop in at Mick's and collect a bacon sandwich to be consumed as he walks back up the hill to the Old Bailey.

By the time court rises at five minutes past four, Charles's case for the Crown is almost complete, with just one remaining witness to be called in the morning. He runs upstairs to the robing room, changes, and walks to London Wall to catch a bus.

He is deposited twenty-five minutes later at Pelican Stairs, the ancient stone steps descending to the river at the back of the pub. He stops for a moment to gauge the tide and remind himself of the effluent-tinged smell of the water, and enters *The Prospect of Whitby* via the back door.

The back bar is low-ceilinged, formed of ancient ships' timbers, and Charles has to bend his head to avoid the beams. He comes to a halt on the stone flags, allowing atmosphere and memories to wash over him.

He doesn't get to the ancient waterside inn very often nowadays. For a little over a year, during the worst of the Blitz, the fifteen-year-old Charlie Horowitz was given shelter in the Shadwell home of his formidable aunt Beatrice and worked with her menfolk in their family lighterage business. Despite the exhausting work, the quotidian dangers of working the Thames and the frequent Luftwaffe attacks through which lightermen worked without pause, Charles remembers those months as the best and most vivid of his life. *The Prospect* had been the Conways' "local" for generations — it was said, as far back as the sixteenth century — and it became Charlie's local too; a home from home in which to relax and laugh after a twenty-hour shift; the place where he was accepted for what he was, as a tough working man among other tough working men.

He is aware of Sean's hand waving from a corner table, but he stays where he is, savouring bittersweet memories. Among the crowd of ghosts in the bar he sees his cousin and best friend, Izzy Conway, laughing, *always* laughing; his powerful uncle Jacob, issuing a drunken challenge to all-comers to be taken on, at anything, dominoes, skittles or arm-wrestling; and great-uncle Jonjo, a sun-bronzed whipcord of a man in his seventies, sitting in that very corner, deep in discussion of communist political theory. All now dead.

Charles shakes himself back to 1966 and goes to join Sloane. Next to his friend is a short, compact man with dark hair.

'Charles Holborne of counsel, this is Detective Inspector Read,' says Sloane quietly. 'Inspector Read is based at City Road. We thought it would be a good idea to meet off our respective patches. I hope this is convenient for you?' He gives Charles a wink.

Read stands and he and Charles shake hands.

'I've told DI Read what you told me about Frank Marshall and asked him for some advice,' says Sloane.

'Please sit down, Mr Holborne,' says Read.

A pint of mild awaits Charles on the pewter-topped table. He takes a seat in front of it.

Detective Inspector Leonard Read, based at City Road police station in the heart of London's East End, is establishing a reputation as that rare beast, a totally incorruptible Metropolitan policeman. So rare indeed that colleagues already predict that his resistance to the prevailing political wind is likely to blight his career, despite his merits as an outstanding investigator. Liked and respected by all who work closely with him, Read has a less comfortable relationship with some of his more nimble and ambitious superiors; superiors who've made successful careers out of side-stepping "difficult" high-profile cases and adroitly claiming the credit for successes.

Read also looks rather different from the typical Met police inspector. For one thing, thinks Charles immediately, he looks too nice. He has an open, pleasant face with brown hair brushed across a square head. At only five and a half feet tall, he also looks too short. It was the small stature which prompted the nickname, acquired as a kid at the Grundy Boxing Club, that has followed him ever since: "Nipper" Read.

'I'm pleased to meet you,' says Read. 'You might not realise it, but I had some early involvement in the investigation into Frank Marshall's disappearance. When it became a murder investigation, it was taken over by DCI Wheatley.'

'Yes. I saw your name on the depositions. You made the arrest.'

'Correct. I have a particular interest in the activities of the Kray twins. As, I think, do you.'

'Me?'

'Your reputation precedes you. No one can work in the Met — certainly not in the East End — without hearing the stories.'

'I don't know what you've heard, but that's all they are: stories.'

This is not how Charles imagined this conversation and he feels a flicker of discomfort. *Not again*, he thinks.

'DCI Wheatley, for example, makes no secret of the fact that he views you as little short of a Firm member.'

'Look, Mr Read,' says Charles, 'I agreed to meet you because I have information that suggests Frank Marshall is alive, which means that Stan Sharpe couldn't have killed him. If you're not interested in that, I think I'll push off. I've not come here to be cross-examined on my relationship with the Kray twins.'

He glares at Sloane accusingly.

'All right, let's get to that,' says Read calmly. 'Why are you so interested in Frank Marshall's disappearance?'

'I was instructed by the Sharpe family to advise on appeal. At that stage I gave it the thumbs down.'

'And since then?'

'I used to know Gracie Williamson before she married Frank. Sharpe asked me to talk to her.'

'And why would he do that?'

'He was grasping at straws, I think. He insists he had nothing to do with Marshall's disappearance, ergo, Marshall wasn't murdered. Yes, I know, not strictly logical, but he's convinced himself it was all a set-up. I think he hoped that if Gracie had heard from Frank, she'd tell me about it, even if she wouldn't tell you.'

Read falls silent, considering Charles carefully.

'If you think I've got some angle here, inspector, you're wrong.' Charles's voice is rising, and those at the tables closest to them glance over.

Read changes tack. 'That "supergrass" case you were instructed in last year. The one the papers called the "Bedpan Murders"?'

'What of it?'

'What was the Krays' involvement in that? There were whispers of jury nobbling.'

Charles tenses and grips the edge of the table, about to stand. 'Okay, I think I've had enough. Sorry, Sean, but you got me here under false pretences.'

Sean places a calming hand on Charles's forearm. 'Easy, Charles, easy.'

'I'm a successful barrister,' says Charles bending his head and speaking directly at Read. He has lowered his voice but speaks through clenched teeth. 'Why on earth would I have need of Ronnie and Reggie Kray? I knew them as a youngster, that's all, and I'd give my right arm to be shot of them!'

Read too leans across the table, keeping his voice low. 'Those who get involved with criminals don't always "need" to.

There're all sorts of reasons. Look at the actors and celebrities flocking to the Krays' clubs to be photographed with them. For reasons which I've never understood, certain people love flirting with dangerous men.'

'And you think that applies to me, do you?'

Read shrugs. 'Perhaps. There can be other reasons.'

'For example?' challenges Charles.

'Well, it could be that you're a messenger, passing information the Krays want me to have, for some reason.'

'That's fucking nonsense! You don't have to look for non-existent conspiracies here, inspector. It's simple: Stan Sharpe was my client, and he's serving life. If I'm told of evidence pointing to his innocence, it's my duty to look into it.'

'Consider it from my point of view, Mr Holborne. Whatever DCI Wheatley may be, he's no fool. He thinks you've got some involvement with Ronnie and Reggie Kray.'

'I think Wheatley *is* a fool. Or so fixed on his own agenda he has a completely closed mind, which amounts to the same thing. Sean can confirm that,' says Charles angrily, nodding towards his friend.

'But the rumours keep coming, don't they? Let's put aside the murder of your wife, then. There was that business on the Thames which led to your cousin's death — yes, we know Ronnie Kray was involved, in some way. Then, last year's case, *your* case, and rumours of jury tampering by the twins. And now who should come to us, out of the blue, with supposed evidence about the continued survival of one of the Krays' murdered lieutenants, but you?'

'Fine,' says Charles angrily.

He pushes back from the table and turns to Sloane.

'Sorry, Sean, I thought I was doing you a favour.'

'Please, Mr Holborne,' says Read, 'just hear me out.'

'Charles. Please,' says Sloane.

'Sean knows me. He knows I *loathe* Ronnie and Reggie Kray and would give anything to see the back of them,' says Charles angrily. He turns to his friend. 'At least, I thought he did.'

'Detective Sergeant Sloane has told me he trusts you and believes you to be straight,' says Read.

'So?'

'Sit down, drink your beer, and listen to me.'

After a moment's deliberation, during which Charles struggles to control his anger and disappointment with Sloane, common sense prevails and he complies. It would be foolish to ignore what the inspector has to say.

'Let me be completely open with you,' says Read. 'I'm going to get Ronnie and Reggie Kray. This city has had enough of them and needs a break from their activities.'

'Best of luck with that,' scoffs Charles. 'You'll never get anyone to testify against them.'

'Historically, that has been the case, I agree. But I'm already gathering statements from certain witnesses whose evidence would see them put away for years. Those statements presently have no names at the top and no signatures at the bottom. They are, if you like, "provisional" statements. Evidence of what certain people *might* say if they were no longer afraid. There will come a time when I have enough of those statements to arrest all of the Firm, every one of them, in one swoop. I shall keep them all separate, so they can't speak to one another or put pressure on anyone. Then we'll see if people start talking; see if we can top and tail those statements. I want them all to realise that if they screw up their courage, come up to proof, they can put the Krays away for good.'

'I wish you luck,' says Charles, and he means it.

'Some of the witnesses are members of the public, people who just happened to be in the wrong place at the wrong time and saw something they wish they hadn't. Some are associates of the Firm; some are actually long-standing members of the Krays' inner circle.'

'Go on then.'

'Go on what?'

'Which category am I in?'

'I don't know yet. My best guess would be that the Krays have something on you. I don't think you're a criminal, Mr Holborne. But I don't think you're totally clean either.'

'If you don't think I'm totally clean, how do you know I won't go straight back and tell them what you're doing?'

'They already know, or at least strongly suspect. I'm fine with that. I *want* them looking over their shoulders, wondering who they can trust, who might betray them. But I don't think you will report back to them. You see, I believe you when you say you hate the twins. I believe if you thought you could help put them away, you would. But you're frightened, like so many who have the misfortune of falling within their orbit. I don't know why, and for the present I'm not asking. But when the time comes I might be able to help you, and you might be able to help me.'

'And that's why you're here?'

'Partly. I thought it would be useful for us to meet. To plant the seed, so to speak. You'd make a very different witness from all the career criminals trying to save their own skins. Someone who'd be believed. As for Frank Marshall, DS Sloane was right to be cautious about who he approached. DCI Wheatley will not take kindly to the suggestion that somehow he got Stanley Sharpe to admit to killing a man who wasn't actually dead. But I will certainly make further enquiries, and if that's where the evidence leads, so be it. You've given us a useful head start.'

Charles doesn't answer. Instead, he stands and points at Sloane. He opens his mouth to speak, but thinks better of it. His hand drops. He is confused, undecided.

He has sought a way out from under the Krays for years, but he's not yet ready to trust Nipper Read. Or, for that matter, Sean Sloane. Once he confesses, he'll lose control of events, and there will be no way back. His conscience is clear; everything he did was to protect the innocent, prevent even greater harm, and circumvent the Krays' schemes. But he has committed crimes, however good his motives, and once he admits that, his career will be over. He will probably find himself in prison.

Lastly, and most powerfully of all, he feels betrayed by a friend.

Without a word, he turns on his heel and strides out of the pub.

'I'm going after him,' says Sloane, standing.

'Off you go, then,' says the little detective inspector, picking up his pint.

'I wish you'd warned me first, guv.'

Sloane runs after Charles. 'Hold up a second, Charles! Please!'

Charles keeps walking.

Sloane catches up with him on the metal bridge over the Shadwell Basin. 'I had no idea any of that was going to happen,' he says.

'Yeah, well, it happened, didn't it?' says Charles bitterly.

'Stop!'

Sloane grabs his arm. Charles shakes it off but he does stop.

'Well?' he demands, turning to face the policeman.

'I've never asked for details of what's gone on between you and the Krays, have I? I trust my gut about people and I do, honestly, believe you're straight. That's what I thought ever since Henrietta's murder, when I saw how you handled yourself, and nothing that's happened over the years since then has made me doubt it. Do you think I'd be your friend if I thought otherwise?'

Charles's shoulders sag and the fight deserts him. He just feels tired. Sloane continues.

'But it's obvious there's more than you let on. I don't pry, 'cos I've assumed that if you needed to, when you're ready, you'd tell me. But if there is something, maybe something you've done which gives the Krays a hold over you, this might be your way out. As far as I'm concerned, you and I can carry on as before. I'd be really sorry to lose you as a mate. As for Read, I think you can trust him. He's not like the others.'

'Maybe.'

'So, are we good?'

'Maybe.'

Charles starts walking off. He calls back over as he walks.

'I'll need to know if you locate Marshall. There's a man still in prison who shouldn't be there.'

CHAPTER SIXTEEN

It's the end of the day and Charles has won his GBH prosecution. He collects his papers from the bench in front of him, shakes hands with the officer in his case and heads for the robing room.

The room is packed with barristers changing out of their court robes. A long firm fraud involving multiple defendants and almost a dozen advocates has just finished in Court 1, and the barristers are in high spirits, schoolboys let out after a lengthy detention. There's a lot of good-humoured banter being shouted across the robing room. Charles pushes his way through to his locker. For once he won't have to take his robes back to Chambers, as he is due back here in a couple of days with nothing but paperwork to do in the interval. He packs away his wig, stiff collar and gown, and heads back downstairs to the main doors.

Out on the pavement of the Old Bailey, he looks up at the small patch of sky between the tall buildings. For the first time in weeks, it is not raining or threatening to rain, and the temperature seems a couple of degrees warmer. It's still a fortnight until the beginning of spring but he senses its approach. He decides to take the long way back to Chambers and drop into Snow Hill police station, so instead of turning left towards Ludgate Hill he turns right onto Holborn Viaduct. It only takes three minutes to walk to the beautiful old building with its polygonal bay windows adorning all five storeys.

He enters and speaks to the station sergeant behind the desk. 'Is PC Collingwood on duty?'

'I think he just arrived, sir. May I ask what it's concerning?'

'Yes, he dealt with the burglary at my chambers in the Temple a few days ago. A couple of witnesses, including me, may be required to make full statements, depending on the results of the fingerprint analysis. And I was going past, so…'

'I see. If you wait over there, sir —' he points to a bench behind Charles — 'I'll see if he's available.'

'Thank you.'

Charles takes a seat and picks up a discarded newspaper, turning to the sports pages. A couple of minutes later, PC Collingwood arrives. Charles stands.

'Good afternoon. Have you not received a call?'

'No. But if it was today, I've been in court.'

'We informed all the potential witnesses, so I expect there'll be a message waiting for you at your office. I'm afraid the fingerprinting turned up nothing.'

'What, nothing at all in any of the rooms?'

'There were a few smudged prints in some of the other rooms, not good enough quality for identification purposes. Your room, however — that's the one furthest from the door right?'

'Yes.'

'Yes, well, your room was wiped clean. Very efficiently. There were no prints anywhere.'

'What do you make of that?' asks Charles. The police officer shrugs. 'Doesn't that suggest to you that my room was the centre of attention?'

'Possibly. Still nothing missing as far as you can see?'

'Nothing.'

'Well, sir, I'm sorry, but there doesn't seem much more we can do at present. If the situation changes, someone will be in touch. '

'Okay, thank you.'

Charles leaves the police station and heads back to Chambers.

Once there he stands in the doorway and scans his room, trying to observe it with an independent eye. As he said to the police on the night of the burglary, there really *was* nothing worth stealing except the decanter and matching glasses, and it looked as though they had been knocked over rather than the thief being interrupted while lifting them. The room is cosy rather than elegant, tatty rather than expensive, and includes few ornaments and no expensive paintings, merely a couple of legal-themed engravings and prints, not one of which would be worth more than five pounds.

So if Charles *was* the target of the intruder, the only thing of potential value would have been the contents of his Instructions. He's never heard of a burglar breaking into a lawyer's office to steal evidence from the "other side", but he supposes it's not inconceivable.

He goes to his desk and pulls towards him the first pile of unopened briefs.

Over the next hour he opens the ribbon on each in turn, skimming the documents, cross-referencing with the index in the Instructions. Nothing stands out; nothing is missing.

There is a knock on the door.

'Come,' he says, his mind still on the problem at hand.

Jeremy enters. 'This just arrived for you, sir,' says the clerk.

He puts something on Charles's desk and makes to leave again. It takes a moment for Charles to focus on what Jeremy has said.

'What's this?'

Charles picks up the document. It's the Rover vehicle manual.

'I don't understand,' he says. 'I've had this for weeks.'

'Yes, sir. But we had a call from the garage saying they'd given you the wrong one, and could they replace it. I said yes, and popped it in the post as requested. This morning some bloke turned up and gave us this.'

Jeremy is again trying to leave.

'Jeremy! Hang on, don't run off. So this one's a replacement, yes?'

'Yes.'

'Where did you find the old one?'

'It was on your desk.'

'No it wasn't. I was looking for it the other night.'

Jeremy blushes and looks slightly embarrassed. 'Well, actually, it *was* on your desk, but it was tied up in one of your sets of papers.'

'Why would it be there?'

The lad looks more embarrassed still.

'I'm afraid that was my fault. Jennie found it on the floor with all the other papers after the burglary. Under your desk, actually. I thought it'd come from your car ringing prosecution. Well, it was a car manual, right? So when we were tidying your room, I put it in with the car ringing papers. It was only when the chap called that I realised it was yours, nothing to do with a case, and I knew exactly where to find it. Sorry about that.'

'No, not at all. I'm not cross. It's a simple mistake. Can you describe the person who came with the new one?'

Jeremy shakes his head. 'Sorry, sir, I was really busy. Youngish, I think. Maybe mid-twenties?'

'Build? Hair colour? Facial hair?'

'Couldn't tell you. Sorry. Dark hair, I think,' says the youngster, but Charles suspects he's guessing. 'Will there be anything else, sir?'

'No, thank you.'

Jeremy leaves Charles turning the replacement brochure over in his hands. Charles leafs through it. It looks identical to the original.

Perhaps the original was for a foreign market?

But then he remembers that the original was only in English and the specifications were all in Imperial, not metric. Charles reaches the final page and then starts with surprise. The minuscule handwriting he saw on the back cover of the original is still there.

This isn't a replacement; it's the same manual.

It is only then that he spots the difference. The penultimate page, the one that looked like blotting paper, is missing. Charles returns to his desk and roots around in his bottom drawer where he keeps miscellaneous odds and ends. He finds what he's looking for, a magnifying glass, and takes the booklet to Peter's desk lamp which is new, modern and much brighter than his own.

Viewed under the magnifying glass it is clear that the blotting paper page has been carefully cut out of the brochure, probably with a razor blade. It has been done carefully so as not to damage the fabric stitching holding the pages together, but a tiny strip of paper reveals where it used to be.

Charles's concentration is broken as the door opens again. Maria enters awkwardly with a pile of law books in both hands, a pen held in her mouth. She's been back at work for a few days and seems fully recovered from her encounter with the City of London police.

'Ah, there you are. I've got a task for you,' says Charles, putting down the manual.

She lowers her burden to Bateman's desk. 'Yes?'

'Do you fancy a walk in the City?'

'Why?'

'It's a lovely day, and I thought you might like a walk to Companies House to do a bit of research.'

'Sure, sounds great. How far is it?'

'City Road? A couple of miles, I suppose.'

'A couple of miles?'

He laughs. 'Yes, half an hour at most. Do you Americans never walk anywhere?'

'Sometimes, but our cities are much more spread out than yours.'

He shrugs. 'Well, I'll give you cab fare if you don't fancy it.'

'What do you want me to look up?' she asks, opening her notebook.

'Remember the fraudulent accounting case you read last week? You made some notes on the law.'

'Yes, I remember.'

'I'd like some background on the directors.'

He hands her a sheet of paper and a five-pound note.

'Here's the address, and that should cover the search fee and cab fares, but let me know if it doesn't. Please get receipts.'

'Isn't this the solicitors' job?' she asks.

'Strictly, yes, but it'll take weeks for them to get a clerk or an agent to do it. Much more efficient if we pop to Companies House and get the answers. Believe me, the solicitors will be pleased we've saved them the job.'

'I can just walk in and ask to make a search?'

'Yes. It's not something barristers often do, but it's a good way for you to learn, first hand, what details are publicly available. And it makes for a pleasant hour or two away from Chambers, especially when the weather's nice. All right?'

'Am I looking for anything in particular?'

'Ask to do an in-person search of the records. Make notes of the date of incorporation, any changes of name since then, the original and current directorships. Any linked companies or directorships also, if they're shown. And if you see anything about charges on the property or assets of the company, like mortgages, make a note of them too.'

'Sure. Shall I go now?'

'Yes, please.'

Maria stands and pulls her coat on.

A thought occurs to Charles.

'You know what…' he starts.

He returns to his desk, opens a drawer and takes out a sheet of paper.

'Just had an idea. Take this too.'

Charles hands her the purchase invoice for his new Rover.

'See this company?'

He points to the name, Sharpe's Luxury Motors Limited, and its company registration number at the bottom of the document.

'Yes?'

'Do the same for them. Anything you can find.'

CHAPTER SEVENTEEN

Charles looks out of his window. The plane trees outside have started to bud and the gardens sloping towards the Embankment and the river have a fresh green sheen to them. The weather is now sufficiently good for members of the Inn and workers from the surrounding offices to have started strolling the gardens during their lunch breaks, although there is still a chill wind off the Thames and most of them wear coats.

He looks at his watch: quarter to six, and time to pack up. He and Sally have agreed to finish work early tonight.

Five minutes later he puts his head into the clerks' room to announce his departure.

'I'm off,' he says.

'Oh, sir!' calls Jennie after him.

'Yes?'

'Fletchers have asked us to return the case of Coleman to them. The fraudulent accounting case?'

'I've already started work on it. And paid a search fee,' he adds, ruefully, reminding himself to ask Maria if there was any change from the previous week's excursion.

'It seems the lay client's done a runner. Last heard of on his way to the Cayman Islands. So the case isn't going ahead. At least not till he's caught.'

Charles laughs. 'That's a fiver I shan't recover. Fair enough. You'll find it on my shelf.'

'Thank you. Goodnight.'

'Have a nice evening,' replies Charles.

He leaves the building to find Sally waiting on the pavement outside Chambers.

Charles's heart sings at the sight of her. She looks inviting, her impish face framed by her dark bob and her figure-of-eight shape accentuated by a waisted jacket. As usual, she's refreshed her make-up in anticipation of seeing him.

I am so lucky!

'Hello, gorgeous,' he says. 'Sorry to keep you waiting.'

'No,' she replies, 'I've just arrived.'

He takes her hand and they join the steady stream of barristers, clerks and secretaries walking northwards, up Middle Temple Lane, heading home for the day. There was a time when he would have avoided the public display of affection for fear of the glances and the gossip. There was also a time, in the first few weeks after they resumed their relationship, when he had specifically to remind himself to make these little gestures. Now they come naturally. Some sort of barrier within him has been smashed, and every day he falls more in love with Sally and cares less about what anyone thinks of it.

As they step out of the gates opposite Temple Bar, an elderly man in a trilby appears suddenly in front of them.

'Hello, Deala,' says Charles, stopping in surprise.

'Evening, Mr H,' he replies. He removes his hat and inclines his head in greeting to Sally. 'Evening, missus.'

'Sally Fisher,' says Charles, 'may I introduce you to Frederick Wheeler, known by everyone in the East End as Wheeler Deala?'

'Pleased to meet you, Mr Wheeler,' she says with a smile.

'So, you're Harry Robeson's girl,' replies the spry old man.

'That's me. You know Dad, then?'

'Deala knows everyone,' says Charles.

'It was me who sold 'im that lovely Austin Princess,' says Deala. 'Gawd, 'e loved that motor! "The poor man's Rolls", he called it.' His face falls. ''Spect he had to sell it when … he…'

'Yes,' says Sally. 'When he went inside.'

'How's he doing?' asks Deala.

'Not too bad. He'll be out soon on licence.'

'That's good. Send him me best, will yer, when you next see 'im?'

'I will.'

'Now, Charlie,' says Deala, turning to Charles, 'I thought I'd pop by 'cos *you-know-who's* been seen again. I thought you should know.'

'Are you sure? When?'

'I heard from two separate geezers that he was watching his boy play football at Weavers Fields, last Sunday afternoon. Bold as brass.'

'Are they sure it was him? Do they know him well?'

'Yeah, they're sure.'

'He must be back in London, then. Would these witnesses give evidence, do you think?'

Deala shakes his head firmly. 'Not a chance. They're not the … witnessy type.'

'Right. Okay, thanks Deala. I owe you one.'

'My pleasure.' He lifts his hat again. 'Evening, miss,' he says, and within seconds he has melted into the rush hour crowd.

Charles and Sally cross the road and continue north up Chancery Lane.

'Was he talking about Frank Marshall?'

'Yes.'

'What're you going to do?' asks Sally.

'I don't know yet. Maybe I'll have a word with Sean. See if there's anything he recommends. But I can't leave Stanley Sharpe in prison for a murder he obviously didn't commit, can I?'

'DS Sloane, please,' says Charles.

Sally and he have finished washing up after dinner and Sally is measuring for curtains in the spare bedroom.

'Who's speaking, please?'

'My name's Charles Holborne. I have some information for him.'

'I'm sorry, sir, but Detective Sergeant Sloane is no longer at West Hendon.'

'Really? Are you sure? He's not been there long.'

'I'm sure. I have a phone number for him if you want to try that?'

'Yes please.'

The officer at the other end gives Charles a central London number which he writes down. Charles gives his thanks and dials again.

'CID office?'

'Is DS Sloane available, please?'

'Hang on.'

A hand is half-placed over the mouthpiece. 'Is that new bloke called Sloane?' hears Charles. The hand is removed. 'Yes. He's in, apparently. Give me a moment.'

It takes a couple of minutes before Charles hears the handset picked up again.

'Sloane,' announces Sean.

'It's Charles. Where on earth are you?'

'Back at West End Central.'

'Jesus, Sean! You've only just got out.'

'I'll explain when I see you. But Nipper Read asked if I'd like to join a new team he's heading up — not Vice. And I agreed.'

'But how does that work? You've only been at West Hendon a few minutes.'

'Formally, I'm on loan. Read had a word with DI Perry at West Hendon and asked if I could come over. I'm potentially useful because I know the ground but I'm not part of Vice.'

'Does that mean your guvnor's lost interest in the twins?'

'Absolutely not. But he's been promoted to DCI and given the task of cleaning up the West End in advance of the World Cup. The eyes of the world will be on us, and we don't want thousands of pissed and silly football fans being ripped off. So we're clamping down on the clip joints and brothels.'

'Right. Well, congratulations, I assume. Are congratulations appropriate?'

'Definitely. But I'm a bit busy, so…'

'Of course. I phoned for a reason. Frank Marshall's been seen again in London.'

'By you?'

'No.'

'By a reliable source?'

'I believe so, although we won't get anyone to confirm it on paper or in court.'

Charles hears Sloane draw a deep breath at the other end. 'Look, mate, I applaud your devotion to duty, but anonymous sightings…?'

'I know, but if he's now back in London, the girlfriend who went off with him might've got bored and come back too. If I give you her address, could you or one of your colleagues see if she's turned up? She was reported missing by her parents at Hornsey Police Station.'

'I'm really busy, but I suppose I could make a call. Maybe get somebody from Hornsey to go round.'

'That would be great, thank you. And if she's there?'

'Let's take it a step at a time. I promise, if we find credible evidence that Marshall's still alive, I'll let you know. My boss is going to want to interview him anyway, as a member of the Firm.'

'Thanks. I can't ask any more than that.'

CHAPTER EIGHTEEN

The Kentucky Club is packed. The usual Saturday night crowd has been supplemented by twenty or more thirsty young men, some with women in tow, who arrived en masse, apparently from some other celebration. They've settled in for the long haul. The club smells of smoke, beer and cheap perfume and noise levels have increased to the point that it's now difficult for Reggie Kray to hear what's being said to him.

He casts a sidelong glance at his twin. Ronnie sways in his chair, his eyes half-closed and his mouth slack. He has drunk far too much, especially on top of the pills, and he's out of it. Reggie looks at his watch — he'll have to take him home soon — but he needs to hear this report first.

'What about the bungalow he was supposed to be renting?' asks Kray, his mouth close to the ear of the little man sitting next to him.

'Trevor took him to look at one, but it went no further'n that. The wench's still at the flat.'

The man, one of Ronnie's latest soldiers, speaks with an Aberdonian accent. He and a few others were recently recruited from outside London to ensure no competing affiliations. His large eyes are protrusive, giving him a constantly startled expression. He reminds Kray of an American cartoon figure, but he can't remember which one.

Ronnie mumbles something inaudible and Reggie casts another glance at his semi-comatose brother. He shakes his head, biting back his anger. This whole strategy was daft from day one. Reg knew it would be nothing but trouble but, as always, once Ron had a bee in his bonnet it was impossible to get him to see reason.

He should have spotted the signs. Ronnie's most bizarre and convoluted master plans tended to herald the onset of another descent into mental illness. Now he is almost out of reach, mixing his medication with huge quantities of alcohol, armed to the teeth and imagining assassination threats all around him. Their mother can't manage him at Vallance Road while he's like this.

Reggie now realises he will have to find his brother somewhere safer to stay, away from the East End. If he can be persuaded to remain on his drugs, where it's quiet, calm, and away from the Firm, the episode should pass. Maybe Doc Blasker can recommend something; more tranquillisers, perhaps. In the meantime, as always, Reggie will have to sort out the mess.

'Is Frank's stuff still at Weston-super-Mare?' he asks.

'Some, but he didn't take much in the first place.'

'What did the girl say?'

'I couldn't get much oot of her and, before you ask, I tried. That wee lass won't be modelling for a while. She says she woke up and Frank wasnae there.'

'Did you believe her?'

'Aye. But for a couple of days before, he'd been going on and on about footie.'

'Football?' Kray pauses for a while, considering the information. 'Got a newspaper?'

The Scotsman looks puzzled. 'No.'

Kray stands and forces his way through the boisterous drinkers to the bar. He shouts at the barman. 'Gerry! Gerry! You still got that *Standard*?'

The barman puts down the pint he is pulling, takes out a well-read newspaper from behind the bar and pushes it across the surface to his boss. Kray muscles his way back to his table and resumes his seat. He turns the newspaper over and leafs back to the sports pages.

'There you go,' he says with some satisfaction, pointing at a football column. There, amid news and gossip about the forthcoming World Cup, is the First Division fixture list.

'What's that?'

'Take a couple of the boys — best make it half a dozen so you can cover all the gates — and go to Upton Park this Saturday.'

'Upton Park?'

'Upton Park, you dozy Scots git! Even you must have heard of West Ham United.'

The other shakes his head and takes a sip of his Scotch. 'I dinnae follow the footie doon here.'

Kray raises his voice over the din. 'Frank's football mad. He used to play in goal for the Hammers' Under Eighteens; that's how he knows all the players. If he's still in London, I'll pay even money he'll be at next Saturday's home match against Aston Villa.'

'Righto, boss.'

'And get someone down to Weston to clear out the flat, including the girl. We don't want any trace of Frank there, got it?'

'Aye. Got it. What do you want me to do wi' Marshall if we find him?'

'Leave that to me.'

'Hi, Mags.'

Ira Meyer, known everywhere in the manor as "Mags", looks up. It's been a disappointing day at Portobello Road market, and footfall has been light. His feet and hands are like blocks of ice and his nose runs constantly. The call of the gas heater, a hot cup of tea and Grandstand on the telly have finally persuaded him to call it a day. He is in the process of collecting his unsold magazines from under the polythene sheet covering his stall when he hears his name.

In front of him stands a tall man wearing a raincoat with its collar turned up. He has short-cropped fair hair and a cigarette hanging from thin lips. Mags knows him as "Tommy", one of the Krays' Firm.

Mags has always been fascinated by the twins and couldn't believe his luck when he found that Tommy frequented the same west London pub as he. He hoped it might provide an opportunity to ingratiate himself to the Krays, and he told Tommy to let the twins know they could always rely on him, if ever they needed to. Tommy seemed uninterested, although not sufficiently uninterested to refuse the drinks Mags bought him.

The only real connection with the twins Mags has managed to forge over the years arises out of his trade in smutty magazines. They're soft porn, nothing compared to what can be acquired behind the counter in plain brown envelopes from most of the shops in Soho, but once in a while Tommy would appear and ask Mags for a handful of magazines to be sent to a certain prison for the "Aways". Tommy always offered a five-pound note, which Mags always declined.

'On the 'ouse,' he'd say, and Tommy would smile and walk off with them under his coat.

Mags assumes this is what Tommy wants, and his hand is already reaching for one of the glossy magazines when Tommy surprises him.

'You still separated from your wife?' asks the tall man.

'Yeah. Why d'you ask?'

'So you're still Jack Jones in your gaff?'

'Yeah, just me.'

'And still at Acton?'

'Yeah, Horn Lane, as ever. What's this about, Tommy?'

The tall man glances to each side. The pitch to the left of Mags's is empty and the owner of the one to the right, a *schmutter* dealer, is engaged in loud haggling with an outraged and apparently deaf old lady.

Tommy leans forward to make sure he's not overheard. 'You always said you'd do anything to help Ronnie and Reg, right?'

'That's right. I would,' says the little man, his eyes shining in anticipation.

'I need your front door key.'

'What?'

'You heard. Reg needs you to give house room to someone for a bit. Just a few days. We'll pay for the extra food, and the inconvenience.'

'When?'

By way of answer, Tommy holds out his hand.

'Right away? But...' Mags thinks desperately for some reason to decline. 'But ... the place is a mess. I ain't tidied up for a bit...'

Tommy smiles, his hand still waiting, and Mags realises that he's not being given a choice. He reaches into his trouser pocket and brings out a latchkey on a ring, putting it in Tommy's palm.

Tommy takes an envelope from his raincoat pocket.

'There's a ton to start with. Reggie said you can have up to a monkey, depending on how long your guest stays. Get some nice grub in — steaks would be good — and plenty of booze.'

'This minute?'

'Yes. We'll be waiting for you.'

Tommy turns on his heel and Mags watches him stride away.

The little man has mixed feelings. At last, his wish to be admitted to the Firm has been granted, and he's excited. On the other hand, he doesn't know exactly what he's let himself in for. A little voice in the corner of his mind wonders if he should have been a little more careful with his wishes.

A couple of hours later he finds himself in the odd position of arriving outside his home, loaded with bags of food from the Co-op, and knocking on his own front door. It is opened by someone he's never seen before, a small man with protrusive darting eyes.

'Aye?'

'I'm Mags. I live 'ere. Can I come in?'

Another voice is heard from inside. 'If it's clear, let him in,' it calls.

The small man leans out and scans the wet pavements carefully. He returns and only then allows Mags to precede him into the hall.

'Thank you,' says Mags.

He sidles sideways through the door to the lounge, the bottles of booze in his bags clinking against his legs. He is surprised to find the sofa made up as a bed. His initial response is of gratitude until he sees his own pyjamas and tooth mug on the occasional table.

The owner of the other voice emerges from the kitchen, a cup of tea in his hand. This man Mags does know, at least by sight and reputation. It's "Scotch Jack" Dixon, one of Ronnie's new lieutenants. Very polite, very Scottish and very dangerous.

'You must be Mags Meyer,' says Dixon. He advances with a smile and an outstretched hand. 'I'm Jack Dixon. Ronnie asked me give you a hand. I'd no idea how big this place isnae! We are going to be cosy.'

'Are you staying 'n' all?'

'Aye. I'll be kipping in the box room.'

'There's no bed in there.'

'Och, that's fine. Gi us a coupla cushions and I'll be right as rain. I've slept in plenty worse. I've put Frank in your room. He's too big for that wee sofa,' he says, pointing at what is going to be Mags's bed for the foreseeable future. 'I hope that's okay.'

'Frank? Frank who?'

'Frank Marshall.'

Mags stares. 'But … but … 'e's dead ain't 'e? Murdered.'

As if in answer, a giant frame wearing a football scarf fills the kitchen doorway. 'Not when I last looked,' smiles Frank.

CHAPTER NINETEEN

It is not much of a coincidence that Charles has also been to the match between West Ham United and Aston Villa. The Hammers were his local team while growing up and he has followed them faithfully ever since. The only unusual feature is that, for the first time in years, he has made it to a Saturday game when he would usually be working in the Temple, when Chambers would be quiet and he would be uninterrupted. As part of their new regime Sally is encouraging Charles to work less and play more, even if that means him going out with a couple of mates from the East End and leaving her alone at home.

In fact, she enjoys being in the house without him.

She has fallen in love with the property and cannot believe her good fortune. She wanders from room to room, appreciating the work already completed and excitedly making notes of what still remains to be done. Her head is full of colours, fabrics and furniture, but Wren Street already feels like her perfect home; a real new beginning for her and Charles. Everything about it, both the house and the relationship, feels much more "right" than it did in the cavernous and rather ostentatious property in well-heeled Hampstead.

So this is how Charles comes to be returning to the house on Wren Street wrapped in his claret and blue football scarf and hat, to see someone loitering by the railings dividing the terrace from the pavement. The figure is small and its outline indistinct, rendered shapeless by a heavy overcoat. It is pacing back and forth immediately next to Charles and Sally's frontage, a large bag slung over its shoulder.

Charles approaches and the figure whirls round, startled.

'Maria?' he asks uncertainly.

The young woman looks up at him. She's been crying.

'I'm really sorry, but I didn't know where else to go,' she says.

'What's happened?'

'It's my father —'

'No,' interrupts Charles. 'Tell me inside. Come on, let's get you out of the cold.'

He climbs the steps to the front door to find it opening for him.

'I heard your voice,' explains Sally. 'Maria?' she adds, surprised to see the pupil below Charles still on the pavement.

Charles turns. 'Come on,' he instructs Maria.

Maria hesitates for a moment and follows him into the house. In the hall Sally takes Maria's coat. She and Charles share a glance as they note the pupil's bag by her feet. It has been hurriedly stuffed with clothes and toiletries, and the trailing end of what looks like pyjamas and the bristles of a hairbrush are visible through the open zipper.

'Come down to the kitchen,' says Sally, 'and I'll put the kettle on.'

'I don't know about you,' says Charles to Maria as they descend the stairs, 'but I'm frozen through and I'd like a hot chocolate. Fancy one?'

'That sounds lovely. Thank you,' replies Maria.

Charles nods to Sally and inclines his head towards the girl. Sally understands and sits opposite Maria at the kitchen table while Charles heats some milk.

'What's happened?' asks Sally sympathetically.

'Has Charles mentioned that I live in my father's apartment in St John's Wood?' she starts.

'I knew you were using your father's flat, yes.'

'He's usually in Brussels. I haven't actually seen him since Christmas, but he came back unexpectedly this evening. I wasn't in.'

She takes off her spectacles and rubs her eyes. She seems less agitated than when she first entered, but she looks very tired.

'He was waiting for me when I got back and we had a terrible row.'

'And you left?' asks Charles from the kitchen counter, pointing at Maria's stuffed bag.

'Well … he sort of threw me out.'

'Oh, I'm so sorry!' says Sally.

'Must've been some row,' comments Charles.

'Is it all right if I use the washroom?' asks Maria. 'I've been out in the cold for half an hour or so, plucking up courage to knock on the door.'

'Of course,' says Sally. 'You know where it is.'

Maria stands and slips out of the kitchen and Sally and Charles listen to her footsteps running up the stairs. She returns just as Charles is pouring the hot chocolate into two mugs. She resumes her seat. Sally notes that her make-up has been repaired.

'I think I probably owe you an explanation, Charles,' says Maria.

'Me?'

'You've been very kind, but … you've probably been able to tell that … well, my heart's not always been in it. The law, that is.'

Charles brings over the two mugs and puts one in front of Maria. He sits next to Sally. 'Sure?' he asks Sally, pointing to the saucepan on the stove. 'I made enough for three.'

Sally shakes her head. 'No thanks.'

Charles reaches behind him to a shelf on which there stands a Scotch decanter.

'It's a criminal waste of single malt, but needs must,' he says, pouring a healthy slug of whisky into his chocolate. He offers it to Maria, who laughs and nods, and he pours another into hers.

'Cheers,' he says and clinks mugs with Maria. 'So, you want to be a jazz musician, right?' he says with a smile.

Maria looks up sharply, puzzled. 'How do you know?'

'You've been doing gigs at Ronnie Scott's. I'm a regular there. In fact, I have to confess, on one occasion I followed you and listened to you practise.'

'You followed me?'

'Yes. I'm sorry about that. But you were frequently leaving Chambers early and it was being noticed. What can I say? I'm a nosy parker, and I was curious. Also, I was concerned for you. I didn't want you to blow your chance of getting a tenancy.'

She nods, accepting his explanation. 'Is that what I've done?'

'Not at all. Or at least, not yet. But you don't really want it, do you?'

She shakes her head. 'I don't think so. My father's desperate for me to carry on, and furious that I've continued playing behind his back. I had a lunchtime gig today, at a hotel in Charlotte Street, and he knew what I'd been doing the minute he saw me.'

'Charles tells me you're very good,' says Sally.

'Really?' replies Maria, looking up at Charles hopefully.

'I think you've an amazing talent. I'm no professional, but I know my jazz and I think you *could* make a career of it. I mean, it's risky, of course —'

'Riskier than the Bar?' she asks.

He smiles. 'No, probably not. There are no guarantees at the Bar either, but once you get started the rewards are probably better for most barristers. Compared to most jazz pianists.'

'That doesn't bother me. Playing music is what I've always wanted to do, since I was three or four.'

'And your parents don't approve?' asks Sally.

Maria turns to her. 'It wasn't a big deal for them, not for a long time. My father's not a jazz fan, so he never got it. In his mind, proper musicians play in concert orchestras, but he didn't actually oppose me until…' She falters and stops.

'Until?' prompts Charles.

'You don't have to tell us if you don't want,' says Sally, looking pointedly at Charles.

'No, of course, I'm sorry,' he says.

'No, I think you're owed an explanation. I just don't know where to start. You see … my brother … no…' She pauses, takes a deep breath, and starts again. 'I had a brother. Spencer. He was five years older than me and he was going to be a lawyer.'

There is another long pause. Sally and Charles allow the silence to lengthen. The kitchen clock ticks steadily.

'Then he was murdered.'

They watch as her lip trembles again and her eyes fill with tears. Sally reaches over and grips her hand. Maria manages to regain her composure.

'Spencer was so enthusiastic about it and Dad thought I might have a similar aptitude, so I majored in law. I didn't love it the way he did, but I was toying with the idea of a career in law too, as long as I could continue playing music. But then Spencer died and all my father's hopes seem to descend onto my shoulders. Suddenly it was my responsibility to take up the reins. The music became "frivolous" and a "waste of my talents".'

'That's not very fair,' comments Sally.

'It wasn't Dad's fault completely. Spencer's death ... well, it changed him. He pushed as hard as he could for an investigation, despite being warned off. It damaged his career. I was just as fired up. We sort of wound one another up, and I thought I saw my path, as a civil rights lawyer. So I was willing, at least at first.'

She falls silent again. Charles sips his drink patiently.

'Do you want to tell us what happened to Spencer?' asks Sally.

Maria takes a deep breath. 'He was shot. He was a student at Ole Miss...' She sees Sally's puzzled expression. 'The University of Mississippi. The first university in the States to take Black pupils. Weren't the riots reported over here?'

'Yes,' says Charles. 'I remember something about it. To do with the registration of a Black student?'

'Yes,' confirms Maria. 'The governor refused to allow integration, even though it was the law. The town was full of Ku Klux Klan and Confederate flags. Spencer was involved — he was volunteering with the NAACP — and there was a riot between the whites and the federal agents. Spencer was shot dead.'

'Who by?' asks Charles.

'We don't know. The local sheriff only pretended to investigate. He's a vile man, a member of the Klan. We assume it was one of the white rioters or local law enforcement.'

Sally reaches across the table and takes Maria's hand again. 'I'm so sorry, Maria. I can't imagine how awful that must be.'

'Thank you.'

'If you want to do civil rights, you're in the wrong chambers,' points out Charles.

'I know. But no one else would have me. Your chambers were going to refuse as well, until Mr Hamilton dug his heels in.'

'Does he know the background?'

Maria nods. 'Yes. He and my father had something to do with one another during the war.'

'But you don't want to be a lawyer at all now, is that right?' asks Sally.

'I don't know. I don't think so. The burglary last month…'

'The burglary?' asks Charles.

'It's why I was so shaken up by that policeman. I was always frightened at home. You won't understand, but it's there constantly, in your face, every day, prejudice, aggression and violence. I was just another uppity Black woman with ideas above her station. And after Spencer's death I was even more on edge. "Scalded cat" my mother called it. She thinks I'm suffering some sort of stress reaction. I was there, you see, not actually where he died, but on the campus that weekend. It was terrifying. All those masked white men running through the street, smashing things! So when Dad was posted to Europe and he offered to let me come, I thought it would be easier here. The Inn accepted my qualifications and I thought, you know, a fresh start. But the way that policeman treated me … it felt just the same. It really shook me up.'

'Did you explain that to your father?' asks Charles.

'No, I didn't get the chance. But he already thinks I'm a coward. He says I have an obligation to see it through, "for Spencer's sake".'

'But what do *you* think?' asks Sally gently.

Maria sighs. 'I loved my brother and I hate them for what they did to him. Of course I want everything to change, and I don't want to let my parents down, but I'm not enjoying the law anymore. On the other hand, I'm really happy when I'm playing. Do you think that's cowardly?'

Charles shakes his head firmly. 'No. You have to do what makes *you* happy. You can't devote your life to doing what other people think you should. Even if they're your parents.'

'But my father will be so disappointed in me.'

Her voice is so desolate that Charles wants to hug her. Instead he leans across the table and fixes his eyes on hers.

'I've been saying this for years, Maria, but I believe that if your parents really love you, they should want to see you happy, even if you don't follow the path they've laid out for you.'

'And there's a man who knows what he's talking about,' laughs Sally gently.

Maria nods and then yawns loudly. 'I'm so sorry,' she apologises. 'I was playing late last night, and today's been … exhausting.'

'There's a bed made up in the spare room if you'd like to lie down,' says Sally, standing. 'Come on, I'll take you up.'

Maria hesitates. 'Would it be okay … for me … to stay? Just for tonight, till I can think what to do next. If not, I completely understand … I can go to a hotel. It's just that I don't know anyone else well enough to ask.'

'You are staying here,' says Charles firmly. 'Tonight, and for as long as necessary until you get sorted out.'

CHAPTER TWENTY

Reggie Kray turns into Vallance Road, Bethnal Green, deep in thought, and heads towards the family home, the second door along the terrace from the corner. To those who don't know, the property is an unexceptional Victorian cottage in an unexceptional street, somewhat blighted by the main railway line to Liverpool Street station which overflies it only a few yards away, creating a long, dingy and very noisy tunnel.

However, to the London criminal fraternity, 178 Vallance Road is an important landmark: the Kray family home.

Since the Krays' tenure began in the 1930s, the property has acquired several nicknames. During and after the war, for example, it was known as "Deserters' Corner", as various runaways from the armed services, including the twins themselves, used it as a temporary hideout.

Now, however, it is commonly referred to as "Fort Vallance" on account of the fact that, hidden under the loose floorboard in Ronnie Kray's bedroom, is the Firm's stash of illegal weaponry, firearms, sabres and other cutting implements.

The house is also where the Firm's inner circle meet regularly to lay their plans, squashed up against one another in the tiny front room, politely thanking Violet Kray for her endless cups of tea. Mrs Kray, the matriarch known to all as "Vi", stubbornly and wilfully insists, despite all evidence to the contrary, that her sons aren't criminals, but misunderstood and persecuted boys.

Reggie is lost in thought. Moving Frank Marshall into protective custody at Mags Meyer's place has kept the big man off the streets so far, but he knows it's only a temporary solution. Marshall is already getting restive. Reggie has bought himself a little time, but no more than that.

He comes to an abrupt halt on the pavement outside his family home. He was so distracted he didn't notice until now, but the house is lit up like a Christmas tree. Every room is illuminated, from the entrance hall to the eaves. He waits for a couple of trains to pass and then hears again the noise he noted but couldn't identify seconds before: it is Ronnie's raised voice, and he is roaring, almost braying, with what sounds like anger.

Reggie opens the front door and rushes towards the kitchen. Ronnie is in the process of coming out, a bottle of spirits in one hand and three glasses in the other. He is in his shirt sleeves, suspended by his trademark silver sleeve garters à la croupier, and his face is flushed. His eyes are dangerously bright, almost wild.

'I did it!' he says excitedly. 'Come and celebrate!'

He leaves Reggie in the hallway and disappears into the front room.

'Where's Mum?' demands Reggie, making sure she can't overhear.

'Out the back,' calls Ronnie.

Reggie follows his brother.

As he enters, two men rise from the couch where they've been sitting, Ian Barrie and Scotch Jack Dixon. They both look embarrassed and apprehensive.

'What're you doing here?' demands Reggie of Dixon. 'Why ain't you at Horn Lane?'

Dixon looks down and inclines his head towards Ronnie, who is handing out glasses.

'Come on,' says Ronnie, gesturing to Reggie to take the third glass.

'Why? What's happened?' demands Reggie.

'I fuckin' did 'im! Just walked up to him and shot him in the head!'

'Who?'

'Cornell.'

'George Cornell?'

Ronnie throws back the entire contents of the glass in one swallow and laughs loudly while attempting to top up the others' untouched glasses. He's exultant.

'It was fuckin' brilliant! Calm as you like, just walked up to 'im and popped him in the forehead with the Luger! It was like something outta a film!'

Reggie is having trouble assimilating the news.

'He shot Cornell?' he demands, looking at Barrie. The man shrugs; Dixon looks away.

'You silly useless bastard!' shouts Reggie. 'What the fuck do you think you're up to?'

The vehemence of Reggie's response and the fury on his face startle Ronnie. He is so surprised, he is rendered speechless.

'Do you know what I've been doing the last few days? Well, do you?' shouts Reggie. 'Cleaning up your fucking mess — as always! Frank Marshall's been wandering around London, in plain view, for anyone to see! I told you over and over, your stupid, *idiotic* plan was never gonna work. And all to get Stan Sharpe banged up? If you felt that strongly, why didn't you shoot *him*? It makes more sense than shooting George Cornell!'

Ronnie shrugs, deflated. His shoulders drop as the excitement drains from him like air from a punctured tyre.

'So what happened?' demands Reggie, still furious.

'Nothing happened.'

'Then why Cornell?'

'He was in the Richardsons' gang,' offers Ronnie, after a pause.

'But since the shootout at Mr Smith's Club they're finished! Everyone else is in custody! It makes no sense!'

Ronnie doesn't answer.

'Where?'

Again, no answer.

Reggie glares at the others. 'Well? Where?'

It's Dixon who replies. '*The Blind Beggar* … in the bar.'

'What? In front of everybody?'

'There weren't many people in,' says Barrie.

'Oh, well, that's all right then! For fuck's sake, Ron. I don't understand why you did it!'

'He called me a fat poof,' mumbles Ronnie, now unable to meet Reggie's gaze.

Reggie's mouth works, but he's so astonished that nothing emerges for a moment. 'That was ages ago! Anyway, you *are* a fat poof. And he was off his pills; you both were! You told me yourself, he didn't know what he was saying!'

Ronnie's voice drops even further. 'He knew. He made me look small, in front of everyone. He 'ad it coming.'

Reggie throws his hands up in exasperation.

'Anyway, shooting was too good for 'im,' mutters Ronnie.

'What?' demands Reggie, confused.

'Sharpe. Arrogant fucker. I want him banged up for life. Make him really suffer.'

Reggie throws himself into an armchair, speechless. When he does eventually speak, it's more to himself than to the other occupants of the room.

'Just how stupid could you be? After everything we've been through in the last few months, you invite the Filth down on our heads with a pointless, idiotic shooting. And in broad daylight!'

'Not exactly broad daylight —' starts Barrie before Reggie gives him a look.

Reggie stands again. After years of damage limitation and nursing Ron through his episodes of mental illness, he knows exactly what has to be done.

'Go on then; upstairs,' he orders.

Ronnie doesn't move.

'Now! Get in the shower and gimme all your clothes. And for fuck's sake, make it quick! We gotta get you out of here.'

Ronnie still doesn't move but stands, dazed, like a stunned animal.

'Go!' shouts Reggie.

Ronnie lumbers into movement, colliding with his mother who enters at the same moment.

Reggie addresses her. 'You know nothing, and you've seen nothing, all right?'

Vi stops on the threshold, looking from one of her twins to the other. She nods.

Reggie calls after Ronnie as he disappears up the narrow stairs. 'Pack a bag. And don't forget your pills!'

CHAPTER TWENTY-ONE

'Well, who will you support, then?' demands Charles.

'I haven't decided yet,' says Sloane. 'Basically, anyone except England.'

'That's bloody charming, to the country which took you in, gave you a good job and put a roof over your head!'

Charles is only mock offended. He has a number of Irish, Scottish and Welsh friends and colleagues, and every one of them will be supporting any team that happens to be drawn against England in the forthcoming World Cup; the sequelae of subjugation, thinks Charles with a grin.

The sense of anticipation is growing. Pubs are filling with armchair experts advocating the merits of their chosen defensive formations, and football stories have begun to migrate from the tabloids' sports pages to the front pages as injuries rule out English players in form and everyone debates who should play. In the next few days Alf Ramsey, the England manager, will be announcing the forty-man squad from whom the final twenty-eight will be chosen. West Ham fans are particularly excited; several Hammers are likely to feature.

Charles has twisted Sloane's arm to meet him for a quick pint at the end of his shift. In truth the detective sergeant is too busy, but he has put Charles off several times and is beginning to feel guilty.

Everyone in Nipper Read's team is exhausted. The clubs, clip joints and brothels they have been shutting down over the last few weeks keep late hours, on top of which they are generating so much paperwork that they've had no choice but to ditch their usual shift patterns. Read is already fretting about the cost of all the overtime.

Sloane has been working for the last seventy-two hours and, like the rest of the team, is out on his feet. Nonetheless, he is happy. For the first time in his professional career in the Met, he is making friends. Read has chosen his team members carefully, and the similarities between them are obvious: each is of unquestioned honesty and loyal to Read himself, not beholden to other senior officers for their ranks, and of a certain independent cast of mind. Sloane has at last found his tribe.

'Has Ireland never made it to the finals?' asks Charles with a twinkle in his eye. He knows the answer.

'Sure, and they were beaten finalists last time out, were they not?' replies his friend. He yawns loudly.

'Okay, now you're overacting,' laughs Charles. 'I'll let you go. I said a quick pint and I meant it. All I need to know is if there's any news about Frank Marshall's girlfriend. I want to get Notice of Appeal filed.'

'I do have a bit of news, but you're not going to like it.'

'Well?'

'Judy Bishop is now back living at her parents' house, but she isn't talking.'

'Why not?'

'It might have something to do with her broken nose and two black eyes,' says Sloane as he lifts his pint.

'A parting gift from Frank?'

'She's not saying but, on balance, I think not. She returned to London alone and the local police at Weston-super-Mare say she was in the flat for at least a fortnight without him. She got that beating after he left.'

'Who, then?'

Sloane shrugs. 'Who knows? It might be completely unrelated. A woman alone, with no money, in an unfamiliar part of the world. There is a suggestion that she was hooking to make ends meet. Dangerous, if you've no pimp and no knowledge of the area.'

'Speak to her yourself?'

'No, Charles, I told you, I'm too busy. One of the uniforms at Hornsey.'

'Do you think I could have my solicitor talk to her?'

'Up to you,' shrugs Sloane. 'We spoke to her father on the phone and he's determined to find out who did that to his little girl. He said he'd talk her round. Maybe give him a few days? Anyway, need sleep. Give me love to your darling girl.'

Sloane downs the last of his pint and hastens to the Tube and, thence, his bed.

Charles sits, nursing his drink in the noisy pub. After a while he reaches a decision and also heads for the Tube.

Gracie's Nissen hut is chaotic again, but this time with packing. She's moving out.

'I found a little flat in Leyton,' she says happily, standing between piles of cardboard boxes. 'It's even got a little garden.'

'I'm pleased for you. How did you manage it?'

She winks at him. 'An old friend came through for me. Anyway, Charlie, it's a bit busy in here —' she steps backwards quickly, out of the way of a man carrying a box towards the waiting van.

'Hey!'

She calls to her two boys who are sitting, heads together, on the floor, reading something.

'What did I tell you? Go and pack those toys! If it isn't in a cardboard box in the next ten minutes, it's being left behind!'

The two lads stand up. The elder boy closes what he was reading and places it carefully on the kitchen counter. Charles recognises the reading material: the programme from West Ham's last match against Aston Villa.

He turns to Gracie.

'Seen anything of Frank?' he asks.

'No, of course not,' she says.

Charles points to the programme. 'Then where did the boys get that?'

Gracie busies herself with closing the lid of a cardboard box.

'Come on, Gracie, I wasn't born yesterday. Frank's been here, hasn't he?'

'No. I told you I'd let you know if I heard anything, and I haven't. Look, I'm busy — you can see what it's like — so you'll have to go. I'll give you a bell once I'm settled, all right?'

'You've no intention of calling me. Know what I think? Frank's back and given you all sorts of excuses, made all sorts of promises, and you're heading off to Leyton to play happy families with him.'

She doesn't answer or look up.

'I bet he didn't tell you where he's been, these last months,' adds Charles.

'Frank's dead.'

'That's not what you thought before.'

'Well, it's what I think now. Don't cause a scene. Just go, okay? I didn't ask you to get involved.'

'He's been living with a woman called Judy Bishop in Weston-super-Mare.'

She finally looks up. 'I don't believe it.'

'Why not? If you've not seen him, he might've been anywhere.'

'Frank's dead. And he'd never cheat on me,' she says, trying to keep her voice level.

'I'm telling you, I've been to see the Bishops. So have the police. Frank and this girl — she was also a Windmill girl, by the way, but some years behind you — it's all over. But that's where he's been all this time. And he'll do it again; it's who he is.'

Charles watches Gracie carefully. She has a saucepan in her hands and stands before a half-full tea chest with its top open. Her shoulders are slumped and she's staring at the bare floorboards. The removal man intervenes, picks up the box and disappears outside, leaving Gracie holding the saucepan.

Charles continues quietly. 'What you tell yourself about Frank isn't my business. But I'll tell you something that *is*: Frank's involved in a conspiracy to pervert the course of justice. There's a man serving life for killing him, it's Frank who's keeping him inside and it's all about to unravel. This is serious, Gracie, and when Frank's found, he'll end up inside again. If you hide him, you'll be getting yourself involved too. Personally, I can't understand why you'd want to protect a man who's lied to you — pretended to be dead, for God's sake! — so he could desert you and the boys for another woman, but that's your call. The question is, what's going to happen to the boys if you're in prison too? Do you want to see them in care? Is that what you want? Because that's a very real possibility.'

She looks up at him. 'Frank's dead,' she repeats for the third time, but her heart isn't in it.

How can she still love him?

'Think about what I've said, all right? But if you go ahead and find yourself in need of a decent brief, you know where I am.'

CHAPTER TWENTY-TWO

Charles smells fresh coffee as he descends the stairs to the kitchen. He is later than normal and still wears pyjamas, slippers and dressing gown. Maria has been no trouble at all as a house guest, but a minor irritating change forced on him by her presence is the requirement to wear more clothes than had he been alone with Sally.

Maria stands by the kitchen counter plunging a fresh cafetière of coffee. It was she who introduced the new gadget into the household.

'Good morning,' she says cheerfully.

She has been at Wren Street for a couple of weeks now, and the change in her is remarkable. No longer the reticent and uncommunicative young woman with whom Charles was familiar, it's as if she's shed an old skin. Gone are the severe tailored court suits and the worried expression, to be replaced by brightly-coloured trendy clothes — today baggy cotton trousers and a maroon top with huge bangle earrings — and a relaxed young woman who smiles a lot. She seems at ease, both with herself and her hosts, and Sally and Charles have enjoyed her company. Now freed of the obligation to go into the Temple every morning, she sleeps late, especially when playing the night before. So, for Charles to find her up and about and apparently showered and dressed by breakfast time is noteworthy.

'I've made coffee,' she says.

'Yes, I smelt it. Thank you. What are you doing up so early?' he asks, taking cereal and bowls from the cupboard. 'Are you having breakfast?'

'No, thank you. Just coffee for the moment. I wanted to catch you before you left.'

'I'm going in late. My trial collapsed yesterday. Anything wrong?'

'No, not at all. But I've made some decisions and wanted you to be the first to know.'

'That's good. Barbara's been very understanding so far, but I don't think you can leave her in the dark much longer. Apart from anything else, Hamilton went out on a limb for you, and I think you owe it to him.'

'I agree.'

'So, are you coming back?'

'I've arranged to meet Mr Hamilton for lunch today, but I wanted you to be the first to know what I've decided.'

Charles continues laying the table as Maria speaks. Sally hops into the room, trying to put on her coat at the same time as struggling with her second shoe. She drops her bag on the floor by the door. Her hair is still damp from the shower. Finally fully shod, she almost runs across the room to kiss Charles on the cheek.

'See you this evening,' she says hurriedly. 'Will you be eating with us tonight, Maria?'

'No, thank you. I may be out, but if not I'll sort myself out.'

'Okay,' says Sally, picking up her bag and heading up to the front door. 'See you!' she calls, and the front door slams.

Charles sits at the table while Maria brings the pot of coffee with two cups and joins him.

'Does your father know your decision?'

'No. I'm seeing *him* this afternoon.'

'Busy day,' says Charles sympathetically. 'So what have you decided?'

She takes a deep breath. 'I'm very grateful to you and everyone at Chambers, but I've decided not to continue with my pupillage.'

'You're going to try full-time music, then?'

'Well, I'm not sure there's such a thing as a "full-time" jazz musician, certainly not at the outset. But in addition to my regular trio spot at Ronnie Scott's I've got a couple of solo gigs.'

'That's great news!' says Charles, his mouth now full of Sugar Puffs.

'It's a start. And I've found somewhere else to stay, so I'll be out of your hair soon.'

'Where?'

'I know some musicians sharing in Shepherd's Bush. The bass player's going on tour soon, so there'll be a spare bed. Will it be okay if I stay here until it becomes available? Probably a few weeks.'

'Of course. If you don't mind me asking, can you manage the rent?'

She smiles. 'I don't mind you asking. Not unless my father helps.'

'And will he?'

'I'll be able to answer that tonight,' she replies, grimly.

The telephone rings and Charles puts down his coffee and reaches over to answer it. 'Terminus one-five-two-five.'

'Mr Holborne?'

'Yes, good morning, Jennie. Everything all right?' Charles can't remember an occasion on which a junior clerk has rung him at home.

'Yes, sir. Sorry to disturb you so early, but Barbara's got an appointment out of Chambers this morning and she left a note asking me to call you as soon as I got in.'

'That's fine. What's the note say?'

'Well, sir, I'm not a hundred per cent sure I understand it. There was a call timed at six forty-five last night from a lady called Mrs Marshall who wanted to speak to you urgently.'

'Yes?'

'The note then says "Reverend Sharpe" and "He's not a murderer" in quotes. Do you understand it?'

'Yes I do, thanks.' Charles's heart lifts; Gracie seems to have changed her mind. 'Anything else?'

'Yes. Barbara seems to have given the lady the phone number of Tindall and Company. The note finishes by asking you to call Mr Tindall as soon as you get the message. Is that okay?'

'Yes. Can you give me the number, please?'

Jennie does so and hangs up.

'Excuse me, Maria, but this won't take long.'

Charles dials Tindall's number. The phone at the other end is picked up instantly.

'May I speak to Mr Tindall, please?' asks Charles.

'Is that you, Charles?'

'Yes. No receptionist?'

'At the dentist. You got the message, then?'

'Yes. Have you heard from Mrs Marshall?'

'Just hung up from her. She's coming in to give a statement at ten thirty. And she's asked us to handle her divorce!'

'Do you do divorce work?'

'We're a small high street firm; we do everything, including matrimonial work, although not me personally. Anyway, she says she believes her husband's still alive and she's had enough of him.'

'I didn't think I'd got through to her,' says Charles reflectively.

'Oh, you spoke to her? She was expecting him to move to Leyton with her and the boys, but he didn't show. Off with another woman, she thinks. So she's finally lost patience.'

'Not before time. So, how can I help?'

'Well, if you can advise favourably on merits, the Reverend Sharpe can get legal aid for an appeal. Would a statement from Mrs Marshall saying she's spoken to him and that he's alive be enough?'

Charles considers. 'On the face of it, yes. But the Crown are bound to say she has an ulterior motive. I don't think I told you, but the police have tracked down the woman who Marshall ran off with.'

'No, you didn't.'

'I saw no point, as she refused to speak to the police or confirm that she'd been with him. But I have her name and address, and if you can show her a statement from Gracie confirming that Marshall's still alive, you might have enough to persuade her to do the same.'

'I'll certainly give it a go.'

'With two witnesses, we should be okay. But the girlfriend will still be reluctant. She's taken a beating and is likely to be scared. On the other hand, if she's now facing a charge of conspiracy to pervert the course of justice, her way out is to tell the truth. The fact that she went off with Marshall doesn't mean the Crown can prove she knew he was supposed to be dead.'

'How could she not know?' asks Tindall doubtfully.

'That's what I'd say. *"I had no idea, I never read about it in the papers."*'

'Hmm,' replies Tindall.

'And Marshall might've been using a false name.'

'Yes, maybe. Okay, I'll reserve judgement for the present. I suppose I'd better find a photograph of Marshall to take with me. Can you let me have her details?'

'She's called Judy Bishop and she was living with her parents on Duckett Road, Haringey, number thirty. Best of luck.'

Charles hangs up. He turns to Maria.

'Remember that chap we saw in Durham?'

'The murdering vicar?' replies Maria with a grin.

'Yes, him. Looks like the victim's turned up, alive and well. So, not a murdering vicar after all. I told you, didn't I? Keep an open mind.'

'Yes. But he's still a wife-beater.'

CHAPTER TWENTY-THREE

Tensions have been rising steadily in Mags Meyer's house. Everyone is on edge, except Mags himself, who seems oddly unaware of it. At last, he's been admitted to the inner circle and he is revelling in his new-found importance as minder to one of the twins' lieutenants, a dangerous man on the run from the police.

He bustles around, cooking, washing up and pandering to Marshall's needs, his scrawny chest puffed up like a little cocky robin. His only regret is that he can't mention his newly elevated status to anyone. He has been sworn to secrecy with such force and so repeatedly that he is under no illusions; blabbing to anyone would have seriously deleterious consequences for his health. So he consoles himself with the thought that, one day, he'll be able to tell the story to awed audiences at the pub. He even finds himself trying out a few phrases in his head.

So, while Mags Meyer daydreams, everyone else in the cramped accommodation is increasingly fractious. Jack Dixon has been there throughout, a consistent presence, but the other minders, at least one and more often two, have changed as dictated by the Krays' wider business needs. For the first few days Marshall was happy to catch up with the old friends who, on the orders of Reggie Kray, slipped quietly in and out of the door of the council house; to eat the enormous steaks bought for him by Meyer; and to drink endless cups of tea. However, gradually, boredom and annoyance have set in.

'When are Ron and Reg coming to see me?' he asks constantly. 'After all I've done for 'em, they could at least have the courtesy to pay us a visit. Everyone else's been, so where are they?'

Dixon has explained patiently that although Ronnie is having another of his "spells" and is out of action for the moment, Reggie is fully occupied making plans for Frank's future, which is going to be rosy.

For a while Marshall was placated. No longer.

Every morning he wakes from his sleep in Mags's bed and stomps downstairs in his pyjamas and dressing gown, irritable and grumpy. Even in his carpet slippers he dwarfs all around him, making the house seem even smaller than it is. The only person to whom he speaks is Mags, and then only to give his breakfast order. He demolishes a mountain of bacon, eggs and beans on toast and a pot of tea while reading the *Sketch*, delivered by the paperboy every morning. The next hour is spent on his ablutions, a good half of that applying hair lotion and combing and re-combing his thick locks before the bathroom mirror until perfectly satisfied with the result. Then downstairs for another pot of tea.

As the morning dribbles away he starts pacing, communicating his agitation to everyone else. By lunchtime he has started on his favourite tipple, Scotch and ginger. Reg has already had to increase Mags's allowance as Marshall's consumption is exhausting the housekeeping budget earlier each week. His capacity for alcohol astonishes everyone — even Jack Dixon, a hardened drinker, no longer tries to keep up with him — but by mid-afternoon Marshall is usually drunk.

He is then at his most unpredictable. Sometimes he is merely boisterous, laughing loudly and, emitting whisky fumes, insisting on demonstrating his strength by lifting Dixon and Meyer off the floor by their belts, one in each hand, or stripping to his vest to undertake a hundred press-ups in the middle of the lounge to an admiring audience. At other times he becomes morose and self-pitying, complaining of being kept hidden away like some criminal (*'I get more fresh air when I'm doing time!'*) and increasingly annoyed that the twins haven't visited.

One of the few subjects on which he can be engaged and, occasionally, distracted when in a foul mood, is the World Cup. Marshall is obsessively interested, and actually knowledgeable, about the competition. The house is already littered with "World Cup Willie" merchandise, bought by minders at various times to keep him happy, and after weeks of incarceration, Dixon and the others can now name the whole of England's likely starting eleven, their positions and the merits and demerits of Alf Ramsey's "wingless wonders" formation.

This afternoon Marshall is obsessing over an article in the newspaper. He is again reading about Pickles, the little dog who found the Jules Rimet Trophy, the World Cup. He has followed the story avidly ever since the trophy was stolen from an unguarded display case at Westminster Central Hall. For days he has been proclaiming that the dog should receive a medal, and he can't understand why no one has thought of it. He even threatened to write to the newspapers himself with the suggestion.

'Doncha agree?' he demands, yet again, of Dixon, who sits opposite him at the table in his shirt sleeves, reading a different section of the same newspaper.

'Eh?' says the Scot, looking up.

'About Pickles.'

'Sorry, pal, can you repeat that?'

'Ain't you been listening?'

Dixon looks blank. 'I was just reading about the election. What're you saying?'

'Fucking Harold Wilson? This is more important than that pipe-smoking commie tosser!' says Marshall, stabbing his beefy finger at the article. 'I'm talking about Pickles. Doncha agree they should give 'im a medal?'

'Back on that wee dog? What's he gonna do wi' a medal?'

'His owner could keep it for 'im. Like, in a box, and show it to him. I bet he'd understand. He's a really brainy dog.'

'He'd be better off wi' a nice juicy bone.'

'He's already had bones galore! Look!' says Marshall, pointing excitedly at the newspaper. 'That's 'im at the Talk of the Town nightclub! He even opened a new zoo! He's full of bones 'n' steak 'n' all.'

Dixon's attention has returned to his reading, and he doesn't answer.

Marshall focuses again on his section of the paper, but within seconds he is back to his principal obsession.

'When's Ron coming?' he demands.

Dixon lowers the paper slowly.

Smiling, and speaking deliberately with exaggerated patience, he says, 'Like I told you, Frank, he's not well. He'll be here as soon as he's feeling better.'

'You keep saying the same thing. Ain't he seen a doctor? He can't still be ill!'

'I'm just as much in the dark as you, Frank. That's what Reg says —'

But Marshall doesn't let him finish.

'Fuck this!' he says, pushing back from the table. 'Where's me jacket?'

'What do you need your jacket for?'

'I'm goin' out. I've had enough.'

That draws Tommy from the kitchen. Dixon stands.

'No, Frank. You know what Reg said.'

'I've had it! What am I doing here? I want to see Gracie and the boys,' shouts Frank, 'and I want a pint, in a proper pub!'

He brushes Dixon out of the way and strides into the hallway. Mags is coming down the stairs, a bundle of used bedlinen in his arms.

Marshall whirls round. 'What you done with me coat?' he demands.

'I 'ung it up for you,' says Mags, nodding to the coat hooks on the wall by the front door.

Dixon and Tommy crowd into the hall after their prisoner.

'It's fucking broad daylight!' protests Dixon. 'You'll be seen!'

'It ain't. It's almost dark. But I'll put on me false beard if it makes you 'appier,' replies Marshall.

'That piece of fluff won't fool no one,' says Tommy.

'I don't care. I ain't staying locked up in 'ere a minute longer unless Ron comes to see me.'

Marshall reaches for his coat and pulls it on.

Dixon considers retrieving his revolver but it's in his jacket pocket and that's hanging off the back of his seat in the lounge. By the time he's fetched it, Marshall will be out of the door and on the busy pavement. He wonders briefly if he could overpower Marshall, but doubts that even the three of them could manage it, particularly in such a small space; they'd never get enough hands on him. He realises that persuasion is his only option.

'Look, Frank, give me fifteen minutes, okay?' says Dixon. 'I'll give Reg a call, right now, and see what he says. He told me the arrangements were almost in place. What if he comes round? If you wander off now you're just going to piss him off.

Maybe even miss your chance. You don't want to do that, do you? After all this?'

Marshall pauses. The others watch with baited breath as the furrows on his handsome forehead deepen, revealing the slow deliberations inside it.

'All right. Fifteen minutes,' he concedes finally.

'Shall I get out the Snakes and Ladders?' suggests Mags cheerfully. 'A quick game while we wait?'

Marshall sighs. 'All right, go on then. But I want to be green this time. And you can make us a Scotch 'n' ginger to go with it 'n' all.'

They all troop back into the lounge, Dixon patting Meyer on the shoulder in approval. He dons his jacket and, as he does so, surreptitiously passes the revolver to Tommy, eyebrows raised. Tommy nods.

Dixon slips out of the front door and heads for the nearest phone box. It's almost directly opposite, on the far side of Horn Lane in front of a small parade of shops. Mags has a telephone in his house, but the line fed to both him and Marshall is that for Mag's own safety, he shouldn't hear all the Firm's business. Marshall agrees; he feels protective of the little market trader and is by now accustomed to his minders popping out to the public call box for orders.

Dixon tries the Regal Billiard Hall first, but the twins aren't there and no one knows where they are. He has no greater success when calling their other club, the Kentucky. He leaves messages at both, emphasising that he'll make sure he's in the call box every hour on the hour until contact is made. He hangs up and is about to cross the road again to return to Mags's house when he hears the telephone behind him ringing. He spins round and gets to the door just before an elderly lady with a shopping trolley. He yanks the receiver off its rest.

'Yeah?'

'This is Reggie. Did you want me?'

'Aye, boss. We're having trouble with Frank. He's getting really antsy. Keeps on asking to see Ron.'

Dixon explains recent events in the house. Reggie Kray has no immediate solution.

'Ron's in no fit state. I'm keeping him tucked up at Finchley Road till he improves,' he says. 'But I'll try to get over there tonight. Just keep Frank happy in the meantime.'

'We're doing everything we can,' insists Dixon, 'but he's no' having it. I thought we'd have to use force this time. I do have a suggestion though, boss.'

'Yeah? What's that?'

'Didn't you say that he's got a big appetite? For the ladies?'

'Yes.'

'Well, it's been weeks now. And we know he's bustin'.'

'Why? What's he said?'

'Nothing. But we're all sick and tired of listening to him wank himself to sleep. Can't we provide him with some company?'

Silence follows at the end of the line while Kray considers the suggestion.

'Not a bad idea. I'm sure we can manage that. Tell 'im there'll be a special visitor this evening, but only if he behaves himself and stays put. Got it? Just a "special visitor". If he asks who, say you ain't been told.'

'Righto, boss.'

The Wellington Club in Bond Street is sufficiently upmarket from the dives in Soho presently being cleaned up and closed down by Nipper Read's team as to have escaped their notice. Nonetheless the Club's business, although considerably more expensive, is identical. Its private bar, full of cigar smoke, leather armchairs and quiet conversation, offers a discreet and comfortable place for wealthy middle-aged men to meet much younger women who are prepared, for an appropriate consideration, to offer their professional affections and their bodies by the hour. The women concerned aren't being pimped by the Club; this is no cheap establishment. They are formally and legally "on the books" — most as waitresses or bar staff, but a few as entertainers — in other words, legitimate employees of the Club. All payments to them, like the tips to bar staff, go to the management. They are paid weekly and fulfil their obligations to the Inland Revenue like any other lawful employee.

Although Reginald Kray knows the Wellington Club, it is not one he personally frequents. He is not as obsessed as his twin with being seen in the company of aristocrats, film stars or important men of affairs and, since Frances left him, he would rather spend his free time at the Regal Billiard Hall or at one of the East End clubs or pubs in which he and Ron have an interest.

However, Will Eckersley, a member of the Firm, has worked as a barman in most of the clubs around London and it was he who recommended the Wellington. The Club was on Eckersley's "milk run", the Firm's regular Friday collection of protection money from West End establishments, and he had come to know both Malcolm Owen, the owner, and the nature of the club very well.

Eckersley and his boss are now leaning on the bar in quiet discussion with Owen. In keeping with his premises, Owen is smartly turned out in a dress suit, crisp white shirt and black bowtie. His black hair is slicked back with Brylcreem and he smells of aftershave. His English and his manners are impeccable, and he reminds Reggie Kray slightly of Lord Robert Boothby, the peer with whom Ronnie has shared several dubious schemes and boyfriends.

'As I said to Will, I've got just the girl,' says Owen. 'She's currently fulfilling an engagement with one of our regular guests, but she should be down soon.'

'What's she like?' asks Kray.

'Not what you'd call gorgeous, but sexy and willing,' replies Owen. 'And she's brighter than most. She'll understand the need for discretion.'

'What have you told her?'

'Nothing. Will asked me to leave it to you.'

'Good,' replies Kray. 'That's good.'

It is in fact over an hour, close to 10:30 p.m., before the door from the upstairs rooms opens and an elegant man whom Kray recognises from the TV steps unobtrusively into the bar. He is accompanied by a young woman.

She is a petite blonde and wears her long hair up, revealing creamy shoulders and a demure dark cocktail dress. Even in high heels, she is tiny. She stands on tiptoe to kiss the man once on each cheek just in time for a woman to emerge from behind the bar with the man's hat and overcoat. The man puts them on and, nodding courteously to Owen, departs.

The blonde is already walking towards the door to return upstairs when Owen calls from behind the bar.

'Louise? Do you have a moment?'

She turns and approaches.

'This is Mr Reginald Kray and his associate. Mr Kray would like to offer you some work.'

She turns to Kray and looks up at him, meeting his gaze. Kray sees recognition in her grey eyes but not fear.

'Good evening,' she says smoothly, offering a dainty white hand for Kray to shake. 'Work?' she asks.

'I've got a rich Arab friend who's just arrived in London.'

'Oh, yes?'

'He's feeling a bit lonely, if you follow me. Do you like Arabs?'

'Sometimes. If they're rich.'

There are dancing pin-pricks of light in the girl's amused eyes. Reggie decides he likes her.

'He was thinking of having a little party, and I wondered if you'd like to come along,' he says.

The woman flicks a glance at Owen. She's not keen.

'I've been working all day,' she says. 'What I really need is a bath, some supper, and an early night.'

'I'm sure you could accommodate a special customer like Mr Kray, couldn't you, Louise?' asks Owen blandly.

She looks from Owen to Kray and back again, her eyes no longer laughing. Owen smiles without humour, and Louise realises that she'll receive no assistance from that quarter.

'Where is your Arab friend?' she says.

'We'll take you there now.'

'And you can have tomorrow off,' adds Owen.

'But I have a regular —'

'I'll sort that out.'

'But how long am I going to be?'

'Not long,' assures Kray. 'But why hurry if you don't have to? Maybe get a lie-in, in the morning, yeah?'

The girl from behind the bar arrives at that moment with Louise's coat and bag. Louise sighs and nods reluctantly.

Within moments of Louise settling on the back seat of the car, Kray sitting uncomfortably close to her, she knows that, whoever she is going to meet, it's not going to be a "rich

Arab”. The car heads away from the West End and the high-class hotels where all of her previous “out of hours” appointments have taken place.

She says nothing. She is frightened, but resigned. She is intelligent enough to know that she needs to keep her wits about her, do as she is told, and look for an opportunity to extricate herself. She watches the shops and business premises of Paddington flashing by. The empty pavements and darkened shopfronts, bathed in yellow sodium light, look sick and jaundiced.

Thirty minutes later the car pulls up outside Mags Meyer’s council house in Acton. Kray gets quickly out of the car, walks round to her side and opens the door for her, handing her out onto the pavement. His courtesy takes her by surprise. He lets Eckersley lead them down the path to Meyer’s front door. Dixon evidently saw them pull up, as the door opens to them and they file into the living room. Frank Marshall has been watching television in his shirt sleeves. When Louise is ushered into the room, he stands.

‘Hello, Frank,’ says Kray. ‘I’m sorry I’ve not been before. As you know, Ron’s not well, and my Frances is in hospital too. So things have been a bit busy.’

‘I thought you’d forgotten me, Reg,’ says Marshall reproachfully.

‘Not at all, Frank, not at all. But we’re almost there. I’ll come back and tell you what we’re planning, but until then I thought you might like a bit of company. This here is…’

Kray turns to Louise, having already forgotten her name.

‘I’m Louise,’ she supplies for him.

‘Yeah, Louise. She’s been looking forward to meeting you. You’ve got plenty of booze in, have you, Jack?’

Dixon answers. 'Yeah, boss. Certainly enough for the night.'

'Well,' replies Kray, taking out his wallet, 'here's another ten, just in case. Have a party.'

He turns to leave.

'May I have a word, Mr Kray?' asks Louise. 'Outside?'

Without waiting for a reply, she walks past him into the hallway. Kray follows.

'What about me?' she asks.

'What about you?'

'Well, I haven't been paid,' she points out.

'But you're employed by the Wellington, ain't you? Doesn't Owen cover your wages?'

'Of course, for normal working hours. But this is extra, isn't it? He's not paying me for this.'

'Don't you worry about that. I'll sort it out.'

The little woman stands her ground. 'No, I'm sorry, Mr Kray, but this isn't the way it's done. I'm a professional, and I'm sure your friend will be happy with my services, but I'm not doing anything until I'm paid.'

'Now, you look here —'

'No, Mr Kray, I'm very sorry, but I have to be paid first. That's only right, only respectful.'

Reggie Kray stares down at the defiant woman in front of him. 'Well, how much?'

'I'm going to be here overnight, right?'

'Yes, probably.'

'And maybe after then?' Kray shrugs, noncommittal. 'I see. I think one hundred's fair, for the present, don't you? We'll have to see after that.'

Kray frowns, his mouth working, but she can see there is amusement in his expression too.

'I ain't got that much on me,' he concludes.

'I'll wait here till you get it, then. And see if you can pick me up a few basics from a chemist's. Like make-up remover and a flannel. I've got a toothbrush and a hairbrush in my bag.'

Kray pauses for a moment longer and then shouts.

'William? I need a lift to Vallance Road.'

He turns back to Louise.

'I'll be back in half an hour.'

CHAPTER TWENTY-FOUR

It's now shortly before seven o'clock and Chambers is still half-full. Peter Bateman lost the toss and has already returned from the "chocolate run" to the shop on the corner of Mitre Court. The biscuits and chocolate bars requested by the tired and stressed barristers — fuel for the next several hours — have been distributed around the corridor. In his absence, Charles and one of the pupils made two pots of coffee and the rooms have now settled in for the evening shift. All that can be heard is the flick of turned legal pages, the scratch of pens and, from the end room, the periodic coughing of someone with a heavy cold.

It is often like this in the run-up to Easter; barristers trying to clear their desks of enough of the most urgent work to allow them a week or two with their families over the school holidays. If the weather remains propitious, the successful and fit juniors will typically be heading east to the high altitude Alpine resorts to enjoy the new holiday craze for the well-heeled — skiing — while the silks, even better heeled but more portly (less athletic) are more likely to be found flying west, long haul, towards a Caribbean beach.

Charles and Sally have no plans to go away. They are having too much fun making the house on Wren Street into a home and, in any case, Sally has been invited to her first Passover Seder at David and Sonia's home.

Sally recognises what an honour this is. She hopes it signifies the start of acceptance of her relationship with the Horowitz first-born. Charles is less optimistic. He notes that the invitation came from his brother, not his parents. Millie

Horowitz will never be reconciled to him living in sin with a *shiksa.*

Nonetheless, he and Sally agree: this is one invitation that cannot be declined.

Peter startles Charles by slamming shut a heavy legal tome.

'Fuck it,' he announces in his posh accent.

'Had enough?' asks Charles.

'I can't concentrate anymore. I've worked until midnight every night this week, and my brain's full.' He stands, extinguishing his desk lamp. 'I'll come in tomorrow morning, fresh.'

He walks to Charles's desk, picks up Charles's packet of cigarettes and lights one without being invited.

'Help yourself,' says Charles.

Peter blows smoke at his friend in answer.

'Look,' he says, 'you don't fancy packing it in, do you, and coming to a party?'

'A party?' asks Charles, looking up with a frown.

'Amanda's been invited by a couple of her musician friends to a party off the King's Road. Very trendy bunch apparently.'

Charles shakes his head. 'No, I don't think so, thanks. I'm meeting Sally in fifteen minutes.'

'Bring her along. I think you'll have fun. These people are … interesting. And there's some poet going, I believe. He's doing a recital, or whatever they call it. One of your lot.'

From anyone else this reference to Charles's Jewishness might have been offensive, but he knows Peter means no harm by it. The two men, so different in their background and upbringings, and so similar in their irreverent attitude to life, are genuine friends and trust each other.

'And which particular *kike* are we talking about here?' asks Charles with a wry lift of an eyebrow.

'According to the papers he's a beatnik, one of those new American poets … hang on, I'll remember in a sec … Bloomberg?'

'A beat poet? Do you mean Allen Ginsberg?'

Peter jabs the cigarette in Charles's direction.

'That's the chap! Well done.'

'Are you serious? Allen Ginsberg's going to this party?'

'So says Amanda.'

Charles puts his pen down and leans back.

'Now that *is* interesting. I read that he was coming over here this summer. He's doing some international poetry thing at the Royal Albert Hall, but he's also offered to read anywhere for free.'

'Yes, well, he's a friend of one of the chaps sharing the house. Also an American, and a bit of a rum bloke, if you ask me; strange religious beliefs. But Amanda went there a couple of months back, and wouldn't stop talking about it.'

'Is it all right just to bring strangers along?'

'Oh,' says Peter airily, waving his hand, 'no one'll notice. Amanda said the place was heaving. All sorts of people popping in and out.'

Charles considers further. 'All right. I'll give Sal a call.'

'Excellent. I'm going to the loo.'

Peter leaves the room and Charles picks up the telephone. He dials his old chambers at Chancery Court and it is Sally who picks up.

'Sal, it's me.'

'I was just putting on my coat.'

'How do you fancy going to a party?'

'When?'

'Tonight. Peter and Amanda have an invitation to some do off the King's Road, and say we can come too.'

He repeats what Peter told him.

'I can't go to some weird trendy party in work clothes,' she protests. 'I'll look right out of place.'

'I doubt anyone'll notice. The place is likely to be packed to the rafters.'

'No, Charles, I'm really not keen. Not tonight.'

Charles falls silent and Sally hears his disappointment.

'Is this important to you?' she asks, with some surprise.

'It wouldn't be, normally, but if Allen Ginsberg's going to perform it's a fantastic opportunity! He's a genuine star, and I've always wanted to hear him read.'

'Then you go. I don't mind.'

Charles pauses again, noting how far he and Sally have come if she is prepared to trust him to go to a party, particularly this sort of party, without her. It's in fact the rush of affection he suddenly feels for her which causes him to reject her offer.

'No, forget it. I don't want to go without you.'

At that moment Bateman returns to the room. He raises his eyebrows at Charles in enquiry.

Charles shakes his head. He half-covers the mouthpiece to say, 'She's got nothing to wear.'

'Could she borrow something of Amanda's?' suggests Bateman. 'Women seem to do that all the time. Amanda's coming from her place, so she could bring a top or something, rather than going straight to the King's Road.'

Charles uncovers the mouthpiece.

'Did you hear that?'

'Yes. But Amanda's tall and slim, which I definitely ain't.'

'Why don't you call her and ask if she has something suitable? If not, we'll go home.'

'Really?' She pauses. 'I'm not sure, Charles. I don't know her that well and she's much more glamorous than me.' There is another pause on the line. 'Oh … all right! I can hear your disappointment. I'll try her. But no promises, okay? I'll call you back in five minutes.'

Forty-five minutes later Sally is led out of the lavatory by Amanda. She wears a tight-fitting red sweater over her work skirt, long leather boots and an enormous necklace made of multi-coloured hoops. On her head is a fluffy white beret with red trim that matches the top, and she wears a shade of red lipstick that Charles hasn't seen before.

'Wow!' says Charles in approval, and Peter wolf-whistles.

'Do I look all right?' asks Sally a little coyly, but smiling because she knows she looks much more than "all right".

'She looks fantastic, doesn't she?' says Amanda. She turns to Sally. 'You fill out that sweater in ways I could never hope for.'

'Where did you get the boots?' asks Charles. 'Surely you're not the same size in footwear?'

'No,' replies Sally. 'They're mine.' She sees his puzzled frown. 'I keep them in Chambers. Most women working in the City have a couple of spare pairs of shoes under their desks.'

'Sorry to nag, folks, but are we ready to go?' asks Bateman. 'Time's getting on. I think we should take a taxi.'

It takes little more than ten minutes to get from Fleet Street to the start of the King's Road at Sloane Square, but twenty minutes later the cab has travelled no further forward than two hundred yards.

It's a pleasant spring evening. King's Road is heaving and in party mode. The street has nose-to-tail traffic, most of it apparently in no haste to go anywhere. In front of their taxi is a sportscar with its hood down, and the sheepskin-wearing driver and passenger are laughing with two mini-skirted young women, who then saunter from their pavement table at Café Picasso to lean on the car while continuing their conversation. The crowds outside Mary Quant's boutique, Bazaar, mill from shop doorway into the road without the slightest regard for the traffic. One woman in a short pink dress, floppy hat and huge sunglasses runs directly towards the cab and opens the door before apologising and giggling when she realises it's already occupied. As she turns back to the pavement she is almost run down by a pair of shiny Lambretta scooter riders buzzing past the stationary taxi on the inside.

The crowds outside the blacked-out windows of Biba are even heavier. One couple is actually dancing across the front of a bus in response to Mick Jagger's prediction of some girl's nineteenth nervous breakdown, which blares across the road from a nearby shop.

Eventually Bateman loses patience, thrusts a pound note through the window at the cabbie, opens the door and drags Amanda out by the hand.

'C'mon,' he says. 'It'll be quicker to walk.'

Charles and Sally climb out after him and join the crowds.

The evening smells of tobacco, food and excitement. Charles feels his spirits lifting. He can't remember the last time he and Sally went to a proper party.

Could this be the first time?

In fact they never do anything this spontaneous. He makes a mental note to repeat it, and then smiles at himself for planning to plan a spontaneous event.

They follow Bateman through the traffic — it's easier to make progress between the cars and buses than on the pavements — and his long legs lead them past The Fantasie Café and round a corner into Shawfield Street.

There is no mistaking the party house when they reach it. The three-storey townhouse *bulges* with young people. There are guests on the pavement, on the steps, in the small front garden and hanging out of upper windows. And the house *rocks*. There's a band playing somewhere inside.

Charles looks up. Through an open sash window on the top floor he sees a musician playing rock music with what appears to be a violin. The fiddler thrashes manically in time to the music, his long black hair flying about his face.

Charles takes Sally's hand so as not to lose her in the press, and they push their way between the people drinking and smoking on the steps and walk through the open front door. As they enter, Charles feels Sally tug at his arm. He pauses and turns on the threshold. Sally inclines her head to his.

'Was that smell…?'

'Grass? Yes.'

'Smoking reefers, right there in the street?' ask Sally, astonished.

He shrugs and laughs. 'It'll be worse inside!'

'But won't I get … you know … stoned?' she asks, embarrassed.

Charles's heart melts at her naïveté. 'No, sweetheart, you won't. But if you're worried —' he shrugs again — 'don't inhale. Come on.'

The main hall of the house is just as busy. A small woman in a baggy jumper and leather jacket approaches them. She is startlingly beautiful, only nineteen or twenty. Her waiflike large eyes and dark hair tied in a scarf make her look like a Russian peasant. She looks Charles up and down.

'You the guy from Verve Records?' she asks.

Her harsh New York accent seems to Charles to be an affront to her beauty.

'No,' replies Charles.

'Oh, sorry.' She points. 'The suit 'n' all. You look like a stiff.'

'Yeah, sorry, came straight from work.'

'Okay. Well, the film's playing on a loop just down there —' she points behind her to a room towards the back of the property — 'there's food and drink in the kitchen, and the guys are playing on the top floor. Have a good time.'

She moves off immediately towards the stairs leading up to the first floor.

'Excuse me,' Charles calls after her, but she doesn't hear him. 'Hey! Brooklyn!' he shouts, projecting his voice as if in court.

This time she and everyone else in the hallway hears him. The noise levels reduce for a moment and everyone looks curiously at Charles. The woman leans over the banister, smiling.

'It's Barbara,' she says, 'Barbara Rubin. And, for your information, it ain't Brooklyn, it's Queens. So, what d'ya want, Stiff?'

'Is Allen doing "Howl" tonight?'

'Sure is. First floor.'

She pushes through those sitting on the stairs and disappears.

Amanda has already met someone she knows and she and the other woman are shouting in one another's ears and gesticulating over the din.

'Look,' shouts Charles to Peter, 'we'll never manage to stay together as a group of four; it's too rammed. Shall we split up? Meet again upstairs when your beat poet starts?'

'How will we know?' asks Sally.

'I guess the music'll stop,' shouts Charles. 'No one'll hear him otherwise!'

The two couples part and Charles and Sally head towards the back of the house to get drinks. They pass a blacked-out room from which repetitive music emanates, and they pause to look in the door.

A film is being projected onto one of the walls. The light from the projector picks out shafts of smoke rising from the floor. The smell of cannabis is overpowering. Only then does Charles realise that the room is packed with an audience of people sitting on the carpet. He turns his attention to the film.

It was shot in black and white but appears to be playing through a rotating sequence of coloured slides. At first it seems merely a jumble of dark, confusing images but, as they watch, Charles and Sally realise that the projection wall is covered in a writhing tangle of actors. But for the masks they wear and some body paint, they are all naked. The deliberate uncertainty caused by the quick cutting between couples and groups makes it difficult to grasp exactly what is occurring on screen, but it is obvious that the actors are having sex, in both heterosexual and homosexual combinations.

Sally inhales in shock and grips Charles's hand. 'Are you seeing what I'm seeing?'

'Yes.'

'It's unbelievable. Have you ever watched anything like this before?' she whispers in Charles's ear.

'At a couple of stag parties, maybe, but nothing so … arty.'

'Yes … it's … art pornography! It's … shocking!'

They watch in silence for a few moments, hands still clasped together.

'It *is* shocking,' says Charles, bending to speak into Sally's ear, 'but it's more than that, don't you think?'

Her hand tightens in his in a quick pulse. 'Yes. It's beautiful … and sexy.'

A woman wearing a flowing blue kaftan gets up from the floor and heads towards the door. Charles steps back to let her pass. She seems older than many at the party, almost Charles's age. She's tall with a thin nose and lips, and Charles notes that her pupils are so widely dilated that her irises are almost invisible.

'What is this film?' asks Charles as she squeezes past him.

She pauses and a small monkey appears suddenly above her shoulder, hanging from her neck and upper arm. Charles and Sally both jump.

'It's Barbara's film, *Cocks and Cunts*,' says the woman, in an extremely posh Home Counties accent.

'No, Detta,' says another woman from the floor. 'She renamed it. She's been calling it *Christmas on Earth* for a while now.'

'There you are, then,' says Detta to Charles. 'Haven't you seen it?'

Charles and Sally shake their heads. Sally can't take her eyes off the monkey.

'You should. It's wild!' she says, and she heads towards the stairs to the first floor, the monkey chittering at Charles behind her back.

Charles and Sally look at one another.

'I think I need a drink,' says Sally.

Two hours later, Ginsberg's reading finishes to wild applause. He and Barbara Rubin make short speeches of thanks — Charles realises for the first time that the little New York Jewess he spoke to on entering the house is responsible for the beat poet's trip to London — and within a couple of minutes the music on the top floor starts again.

Peter and Amanda lead the way up the stairs and force their way into the sweaty room. Bateman's jaw drops, and he turns to the others.

'I don't believe it! Do you know who that is?' he shouts, pointing at the rock group.

The others shake their heads.

'It's the Velvet Underground! The guy on the viola is John Cale!'

He points across the room, past the dancers, to the man Charles saw a couple of hours earlier through the window.

Charles's attention is drawn to a young woman wearing a trouser suit and a pink hairband dancing in front of him. A tall skeletal man with long hair and a goatee beard, stripped to the waist and wearing nothing on his feet, comes up to her, inclines his head, and starts speaking. In his hand is what looks like a sheet of torn paper. The music is so loud that Charles can't hear what's being said despite the couple's proximity, but the man is excitedly showing the girl the paper. His eyes shine and his chest is sheened in sweat. He is so emaciated that Charles could count his ribs. He sways, but in time to music that no one else in the room can hear. He offers the paper to the girl, she nods, and he tears off a tiny pea-sized corner of it which he places on her tongue.

The man stumbles towards the door and collides with Charles. Both apologise.

'You want a tab, man?' asks the guy, thrusting the paper at Charles.

Charles takes it. The man raises both hands on either side of Charles's head and starts tracing Charles's outline.

'Wow...!' he says in awe. 'You got some aura, man!'

Charles examines the paper in his hand.

'It's good stuff!' shouts his new friend. 'Victor made it!'

'Victor?'

'Victor Kapur.'

Charles feels the paper; it has the texture of blotting paper and has faint horizontal and vertical lines on it which divide the sheet into tabs, tiny squares, like graph paper.

Then, unexpectedly, machinery in his head clicks, gears whirr and a piece of jigsaw drops neatly into place.

This is blotter acid, impregnated with LSD.

Every tab provides up to twelve hours of kaleidoscopic, hallucinogenic, illegal rapture.

CHAPTER TWENTY-FIVE

Charles settles at his desk with a pot of coffee, and some anticipation, to read the new Instructions from Tindall and Company, found in his pigeonhole fifteen minutes earlier. Before he can open the ribbon, the telephone rings on his desk.

'Mr Holborne? I've your brother for you.'

'Thank you, Barbara. Put him through. Sorry about this, Peter,' says Charles to Bateman, sitting opposite him.

Bateman, deeply engrossed in some research, waves his hand airily without looking up.

'Charles?' says David, a single syllable of tension and anxiety.

Charles suddenly feels as if an icy hand has encircled his heart and squeezed.

'What is it?' he asks.

'It's Dad. He's collapsed at home. The ambulance men are with him now. It looks like a stroke. We're on our way to New End Hospital in Hampstead.'

'Is he conscious?' asks Charles.

'No.'

'I'm coming. Half an hour.'

Charles enters the ward with a tray laden with paper cups of tea. It is four hours since Harry arrived in the hospital and he is still in a booth in Casualty.

'Well?' says Charles. 'Any sign of a doctor?'

'You just missed him,' says David, 'but he's coming back.'

There are three people around Harry's bed, his mother, clinging to Harry's hand and weeping and, on the other side, David and Sonia. Harry Horowitz is still unconscious. He looks peaceful, his face in repose, despite the tubes emerging from his arm and the oxygen mask covering his lower face. The department is busy and noisy. The area around Harry's bed is an island of petrified calm in the midst of an angry crowd.

David stands. 'It's definitely a stroke,' he tells Charles quietly. 'They're giving him some drugs.'

'I want to talk to the doctor,' says Charles, looking around.

Uniformed nurses scurry back and forth but there is no sign of anyone resembling a doctor.

There is something about David's expression, particularly his eyes, which prompts Charles to beckon, and David follows Charles to the door.

'What did he say?' asks Charles quietly when they reach the corridor.

David shakes his head. 'It's not good. They've no way of knowing how severe the damage is, but it's likely to be bad. Dad may have been on the floor of the bedroom for over an hour. His brain was starved of oxygen…'

A sob escapes David's chest, and his eyes fill with tears. The brothers hug briefly, then David stands back and fishes a handkerchief from his pocket. He blows his nose noisily. Footsteps approach from behind them. Both turn, and David addresses the man in the white coat about to pass them.

'Oh, doctor, this is my brother, Charles.'

The doctor comes to a reluctant halt. 'What's the situation?' asks Charles.

'As I explained to your brother,' replies the other, a squat man in his mid-fifties with very dark eyes, 'your father seems to have suffered a severe ischaemic stroke. He may or may not recover consciousness.'

He speaks quickly, his eyes flicking to the ward door. He is obviously in a hurry. Charles wonders if he is irritated by having to deliver the same news twice.

'What are his chances?' persists Charles.

The doctor takes a deep breath and, apparently resigning himself to the conversation, speaks more calmly.

'Well, he seems to be holding his own for the moment. His heartbeat is strong and regular, his blood pressure's a little high but nothing of major concern, and we don't think he's suffering from atrial fibrillation, which can be the cause of a stroke. We've put him on aspirin to thin his blood and break up any clots. There's a history of angina, I believe?'

'He had some procedure to clear one of his arteries a few years back,' says David.

'I didn't realise that. I don't think it's on our records,' says the doctor. 'But he's going for a chest X-ray so we'll know more shortly. But, I must warn you that even if he does survive…'

'What?' demands Charles.

'I'm sorry to say he's very likely to have some permanent neurological damage.'

'What does that mean?'

'Some brain damage. After a stroke of this severity it's almost unavoidable. Although, some patients do make a partial recovery. *Partial*,' he emphasises. 'I'm very sorry to give such bad news in a sprint, but I must go. And so should you. Visiting times are on the board,' he says, pointing quickly and vaguely towards the end of the corridor.

The doctor turns and enters the ward. Charles and David follow.

Charles goes and stands behind his mother and puts a hand on her shoulder. She reaches up without turning round and pats his hand. She doesn't speak.

A few minutes later two men arrive to wheel Harry's bed to the X-ray department and the family are told to return later that evening. If there is any urgent news, someone will telephone.

Outside, Charles and David resume their private conversation.

'Okay,' says Charles. 'What about Mum? She can't manage on her own at home.'

David shakes his head. 'I can't believe how matter of fact you're being when Dad's life's in the balance!'

'You know me. Practicalities first; emotion comes later.'

'This is something I've never understood about you.'

'Please, David, let's focus on what needs to be done. We can explore my deficiencies as a human being later. Mum can't go back home, on her own, can she?'

David shakes his head, whether at Charles's heartlessness or in answer to the question, Charles is unsure.

'No. She'll have to stay with one of us,' says David eventually with a heavy sigh.

'So it's your place or mine. I'm happy to have her but, remember, we've a lot of stairs. And we're not kosher.'

David considers and shakes his head again. 'No, she'd struggle to get to your top floor. And, in any case, Wren Street's too far.'

'Too far?'

'From Mrs Weinstein — she doesn't drive, you know, and we're going to need her to increase her hours, not stop altogether — from the *shul*, and from us. And there's the *kashrut* issue. She may be a bit forgetful, but she's knows a bacon sandwich when she sees one.'

'"*A bit forgetful*"?' exclaims Charles. 'She's got dementia, Davie, and it's galloping away with her!'

Charles watches David's expression. He looks as if he's just been punched. Charles moderates his tone.

'Oh, boychick, I know you find this difficult, but we've got to face reality. She can't live independently, which means she can't go back home. I agree, now's not the time for long-term decisions, but for the moment, can she stay with you?'

'Of course. I'll speak to Sonia. I'm sure she'll be fine with it.'

Charles manages to return to his desk in Chambers after eight o'clock that evening. Peter Bateman is still at his desk, shirt-sleeves rolled up, piles of law books around him.

'How's your Dad?' he asks as Charles enters.

'Still here? I thought I'd have the place to myself. Sorry about this,' he says, showing Bateman the bag containing hamburger, chips and coffee bought from the Wimpy Bar at Charing Cross.

'Doesn't bother me. How is he?'

'Still unconscious. They've moved him to a ward but we can't find out what the X-ray and tests have shown.'

'I'm surprised you're not still there.'

'Bastards threw us out. "*Visiting times are strictly enforced regardless of the condition of the patients.*" David and Sonia had to drag Mum away. But she's not eaten since breakfast and we've got to pack her suitcase. Don't let me disturb you.'

Charles settles himself in to burn the midnight oil, his dinner forming a cold greasy lump on his desk.

IN THE MATTER OF AN APPEAL TO THE COURT OF CRIMINAL APPEAL

THE REVEREND STANLEY SHARPE

Proposed Appellant

- and -

THE CROWN

Proposed Respondent

INSTRUCTIONS TO COUNSEL

Enclosures:

1. *Proof of Evidence of Gracie Marshall*
2. *Proof of Evidence of Judy Bishop*
3. *Bundle of Crown evidence led at first instance*
4. *Original statement of the Rev Stanley Sharpe*

Counsel will be familiar with this case, having advised Rev Sharpe in conference at HM Prison, Durham, and having offered some informal advice on evidence since then.

Instructing Solicitors are delighted to report that (1) Gracie Marshall, the wife of Frank Marshall, and (2) Marshall's former lover, Judy Bishop, have now agreed to give evidence of having seen Marshall, alive, in the recent past. Counsel is directed to their statements.

As Counsel will know, it is only in exceptional circumstances and subject to exceptional conditions that the Court of Criminal Appeal will admit new evidence. Before granting an application for permission to call such evidence, it must firstly be shown that the proposed witness was not available to give evidence at the trial. Clearly, although both of these witnesses could have been called to give evidence at trial, they had no relevant evidence to give at that stage. Counsel is asked to confirm his opinion, but Instructing Solicitors believe that evidence of sightings of the supposed victim of the murder following Rev Sharpe's conviction should be sufficient to overcome this hurdle.

The second requirement is that the additional evidence must be such that, in the opinion of the appeal court, it probably would have affected the verdict which the jury returned. It is difficult to see how evidence that the supposed victim was actually alive at the time could not have affected the verdict, which is based on the presumption that Frank Marshall was dead.

At Counsel's request, Instructing Solicitors made contact with the retired car salesman, Mr Frederick Wheeler (known in the trade, we understand, as "Wheeler Deala"). He has confirmed seeing and speaking to Frank Marshall in the recent past, but unfortunately he was not prepared to give a statement. Instructing Solicitors will continue to press Mr Wheeler to change his mind.

For the sake of completeness, those instructing have included a bundle of the original depositions which set out the Crown's case at trial. It is not thought that they will detain the Court of Criminal Appeal long, as they are all fatally undercut by the new witness evidence. Finally, we have included the original statement of Rev Sharpe upon which he gave evidence at the trial, and in which he asserts his innocence and denies that he gave the interview attributed to him by DCI Wheatley. Rev Sharpe has nothing new to add.

Counsel is asked to advise if, in his opinion, the evidence now produced is sufficient to draft an application for leave to appeal out of time together with grounds of appeal. If so, he is requested to draft the relevant documents and represent the proposed Appellant at the application. It is intended to bring a bail application at the same time. Including the period spent on remand, Rev Sharpe has now served over a year of his sentence. Reverend Sharpe remains clinically depressed and on suicide watch.

Lastly, Instructing Solicitors have been put in funds to instruct an enquiry agent, and one has been instructed. If he locates any other willing witnesses to the continued survival of Mr Marshall, Counsel will be the first to know.

If Counsel requires any further information, he should not hesitate to contact his Instructing Solicitors.

Tindall & Co.

PROOF OF EVIDENCE OF GRACIE MARSHALL

I live at 165A Farmers Road, Leyton, London E10. I am a full-time mother presently seeking employment. My husband is Frank Marshall. In late 1965 I was a witness for the Crown in a prosecution against Rev Stanley Sharpe who was accused of murdering my husband. As set out in my deposition, I returned home from collecting our sons from school to find my husband missing from the home and what appeared to be evidence of a fight. I have read my deposition again and would wish to change nothing in it. As far as I knew at the time, and continued to believe until recently, my husband had disappeared in circumstances unknown to me. I was told by DCI Wheatley that Frank had been murdered by Reverend Sharpe and that Reverend Sharpe had confessed to the crime, and I believed him.

In February or March this year I began to receive reports from local people that they had seen someone whom they believed to be my husband, albeit in disguise. My husband is an unusually large and broad man, and very well known in the East End of London. Nonetheless, I treated those reports with scepticism.

On the evening of 16 March 1966, I was at home with my sons in temporary accommodation in Stratford when there was a knock on the door. I opened the door and was astonished to see Frank. I was very angry with him at first for having let me and the boys believe he was dead, but he told me he had no choice but to pretend to be dead because his life had been in danger. That explanation was not completely incredible, bearing in mind his work and some of his associates, who are career criminals. The boys were so pleased to see him and had missed him so much I put my reservations to one side. I too had missed him, and wanted us to resume our married life together.

Frank promised me that we would have a new start together as a family, and he gave me some cash to use as a deposit on the flat where I now live. He said he had to go away for a few more days but would then join me and the boys. However, weeks have gone by since then, and all my attempts to contact him have met with failure. I do not believe that he is coming back. I have seen the draft deposition of Judy Bishop, the woman with whom my husband went away at the end of last year when he was supposedly dead, and I no longer believe his account of being in fear of his life. I have decided to divorce him on the grounds of his adultery.

I am absolutely sure that the man who came to my flat was my husband, and I realise that he was not murdered at all.

I am making this statement, which is true, of my own free will, and I am prepared to give evidence if requested.

'So that's what he told her!' says Charles out loud.

Bateman looks up from his desk. 'What's that?'

'Frank Marshall. I wondered what cock and bull story he gave to Gracie when he turned up on her doorstep, months after being murdered.'

'What did he say?'

Charles laughs. 'He was frightened of being murdered.'

PROOF OF EVIDENCE OF JUDY BISHOP

I am an exotic dancer and I used to work at the Windmill Club, Windmill Street, London. It was while I was working there that I met a man who called himself Freddie Markham in late 1962. He invited me out for some drinks and we started an affair. I knew that he was married and had two young children, but he told me he was separated from his wife and he only ever returned to the family home to see his boys.

In October 1965 Freddie told me that there was a plot to kill him and that he had to disappear. I knew from certain things he had said during our relationship that he had worked for some unsavoury criminals, and so his announcement did not seem particularly strange to me. He told me he had to get out of London and begged me to go away with him to pretend I was his wife. He said that if we posed as a couple he would be less at risk. I was between jobs at that time, and I really believed that this pretence would help to save Freddie's life, so I agreed.

'Clever,' mutters Charles admiringly.

This is the beginning of a defence, that of self-defence of another. If Judy were to be believed that she thought she was helping to protect Marshall when under a reasonable, even erroneous, belief that he was about to be murdered, she might escape conviction for assisting him to pervert the course of justice.

I wonder if she came up with that on her own? wonders Charles. *And how will she explain away the fact that Sharpe was on trial for her boyfriend's murder?*

He returns to the statement.

He took me to a bed and breakfast in Weston-super-Mare where we stayed for a short time, and we then moved to a series of flats. Freddie told me that we had to move frequently for his protection, and I believed him. In retrospect, I think the real reason was that he kept running out of money, which forced us to move into increasingly cheap accommodation.

I have been asked if I read about the murder trial of Rev Stanley Sharpe, and if I knew that a man called Frank Marshall was supposedly the victim of that murder. I did not know anything about that trial. I don't usually read the newspapers, and none of the accommodation where we lived had a television. On the odd occasion that I do read a newspaper, I avoid the reports of crimes and criminals, because they upset me. I therefore did not know anything about that trial or what happened to the Rev Sharpe. Even if I had known, the name of the man I was with was

Freddie Markham and not Frank Marshall, so even then I wouldn't have made the connection.

From around March 1966 our relationship deteriorated, and Freddie began spending time away from me. I suspected he was returning to London to see his family. Eventually he left without a word for the last time and, after waiting for a further few days, I returned to my home in London. It was only then that I got to learn that someone called Frank Marshall had supposedly been murdered and the Rev Sharpe sent to prison for it. I saw a photograph in a newspaper and realised that my Freddie Markham was in fact Frank Marshall. I decided to report what I knew to the police, but before I could do so I was approached by Tindall's solicitors, to whom I gave this statement. I have subsequently made a full report to the local police station at Hornsey.

I am making this statement, which is true, of my own free will, and I am prepared to give evidence if requested.

Charles leans back in his creaking leather seat and stares at the ceiling.

'Enough?' asks Bateman, without looking up from his own work.

'Definitely enough to draft grounds. And, I think, enough to set aside the conviction as unsafe and unsatisfactory.'

'Bear me in mind if you need a junior, won't you?' Peter says with a grin. 'I've not been to the Court of Criminal Appeal yet.'

'Happy to, if you'll do it for free. But we'll never get legal aid for two counsel.'

Charles bends to his task and starts drafting.

CHAPTER TWENTY-SIX

A week has elapsed. The news from the hospital is good or, at least, better. The good news is that Harry is conscious and, although his speech is slurred, it seems as if he is intellectually undamaged. The bad news is that he is likely to be left physically handicapped. His right arm is weak and jerky; his right leg almost useless. His trunk is affected, so he cannot sit upright in a chair without support. "Hemiplegic" the doctors say. He might still recover further with speech therapy and physiotherapy but it seems obvious to Charles that his father will never be able to care for Millie in their own home.

Charles and Sally walk hand in hand round the corner from Wren Street and into Gray's Inn Road. It is a cool and blustery spring morning, but the sun is out and the trees lining the streets are in full leaf. They are leaving home a few minutes earlier than normal to cast their votes in the General Election while the voting station is quiet.

Traffic is building to its peak, but is not sufficiently loud to prevent them talking.

'Is today Maria's moving day?' asks Charles.

'No. She left a note on the fridge saying it's been put off for a week as the other chap's tour has been extended. Have you spoken to her?'

'No. She's been playing late at the new venue. I heard her come in at about two the night before last.'

'I assume her father must've come through on the rent, or she'd not be going,' says Sally.

'I guess so. Don't let her go without saying goodbye, will you?'

‘I’m sure she wouldn’t do that.’

They walk the couple of hundred yards to the Victorian redbrick building, usually a technical college but today being used as a polling station, and climb the steps. There is no one in the room except two election officials sitting silently at a table.

Charles and Sally hand over their ballot cards and have their address checked, which causes the female official to look up to examine this unmarried couple apparently living together in sinful circumstances. Their names are ticked off a list and they take adjoining booths. The booths remind Charles of fold-out deckchairs. They are three-sided, hinged, wooden structures that hide voters from the thighs up, but they are so flimsy, and their legs so spindly, that a gentle nudge from one end would collapse the lot like a line of dominoes. Charles has been tempted.

He taps on the wooden partition separating his booth from Sally’s.

‘Knock once for Tory and twice for Labour,’ he whispers.

‘Sir!’ chides an elderly moustachioed man in a bowler hat waiting behind Charles.

‘Only joking,’ protests Charles, but the other harrumphs.

He and Sally take their completed ballots and slip them in the slotted metal box on the officials’ table.

‘That was easy,’ says Sally as they step back into the traffic noise and sunshine.

‘Did you vote for the pipe-smoker?’ asks Charles

Sally grins. ‘Mind your own business.’

She stops on the pavement and turns to Charles. ‘I’ll see you tonight. Good luck.’

‘With Sharpe?’

'No, actually. I was thinking of your visit to the care home.'

'Oh, that.'

He bends to kiss her. 'Thanks.'

They part. Instead of heading south down Gray's Inn Road with Sally, Charles turns towards Guilford Street and Russell Square. He has a task to complete before going to court.

Five minutes later he feels the first drops of rain and, within a minute, it is pouring. He sees a cab speeding by and hails it.

'Savile Row police station, please,' he says as he closes the door behind him.

The front desk at Savile Row, West End Central, is heaving. Four harassed uniformed officers are trying to corral several rowdy people into sitting down quietly, and they're having none of it. Five women, who Charles thinks must be prostitutes from their clothing, appear to be fighting among themselves, while two men are shouting at them and each other while trying to keep the women apart. The desk officer sees Charles over the heads of the melee and shouts towards him.

'Sir?'

'DCI Read or DS Sloane?'

'Mr Read's in — not sure about Sloane,' he shouts. 'I'll call upstairs. May I suggest you wait outside?'

He points to the group in front of him, in which fists are now flying. Charles waves and nods. He turns and opens the door again and stands outside on the steps, just under cover from the downpour.

People come and go through the doorway, police officers and members of the public, and each time Charles steps out into the rain and then, as promptly as he can, back onto the step. After ten minutes or so the shower passes, and he moves onto the pavement out of everyone's way.

A few minutes later he feels his shoulder being tapped, and he turns. To his surprise he is greeted not by Sean Sloane but by his friend's boss, Detective Chief Inspector Nipper Read.

'Mr Holborne,' says Read. 'You wanted to talk to me?'

'Yes, chief inspector. Although it's not about the Krays, I'm afraid.'

Read's face is impassive, but Charles thinks he detects some disappointment in the square face.

'What, then?'

Charles digs into his briefcase.

'This is the manual for the second-hand Rover I bought from Sharpe's Luxury Motors a couple of months ago. You know? Robin Sharpe, the son of Reverend Stanley Sharpe?'

'Yes?'

'Out of the blue, the garage asked to replace it, saying it was the wrong one. When I looked at the replacement, I realised they'd sent me back the original, *but* with an unused page razored out.' Charles opens the manual from the back. 'The page was in here, and if you look carefully along the stitching you can see where it was.'

'Look, Mr Holborne, if you've got some complaint about the garage which you think might be evidence of a crime, by all means make a report, but I really am too busy —'

'The excised page had an odd texture, like blotting paper,' persists Charles. 'I think it was impregnated with LSD, and if you analyse what's left inside the manual, my guess is you will find LSD residue.'

Now Charles has the policeman's attention. Read starts digging into his jacket pockets.

'I wouldn't worry about gloves, if I were you,' says Charles. 'It's bound to have prints from personnel at the garage, including Sharpe's.'

Read looks up at Charles and gingerly takes the manual from him, touching only the edges of the book. He peers closely at the stitching inside the back cover.

'If you want my guess, and it is only a guess, I think Sharpe's supplying LSD under cover of the garage,' continues Charles. 'It's a brilliant piece of laundering, if you think about it. He sells a shiny second-hand car, a classic with an arguable market value, together with the LSD tabs in the manual; receives above market price for the car because of the drugs, and — hey presto! — he has clean money. No need to pass it through some cash business, because it's the gross takings of Sharpe's Luxury Motors. I'll bet he even pays tax on it! He's selling drugs, with the car as a free gift.'

Read closes the manual.

'Thank you. I don't suppose you have any idea who might have been manufacturing the lysergic acid?'

'No. But I do have a name you might like to look into. I'm given to believe that he is manufacturing, but whether he's supplying Sharpe or not, I couldn't say. Victor Kapur.'

Read nods. 'I'll need to keep this,' he says, brandishing the manual.

'Of course.'

'Why are you doing this?' asks Read suspiciously.

Charles sighs. 'I know you have a problem believing this, chief inspector, but I'm a good citizen. I believe in the rule of law, and I've devoted all my professional life to it. And it's my public duty to report crime, isn't it?'

'And you'll give a statement, will you, in relation to this?'

'Of course.'

Read pauses. 'You know that *this* —' he brandishes the book in his hand — 'is not going to buy you any favours, don't you?

Any arrangement we might come to will be in return for you giving evidence against the Krays.'

'You've made that perfectly clear,' replies Charles. 'Good day.'

Charles strides off, eastwards, towards Piccadilly Circus and thence the Royal Courts of Justice.

CHAPTER TWENTY-SEVEN

'Is this where you work all the time?' asks Mrs Sharpe, looking up at the vaulted ceiling. 'You're so lucky! It's a fairy tale castle!'

'I don't work here very often,' says Charles. 'I'm mostly in the criminal courts, like the Old Bailey. The Royal Courts of Justice are for civil matters, but it's also where the Court of Criminal Appeal sits. It is wonderful, isn't it? This way.'

He settles his gown on his shoulders, tucks his wig under one arm and leads Mrs Sharpe across the marble floor and up one of the staircases. He stops outside Court 10. As he checks the Cause List, she peers over the stone balcony at the patterned floor, Victorian gothic windows and massive oil paintings below her.

'Here we are,' reads Charles, 'not before three thirty. Lord Justice Bennett.'

'Do you know the judge?' asks Mrs Sharpe.

'No, I'm not familiar with him.'

He pushes at the double swing doors and steps into the court vestibule. He returns a few seconds later.

'It's empty. We can go in if you like.'

He holds the door open for his client and they enter the empty courtroom.

'Gosh!' says Mrs Sharpe, looking around at the dark wood panelling and stone walls above. 'It's very grand.'

'Have you never been inside a court before?'

'No, never.'

'I'm surprised. Even when your husband...'

'No.'

Charles is sceptical — surely she would have been in court to support her husband on one of his many brushes with the criminal law? — but her tone of voice makes it clear it's time to change the subject.

'I sit here,' he indicates, 'and you can sit on the bench behind me.'

'Where does Mr Tindall sit?'

'Normally, directly behind me, but he won't be here today.'

'Oh?'

'The solicitor doesn't always have to be present, and this is a straightforward *ex parte* application, so we thought it sensible to keep costs down.'

Charles sits at the barrister's bench and swivels in his seat to regard Mrs Sharpe.

He has not been this close to her before. He sees a plump middle-aged woman, perhaps a decade older than he, with thick light brown hair which Charles suspects is tinted and spectacles dangling from a chain around her neck. She is wearing conservative sensible clothes, all shades of unobtrusive blue. She has a wide mouth, full lips and grey eyes. There is a calmness about the set of her pleasant features which Charles likes. She would have been a striking young woman, he thinks, and he can see what might have attracted Sharpe to her. But what on earth did she see in the criminal she married?

Charles notices that the large diamond ring she wore the first time he met her has disappeared; her finger bears only a simple gold wedding band. She sees his glance and covers her left hand.

'Yes, I pawned it. To pay Mr Tindall's fees … and to instruct the private investigator.'

Charles opens his mouth but falters, not certain how to frame what was to be his next question.

Mrs Sharpe smiles.

'And you're wondering why I would do that, yes? Part with my only valuable asset when I have no income and no home? And when you suspect my marriage has been … difficult?'

Charles shrugs.

'You love your husband. Although … it is puzzling that you've never been in court before, considering his history. Of course, it's none of my business…'

'I don't love Stanley, Mr Holborne. I feel … a responsibility towards him and, I suppose, some remaining affection. He's capable of immense charm and great warmth, you know? And he's been a wonderful father to Robin, despite everything. But we haven't been close for many years. I made the schoolgirl error of thinking I could change him, you see? I was in love; everything seemed possible. But you can never change anyone, can you? Not unless they want to change themselves, and often not even then. And by the time I realised that, it was too late.'

'Divorce wasn't an option?'

'I'm a Catholic,' she says simply. 'Not a very good one, I accept, but that would've been impossible for me.'

'Even if he … mistreated you?'

'Even then. And you shouldn't take Robin's opinion too literally. I was far from blameless. Children don't understand the nuances, do they? They hear the shouting, maybe even see some … aggression, and they blame the shouter.'

'Given his history and what you've told me, what convinces you that Stanley is innocent of this crime?'

'For years I made sure I had nothing to do with his business affairs. I had my life, and he had his. If he got himself arrested, that was due to his choices, and I wouldn't support him. His solicitors sometimes asked me, but I always refused to go to court with him. But this time it's different. I *know* he's innocent.'

'How can you be so sure?'

'You're not a Christian, so you might find this difficult to understand. I know, because his conversion was genuine. I witnessed it in action for several years, long after the police, the probation service and the press were no longer there to see it. I saw Jesus enter his heart and Stanley find his calling. It was profound, and unmistakeable. It didn't affect how I felt about him personally — we'd been too far apart for too long — but it's *my* duty to do whatever I can to right the injustice. Do you understand? *My* Christian duty. He should be free to … continue his ministry.'

Charles looks at the kind face and smiles slowly.

He envies Mrs Sharpe's quiet confident faith. In a way he even envies her imprisoned husband. Their certainty is like that of his own parents, his brother David too. Their steadfast Jewishness washed over him, leaving him dry as dust, certain of his rationalism, impatient of their beliefs and at the same time vaguely troubled that he was missing something important, something just out of sight.

The door behind them opens and a young man in a court gown enters with a pile of files in his arms. He goes to the desk in front of the judge's bench, puts the files down and picks up a clipboard.

'Are you in the appeal of Sharpe?' he calls across to Charles.

'Yes. Charles Holborne of counsel.'

He notes Charles's name. 'And it's just you?' he asks.

'Yes.'

'Are you ready?'

'Whenever you are.'

The man disappears. A few minutes later, a woman appears through a door in the panelling behind the judge's bench carrying a huge ledger. She takes a seat in front of it. The young man reappears and places a red notebook and some pens before the judge's seat, returns to the door from which he entered and exits again without closing it fully. He raps on the door.

'All rise!'

Charles and Mrs Sharpe stand. Other than the court staff, the court is deserted. A judge in red robes enters, bows to Charles and takes his seat. Charles does not recognise him.

'Application in the appeal of Stanley Sharpe versus the Crown!' calls the usher.

'Mr Holborne,' starts the judge, 'let me try to save us some time. I have read the application and the witness statements of Mrs Marshall and Miss Bishop. As I see it, there is a very simple issue before me today, is there not? If I am of the opinion that such evidence, had it been before the jury, would probably have affected the verdict the jury gave, I have a discretion to extend time for the appeal and to admit the evidence. Do you agree?'

'I do, my Lord. The words of the Act are that the court "may" admit the evidence if it is "necessary or expedient in the interests of justice." It's my submission that the interests of justice must include freeing a man imprisoned for murdering someone who, it turns out, is not dead at all. One would struggle to provide a better example of when the discretion *should* be exercised in favour of an appellant. Mr Marshall's continued survival is not a matter of opinion or shades of grey. If it is a fact, as we believe we can prove, the Reverend Sharpe is, unequivocally, innocent.'

'Notwithstanding the fact that he admitted the murder?'

'Even then. Indeed, the continued survival of the alleged victim raises very significant questions as to the honesty of the police officer who claims to have obtained the confession. I rely on that, too, in saying that it's necessary and expedient in the interests of justice for there to be an appeal.'

'I have no doubt that counsel for the Crown will argue that that is a collateral issue, but time will tell. Very well. Mrs Watkins, who works in the office of the Registrar of Criminal Appeals has kindly attended —' he indicates the woman with the ledger sitting below him — 'and she will ensure that the original prosecutor and the officer in the case … Detective Chief Inspector Wheatley … are contacted.'

The woman below the judge turns in her seat and nods.

'It was the Director of Public Prosecutions who conducted the trial on behalf of the Crown,' says Charles.

'Thank you. I am disposed to extend time to appeal up to the date of your draft application, which will be treated henceforth as the actual application, and to give you permission to have the witnesses examined by the court under section nine of the Act. Are there any further applications?'

'Yes, my Lord. I seek legal aid on behalf of the Reverend Sharpe. The questions relating to his means have been answered in form thirty-four, which should be before you. As you will see, he was on a vicar's pay prior to his arrest and incarceration, and he has no savings or other means.'

The judge leafs through his papers and finds a form. He reads for a moment.

'Is that all a vicar in the Church of England earns?' he asks in surprise. 'Good heavens.'

'My Lord is too generous. It's "adequate heavens" at best,' comments Charles with a smile.

'Indeed. On that basis I grant legal aid for the appeal, limited to solicitor and junior counsel. Or are you seeking legal aid for a leader as well?'

'No, thank you, my Lord. As you say, this should be a simple matter and I feel competent to deal with it without a QC.'

'I agree. Anything else?'

'Yes, my Lord. I seek bail on Reverend Sharpe's behalf. Taking his time on remand together with the time spent as a convicted prisoner, he has served considerable time for an offence of which he should not have been convicted.'

'No, Mr Holborne, I can't decide on bail today. There may be objections or conditions from the police and I need to hear from them. But I shall list the matter for a separate bail application once the position of the Crown is known and they have appointed counsel.'

'Very well, my Lord. Thank you.'

'Well, if that's all, I shall rise.'

'All rise!'

The judge and his officials leave court and Charles turns to Mrs Sharpe with a smile. 'So far, so good. As I warned you, Stanley was very unlikely to get bail today.'

'No, that's fine. As long as we can bring an application as soon as possible.'

They leave court and Charles is about to bid farewell to Mrs Sharpe when he realises she wants to say something further.

'Do you have a minute, please, Mr Holborne?'

'Yes.'

'It's about Robin. He's been arrested, together with other people working at the garage. I don't know the details, but it's something to do with drugs. I wanted to ask if you'd consider representing him.'

'Has he asked?'

'No, I just thought…'

Charles pulls a face. He knew this moment would come. His discovery concerning the Rover manual was not covered by legal professional privilege — Robin Sharpe was not his client — and so in giving the information to Nipper Read he was doing his public duty. The illegal manufacture and supply of drugs is a serious offence and Charles is, after all, an officer of the court; were he to be discovered withholding this information, he would certainly be in professional difficulties. He is nonetheless uncomfortable at having triggered his client's son's arrest. It is that discomfort which causes him to edit his response.

'I'm very sorry, Mrs Sharpe, but I can't. I bought a car from your son's business, you see, and it's not impossible I shall be a witness in the case. So I'm conflicted. I expect Robin realises that.'

The truth but not the whole truth, thinks Charles grimly.

'Is he on bail?' asks Charles.

'Yes, they were all released pending further investigations, but the garage is closed while they do tests or something.'

'Well, I can certainly recommend another barrister, from my chambers if you like, one who'd do a first-class job.'

'When I told Stanley he said to ask you.'

Charles shakes his head. 'Like I said, I'm conflicted. It's not possible. But I promise, there are some excellent barristers in Chambers. I'll get some recommendations to Mr Tindall.'

CHAPTER TWENTY-EIGHT

Louise pulls her silk dressing gown tight around her and slips out of the bedroom. She uses the toilet in the cramped bathroom, flushes, and walks softly downstairs to the kitchen. She doesn't want to wake Marshall, who she left, snoring quietly, lying diagonally across the double bed.

For the first few days she was terrified of the big man. He was always respectful and he never forced himself on her, but his needs were insatiable. It was as if he felt a compulsion to prove himself, his strength and his stamina, and his technique was at times little short of brutal. Louise ached from neck to calves and her private parts were dry and sore from his repeated pounding. More than once she complained to Dixon, who appeared in the absence of Reggie Kray to be in charge, that she couldn't endure it any longer. He shrugged, uninterested, and Louise was forced to change tack.

She started treating Marshall not like a client but like a genuine lover. It involved another, deeper, layer of pretence, one with which she was profoundly uncomfortable at first, but it worked. The more intimate she became with him, the more he responded in kind. Now, although he still insists on sex four or more times a day and some sessions last over an hour, he is tender and gentle with her. Once or twice he has cried during or after sex, and her heart has gone out to him. She realises that beneath the formidably powerful body is a frightened little boy, one who responds to kindness with tears.

They both know that she is a temporary pastime and he a client, but within the strained confines of the artificial world created by Mags Meyer, his small council house and the ever-changing guards, they have begun to develop genuine affection for each other. They tend to eat together, alone, in the bedroom, rather than downstairs in the kitchen with the others, and Louise does her best to enter into his world. She listens to him as, haltingly, he reads the newspapers to her and, unlike the men, she pretends to be interested in his obsessions, principally the World Cup and the part that West Ham United players will play in it. He also talks affectionately of his two sons, sometimes of his wife. The cognitive dissonance is something with which Louise is familiar. Many clients talk of their wives and how much they love them, even during their sexual throes with her.

At first she thinks the kitchen is deserted, but sitting in the shadows on a stool, looking out into the garden, is Dixon. He smokes a cigarette, apparently lost in thought, and only half-turns to acknowledge her presence.

At the start Louise was embarrassed to pad about the house half-naked. She was acutely aware of the other men's gazes and where they lingered; she knew they heard the exertions and cries from the bedroom above them.

Now, weeks later, they have all settled into the arrangement. The Firm members pose no risk to her and Mags is actually rather sweet. They're all playing their parts, working with the same aim and for the same demanding master. Reggie Kray obviously made it clear that she was out of bounds to everyone except Marshall, and all the men have respected that.

Louise fills the kettle and places it on the gas ring. 'I'm making tea. Do you want one?' she asks.

'No ta, hen,' says Dixon, softly. 'I'm away to ma bed. All okay up there?'

'Yes. He's asleep. Still banging on about going to the matches, though.'

'When's the first one?'

'In a couple of weeks. Difficult match, against Uruguay.'

'Ha! He's got you going 'n' all!'

She smiles. 'You all think he's stupid, but he's not. When he's interested in something, he remembers all of it. It's actually fascinating. Do you want me to explain the offside rule?'

Dixon laughs, stands and stubs out his cigarette on a dirty tea plate. 'No thanks, hen.'

He stretches and yawns, pats her gently on the backside as he passes her, and leaves the kitchen. She listens to his footsteps climbing the stairs.

Louise turns on the strip light. It flickers hesitantly to life. She sits at the tiny kitchen counter and drags over a newspaper discarded by one of the men. She turns the pages idly as she waits for the kettle to boil, skimming the speculation on where the Moors Murderers, Ian Brady and Myra Hindley, buried the missing bodies, and pausing briefly at an article under the headline "Swinging London".

The page is full of photographs: young people dancing in clubs; brightly dressed hippies; the Beatles being chased by fans into Paddington station; and a stylish couple posing on a scooter in Carnaby Street, accompanied by a full-grown cheetah on a lead. She snorts and turns the page. If London's swinging, it's not swinging much in Acton. The photographs irritate her; they represent a life so distant from hers as to be untouchable.

'Oh, sod it!' says Louise quietly, giving up on waiting for the kettle to boil.

She turns off the gas with an irritated twist of the wrist and heads back to bed.

CHAPTER TWENTY-NINE

'Charles! My dear fellow, how are you?'

The unmistakable plummy voice on the other end of the telephone is that of former Metropolitan police officer, now senior crime correspondent, Percy Farrow. The gargantuan Farrow, perhaps the most famous gourmand in London, has been covering crime for the Mirror Group for over a decade. He has a professional reputation to match his size. Constantly the head-hunting target of other editors, Farrow has been responsible for some of the biggest scoops of the 1960s, including Ronnie Kray's gay sex orgies and the involvement therein of several high profile men from both sides of the political fence.

Farrow has been Charles's friend since he covered a couple of Charles's early cases and is responsible for introducing Charles to some of the small but growing band of elite chefs now working in London. However, Charles suspects that this impromptu telephone call might herald bad news.

'Good afternoon, Percy. To what do I owe this honour?'

'Always a pleasure to speak to you, old chum. And I'm cognisant of the fact that I still owe you that dinner for your interview following the Greene and Cathcart prosecution.'

'But?'

'But I thought you should know that news of Reverend Sharpe's forthcoming appeal has leaked.'

'Yes, thank you, Percy. I thought it would. In fact, a little bird in Chambers warned me that, not only does the office of the Registrar of Criminal Appeals leak like a sieve, but it leaks specifically in your direction.'

Farrow laughs. 'Yes, well, we all have our sources of information, don't we, Charles?' he says pointedly. 'And at least I'm warning you, which many others wouldn't.'

'Thank you. I do appreciate that.'

'The bail application is at noon tomorrow, I gather.'

'Fucking hell, Percy, we haven't heard from the list office yet! Are they giving the list to reporters before the parties themselves?'

'Now, now, Charles. You know I'm not keen on that sort of language.'

Charles does know. Farrow is the son and nephew of churchmen and, uniquely among the many police officers and journalists Charles has ever met, is extremely uncomfortable with profanity. Charles has often thought that Farrow must've suffered mightily in both of his foul-mouthed professions; the favourite adjectives of the *Mirror*'s present editor only run to four letters, and multiple examples punctuate every sentence he utters.

'Yes, Percy, I'm sorry.'

'The list was published five minutes ago. I expect your delightful clerk is at this very moment on the phone to the list office. Anyway, I'm afraid you can expect quite a circus tomorrow at the RCJ.'

'Okay. Thanks for the heads-up.'

'My pleasure. I'll see you there. Perhaps we can grab a late lunch after you're done?'

'Maybe, although I can't commit to it, I'm afraid.'

'Understood. Well, pip pip!' he says cheerfully, and hangs up.

Charles has barely replaced the receiver when the telephone rings again. He picks it up and speaks immediately. 'Yes, I know: the Sharpe application is at twelve noon tomorrow,' he says.

'How on earth do you know that?' demands Barbara, somewhat peeved.

'Psychic,' he says. 'And you're going to meet a tall dark stranger.'

'What would I want with a tall dark stranger?' mutters Barbara impatiently as she hangs up.

The following morning Charles is in Chambers early. The bail application is not especially difficult and has been prepared, but in an attempt to clear the urgent matters from his desk in hopes of enjoying a good long lunch with Percy Farrow, he thought he would get a head start. So, for a change, rather than walking in with Sally, he left home by half past seven and was at his desk with a cup of tea and two rounds of buttered toast from Mick's half an hour later. It is now just gone nine, and Chambers is filling up. There is a knock on Charles's door and a head appears.

'Got a moment?' it says.

In walks Piers Roth QC, a barrister colleague from Temple Gardens, also Jewish. Charles doesn't know Roth well, but there are so few Jews at the Bar — all of whom have faced the same prejudice — they tend to recognise one another.

'Roth? What on earth are you doing here?'

To Charles's surprise, the tall man is not alone. Following close behind him is another barrister, one who Charles knows by sight alone.

'Have you met Jonathan Cohen?' introduces Roth. 'He's one of the youngsters in my set, also in crime. You may remember…'

'I certainly do. Pleased to meet you in person,' says Charles.

'We've come to give a word to the wise,' announces Roth, drawing up a chair without being asked, plonking himself in front of Charles and lighting a small cigar.

Charles looks from one of his guests to the other and a suspicion develops.

'Are you trying to get up a *minyan*?' he asks with a grin.

A *minyan* is the quorum of ten Jewish men required to form a congregation for religious purposes. That fact that women don't count is one of the myriad causes of Charles's impatience with his family's religion.

'In a manner of speaking,' replies Cohen.

'Your bail application is today, isn't it?' says Roth.

'It is,' confirms Charles.

'We don't know who's hearing it, but we've learned on good authority who's going to be sitting on your appeal.' Roth pauses for dramatic effect. 'Lord Justice Greenidge,' he announces with a flourish.

'Shit. Really?'

'Really.'

Lord Justice Richard Greenidge's name is known to most members of the public. An outspoken and eccentric member of the Court of Appeal, he is also a virulent anti-Semite. Once, after inviting counsel into his chambers at court for a post-trial drink, and belatedly realising that one of them was Jewish, he demanded, in earshot of the departing barristers, that his clerk open a window to "clear the Hebrew atmosphere from the room."

Charles has never had the misfortune to conduct a case before him but, memorably, Cohen has. It is a story known throughout the Bar, oft repeated as a cautionary tale by Jewish barristers, especially those who witnessed it. Charles was amongst them.

Greenidge was sitting as a circuit judge, before his elevation to the High Court. Cohen, then a very junior barrister, was representing an innocuous Jewish jeweller from Hatton Garden who, on rather slim evidence, was charged with handling a stolen necklace. It was a very simple case, expected to last a day. Almost before he had risen to his feet for the first time, Cohen was subject to a barrage of aggressive questions and comments from Greenidge. He could barely open his mouth without being interrupted. Greenidge took against Cohen, his defence, his client, and even the independent expert called on behalf of the accused who, unfortunately, also happened to be Jewish and was wearing a skullcap.

By lunchtime Cohen was so rattled he could barely ask a question without stammering.

News of his ordeal travelled back to the Temple. Middle Temple Hall and Inner Temple Hall were full of barristers eating their lunches, their heads together as the gossip raced through the dining halls.

'Young Jonathan Cohen from Temple Gardens is getting a terrible kicking from that bastard Greenidge,' they said.

When, at just after two o'clock, Greenidge resumed the trial, he noticed that the barristers' benches were rather fuller than before. What had been a half-empty courtroom was filling up with other members of the Bar, including Roth and Charles. Within an hour the benches were packed. Numerous Jewish barristers who had heard the story, together with a handful of their decent non-Jewish colleagues, were there to lend moral support to the beleaguered Cohen.

Defiant, initially Greenidge doubled down on his attacks but, as the numbers on counsel's benches grew, he quietened down and began to be more circumspect in his interruptions. The sniping eventually ended altogether and Cohen was permitted to complete his defence of the accused without further interruption.

Perhaps some of the jury members were Jewish; perhaps they just didn't like the prosecution's case. Either way, at quarter past four, after retiring for only ten minutes, the jury returned with a verdict. They acquitted the unfortunate jeweller, who broke down in tears of relief. Without a word, the massed ranks of barristers rose as one, bowed to the judge, and filed out of court.

'Do you know who the other judges are?' asks Charles.

'Mr Justice Davies and Lord Justice Linnard,' answers Cohen.

'I know Davies,' says Charles. 'I was against him a couple of times while he was still at the Bar. Perfectly reasonable chap. I've never encountered Linnard.'

'He's old school,' says Roth. 'Not mad like Greenidge, but if we had to guess, we'd say he shares many of the same prejudices.'

'They're both benchers of Gray's Inn and members of the same club,' adds Cohen. 'And when they were at the Bar they shared a room for ages.'

'Shit,' repeats Charles. 'They're mates.'

'Yes,' replies Cohen.

'So we came to ask if you'd like some moral support,' offers Roth. 'I'm finishing a robbery trial tomorrow or the day after, and I'm out of court for at least a fortnight after that to prepare a long firm fraud. Jonathan here is a bit busy, but there are two other Yiddisher chaps in his chambers who can make the time. I'm sure we can round up some others. What do you think?'

Charles considers. 'It's a very simple case,' he muses, 'only two witnesses and a simple case of identification. If the witnesses come up to proof, it's a stone-cold certainty that the appeal will be allowed.'

'Famous last words?' asks Cohen.

'Maybe,' concedes Charles, 'but I don't want to up the ante unnecessarily. If a load of our brethren crowd into counsel's benches, it'll look obvious. Like a challenge. And Greenidge's just bonkers enough to rise to it.'

Roth turns to Cohen. 'I did wonder about that.'

'I think on balance I will decline, at least for the present,' concludes Charles. 'But thanks for thinking of me. The solidarity is much appreciated.'

Tindall and Mrs Sharpe arrive in Chambers at 11:15 as arranged. Charles didn't want Mrs Sharpe to face the press alone, and so it was more convenient for the team to assemble in the Temple.

For the sake of convenience, Charles changes into his fancy dress in Chambers and leads the group across the Strand to the Royal Courts of Justice. A large crowd of Christian supporters, protesters and press can be seen from some distance away. Charles recognises the young deacon he interviewed some weeks earlier, leading a group of his parishioners.

As Charles steps off the zebra crossing right outside the main entrance he is accosted by journalists brandishing notepads, cameras and microphones. A barrage of questions is shouted to both him and Mrs Sharpe, but Charles uses his bulk to push through without response and the others follow in his wake.

The interior of the court building is relatively peaceful. The protesters and supporters are being kept outside behind a line of policemen, and Charles assumes that the number of reporters allowed is being controlled; only two approach, but

Charles ushers Tindall and Mrs Sharpe away too quickly for them and runs lightly up the stone steps to Court 6.

Charles pushes open the doors.

The courts at the Royal Courts of Justice have a different atmosphere to those at the Old Bailey. These hallowed temples of justice are unused to witnessing the everyday dramatics, even histrionics, that are meat and drink to the criminal courts. They have a solemn air, as befits a place where really important matters — namely, money — are the daily subject of dispute.

Not today.

The two benches at the back of the court, usually reserved for members of the public, are full of noisy journalists. The dedicated press bench, closer to the judge and along one side of the court wall, has twice the number of bottoms squashed into it as there are leather seats, and the court associate is in the process of moving a group of men and women unlucky enough to arrive too late for a seat to a small space at the back of the court where they may stand without getting in anyone's way.

The associate catches Charles's eye and scurries over. 'Mr Holborne?'

'Yes.'

'Your client was to be produced from prison this morning, is that right?'

'Yes. Is he here?'

'No, I'm afraid not. That's the point. He was supposed to be moved to Pentonville yesterday ready for his escort here, but apparently he hasn't arrived.'

'Why not?' demands Charles.

'I'm very sorry, sir, I don't know. There's a suggestion he refused to leave Durham, but that's just gossip and I haven't yet been able to get to the bottom of it.'

Charles shakes his head in frustration. If Sharpe did refuse to leave HM Prison Durham, the judge might infer that he doesn't want to pursue the application.

'All right, thank you,' says Charles.

He slides into counsel's bench, looks across at his opponent and a bad start to the morning gets a lot worse.

It's The Great Toad!

Now in his seventies, Barnabus Warboys, QC, has prosecuted for the Crown for a generation and remains a firm favourite of the Director of Public Prosecutions. He is a squat man with a pox-scarred face, no apparent neck and an extraordinarily wide mouth surmounting flabby jowls. Although he does look strikingly like Mr Toad of Toad Hall, it was his croaky voice which prompted Charles to nickname him "The Great Toad" after contesting a case against him. As will happen when nicknames unerringly strike the bull's-eye, the moniker stuck and gained widespread currency in the Temple. Warboys knows who started it. He has loathed Charles ever since.

'Good morning, Warboys,' says Charles.

The QC looks across and frowns. 'Have we met?' he croaks, pretending not to recognise Charles.

'We have, actually, on that manslaughter insanity plea, Alice Wheeler, but it was brief.'

'Indeed? And you're for the appellant today?'

'I am.'

'Name?'

'Charles Holborne,' replies Charles patiently.

Warboys makes a note and looks up. 'No leader?'

'No. To be honest, I'm surprised to see you dealing with a bail application.'

'It's not every day that judges are asked to free convicted murderers,' says Warboys dismissively, turning his back on Charles and starting to talk to someone behind him.

Charles realises, with a shock that starts in the pit of his stomach, that in the bench behind the old QC stands Detective Chief Inspector Wheatley. Wheatley has his head turned away from Charles and covers his mouth as he speaks, but it's obvious that Charles is the subject of conversation, because both men turn at the same moment and stare at him.

Charles knows he shouldn't be surprised; Wheatley was bound to be present both for the bail application and the appeal itself. It is nonetheless a shock to see the man who tried so hard to have him hanged. This is the first time Charles has seen Wheatley since he escaped his custody nearly four years ago; forced on the run to extricate himself from the frame into which the corrupt policeman had placed him.

Tindall, now sitting next to Mrs Sharpe directly behind Charles, must have noticed Charles's expression. He leans forward.

'Are you all right, Charles?' he asks quietly. 'You've gone quite pale.'

'A bit of my past suddenly popped up, that's all,' he says, forcing a smile. 'This case seems to be doing that rather a lot.'

He looks down at Mrs Sharpe and gives her a genuine, reassuring smile.

'I'm fine. But I'm sorry to say that Stanley isn't going to be produced.'

'What? Isn't he here?' asks Mrs Sharpe anxiously.

'No. And at the moment it's not clear why.'

The familiar rap comes on the door.

'All rise!'

A judge enters. It is, again, Lord Justice Bennett, before whom Charles appeared the previous week. Charles doesn't expect the application to be any less difficult before this judge, but at least he is younger and more reasonable than some of his older and more conservative brethren.

Once the court settles, the judge addresses Charles.

'Mr Holborne.'

'Yes, thank you, my Lord. As you know, I appear on behalf of the appellant, the Reverend Stanley Sharpe, and the Crown is represented by the DPP in the form of my learned friend, Mr Warboys.'

Warboys half-rises from his seat to bow to the judge.

'You granted leave to appeal against conviction last week and deferred the issue of bail pending the appeal. Today is the bail application.'

'Is it being pursued?' asks the judge. 'I understand your client is not present.'

'I have just been informed that he is not here, my Lord. I have no idea why that is the case, and the court associate has no confirmation either. Arrangements were made for him to be transferred from Durham to a London prison in time to be produced at court today. But my Instructions throughout have been to seek bail, my Instructing Solicitor is here, and our Instructions haven't altered since we were last in contact with Mr Sharpe. Accordingly, I take it that I am still to pursue the application, even in the absence of my client.'

'Very well. Mr Warboys, is the application opposed?'

'It is, my Lord. As will be the appeal.'

'Very well. Mr Holborne, if this is convenient to you I would prefer to hear the objections to bail first. Mr Warboys can call any witnesses on whom he relies, and you can cross-examine and then address me at the end.'

'I'm happy with that approach, thank you, my Lord.'

'Excellent. Mr Warboys, then.'

The Great Toad lumbers to his feet.

'Thank you, my Lord. I propose calling Detective Chief Inspector Wheatley, who led the investigation and who took a verbatim record of the prisoner's full confession. He will deal with, if I may put it this way, the granularity of the application. However, I start with a matter of principle. I invite the court to address this application on the basis that this is a substance-less appeal, most unlikely to succeed, and that Sharpe is a dangerous criminal who must remain in custody for the protection of the public and potential witnesses. So lacking in merit is this proposed appeal that one is tempted to wonder why it was brought. Your Lordship may have some knowledge of my learned friend's history, his extraordinary predilection for the limelight, but if not I am in a position to put bèfore the court some of the highlights in which he has found himself on the front pages of various scandal sheets in an apparent attempt to bolster his career. This is another example of the same. An unmeritorious publicity stunt.'

'Let me stop you there, Mr Warboys. We are not here to consider Mr Holborne's practice or his motives in bringing this case. I granted permission to appeal on the basis of what appeared to me to be perfectly proper evidence of two witnesses which, if accepted, means that the alleged victim of this murder remains alive to this day. The court can only work on the basis of *evidence*. Please confine yourself to that.'

The Great Toad draws a deep breath, his enormous chest puffing itself up, and Charles has to hide a smile behind his hand.

'As your Lordship pleases,' he croaks. 'Moving on, then. Firstly, my Lord will be aware that although the court has the power to award bail pending an appeal, it will only be exercised in exceptional cases. My Lord knows of the authorities, starting with R *versus Gordon* and ending with R *versus Starkie*. They are all to be found in paragraph 882 of Archbold, and I need not dwell on them.

'Secondly, the so-called "evidence" upon which the appeal is brought is untested. By contrast, the evidence of conviction was rigorously tested before a jury, which had no hesitation in convicting. Unanimously. They were undoubtedly right to do so, in light of the full and detailed admissions made by the prisoner. Thus, until the new evidence is tested and accepted, the prisoner remains a convicted murderer.

'I now turn to the safeguards my learned friend will say may be put in place to mitigate the risks to the public should bail be granted. Even without the instant conviction, it is undeniable that Sharpe's criminal record, which DCI Wheatley will go through in detail, was utterly appalling, indeed frightening. It includes robbery with violence, wounding with intent, and intimidation of witnesses. In addition, I counted over a dozen serious offences of dishonesty.

'Mr Sharpe is therefore both violent and a man whose word cannot be trusted. Whatever he or his counsel may promise in respect of remaining in this country, reporting to the police or whatever, I invite my Lord to place little or no reliance on it.

'Lack of ties: until his incarceration, the prisoner was, or claimed to be, a Church of England vicar. On his conviction he was stripped of his office and he lost his church accommodation. He has no home, no ties to a particular area. DCI Wheatley will give evidence concerning this, but it is understood that he has separated from his wife. The court should not be misled by the presence of Mrs Sharpe in court today. We submit it is a ruse to paint a false picture of matrimonial harmony.

'So, we have a career criminal with a record demonstrating merciless violence, total disregard for the law and the truth, who may spend the rest of his life in prison if his appeal fails, and no reason to remain in the jurisdiction and face justice. The flight risk is simply enormous, whatever conditions my learned friend might suggest. Never can there have been a less meritorious application for bail. Unless my Lord has any questions of me, I will call DCI Wheatley.'

'Yes, thank you.'

Wheatley steps down from the bench behind counsel into the well of the court, climbs into the witness box, picks up the Bible without being prompted and, holding it high, recites the oath in a firm voice without having to read it from the card.

As expected he is taken by Warboys through Sharpe's litany of evildoing, without drawing attention to the decade-long gap between his regular offending and his conviction of Marshall's murder. He tells the court that the police have been unable to find any significant connections that would induce Sharpe to remain in the country were he given the opportunity to abscond, and he has no assets to offer as a security for his attendance. In an almost apologetic tone he relates how Mrs Eileen Sharpe is now living with her sister and how Sharpe's only other close relative, his son Robin, is estranged from his father.

After ten minutes of damning evidence, Charles rises to cross-examine the police officer. As he stands, he is still making up his mind as to how far to take his attack on Wheatley. He and the policeman both know that the assault on the veracity of Sharpe's alleged confession must come at some point. But now, or later? At the last second Charles decides to keep that powder dry for the appeal itself.

'You gave evidence, chief inspector, that Mr and Mrs Sharpe are separated.'

'That is what our enquiries have revealed.'

'Yet here she is today.'

'Well, of course. Mr Sharpe is a violent man, my Lord. He has bullied his poor wife for years. He has three convictions arising out of that behaviour and has been bound over to keep the peace on three more. Mr Holborne knows as well as I that career criminals such as Sharpe can exercise their control from inside prison as much as from outside.'

'I am in a position to call Mrs Sharpe,' says Charles, 'to prove that she pawned her engagement ring to pay for her husband's legal expenses today. Does that sound to you like a woman who is separated from her husband?'

'It sounds like a woman put under pressure, to me.'

'If released on bail, Mr Sharpe could be ordered to reside at a bail hostel, to surrender his passport and to report to the police as much as twice a day, could he not?'

'My Lord, the court could order those and other restrictions, but it is the police's firm opinion that nothing would be adequate to guarantee Sharpe's attendance at the appeal. He masterminded a complex and sophisticated criminal network. The acquisition of a false passport would be child's play for him. He would be out of the country before we even knew it.'

Charles continues to cross-examine for several further minutes but gets nowhere.

He has already advised Tindall and Mrs Sharpe that to persuade the court to give reduced weight to Sharpe's previous criminal record, they have to prove that his conversion and years of practising Christianity were a mark of the true man.

That argument is, at least for now, fatally undercut by the conviction for murder which postdates it. The conviction implies that the conversion and good deeds that followed were, as the newspapers screamed, part of an elaborate pretence: Stanley Sharpe was a hypocrite whose attempt to fool the public and the parole board have been rumbled.

Charles is therefore deflated but not surprised by his uphill struggle. In his heart he knows that unless and until Gracie Marshall and Judy Bishop give evidence, and survive cross-examination, the court is bound to take a cautious approach.

And so it proves.

'No,' concludes the judge as Charles resumes his seat, 'I'm not satisfied that it would be appropriate to grant the prisoner bail at this stage. Notwithstanding the apparent hiatus in offending for several years while he worked as a vicar, bearing in mind his very serious history of criminality and the lengthy period of imprisonment he will face if the appeal is unsuccessful, I believe the risks of his absconding are too great, whatever safeguards might be imposed. The prisoner will remain in custody until the hearing of his appeal.'

CHAPTER THIRTY

It is late evening at the house on Horn Lane. The faint sounds of the Beatles' "Paperback Writer" drift downstairs from the bathroom where Louise is relaxing in a hot bath and shaving her legs. The song has been at number one for a fortnight and has been on all the music stations.

All the men in the household have been sitting around the kitchen table, playing cards and drinking whisky. The atmosphere is comfortable, as if the formal roles of prisoner, gaoler and guards have been put aside and they are just four friends meeting to chat and gamble for a few pennies.

Mags Meyer announces that he is peckish and fancies a sandwich, to which he receives an enthusiastic order from the other players. Mindful as always of his duties as host, he calls up the stairs to ask if Louise wants anything, but she is singing along with Paul McCartney and doesn't hear him. He will do another round for her when she comes down, he decides.

Marshall has been in unusually good humour since he read the *Evening Standard*'s report on the World Cup preparations. Alf Ramsey has named his final squad and it includes three Hammers.

'I'm going,' he announces, 'no arguments.'

'You'll never get tickets now,' replies Tommy, collecting the discards after another completed hand.

'I bloody will,' replies Marshall confidently. 'Budgie will've left 'em at me mum's.'

'Budgie?'

'Yeah, me mate Johnny Byrne. Top goal-scorer; plays at number nine.'

'You'd best ask Ronnie about that,' warns Dixon.

Marshall leans forward menacingly and raises a thick forefinger, jabbing it in the direction of Dixon's nose.

'Like fuck I will,' he growls, and suddenly the tension in the room has returned. 'I've been waiting for this all me life, and no one, not even Ronnie Kray, is gonna stop me.'

Dixon raises his hands in submission. 'Yeah, sure, whatever you say, pal.'

'Ron? Where are you?'

Reg Kray closes the front door of the Finchley Road apartment with his foot and puts his shopping on the hall table. He slips off his shoes and pads down the plush corridor in search of his twin.

'Ron?'

Reg finds him asleep in the armchair. Ronnie wears creased trousers, a sleeveless vest and slippers. The curtains are closed and the room is in darkness but for the light emitted by the television, its sound turned right down. Beside him on the occasional table at his elbow is an empty tumbler and two large bottle of pills without labels. Doc Blasker has evidently been to replenish the tranquillisers, which are always delivered in unmarked bottles. Reg now recognises the different sorts by their colours and shapes.

Reg removes Ronnie's glasses, which are about to fall off his nose, turns off the television and goes into the kitchen to wash up. The plates and utensils he left there after breakfast have been supplemented by others, simply piled in the sink on top of the older ones. He takes off his jacket and rolls up his sleeves.

He has almost finished when he realises Ronnie is standing behind him in the doorway, yawning.

'How're you feeling?' he asks over his shoulder.

'Bit better. Gotta few hours kip.'

'Good.'

'How're things in Acton?'

For over a week Ronnie hasn't been able to engage with anything at all, so the fact that he enquires is in itself good news.

'Dixon reckons we've got problems coming. Frank's insisting he's going to all the England matches. I don't think keeping him at Mags's will wash for much longer.'

'What then?'

Reggie removes his orange Marigold gloves with a double-snap and leans back on the sink.

'Well, we need to talk about that. I don't know. I like Frank. There's not many who go all the way back with us.'

'Yeah. He's family.'

'And a good loyal soldier. But 'e's never going to get it. He won't stay hidden and he won't stay away. Sooner or later he'll be picked up by the Filth. Just a matter of when.'

'We can't let that 'appen, can we?'

Reg sighs and shakes his head. 'No.'

'Tell 'im if he stays put, we'll let 'im go to the matches. Chances of 'im being seen in them crowds is pretty slim. That'll keep 'im quiet for a bit.'

'There's loads of matches,' points out Reg.

'Yeah, but not for England. We'll be knocked out pretty quick.'

'And then?'

'Make some calls. We'll need a van.'

CHAPTER THIRTY-ONE

Charles hurries around the corner from Gray's Inn Road into Wren Street. Tonight is the first match of the World Cup and the hosts, England, are playing Uruguay. Charles is determined to be front of the TV, a beer in hand, before kick-off.

As he approaches his front door, he sees a car that he recognises parked behind his Rover. He halts.

'Oh shit!'

The Volvo belongs to David.

What's happened?

But then he remembers: he invited David round to watch the match. The invitation was issued weeks ago, but so much has happened in the meantime it had slipped completely from his mind. Most importantly, he forgot to tell Sally.

I'm going to be in trouble.

David will only eat kosher food and not off plates that, like those of Sally and Charles, have been used for *treif*, non-kosher food. Unless he is only to drink tap water, inviting him to the house requires planning and preparation.

Charles runs up the steps and opens the front door.

'Hi!' he calls apprehensively.

Sally appears from the lounge. She walks towards him and places a kiss on his cheek.

'You're in the doghouse,' she says, but she doesn't sound as cross as she ought to given the circumstances, and there is a smile crinkling the corners of her eyes.

'I'm so sorry, Sal, I completely forgot I invited him.'

'Just as well I happened to call Sonia this morning, isn't it?'

'You did?'

'Yes. And she's provided food for all of us.'

'She has?'

Sonia, David's wife, sticks her head out into the hall.

'She has,' she confirms.

'You're here too!' exclaims Charles, and he runs over to her to give her a warm embrace and a kiss on each cheek. 'I imagined it'd just be David.'

Sonia is tall, dark and statuesque with large almond-shaped eyes. She and David are very well-suited and extremely happy.

Charles has a soft spot for his sister-in-law. Although she grew up in a devoutly Jewish family and maintains a strictly Orthodox household with David, she has always been a silent but steadfast ally to Charles in his long-term battle with Millie. Sonia pities him and admires the way (for the most part) he maintains his good humour in the face of Millie's endless goading.

'It's not much,' she says, 'but there's a large tureen of chicken soup on the hob, and I've brought bowls and cutlery.'

'Thank you so much, Sonia. You've saved my —'

'Kosher pressed beef?' she offers.

'Exactly. But where's the baby?' asks Charles. 'Do I get to see my nephew as well?'

'Afraid not,' says a voice.

Charles looks over the heads of the women in the hallway to see his younger brother, tall and fair, emerging from the lounge.

'Mum and Jonathan are being babysat by Mrs Weinstein,' says David, 'giving Sonia and me our first night out in months. And, if you don't mind me mentioning it —' David jabs his wrist pointedly — 'kick-off's in thirty-five minutes.'

A disappointing nil-nil draw having been played out, the television pundits remain on screen, muted, trying to make something interesting out of the sparse highlights. The four family members sit in the lounge drinking lemon tea out of the glasses brought by Sonia, and chat.

Charles has tried on several occasions to discuss Millie and Harry's living arrangements with David, but his younger brother, clinging to the hope that Harry would make a full recovery, refused to discuss it. Charles backed off. Sooner or later decisions would have to be taken, but there was no point forcing their pace. The whole family would have to be in agreement.

The hospital has now indicated that Harry will be discharged in a fortnight, and David realises that there is now no avoiding it. Plans have to be made. Having had time to reflect, he now agrees that the best course is for both Millie and Harry to move into one of the care homes identified by Charles, initially for respite care. Charles suspects that Sonia has had a lot to do with his brother's change of mind. The four of them have narrowed down the choice of care homes to two, and a further visit is proposed for the weekend, this time with Millie and Harry.

The front doorbell sounds, surprising all of them.

David looks at his watch. 'Almost ten o'clock? One of your clients, perhaps?' he suggests to Charles, only half-joking.

Charles frowns and is about to speak when the doorbell sounds again, followed immediately by a loud rap with the door knocker.

'Someone's impatient,' he says, rising.

He goes into the hall and opens the front door.

'Charles Holborne?'

The speaker is a thin middle-aged man. He is well-dressed and sports a tailored overcoat and cashmere scarf, the latter evidently worn more for style than comfort as the spring evening is warm and balmy, and the weather would surely not demand it.

'Yes. What can I do for you?' asks Charles.

'My name's Dominic Hudson. I'm Maria's father.'

There is an urgent tenor to his American-accented voice.

'Is she all right?' asks Sally, concerned, as she joins Charles at the front door.

'I don't know,' says Hudson. 'That's why I'm here.'

Charles opens the door wider and steps back.

'You'd better come in.'

Hudson enters and sees David and Sonia emerging from the lounge.

'Sorry to interrupt,' he mutters perfunctorily.

'Follow me,' says Charles, leading the way down the steps into the kitchen.

David and Sonia retreat to the lounge and Charles, Sally and Hudson descend to the kitchen.

'Take a seat, please,' offers Charles.

'No, thank you, I shan't be long. Do you have Maria's address?'

Charles frowns. 'Don't you?' he asks.

'No, obviously, or I wouldn't be asking,' says Hudson with exaggerated patience.

'As a matter of interest, Mr Hudson, how did you obtain *our* address?' asks Sally.

'I asked at your husband's office,' he answers shortly. 'So, please may I have Maria's whereabouts?'

'And my chambers gave you our address, did they?' asks Charles, pressing the point.

It is strictly forbidden for clerks to give out barristers' contact details without permission. In the case of those practising in crime, particularly those whose daily business is to incarcerate violent gangsters, it carries obvious risks.

'That Scottish woman did, eventually.'

'I'm surprised,' says Charles.

'She had no choice when I told her I thought that Maria was in danger.'

'Please, do sit down,' says Sally, trying to smooth what appear to be increasingly ruffled feelings. 'May we offer you a drink?'

'No, I told you, I shan't be long,' says Hudson. 'I want you to give me Maria's address, and then I shall leave.'

'Mr Hudson,' says Charles, 'what makes you think that Maria is in danger?'

'She is alone somewhere in London, out of contact with her family and, apparently, with the chambers where she was supposed to be trained! As far as we know, she's disappeared altogether.'

'I see,' replies Charles. 'So there's no suggestion she's actually in danger; you just don't know where she is.'

'We thought she'd spoken with you and you'd agreed to help with her rent,' says Sally. 'So, that's not right?'

'We had an … interview, but I certainly did not agree to any such thing. I haven't seen her since.'

'And she's not given you her new address,' says Charles, now understanding the situation.

'Exactly.'

'Well, Mr Hudson, I'm very sorry, but if Maria hasn't chosen to tell you where she is, I don't think we should go behind that.'

'She's my daughter, Mr Holborne. I have a right to know.'

'She's a grown woman, sir, capable of making her own decisions.'

Hudson's pale face colours.

'You have absolutely no right to withhold this information from me!' he shouts. 'It seems to me that you have let her down disgracefully. Your Mr Hamilton assured me, and Maria's mother, that she would be educated and supported during her training! She's in a foreign country where she knows no one! You've allowed her to wander off, abandoning years of education and hard work. I shall report you to the authorities if you don't provide me with her contact details this minute.'

'Like I said, Mr Hudson, I'm sorry, but I feel obliged to respect Maria's decision. I'm happy to get a message to her and explain that you wish to make contact, but it's for her to decide what she wants to do.'

Hudson raises a warning finger at Charles. 'Now, you look here —'

'No, Mr Hudson! I'm sorry, but you're going to have to leave. I understand you're upset and concerned for Maria's well-being. But I've no reason to assume she's in any danger at all. She's living her life, in the way she wants. And as for the suggestion that she knows no one, you're quite wrong. She's made a lot of new friends, we among them. But you really can't come into our home, shouting and making threats like this.'

'Friends?' asks Hudson scornfully. 'You mean beatniks and hippies.'

Charles does not reply.

There is a pause. Hudson looks from Charles to Sally. Sally looks apologetic, but she agrees with Charles.

Charles takes a step forward, ushering the irate man towards the staircase. For a moment it seems as if Hudson will stand his ground, but then he whirls round angrily and stomps back up the steps. He strides to the front door, opens it himself and closes it behind him with a bang.

Charles and Sally follow him into the hallway.

'There goes Mr Dominic Hudson —' starts Sally.

'The diplomat,' completes Charles.

Sally laughs quietly.

'But,' she says, more seriously, 'if he's not paying her rent, how's she managing? Do you think she's earning enough to make ends meet?'

Charles frowns anxiously. 'That's a really good point. And I don't know. I don't think there's a telephone at her house, but I'll get a message to her via Ronnie Scott's.'

CHAPTER THIRTY-TWO

'Sharpe? Is that you?'

It is almost eight o'clock in the evening and Robin Sharpe is still at his desk. The police left the day before and, a week after the garage was forcibly closed, there is now a mountain of paperwork — sales and purchase orders, service files, letters from HP companies — to get through. The premises were closed down in the space of five minutes and every person present arrested and taken for questioning. Sharpe was barely allowed time to get his coat. The search made even more mess and only now, after a day of tidying up, is the place almost back to normal. The smell of fresh paint and new carpet are reassuring, a promise of orderliness and business to come once the crisis is over.

It is unusual for the telephone to ring this late and more unusual still for someone to come through on his direct number. Unless Gloria has forgotten to do it, calls at this hour should be routed direct to the answering service.

'Yes?' he says.

'It's me.'

Sharpe becomes suddenly still as he recognises Reggie Kray's voice. He lowers his pen and sits back in his seat.

'Yes, Mr Kray.'

'I ain't calling about the raid. I'm calling about something special. I need a van for Saturday week. It's got to be reliable; it can't go breaking down, got it? And it's got to be anonymous, no signage, nothing like that. Can you arrange that?'

'I've got two or three that match that description on the forecourt. Do you want to borrow one of those?' asks Sharpe.

'Borrow? No. You won't be getting it back.'

Sharpe does not answer for a moment.

'Are you saying that … there should be no connection … with the business?' he asks.

'You got it. I'll tell you where to take it in good time. You'll leave it there the night before, right, put the keys on top of the rear nearside wheel, and walk away, okay?'

'You want me to do this personally? Can't I get one of the drivers to —'

'You're doing it. No one else. And no one else to know. Do you understand me?'

Sharpe sighs, but answers quickly.

'Yes, Mr Kray. I understand you.'

'Oh, and no windows.'

'Sorry?'

'The van. No windows in the back. It's moving something … valuable. Can't have anyone looking in. Got that?'

'Yes.'

'Good. I'll be in touch.'

The dialling tone purrs as Kray hangs up.

Sharpe walks round his desk, goes to the window and gazes out over the forecourt.

Two of the three small vans at the back, just inside the chain-link fence, would meet Kray's description, but all of them have gone through the business's books. Sharpe doesn't know what Kray's purpose is with the vehicle — although he could guess — but whatever it is, he won't allow it to be traced back to Sharpe's Luxury Motors.

This is how the Krays work. They ask a little, then a little more, then a lot more. Soon you find they've secured your silence and complicity for whatever they demand. By then you're in too deep. Walking away is no longer possible, and running to the police is inimical to continued breathing.

Sharpe shakes his head and sighs deeply. He slips off his jacket and tie and hangs them on the hook on the back of his office door. Then he bends to the bottom shelf of a metal cabinet and retrieves his overalls. He tests his fingers — no grease — and remembers that he had them washed a couple of months back, after they were last used.

He slips them on over his trousers and crosses to the perforated hardboard that covers most of the back wall. Of the sixty sets of keys which usually hang here, representing every vehicle on the company's books, only a handful remain. The rest are in the possession of the police. Luckily, those still hanging here include the half dozen oldest of the stock, including the vans; the stock the police considered unsaleable.

Sharpe selects a key, pockets it and walks through the showroom towards the workshop. He hits the main lights and after a pause they reluctantly flicker to life.

He pulls on a pair of gloves as he crosses the workshop towards the metal benches and drawers housing the tools. It takes him no time to find what he seeks, an angle grinder. He examines the disc carefully and decides that it is still new enough for his task.

Now he will drive one of the vans into the workshop, close the doors carefully against prying eyes, and grind the vehicle identity numbers off the several places where the police might look for them. Then he will make up false registration plates, ensure they look suitably grubby, and substitute them for those on the vehicle, placing the genuine ones in his bag to be taken home and disposed of safely elsewhere. Finally, he will place a "Sold" sign on the van's dashboard and wipe down every inch of her to remove any tell-tale fingerprints.

Then, once the "dirty" work is finished, he will return to the office, change back out of his overalls, wash his hands carefully, and sit at his desk to create a false paper trail. With luck, before he leaves for the night, the company files will demonstrate that during the previous month the van was sold for cash to a man whom, it subsequently appears, must have given a false name. Not the usual files, of course — the police seized all of those — but Sharpe has an idea to overcome that too. He will crumple and dirty this document and slide it behind the heavy pre-war filing cabinet where it can be "discovered" in due course, if and when questions are asked.

As long as he is methodical, by the time he extinguishes the lights in the office and sets the alarm for the night, it should be impossible to trace the vehicle back to him or to the company. For the last few months, perhaps for the first time in his life, despite the existence of his new business partners and this recent setback, Robin Sharpe feels in control of his life. He will allow nothing, nothing at all, to destroy that. He has sacrificed too much; he has gone too far.

CHAPTER THIRTY-THREE

Charles Holborne is an extremely happy man.

He was only able to find a ticket for one match, just one, but his stars must have aligned, because of all the matches — bar the final, of course, where disaster could still lie in wait — this was the one to attend. Everyone agrees that the match they've just witnessed, England's semi-final against Portugal, was the best match of the tournament so far, and a classic. Two well-matched teams and a game conducted with perfect sportsmanship on both sides. Charlton played a blinder and scored both of England's goals, the second in particular a thing of absolute beauty, rifled high into the net from twenty-five yards out. The quality of play and the result were only slightly tarnished by England conceding their first goal of the entire tournament, seven minutes from the end, but to Charles even that seemed appropriate. Eusébio, Portugal's genius of a striker, was in tears at the end of the game and deserved a consolation prize. He'd have that goal to take home to Benfica, together with his stunning four-goal performance against North Korea in the quarter-finals at Goodison, scored after the Koreans had rushed into a three-goal lead.

And now, the final!

Could it be that, for the first time in the history of the nation which gave the sport to the world, England might just win the World Cup?

Although Charles went to the match alone — the single ticket had miraculously found its way to him through numerous hands after its original purchaser broke his leg falling off a scaffold two days earlier — he is now chatting and laughing with the other fans on the Metropolitan line tube train as if he had known them all his life.

In a way, he has. These are the sort of men and boys, and some women, with whom Charles used to stand every week on the freezing terraces at the Boleyn Ground, Upton Park, to watch West Ham United. He knows them. While they may support different clubs and, on another day, Charles's love affair with the Hammers might have led to some good-natured (sometimes less than good-natured) banter from supporters of Chelsea, Arsenal or Tottenham, this evening they are united in their admiration for Bobby Moore, captain of both West Ham and England, Jackie Charlton of Leeds United and Nobby Stiles of Manchester United, whose marking of Eusébio was so crucial to England's success.

Charles would be astonished to know that a mere three carriages further down the packed tube train, also engaged in a great deal of laughter and camaraderie, is the man whose continued existence he has been desperate to prove for several months. Frank Marshall, his ridiculous false beard mostly hidden by an England scarf, is on his way back to Acton with his minders, having watched the same match.

Marshall's high spirits carry him all the way back to Mags Meyer's front door and he's still gabbling, talking through the game in tedious detail, as he enters the living room. His stride and words falter simultaneously.

'Ronnie?' he says.

For a second he has mistaken the Kray twin sitting in the armchair awaiting him, but as soon as the man moves, he sees that it is in fact Reggie. Not all members of the Firm can tell them apart immediately, but Marshall can; he has known them since he was a boy.

'Good match?' asks Kray.

'Great,' replies Marshall, but his voice is flat.

'No problems?' Kray asks of Dixon, who has followed Marshall into the room.

The Scot shakes his head and goes directly to the kitchen to put on the kettle.

'Well, Frank, I've some good news,' says Kray cheerfully.

'Where's Ronnie?' asks Marshall.

'He's still not well. But he's written you a letter. Here.'

Kray holds out an envelope, which Marshall takes excitedly.

The huge man perches on the arm of the couch which tips alarmingly at the assault, and tears open the envelope. Two sheets of paper covered in handwriting are extracted. Marshall leans with his elbows on his knees, the letter held between both hands.

A deep furrow of concentration appears on his forehead as his lips move wordlessly. Kray waits patiently. Marshall's reading is slow and laborious and the letter, which the brothers crafted together, is complex, containing as it does a lengthy series of outright lies.

It starts, however, with a truth: Ronnie has been ill, it says, under a lot of stress, and Doc Blasker has ordered several weeks of rest. However, despite resting, Ronnie has not been idle. He has acquired a country house and is on the verge of beginning his new life as a squire in the far reaches of Essex. The house has been prepared and Ronnie will be moving there on Friday. He cordially invites Frank to join him. A lovely bedroom is waiting and Ronnie expresses the hope that Frank will make the place his home. There, he will be safe; they'll play billiards on the new table, swim in the pool and go hunting and walking in the countryside. He can even join Ronnie in learning to ride a horse. Frank is to be an indispensable part of the household, Ronnie's head of security and personal confidant.

Reggie Kray watches Marshall's face change as it dawns on him that his every wish has been granted. It's as if a light has been illuminated inside the big man's heavy, handsome face. Marshall always said he was Ronnie's special friend; that he alone in the Firm (except, perhaps Reggie) understood him; that he was prepared to serve him in any way he could. Now, at last, his value has been recognised.

A smile plays about his moving lips as he continues to read about how Gracie and the boys will be there too, ready to begin their new lives. Ronnie signs off "my dear friend", words which Marshall reads several times in succession beneath his breath.

All is going to be well.

'You see, Frank? I told you it was all going to work out,' says Kray, standing. 'Now, you'll need to be ready Saturday morning. Okay? The van'll be here really early, before the roads start getting busy.'

Frank too is now standing, but he's not listening. He's re-reading the last few lines of the letter.

'Frank?'

Marshall finally looks up. 'Saturday, Reg? I can't go Saturday.'

'It's the best time. As long as we're careful, the Filth'll be looking elsewhere, too busy with football fans.'

Marshall's mouth opens but the first attempt produces no sound. His face, so happy a moment ago, is clouding.

'I can't on Saturday! It's the final!'

'Come off it, you've been on at us non-stop to get out of here and see Ronnie. And now we've arranged it!'

'Yes, but this is the World Cup! D'you know how long I've waited for this? All me bleedin' life! Surely it can wait a coupla hours?'

'It's just a football match.'

Marshall looks at Kray as if he is speaking a foreign language, his mouth open and his head shaking in complete disbelief.

'You just don't get it,' he manages eventually. 'I'm sorry, Reg, and I do appreciate the efforts you and Ronnie've gone to, but I ain't going before the match. I've got a ticket!'

Kray opens his mouth to argue further but realises it's pointless. He sits down again, his hand massaging his forehead as he thinks.

'All the arrangements are made,' he says quietly, 'so it's got to be Saturday. But maybe…'

'Maybe what?' says Marshall, hope flickering in his childlike face.

'Well, maybe we could pick you up, keep you outta sight 'til just before kick-off, and pick you up again after.'

'Yeah, yeah! That'd work! That'd be brilliant!'

'You'd be in the van for quite a few hours —'

'That's fine! I don't mind that.'

'And then, after the match, head off for Essex.'

'Perfect!'

'Okay,' says Kray, standing again, this time with a smile. 'That'll still work. Make sure you clear out everything you have, okay, because you won't be coming back here again.'

'Sure. What about Louise?'

He drops his voice to speak confidentially, but everyone in the house can still hear him.

'She's a nice girl, Reg. You'll make sure she's all right, won't you?'

'Course I will,' replies Kray. 'She'll be looked after.'

'She'll never talk,' assures Frank. 'I guarantee it.'

'I'm sure you're right. Okay, if we're all settled, I gotta make tracks.'

Kray moves towards the hallway. Mags, waiting by the front door, has been listening. Kray leans his head towards the little market trader.

'Make yourself scarce. Don't be here after tomorrow afternoon. We'll clean up.'

Mags frowns. 'But I live 'ere. How long for?'

'A week or two. You've got a sister in Southend, yeah? Go there.'

'Whatever you say, Reg.'

CHAPTER THIRTY-FOUR

'Have you seen my notebook?' calls Charles from the back bedroom, the one he uses as a study.

It's the day of Sharpe's appeal and Charles's bags are packed, by the front door and ready to go, except for the fact that he can't find his blue counsel's notebook.

'I've no idea,' shouts Sally from two floors below.

'I'll bet you're using it for a shopping list,' says Charles as he runs out of the study and down the flights of stairs into the kitchen, where Sally is packing her own bag.

'What was that?' she says.

Charles doesn't answer but opens, inspects and closes each of the three drawers in the kitchen dresser in turn, without success.

'I am not using it for shopping lists,' says Sally.

'You heard me, then?'

'Yes, I did. And I only did that once when, you'll recall, you removed the notepad from the kitchen.'

Charles comes to a halt in the centre of the room.

'Fuck knows where it is, then,' he concludes.

'Have you looked in Maria's room?'

The spare bedroom has been known as "Maria's room" ever since she stayed with them.

'No. Why?'

'There was one up there on the dressing table. It's been there since she left.'

'Great!' says Charles, and he runs back upstairs again, his feet thundering on the wooden staircases.

He returns a minute later, a notebook clutched in his hand.

'Thank you. Well spotted. Are you ready?' he asks, picking up the red cloth bag used to transport his robes and swinging it over his shoulder.

'I'll be another five minutes or so. Need the loo.'

'Do you mind if I go? Maria's offered to help, and she's coming into Chambers first thing.'

'That's nice of her.'

'I think she's grateful to me … us. She's met the client and read the papers. And she'll be able to tell her grandchildren that her legal career ended, fully robed, in the English Court of Criminal Appeal on a murder case. We're going over the road early.'

"Going over the road" is barrister shorthand for walking across the Strand from the Temple to the Royal Courts of Justice.

'Another con?' she asks. 'Didn't you see him last night?'

Charles and Tindall did indeed visit Sharpe the night before at HM Prison Pentonville. The meeting was, in truth, more a courtesy than a legal conference as Charles required no further instructions. Sharpe would be a mere spectator at the hearing; many appellants don't even bother to exercise their right to attend.

Sharpe offered no explanation of why he was not transported south in time for the bail application, but Charles didn't press the issue. It was obvious that his client's mental state had declined dramatically since they met in Durham. Sharpe refused to speak and made no eye contact; he merely sat in front of his lawyers in the tiny conference and wept silently for half an hour.

'I'm concerned about him,' explains Charles. 'I'm not even sure he's fit to instruct us, to be honest, not that we need further instructions.'

'You get off, then,' says Sally. 'And tread carefully with Maria. We don't know how things have been resolved with her father.'

She approaches him and kisses him lightly on the lips. 'Good luck.'

'Thanks.'

Unknown to many, although they are principally civil courts, the Royal Courts of Justice do have a small suite of cells in the basement, and criminal appeals are usually listed in one of the few courts with connecting passages to them. Charles has led the defence team — Mr Tindall, Mrs Sharpe and Maria — to the far end of the Great Hall and installed them on a bench close to the steps leading down to the cells. At intervals he has left them to ring the bell and inquire about the arrival of his client. On every occasion he has returned empty-handed. Sharpe has not yet been produced and no one in the cells seems to know why. Their case has been progressively moved back in the list and is now due to be called at two o'clock.

'Shall I call Pentonville again?' asks Tindall.

Charles checks his watch. 'No,' he says, 'we have to go in shortly. Maria, if Mr Tindall gives you the number, could you give Pentonville another call? See if you can find someone who knows when the transport left and when it should be arriving.'

'Of course,' she replies.

Tindall hands Maria some change for the call box and a note of the number and who to ask for.

'They've listed us in the Chief's court,' says Charles.

Maria looks puzzled.

'Court 4, the Lord Chief Justice's court,' clarifies Charles.

'Got it,' she says, and runs off.

'Right, we need to go in,' says Charles. 'They'll be calling us any second.'

'What do you think's happening?' asks Mrs Sharpe, concerned.

'I doubt it's anything to worry about,' reassures Charles. 'It's usually some muddle about laying on transport, or staff rotas. Come on.'

He leads them up the stone staircase and into Court 4.

The courtroom is heaving, even busier than for the bail application. Charles pushes his way down junior counsel's bench and the rest of the team follow him, one bench higher up. Charles has barely gained his seat when the judges enter.

'All rise!'

The sound of so many people rising to their feet is like the rumble of distant thunder. The three red-robed judges file into court, take their places in front of their tall seats and, almost in unison, bow to the crowded court. The barristers, solicitors and a few of the others present reciprocate, and everyone sits.

Charles eyes the tribunal which will decide Stanley Sharpe's fate. In the centre is the senior of the three Lords Justice of Appeal, Lord Justice Linnard. To his left is his long-standing friend and colleague, Lord Justice Greenidge. To his right, the "baby" of the court, sits Mr Justice Davies. Davies was appointed to the High Court bench less than a year earlier. Although he can be expected to demonstrate some deference to his more senior colleagues, Charles knows him as a man of powerful intellect and fierce independence. He was also, in contrast to his colleagues, a criminal practitioner while at the Bar.

'Mr Holborne,' says Lord Justice Linnard. 'Is your client joining us?'

As he speaks, there is a noise from above and the hundred occupants of the court look up. The dock in Court 4 is reached by a narrow winding passageway from the cells and emerges high on the wall to the right of the judges' bench, from which the condemned man can look down on the proceedings, as if from a royal box.

A metal key turns in a lock and a head appears, wearing the uniformed peaked hat of the Prison Service. A prison escort climbs into the dock, dragging behind him Stanley Sharpe. Sharpe is attached to the escort by handcuffs. As Sharpe himself ascends the stone steps it is apparent that he is also connected, via the other wrist, to a second escort.

'Sorry, my Lord,' says the first uniformed man, plainly out of breath. 'We got held up.'

Charles rises. 'I've had no opportunity to speak to my client this morning; it appears he has only just arrived.'

'Do you need to speak to him?' asks Linnard. 'We could give you fifteen minutes.'

'No, thank you, my Lord. My concern is my client's state of health. Mr Sharpe does not look at all well.'

Everyone stares upwards. Sharpe's shoulders are slumped, his arms dangle loosely by his sides and his head lolls on his chest. It looks as if, without the support from his two escorts, he'd fold up onto the floor. His eyes seem rolled back in his head.

The second escort raises a hand as if he were a schoolboy.

'Yes?' says Linnard.

'He was like this when we took charge of him, my Lord,' says the man. 'We were told he'd been sedated, but we weren't given any details.'

'There we are, Mr Holborne. That seems to be as much explanation as we shall have. What is your position?'

'May I take instructions, please, my Lord?'

'Yes, if you are quick.'

Charles turns and speaks in a low voice to Tindall and Mrs Sharpe.

'I don't like to worry you, Mrs Sharpe, but I doubt they would have sedated him unless he was violent —'

'Or, perhaps, suicidal,' adds Tindall.

'Yes,' says Charles. 'I suppose that too. The question is: proceed or seek an adjournment?'

'I thought you said he's just a spectator,' says Mrs Sharpe.

'That's right,' responds Charles, 'but I'm not used to proceeding while my client's semi-conscious. Look at him!'

As the others lift their heads, a thin line of saliva dribbles from Sharpe's slack mouth, runs down his chin and lands on his chest. He seems oblivious to it.

'Please don't put the case off!' whispers Mrs Sharpe urgently. 'He's been in a terrible way the last few weeks, in some sort of spiritual crisis. Whatever the result, he needs this to be over as soon as possible.'

'So, we press on?' asks Charles

Tindall shrugs and then nods uncertainly.

Charles turns back to face the bench. 'My Lord, we wish to proceed with the appeal. But my client is evidently in no condition even to observe the proceedings. Would it be in order for his escorts to take him down, so he might lie down in one of the cells?'

Lord Justice Linnard inclines first to his left and then to his right to seek his brethren's views.

'Yes, very well. There's no point having him here if he's just going to drool all over the furniture. Officer,' he adds, addressing one of the escorts, 'I shall require a full report as to how this prisoner came to be brought before the court in this condition, do you understand?'

'Yes, sir.'

The reporters scribble away as Sharpe is removed from the court.

'Very well,' says Linnard. 'Perhaps we can now start, Mr Holborne.'

'Thank you. My Lords, I act on behalf of the appellant and Mr Warboys QC appears on behalf of the Crown, instructed by the DPP. This is the appeal against conviction in the case of the Reverend Stanley Sharpe —'

'He's not "the Reverend Sharpe", is he?' interrupts Lord Justice Greenidge. 'He was stripped of that office on his conviction.'

Here we go. Less than five seconds in.

Charles draws a deep breath. 'No, my Lord, you are correct. He *was* Reverend Sharpe before his conviction, and if this appeal is successful he will probably be so again.'

'Let's not get ahead of ourselves,' growls Greenidge ominously.

Charles continues. 'On the ninth of February this year, Mr Sharpe was convicted of the murder of Frank Marshall. Permission to appeal out of time was granted by Lord Justice Bennett sitting as a single judge of this court, based upon the evidence at pages six to ten of your bundles. The appeal is simplicity itself. Two independent witnesses who know Frank Marshall intimately will give evidence before your Lordships that they have seen him recently, certainly after the time when the Crown say he was murdered by my client. Leave to rely on their evidence, which, by definition, was not available at the time of the trial, was given by Lord Justice Bennett —'

'When one reads the section in Archbold,' interrupts Lord Justice Greenidge again, 'it says that it must be shown that the proposed witnesses were not available to give evidence at trial. But both of these witnesses could have been called at the trial, could they not?'

'Yes, although they'd have had no evidence to give. It's our submission that that proposition in Archbold is unsupported by any authority and, at least as set out, is wrong. It is not the existence of the *witnesses*, before or since trial, that is important. It is the existence of their *evidence*. Evidence of Mr Marshall's survival *after* the trial could not, by definition, have been given at the trial.'

'Always an uphill task to demonstrate the editors of Archbold are wrong, don't you agree, Mr Holborne?' adds Lord Justice Linnard with a smile.

'I would say, my Lord, that they were not "wrong"; they merely failed to foresee our novel circumstances. I can find no authority in which the facts were the same as these, namely discovery that a murder "victim" was not actually deceased at all. We submit that had such a circumstance occurred before, the editors of Archbold would have qualified their analysis.'

'Hmm,' grunts Greenidge unsympathetically, but the Lords Justices seem to have nothing further to say at this juncture, and Charles is allowed to continue.

'I propose, with your leave, simply to call the two witnesses. If after cross-examination your Lordships consider their evidence to be credible, and would probably have affected the verdict of the jury, the appeal must be allowed.'

The court falls silent as Charles awaits permission to call his first witness. Linnard leans into Greenidge to whisper something to him. For a moment, it appears that he is not going to consult the junior judge, Davies, but after waiting a few seconds Davies himself turns and says something *sotto voce* to Linnard.

'Very well,' says Linnard. 'Call your first witness.'

'I call Judy Bishop,' says Charles.

The usher slips out of court and everyone inside hears Judy Bishop's name being called. After a short pause, the door opens again and a young woman enters.

This is the first time Charles has laid eyes on the former girlfriend of Frank Marshall, and he is immediately struck by her resemblance to Gracie Marshall or, to be more precise, to Leonora, Gracie Williamson as she once was. As might be expected for a former Windmill Girl still in her twenties, she is slim and tall, with long legs. Her hair is blonde and fashionably short, and she is well turned out in a pale blue trouser suit. As she descends the steps from the door and passes the end of Charles's bench, Charles thinks he detects the remaining shadows of bruising on her cheek and under one eye. He hopes the young woman will turn towards him and Tindall so he can give her an encouraging smile, but she keeps her eyes fixed rigidly ahead as she descends. She is escorted across the well of the court and up into the witness box.

'Religion?' asks the usher.

'C of E,' replies Miss Bishop, her voice very quiet.

The usher offers her the Bible, which she takes in one hand, and the card bearing the oath, which she takes in the other. She reads the oath off the card in a faint voice without halting and hands both Bible and card back to the usher.

When Charles speaks she seems startled and looks around to find the source of the voice.

'Your name is, I believe, Judy Bishop?'

'Yes.'

'Miss Bishop, I would be grateful if you would keep your voice up so everyone can hear you. Please could you give the court your address?'

'Thirty Duckett Road, Haringey, north four.'

'And your profession, please?'

'I trained as a dancer. I'm presently unemployed.'

'Did you ever work at the Windmill Club in London?'

'I have worked there.'

'And while you were working there, did you meet a man with whom you subsequently formed an attachment?'

'I worked there for several years and went out with a number of men during that time.'

Charles experiences a first flicker of concern. Miss Bishop might just be nervous, but on the other hand she knows full well who she is there to identify. Her non-committal answer is troubling.

'Was there a particular man with whom you recently went away to Weston-super-Mare?'

'Yes.'

'By what name did you know that man?'

'He said he was Freddie Markham.'

'Thank you. When did you first meet him?'

'In 1962.'

'What was Mr Markham's situation?'

'I don't know what you mean.'

'Well, did he say if he was married?'

'He told me he was separated from his wife.'

'Did he say what he did for a living?'

'He never told me exactly. But I gathered he worked with some nasty people. People who ran nightclubs and so on.'

'Was your relationship with him still continuing at the end of last year?'

'Yes.'

'Tell us what caused you to go to Weston-super-Mare with him.'

'He told me he needed to leave London for a while and asked me to go with him. He said he was in danger from some business associates.'

'Why did he want you to go with him?'

'He said if we posed as a couple there was less chance of him being identified.'

'Did you agree to go?'

'Yes. I was very fond of him and I didn't want him to be hurt. So I thought I should help him.'

'How long did you stay in Weston-super-Mare?'

'I don't know the exact dates. We were there before Christmas and I came back to London in March, maybe early April.'

'Did you come back together?'

'No. We'd not been getting on and there were some arguments. Freddie came and went for a while, and then he didn't come back at all. I waited for a few days and then thought I'd come back to London, as it seemed the relationship was over.'

'Were you aware that, at the end of last year, the Reverend Stanley Sharpe was accused of murdering a man called Frank Marshall?'

'Not at the time. I don't read the newspapers much, especially not crime reports.'

'And subsequently?'

'After I came back to London, that man sitting behind you came to the house and made me aware of it. And the police did.'

'Were you shown a picture of Frank Marshall?'

'Yes.'

Charles turns. Maria is now behind him and ready, a sheaf of enlarged head and shoulders photographs of Marshall held out to Charles. Charles winks at her and takes the glossy photos.

'Usher,' he says, 'there are five photographs here. Please ensure that their Lordships have one each, that one is given to my learned friend and one to the witness.'

Charles waits for the photographs to be distributed.

'Now, Miss Bishop, please look at that photograph. That is a picture of Frank Marshall, the supposed victim of the Reverend Stanley Sharpe. Do you recognise it?'

There is a moment's hesitation before she answers. 'Yes.'

Her intonation rises at the end of the word as if she's asking a question. The flutter of anxiety in Charles's stomach repeats, stronger this time.

'And who is portrayed in that photograph?' he asks.

'It's … Mr Marshall, isn't it? The man who was killed?'

'It is Mr Marshall, yes. But is it also the man with whom you went to Weston-super-Mare?'

This time the pause lengthens. And lengthens.

'I'm … not sure. Possibly. There is definitely a likeness. But … you know, I'm not sure, now I see it again. Actually, now I look really hard, I don't think it is the same man. No, it's not. There's something different about the eyes. And maybe the hair.' She looks up at Charles, her face blank.

Charles's heart is thundering in his chest, but he smiles as if the answer was exactly what he was expecting.

'Did you give a statement to the man sitting behind me, Mr Tindall, a couple of weeks ago?'

'Yes.'

'Please have a look at this document,' says Charles, and he hands a copy to the usher for transmission to the witness box.

'Could I ask you to read that, to yourself?'

He watches as her eyes skim left to right, left to right, until she has reached the end of the document.

'Yes?' she says, looking up again.

'Having read that statement, would you like to reconsider your answer?'

'N-no, I don't think so.'

'This time last week, Miss Bishop, you gave a statement saying you were sure that the two men were the same.'

Warboys leaps to his feet to object, but Lord Justice Linnard raises a hand like a policeman stopping traffic.

'Now, stop there, Mr Holborne,' he says. 'You're not allowed to cross-examine your own witness. She says she is not sure of the identification. That's her evidence.'

'I apply to treat Miss Bishop as a hostile witness so I can put to her, in terms, what she said in her sworn statement,' says Charles.

'No,' intervenes Lord Justice Greenidge firmly. 'This witness is not hostile to you within the authorities. She hasn't come up to proof, and you may not be happy with her evidence, but to fail to identify two people as the same man is not "hostile".'

Linnard leans over to discuss the point quietly with Mr Justice Davies, who nods.

'No,' concludes Linnard. 'We're all agreed. Miss Bishop isn't even remotely "hostile". It seems to me she is simply doing her duty to answer your questions carefully, a matter of particular importance in an identification case. Your application is refused. Do you have any further questions for her?'

Charles pauses and in the interval notices a glance flick from Judy Bishop to the DPP's team sitting across the court. In response, DCI Wheatley gives the most minute nod of his head. Charles turns and bends to speak to Tindall.

'She's been nobbled!'

'By Wheatley?'

'Or whoever beat her up. But I can't see any point continuing with her.'

Tindall nods reluctantly.

Charles turns back to the bench. 'No, thank you, my Lord.'

'Cross-examination?' Linnard asks of Warboys.

The Great Toad barely rises from his seat to answer.

'No thank you, my Lord,' he says cheerfully.

'You are free to go, Miss Bishop,' says Linnard with a smile. 'Thank you for your evidence. Your next witness, please, Mr Holborne.'

'Mrs Gracie Marshall,' says Charles.

Charles watches as the usher climbs the stairs next to him and leaves court. He hears Gracie's name being called and then notices someone has slipped in at the back of the court and is standing half-hidden by the overflow of journalists. The white-blond hair and piercing blue eyes are unmistakable: Robin Sharpe.

The door opens again and Gracie enters. She has clearly made an effort with her clothes and her make-up and she looks a decade younger than when Charles last saw her, as she packed up to leave the Stratford Nissen hut. She wears white gloves and a little pillbox hat at a jaunty angle, and Charles wonders if she's had her hair coloured, as this time he can see no grey in it.

She gives the oath in a steady voice, folds her hands on the rail of the witness box and waits patiently.

'What is your name, please, madam?' asks Charles.

'Gracie Marshall.'

'Your address, please?'

'165A Farmers Road, Leyton.'

'Your occupation?'

'I've just started part-time work at the Labour Exchange in Stratford as a clerk. Otherwise, I look after my two young children.'

'In front of you there should be a photograph of a man. Could you look at it, please?'

Gracie picks up the photograph left there by Judy Bishop and studies it.

'Yes?'

'Do you recognise that man?' asks Charles.

'Of course. It's my husband, Frank.'

'When did you last see him?'

'About four weeks ago.'

'In what circumstances?'

'I was staying in temporary accommodation in Stratford with the boys and he just turned up one evening.'

'How long were you with him on that occasion?'

'About half an hour.'

'Where were you, exactly? Were you inside or outside?'

'We were inside. I made him a drink and we talked. He also played with the boys for a while.'

'Did you have any doubts that it was him?'

'Of course not. He's my husband.'

'Did he explain where he'd been over the last months, while he was supposedly dead?'

Warboys leaps to his feet, moving surprisingly fast for a man of his bulk.

'I object to that question, my Lords. My learned friend is inviting this witness to give hearsay evidence.'

'No, my Lords,' replies Charles. 'I am not putting forward any answer given by Marshall as evidence of the truth. Exactly the opposite, in fact.'

'You may continue, Mr Holborne,' says Linnard.

'Well, Mrs Marshall, what did your husband say?'

'He said his life was in danger and he had to lie low. Pretend to be dead.'

Charles takes a deep breath and begins to relax a little. Things are beginning to get back on track.

'How did that conversation end?'

'He said he wanted us to get back together again and that we'd have a new start. He gave me some cash and said he'd be back in a few days. We'd start living together again, with the boys.'

'Is that what happened?'

'No. He didn't get in touch again. I tried to speak to his friends and work colleagues, but no one knew where he was.'

'Did you form any conclusion about where he was?' asks Charles.

'Well, I saw a statement from that woman.'

'Which woman?'

Gracie nods towards the door of the court. 'The one who gave evidence just now. Judy something. She said she'd been off with him at the seaside and I thought, well, Frank's probably gone off with her again. Or perhaps someone else.'

'Did that affect your mind about what was likely to happen in the future?'

'Yes. I didn't believe him anymore. He lied to me for all that time, letting me and the boys think he was dead, when all the time he was … with someone else. I decided I'd had enough.'

Charles pauses, allowing the pens of the three judges to catch up with the evidence. Then he asks his final question.

'How sure are you that the man who came to your accommodation in Stratford and spoke to you was Frank Marshall?'

'One hundred per cent. I'd know my husband anywhere. He sat with me for half an hour, chatted to the kids and made us all sorts of promises. There's no doubt. Frank is alive and well, somewhere.'

'Thank you. Please remain there.'

Warboys rises to his feet, hauls his massive gown, which has slipped down somewhat, over his shoulders, clasps his hands behind his back and, looking not at the witness but at some feature of the wall above his head, asks his first question.

'Mrs Marshall, you were once a dancer at the Windmill Club, Windmill Street, Soho, is that right?' he croaks.

Gracie pulls a face and shakes her head sorrowfully. Her expression eloquently says that she anticipated this line of attack and it is all so predictable.

'Yes. Many years ago, before the boys were born.'

'You were dancing there, I believe, before you even met your husband?'

'That's right.'

'Is that where you met Stanley Sharpe?'

The effect on Gracie is as if someone stuck her fingers into a live electrical socket. She tenses and her eyes open wide. *That* was not a question she anticipated.

Charles feels someone tugging the back of his gown and he turns. Tindall leans forward.

'Where's this come from?' he whispers.

'I don't know,' replies Charles, 'but I have an awful suspicion I know where it's going.'

'Er…' stammers Gracie, 'I … I met a lot of people there. I worked there for years.'

'And one of those people was Stanley Sharpe.'

'If you say so.'

'I do say so. You know Stanley Sharpe very well, don't you, Mrs Marshall, because he used to be your pimp?'

'That's nonsense!' replies Gracie, outraged. 'Are you saying I'm a prostitute?' She turns to the judges. 'Is he allowed to say that?'

Lord Justice Greenidge answers smoothly. 'Just answer the questions, if you please, Mrs Marshall.'

'I'm saying that during your professional life, you have acted as a prostitute at the disposition of Stanley Sharpe.'

'That's a lie,' says Gracie.

Charles notes that her eyes are dancing around the courtroom looking for a safe haven but, wherever they land, she manages to avoid looking at him.

'Do you deny that on the seventh of January nineteen-fifty you were convicted at the Bow Street Magistrates' Court of theft?'

'No. But that was a mistake.'

Charles rises.

'I object to this line of questioning, my Lords. This is an identification case. Whether this lady has a conviction for theft sixteen years ago is irrelevant.'

'I'm impeaching this witness's credibility,' replies Warboys confidently, 'and I'm entitled to do so on the basis of a previous conviction for an offence of dishonesty. However, not only will I be suggesting that her evidence on oath should not be trusted, but I intend to establish a connection with Stanley Sharpe which provides a motive for her perjured evidence today.'

'You may continue, Mr Warboys,' says Lord Justice Linnard.

Warboys does so.

'You were found guilty of stealing five pounds from the wallet of a man named Byng at the Savoy Hotel.'

'Like I said, it wasn't theft.'

'Did you take five pounds from Mr Byng's wallet?'

Gracie looks troubled but she does answer. 'Yes. But he owed it to me.'

'For what?'

Gracie looks down at her feet and this time does not answer.

'For what?' repeats Warboys in a loud voice, now staring hard at her.

Still Gracie does not answer.

'You took five pounds from Mr Byng's wallet because you had agreed to have sexual intercourse with him for that sum, did you not?'

Charles hears Tindall whisper 'Jesus!' under his breath behind him and feels another yank on the back of his gown.

'Did you know about this?' he asks Charles.

Charles turns slightly in his seat and shakes his head.

'Not specifically, and nothing at all about the conviction,' he mutters.

'No … I mean, yes,' stumbles Gracie, 'but he was a gentleman friend. I'd been seeing him for a while … he wasn't…'

'He wasn't a client?' suggests Warboys.

Gracie shakes her head.

'But you still charged him for intercourse?'

'It wasn't like that. I was struggling, and he used to take me out for a meal every now and then. He would always give me something to help me out, like with the rent, or food. He always did. But this time he forgot…'

'So you took the money without asking?'

Gracie nods shame-facedly.

'While in the hotel room?'

'Yes.'

'And then you left without waking your client?'

'I told you — he wasn't a client. Not the way you mean.'

'Mr Byng was at that time, before his dismissal, a civil servant working in a senior position in the War Office. How did you come to meet him?'

'I … I don't remember.'

'Let me refresh your memory, then, Mrs Marshall. You were introduced to him by Stanley Sharpe at the Windmill Theatre, were you not?'

'I don't know. Maybe.'

'So you do now admit that you know Stanley Sharpe?' crows Warboys, transferring his gaze to Lord Justice Linnard.

'I know lots of people. I can't remember if I knew Stanley Sharpe back in nineteen-fifty,' she answers desperately.

'Usher,' says Warboys, holding out a sheaf of papers, 'please hand this document to the witness. My Lords, this is a copy of the criminal record of Mr Sharpe which is already in your papers starting at page seventeen of your bundles. Now, Mrs Marshall, please turn to the second page of that document and look for the date of August nineteen fifty-two in the left-hand margin. Tell me when you have got it.'

'Yes, I see it.'

'Now, read across with me from the eighteenth of August nineteen fifty-two. It says: Inner London Sessions, a conviction for demanding money with menaces contrary to the Larceny Act nineteen-sixteen, known in general parlance as blackmail. Do you see that?'

'Yes.'

'Six such counts. Now I have the sentencing remarks of the judge who sent Sharpe to prison on that occasion, which I am happy to show you if you need me to refresh your memory. One of the offences was the demanding with menaces from a

Mr Byng arising out of information passed to Mr Sharpe by a woman named Gracie Williamson. What was your maiden name please, Mrs Marshall?'

Gracie's lips move but no sound can be heard.

'Louder, please, Mrs Marshall.'

'Gracie Williamson.'

'You were set up by Mr Sharpe to meet Mr Byng as a — let's not use the word if you object to it; instead, let us instead say "escort" — and thereafter Sharpe would use the encounter and anything you learned from it for blackmail.'

Gracie shakes her head.

'It wasn't like that. I liked Frederick … Mr Byng … he was good to me. The five pounds was a mistake. I knew if I asked him he'd say yes, but he was asleep … as for getting information, you make me out as if I was some sort of spy. But he never told me any secrets.'

'But the fact of your liaison with Mr Byng, a married man … *that*, Mrs Marshall, was passed to Mr Sharpe, wasn't it?'

Gracie does not answer. Finally, she looks up at Charles with an apologetic expression.

'Yes,' she says quietly.

There is a long pause, finally broken by Lord Justice Linnard. 'Is that a convenient moment, Mr Warboys?' he says, looking up at the clock.

Charles follows his gaze and realises that it is only a couple of minutes before four o'clock.

'I have one or two further questions, my Lord,' replies Warboys, 'so if the court would consent to sit until, perhaps, five past, I think I shall finish in time.'

'Yes, very well.'

'Now, Mrs Marshall, until this afternoon, did anyone else, other than Mr Sharpe, know you'd been an … escort?'

'It was only that once,' she says, dabbing the tears now emerging from her eyes. 'I twisted me ankle so I couldn't dance. If you didn't dance, you didn't get paid. It was a terrible time. I was starving.'

'Answer the question, Mrs Marshall! Did anyone other than Mr Sharpe know that you'd acted in this way?'

'Well, the police knew, as you've shown me that document … but otherwise, no. I was ashamed. I never told no one.'

'Did Mr Sharpe put pressure on you to give evidence today?'

Gracie looks up sharply.

'No, of course not. I ain't seen him in years!'

'You don't have to have seen him personally, though, do you? Did anyone at all approach you and ask you to give this evidence?'

'Absolutely not. Never.'

'Nobody approached you and offered you money to give this false evidence?'

'No. It's not false.'

'Nobody approached you and threatened that unless you gave evidence that you'd seen your husband, the story of your acting as an escort, having sexual intercourse for money, would come out?'

'No.'

'That would be precisely Mr Sharpe's method, would it not? He has convictions for blackmail exactly like this.'

Charles rises swiftly to forestall an answer.

'This witness cannot be asked to comment on Mr Sharpe's criminal methods. That is a matter for my learned friend's closing arguments.'

'Yes,' says Lord Justice Linnard, 'you've made your point, Mr Warboys, and you may make it again in your submissions, but I don't think it is for this witness to pass comment.'

'Very well, my Lord. Mrs Marshall, it is my unpleasant task to suggest that you have made up the story of seeing your husband recently. You have told us a pack of lies.'

'No, that's not true. I did see him, he came to the house. You can ask the boys.'

'The Crown shall not be asking two small boys to give evidence,' says Warboys. 'I further suggest that you did it at the behest of Stanley Sharpe, either because he had a hold over you or because he offered you money.'

'No. That never happened. Frank came round and said he'd been in hiding. He left a football programme with the boys and promised me we were going to get back together. I did see him.'

'Thank you, Mrs Marshall. And thank you, my Lord, for allowing me to finish.' Warboys resumes his seat with a satisfied grunt.

Lord Justice Linnard addresses Charles.

'Mr Holborne, you can close your case Monday morning at half-past ten. Mr Sharpe shall remain in custody.'

'All rise!'

CHAPTER THIRTY-FIVE

Charles sets Tindall the task of finding an available conference room and he heads straight for the cells. The pattern of the day is repeated: Sharpe is not there. The custody officer informs him that Sharpe fell asleep and couldn't be roused, so he was returned to the prison hospital wing. Charles insists that the officer rings HM Prison Pentonville while Charles waits.

When Charles emerges from the cells, Maria is waiting for him and she takes him to the conference room.

Littering the table are several used polystyrene cups, many with cigarette butts floating in them, and a well-thumbed newspaper, bearing testament to a long, boring day for someone. The room smells of stale food and stale smoke. Mrs Sharpe is stacking the used cups to make space on the table and Tindall is slumped in a chair. Maria closes the door behind them and stands with her back to it.

Charles also sits. He takes off his wig and scratches his scalp. He hates the ancient horsehair headpiece and the way it makes his head itch.

'I've spoken to Pentonville,' he reports. 'Stanley's okay. He's in the hospital wing, awake now, although still drowsy. I'm sorry to tell you, Mrs Sharpe, but he tried to commit suicide this morning.'

She gasps, and her hand goes to her mouth. 'What … how?'

'They found him hanging in his cell.'

'Oh my God!' she whispers.

'The idiots got him down unharmed, and then sedated him as he was leaving. Anyway, he'll stay there for the present so they can keep an eye on him. I suggest we don't ask for his production on Monday.'

'I agree,' says Mrs Sharpe.

'Are we sunk, Charles?' asks Tindall.

Charles nods. 'I'm afraid so. I don't think today could've gone any worse.'

'Mrs Marshall stuck to her story,' says Mrs Sharpe hopefully.

'Yes, she did. But her evidence is useless.'

'She shouldn't have lied about not knowing Sharpe,' says Tindall angrily.

'No, she shouldn't,' replies Charles, 'but even without the lie, the fact of the connection with Sharpe — and his potential hold over her — wound her fatally. If only she'd told me the full story!'

'I can't blame her, entirely,' says Mrs Sharpe. 'She's obviously deeply ashamed of what she did, and if the poor girl was reduced to doing … *that* … to keep body and soul together…'

Charles looks up at her in surprise and with some admiration.

'Well,' she continues, 'it's easy to judge, isn't it? But powerless women have been forced into prostitution since … well, forever. One cannot blame them.'

'Well, the bottom line is, we're sinking. I'll do the best I can on Monday, but I'm afraid you need to resign yourself to it. I don't see how we can win this appeal.'

'It just seems so unfair that something from Stanley's past, for which he has already paid, should come back to haunt him like this,' says Mrs Sharpe.

'I agree. I think one of us should go and see him over the weekend,' says Charles to Tindall.

'Yes. I'll go.'

'I'm very sorry, Mrs Sharpe,' says Charles.

'It's not your fault.'

'I think it is, to some extent,' replies Charles. 'I should've pressed Gracie further when she first hinted at having been on the game. But I had no idea it had any connection to Sharpe. Or that such ancient history could affect her evidence. It seemed indelicate, even cruel, to ask.'

'Don't blame yourself,' says Mrs Sharpe. 'If you'd known she had a previous conviction or that she'd been an escort, what could you have done about it? You'd either have to call her, and Mr Warboys would've asked the same questions, or not call her at all. It would have made no difference to the outcome.'

'Thank you; that's very … Christian of you.'

She smiles at Charles.

'I'll see if I can think of anything over the weekend,' he says.

'And I'll pray,' says Mrs Sharpe, as if it were an entirely practical step, like doing further legal research.

Tindall escorts Mrs Sharpe out towards the Strand, leaving Charles sitting morosely. When she realises that he's not going to get up immediately, Maria joins him at the table.

'Oh, well. You can't win them all,' he says.

'Isn't this the reverse of the coin?' asks Maria, sympathetically.

'What?'

'You told me it wasn't for us to make a decision. We had to put the story the best way we could, but then leave it to the jury. Isn't that the same for an appeal?'

'Yes, you're right of course. But it's hard when you're convinced your client's innocent and the jury, or in this case the judges, disagree. Come on,' he says, rousing himself. 'Let me buy you a coffee. Or maybe a drink, if it's not too early for you.'

'Coffee would be nice. Can we go to that place on the other side of the zebra crossing? They've some nice-looking cream cakes in the window.'

Charles grins. 'Good idea.'

He gathers together his papers.

'By the way, thank you for the use of your notebook.'

He offers her the blue counsel's notebook he took that morning from her former bedroom.

'You might as well keep it. I shan't need it,' she replies. 'Did you see my notes?'

Charles frowns and opens the front cover. There are two or three pages full of Maria's rounded handwriting.

'Oh,' he says. 'That fraudulent accounting case. No, I'd forgotten all about it. The solicitors took the papers back.'

'So my trek to Companies House was pointless after all.'

''Fraid so.'

Charles rips the first pages out of the book along their perforations.

'Just a sec,' intervenes Maria. 'Don't you want that either?'

She points at the last torn page. Under a bold line marking off the previous notes there are some additional names and dates.

'You asked me to look up that company; the one where you bought your car.'

Charles reads the notes and suddenly his eyes open wide.

'This is the research you did on Sharpe's Luxury Motors Limited?' he asks urgently.

'Yes.'

'I don't believe it!' Charles exclaims. 'Quick! Run out to the front and see if Tindall and Mrs Sharpe are still there! Bring them back if you can!'

A few minutes later Maria reappears at the door, breathless but triumphant.

'I got them! Just as they were getting into a cab!'

'Well done.'

It takes Mrs Sharpe another thirty seconds to arrive, followed immediately by Tindall.

'Sorry to call you back,' says Charles, 'but I just stumbled on something. Sit down, everyone, this will take a few minutes.'

Charles allows them to settle. All of them are looking at him expectantly.

'Mrs Sharpe, did you speak to Robin today?'

'Was he here? I didn't see him.'

'Yes, he was watching from the back of the court. When did you last speak to him?'

'Not since our first conference with you. He's been very busy with his new investors. Why?'

'You know I bought a car from Robin's garage?'

'Yes?'

'I asked Maria to do a search at Companies House into Sharpe's Luxury Motors. I wasn't sure exactly what I was looking for, but I was curious about its sudden change in fortunes. There was also something that bothered me, which I needn't go into here. To be absolutely honest with you, I forgot all about it until I just saw Maria's notes.

'Mr Tindall, you need to do a full Companies House check first thing on Monday morning, please, but I'm fairly certain of what I've discovered. According to Maria's notes, Robin resigned his directorship around the time that Stanley was convicted. Two new directors were appointed in his place. The first is Alan Bruce Cooper. If he's the Alan Bruce Cooper I know, he's a strange chap, an American. He has connections both with organised crime and the American government.

Most importantly, however, he's a very close business associate of Ronnie and Reggie Kray *and* ... he's known to have an involvement in the manufacture of LSD.'

'Are you saying —' starts Mrs Sharpe, but Charles raises his hand to stop her.

'Let me finish, if you please. The second new director, the one who's now company secretary, is a man called Leslie Payne. He's also an associate of the Krays, an accountant by training.'

'Wasn't Payne involved in the Krays stealing a club or something?' asks Tindall.

'Yes. He was instrumental in them acquiring the majority interest in Esmeralda's Barn a few years ago. The point is, Mrs Sharpe, whereas one might just be a coincidence, the two together can't be.'

'What does this mean?' asks Mrs Sharpe.

'It means the Krays now control the garage. That's how it turned overnight from a loss-making, rather second-rate yard into a bright shiny new showroom with expensive classic cars.'

There is a long pause before Mrs Sharpe responds.

'I can't tell you how disappointed Stanley will be, if that's true. He hated the Krays, particularly Ronnie. But…'

'But what does it have to do with Stanley's appeal?' suggests Charles for her.

'Exactly.'

'You've given the answer yourself. Would Stanley have allowed Ronnie Kray to act as your son's backer?'

'No, never, not if he knew about it.'

'Would he have allowed the Krays to use his garage as a front for selling hard drugs?'

'Of course not.'

Charles shrugs as if the answer is obvious. 'So, Mrs Sharpe, who gains if Stanley is no longer around? If he's locked up for life?'

'Well, the Krays, obviously.'

'And?'

'Robin? You're saying Robin was party to implicating Stanley?'

'Like I said, who gains? Stanley — who Robin blames for making you unhappy — is removed from your life, and Robin gets new investors to turn around a failing business.'

Charles considers his next words carefully.

'I'm in a difficult position here, because I may have to give evidence against Robin eventually. All I can say is that I stumbled across some probable criminality regarding LSD, arising out of my buying that car, and as far as I can see, Robin was involved. So, yes, I'm afraid to say I think Robin was a party to getting Stanley out of the way. Or, if he wasn't, he knows much more than he's admitting.'

'But he'll never give evidence for us, will he?' points out Tindall. 'Admitting he knows that Marshall is still alive means admitting conspiracy to pervert the course of justice. With Ronnie and Reggie Kray, no less! That would be —' the young solicitor looks towards Mrs Sharpe nervously — 'a dangerous thing to do.'

'And in any case,' contributes Maria diffidently, 'wouldn't his evidence be weakened because, like the other witnesses, the Crown can say he has a motive for lying? Trying to save his own father?'

'Yes, Maria, that's a good point,' replies Charles. 'He'd be damaged both by his association with the Krays and by an impugnable motive. On the other hand, as admissions against interest are concerned, it's about as powerful as you can imagine. People don't admit perverting the course of justice, facing prison and crossing the Kray twins — all in one hit — unless they're telling the truth.'

'So, can we use it?' concludes Tindall.

Charles looks pointedly at Mrs Sharpe and waits.

'I can,' she says in a small voice.

Everyone else in the room turns to look at her.

'You?' asks Tindall.

'I think it's time I had an honest discussion with my son,' she says quietly.

'Thank you,' says Charles. 'I hoped you'd say that. But it has to be soon. The appeal will be rejected on Monday unless Robin's prepared to help.'

'I'll do it this evening. How do I contact you if I have any news?'

Charles writes down his home telephone number in his notebook and tears off the page. 'Call me at home,' he says.

CHAPTER THIRTY-SIX

As she told Charles, the last time Eileen Sharpe spoke to her son was at the conference in the Temple, and it did not end well. She was therefore a little surprised when Robin agreed to come to Theresa's flat, even if for only an hour or so. But then Theresa, known throughout their large Irish family as "Auntie Terry", is Robin's favourite aunt and he her favourite nephew.

Eileen feels guilty that she's not mentioned that Auntie Terry won't be in attendance, but she has no choice. She will confess on Sunday. No, she corrects herself; she'll confess now and again on Sunday.

She bustles about her sister's kitchen. It took her a while to find the best china, but it is now mostly washed and dried, ready to be laid out. Terry didn't take kindly to being asked at no notice to vacate her own flat on a Saturday morning, and the sisters almost rowed about it, but Eileen was gently insistent and eventually Terry agreed to visit one of the elderly ladies from her church. This is going to be the most difficult conversation Eileen has ever had with her son — with anyone, in fact — and she knows that her nerve would have failed her in the presence of witnesses.

Eileen stands back and surveys the table, laid for lunch for two. The inviting aroma of fish pie, Robin's favourite, drifts from the kitchen. Stanley wasn't keen on the dish, so it became Robin and Eileen's special treat when he was away "on business." After a couple of hours of cooking, Terry's lounge now smells of Robin's childhood.

The doorbell sounds its cheerful *ding-dong!* and Eileen dries her hands and, taking off her pinafore, goes to the front door. Robin stands on the threshold, a bunch of flowers in his hand.

'Hello, Mum,' he says, a little apprehensively.

She leans forward and kisses him on the cheek.

'Hello, darling. I'm afraid Auntie Terry had to go out. Something about the church. So it's just the two of us.'

'Oh, really?' he replies, disappointed. 'I was looking forward to seeing her.'

'Well, there'll be another time. Go on in.'

She closes the door and follows him.

Terry's second floor lounge is full of summer sunshine but, as ever, it is over-stuffed with furniture and her collections of fussy china ornaments. The tiled 1930s mantelpiece, the windowsills and a large display cabinet are loaded with a glazed shepherdess, horses, dogs and other small animals. Every fabric surface has its own antimacassar and the occasional tables their own doilies. It is the room of a middle-aged single woman who has always lived alone.

Eileen takes the flowers into the kitchen and Robin throws his coat over the arm of a chair. Eileen returns with warmed bowls and lays them on the table.

'Can I smell fish pie?' he asks.

Eileen laughs. 'Yes, you can, and cabbage soup the way you like it. I wanted to make it special. How are you?' she calls as she walks back to the kitchen.

'I'm all right,' he says noncommittally. 'But very busy,' he warns, 'which is why I can't stay long.'

'I understand,' she says, 'so I'll bring in the soup now and we can chat while we eat.'

Robin picks up a newspaper from the table and opens it.

'Did you read this?' he asks as his mother enters the room with a large tureen.

'What's that, dear?'

'John Lennon's interview. He reckons the Beatles are more popular than Jesus.'

'Is that what he said?'

'According to the *Evening Standard*.'

'I don't suppose Auntie Terry would approve of that. Come and sit at the table.'

They talk inconsequentially as they eat. Both are aware of the falsity of the situation. By the time they reach the main course, Eileen has started glancing up at the clock. She knows she has to take the plunge, and before Terry returns. The conversation falters, and then ceases.

'Look,' starts Robin, 'I know you want to know about the police raid, but —'

'No, I don't. Or rather, I'm happy to talk about it if you want, but I have something more important to say to you.'

'What's that?'

Eileen looks down, takes two deep breaths to steady herself, and starts. 'I think you were in court yesterday for your … dad's appeal.'

'Yes.'

'So you saw the state he was in.'

'Yes. Is he all right now?'

'You've not been to visit him, then?'

'No.'

She looks up and locks eyes with her son. 'No, Robin, he's not all right. He tried to hang himself.'

Robin Sharpe becomes very still.

'That's why he was sedated,' she says.

'Is he okay?'

'For the moment, I suppose, while they're observing him in the hospital wing. But … he's in absolute despair.'

'You think he'll try again, then?'

'Oh, yes,' she replies, as if the answer were obvious, 'I do.'

'And you want me to go and see him?'

'Well, you've not visited him once since he was sentenced, have you? He feels abandoned by … well, by everyone. And he loves you more than anyone else in the world.'

'I don't want to see him,' says Robin firmly, a tremor in his voice.

Eileen can't decide if he's angry or upset.

'Whatever you think of him, he's been a very good father to you, you know that. He loves you more than he can say. Certainly more than he ever loved me.'

Robin makes a scoffing noise. 'Did he ever love you? If so, I never saw it.'

'Yes, I think for a few years he did love me.'

'Until he started hitting you.'

Eileen pauses, gathering her strength.

'You mustn't be too quick to blame him, darling. I … I made it very difficult for him.'

'You?' Robin cries in astonishment. 'What did you do?'

Eileen lowers her head. She can no longer look at him.

'This is what I need to explain. I had an affair.'

Robin looks as if he didn't understand her words at all; as if his mother had suddenly turned into a foreigner or was speaking in tongues.

'What did you say?'

'I said I had an affair. In fact, I suppose, I'm *having* an affair.'

Robin drops his knife and fork and moves his chair back from the table sharply, as if he can only comprehend this discrepant information by viewing it from a distance. He stares at his ordinary, plain mother.

'"*Having*"? You're still seeing this … man?'

'Yes. We've been friends for over thirty years. Really ever since I realised … when I'd been with Stanley for a few months, and I'd understood … who he was, and what he did.'

At last she looks up at her son's uncomprehending face. Her expression pleads for him to understand.

'I was so young, darling! Full of romantic nonsense, bowled off my feet by this older, confident man in a smart suit and smart car! I suspected he was … a bit fly —'

'*Fly*?'

'Yes, but I could never have comprehended the reality. It was months before I began to see the truth. And *then* I thought I could change him. That's how naïve I was!'

'So?'

'I didn't know what to do. I couldn't say anything to your grandparents. I'd run away and married against their wishes and I'd never admit they'd been right. I had no one to talk to. Aunty Terry was still in Ireland then. I spent months crying and your fa… Stanley … he just got on with it. He promised me I'd never have to have anything to do with the business … he'd keep me out of it completely … I suppose he hoped I'd come round. But I was so lonely! You've got to remember, I was only a teenager. I knew nothing about the world. And then I met someone at church.'

'The man you had … you're *having* an affair with.'

'His name's Andrew. I don't think one could call it an "affair" really. Not now. He's my best friend, my companion.'

'And Dad knows about him.'

She nods. 'Yes, almost from the start.'

'And that's why he hit you?'

'No. He was very angry, of course. He tried to intimidate Andrew into not seeing me again. But he didn't hit me…'

'I saw him! I saw him hit you at least twice. When we were on holiday in Bangor when I was about five —'

'He never hit me until after I told him I was pregnant.'

Robin opens his mouth and then halts as what his mother is trying to tell him finally hits home.

'Pregnant?' he says eventually. 'With me?'

She locks eyes with him again and nods.

'So Dad … Stanley … isn't my father?'

'No,' she whispers. 'Andrew's your father.'

'How can you be sure?' he demands.

'Wait till you meet him. You're so like him, it's uncanny. Same hair, same blue eyes, even the same temperament. So after you were born, although Stanley and I lived in the same house, we agreed to have separate lives.'

'But you shared the same bedroom! For all the time I was growing up.'

'Yes. He insisted. He didn't want you to know anything was wrong. He wanted you to grow up in a normal home, with a mum and a dad.'

'Fathers don't hit mothers in a "normal home"!'

'No, I suppose not. But he had to look at you, your blue eyes and fair hair, every day of his life. The evidence of my unfaithfulness. He could never forget it because every morning, there you were, at breakfast. And he loved you *so* much despite all that. He…'

For the first time Eileen loses control, and the breath catches in her chest as she sobs.

'He *begged* me not to take you away,' she cries, tears now running freely down her powdered cheeks. 'On his knees. I've never seen a strong man so distraught, so … *unmanned*! And I couldn't do it to him. I'd betrayed my marriage vows, and I knew I'd never give Andrew up, but I couldn't deprive your dad … Stanley … of his son.'

'But I'm not his son!' cries Robin, standing up suddenly.

'No, not biologically. But in every other sense, you are. He adores you. You know that's true.'

Robin spins round, searching for his coat.

'I've got to go!' he says wildly. 'I can't deal with this! It's too much!'

She too stands and reaches over the table to grab her son's arm.

'Yes, but I have to say one last thing! Please, darling, wait!'

'You mean there's more?' he cries, yanking his arm from her grip.

'I know you know more about this man, Frank Marshall, than you're telling.'

Robin's face contorts in disdain. 'You don't know what you're talking about,' he sneers.

'Yes, Robin, I do. I know about the Krays, about the drugs and about Mr Marshall. And I'm not judging you or asking for any explanations. But please, I beg you, don't punish Stanley because of what you think he did to me. Don't allow your anger towards him let you make a terrible mistake.'

'He's a monster!'

'He was a monster, yes, but that was a long time ago. And even when that was true, he loved and cared for you, when most men wouldn't even have had you in the house!'

Robin is still for a second.

'I've got to go,' he repeats, and he blunders out of the flat, the door slamming shut behind him.

Sally shoves Charles. 'Charles. Charlie!'

Charles turns over in bed, wondering if he's missed the alarm. He opens a bleary eye to the clock on his bedside table.

'It's quarter to two,' he says groggily.

'I know. But the phone's ringing.'

Charles listens. The only phone in the house is in the kitchen, and although they both want some extensions installed, they haven't got round to it yet.

'No it's not,' he says. 'Go back to sleep.'

'It was ringing! Someone's tried at least twice,' she insists.

The ringing starts again from downstairs.

'See?'

Charles sits up and swings his legs out of bed. He runs down the three flights of stairs, expecting the phone to ring off before he gets there.

'Yes?' he says, picking up the receiver.

'Holborne?' says a muffled, hoarse voice.

'Who is this?'

'Listen carefully. Frank Marshall's going to be moved from somewhere on Horn Lane, Acton. I don't know the number.'

Charles is now suddenly and completely awake.

'When?'

'Sometime early this morning.'

'Who is this?'

'You'll only have one chance. Don't fuck it up.'

The line goes dead. Sally appears in the kitchen doorway in her nightdress.

'Who was it?' she asks.

'Not sure, but if I was a betting man, I'd say Robin Sharpe.'

Charles clicks the receiver rest to get a new line and starts dialling.

'Who are you calling now?' asks Sally.

'Sean Sloane. Go back to bed. I won't be long.'

CHAPTER THIRTY-SEVEN
...IT IS, NOW

'Is he dead?' calls Vince from the front passenger seat. His voice is muffled by the hardboard bulkhead separating the rear compartment from the front seats.

'Yeah,' confirms Gerry.

Vince turns to the driver. 'C'mon, Tony, let's move. But for Christ's sake, take it easy. Stick to the speed limit, watch for red lights and stay a good distance behind the car in front.'

'You think I ain't done this before?' says Tony, offended, as he moves off. 'Where we taking him, Gerry?' he shouts over his shoulder. 'Canvey?'

'Not this time,' Gerry shouts back. 'The paper mill in Purfleet. D'you know it?'

'Yup. I've delivered there before.'

Vince shouts from the passenger seat.

'Can we stop for a cuppa, Gerry? I've been up since before four, and I'm parched.'

'No. Reg said go straight there.'

'But it's a coupla hours!'

Cliff Stewart chirps up. 'I wouldn't mind stopping for a bit, Gerry. I need a slash.'

'Wanna go to Katie's?' calls Tony. 'It's not far off the route.'

'Oh, yeah!' replies Vince enthusiastically. 'Her full English is brilliant! You ever been there, Cliff?'

'Nah, but I've heard you lot going on about it. I wouldn't mind a full English.'

'C'mon Gerry,' wheedles Vince. 'Reg ain't gonna know.'

'And Frank 'ere ain't gonna care,' adds Cliff, to general laughter.

Gerry thinks for a while. He too is hungry.

'Have a look under the seats,' he says. 'See if you can find a tarp or something.'

He crawls to the back of the van. 'Bloody hell, Tony, take it easy!'

'I ain't doing more than twenty-five,' protests the driver.

'Well, we've got nothing to hold onto back 'ere!'

Gerry lifts the board covering the compartment for the vehicle's spare wheel.

'I've got something.'

He drags out an old blanket. A wheel brace and jack roll out of it as he pulls.

'This'll do,' he says. 'Okay. We'll have a short stop at Katie's. One of us'll need to stay in the van.'

'We'll take it in turns,' suggests Vince.

Katie's Transport Café at Greenford is well-known to locals and long-distance drivers alike. An institution since the First World War, it serves huge meals for hungry working men at reasonable prices. Only half a mile off the A40, it's a favourite round-the-clock truck stop for goods vehicles hauling into and out of London.

Two or three years earlier, its present owner, Helen, the granddaughter of the original Katie, bought the adjoining land and extended the car park, but even the enlarged area is today overflowing with vehicles of all shapes and sizes. Tony finds a small space between two heavy goods vehicles to park the little van out of sight and offers to stand guard for the first period as long as someone brings him a cup of tea. The others go inside.

Vince, the first in the door and the hungriest, grabs the only unoccupied table while the others queue to place their orders at the counter. In addition to taxi and truck drivers, today the café is half-full of football fans on their way to Wembley. Most wear "England" rosettes, and Vince counts a dozen flags and banners identifying fans coming in from the west, one as far away as Bristol. There is football talk at every table.

What with the time it takes to order and the kitchen being under pressure, the "short stop" in fact becomes an hour and a half. Tony, the last to have his order shouted from the counter, eats hurriedly, but then declares that he's going to the toilet. All the others groan, but the risk of being trapped in a small van for hours with a man who desperately needs to empty his bowels eventually persuades everyone to give him time.

Of course, there's a queue for the single cubicle and by the time Tony has finished his business, it is 8:45 a.m. before the van is pulling back out onto the A40, now heading east to join the North Circular at Hanger Lane.

It is here that they hit real trouble. The weight of traffic heading towards Wembley for the World Cup Final that afternoon is incredible, and they find themselves in stationary traffic half a mile before the junction.

'Can you see what's up ahead?' Gerry calls to the driving compartment.

Tony calls back. 'There's a couple of police cars at the lights, but I can't see if there's been an accident.'

'Jesus!' swears Gerry under his breath. 'I knew we shouldn't have stopped.'

'They ought to do something about this junction,' grumbles Tony. 'Been like this for years.'

The pavements are now also becoming busier with football fans heading towards the underground station.

Eventually the van is able to move forward by a hundred yards or so. Tony and Vince can now see uniformed police officers ahead.

Tony calls back. 'Gerry, there's rozzers up ahead.'

'What're they doing?'

'Nothing much. Directing traffic and football fans, looks like.'

'Can you turn off?'

'Yeah, there's a turning on the left coming up, but I don't know where it goes.'

'Don't worry about that. Just get off the main road.'

It takes them another ten minutes to be able to turn off, but the side road into which they've driven curves immediately back on itself. They are now travelling down an unknown street in the wrong direction.

Gerry calls from the back. 'Stop as soon as you see a call box. I'm going to phone Reg for instructions. One of you will need to get out first and make sure it's safe.'

The van drives aimlessly for the next fifteen minutes until they see a telephone box. Even Tony, who knows this part of London like the back of his hand, isn't exactly sure where they are. Vince gets out and looks up and down the pavement to check they are not being observed.

'You're okay,' he calls, and taps on the back door.

Gerry climbs out. 'Wait there,' he instructs, striding across the pavement towards the red call box.

Charles and Sally are in the garden at Wren Street. It is a beautiful summer's morning, the city is quiet and Charles is about to start the lawnmower when he hears the phone ring. He runs back into the kitchen.

'Charles?'

'Hi Sean. Any joy?'

'We missed him. House to house enquiries identified the property, and we're sure it's the right place. Lots of reports of a giant with a false beard coming and going in the company of different minders. And we think we've identified one of them, too. But the place has been wiped clean, by experts. Not a single fingerprint from top to bottom. And the owner hasn't been seen for three days.'

'Okay. Thanks for letting me know.'

'We've circulated descriptions and there are uniforms all over the metropolis for the football. We might get lucky.'

Gerry climbs back into the van, slams the door behind him and crawls up to the bulkhead so Tony and Vince can hear him.

'Okay, new plan,' he says. 'He's given me an address in Ruislip. A bloke he knows has an empty lock-up and he'll be waiting. We're to put the van in, lock it up, and leave it till after the match, when the streets are quieter. He says we've gotta be at the mill by six thirty at the latest.'

'Was he cross?' asks Vince nervously.

'Not with us he weren't. I told him the van had no petrol in it and we had to push it till we found a service station. Okay, everyone? We went to BP in Neasden, just off the North Circular, right?'

'Fuck me,' says Tony. 'Someone's going to catch it.'

'Yeah,' agrees Gerry, 'but better him than us, eh?'

'What are we supposed to do between now and five o'clock?' asks Cliff.

'Do you think this geezer might have a telly?' asks Tony hopefully.

It turns out that the "geezer" does have a telly and is already preparing to watch Grandstand and the football match. Having hidden Frank Marshall's temporary coffin out of sight in his garage and locked up, he invites the members of the Firm to join him. At noon, Gerry sends Cliff out to the local off-licence to supplement the geezer's stock of beer and cigarettes. By one o'clock, when the familiar theme tune of Grandstand starts, the four members of the Firm and their host have settled in, along with most of the country, to watch a day of sport, starting with the Red Arrows fly-past.

The tension builds, more beers are drunk and, finally, the football match starts.

'It's like a bleedin' holiday,' says Vince, his feet up and a bottle in his hand. 'We should do this more often.'

He slaps his thigh with his palm in time to the rhythm of the drummer in the Wembley crowd — *Bang-bang! Bang-bang-bang! Bang-bang-bang-bang!* — and all the men finish with the shout: 'England!'

The holiday spirit continues, helped by an England lead, until the 89th minute of the game, when West Germany equalise with a goal from a dubious free kick.

Everyone in the room groans and slumps in dismay.

'We had it won!' says Tony. 'It was in the fucking bag!'

'I'll bet we lose it now,' comments Vince morosely. 'Look at them. They look totally knackered.'

He's right. The black and white figures of the England players on the screen have their heads down, still reeling at having had victory snatched from them at the last second.

Gerry looks across at Tony. 'You know what this means, Tone?'

'What?'

'Extra time.'

'So?'

'We can't stay for it.'

The announcement produces a chorus of dissent from the others.

'It's half an hour, right, plus turnaround time,' insists Gerry. 'It means we won't leave 'ere till, what? Almost five thirty.'

'I can do it,' says Tony.

Gerry notes with concern that his eyes are bright and his cheeks flushed. *One beer too many?* he wonders.

'What? Ruislip to Purfleet in an hour?' says Cliff.

'Easy,' assures Tony confidently.

'Don't talk bloody nonsense!'

'Cliff's right, Tone. You can't do it in that time. We should go.'

'Aw, c'mon, Gerry! We can't leave now!' protests Vince.

'We could stay for the first period of extra time, couldn't we?' suggests Cliff. 'That'd give us an hour and a quarter before the mill closes.'

Gerry considers the suggestion. He too wants to watch the conclusion of the match, but if they're late at the mill it will be he who catches it from the twins. Finally, he says uncertainly, 'Yeah, I s'pose that'd be all right.'

In fact, they stay for the first half of extra time and a good part of the second. Then Geoff Hurst scores in the 101st minute to make it 3–2 to England, and a roar of approval goes up from every house on the street, including theirs.

Gerry rises. 'C'mon. That's it. Let's go!' he orders.

Reluctantly the others put bottles down, stub out cigarettes and rise. Vince takes a last handful of crisps. With his eyes still on the screen, their host reaches into his pocket and throws the key to the lock-up towards Tony, who catches it neatly.

With lingering backward glances at the screen and shouted thanks to their host — who at no time was asked or offered his name — the team files out the front door. The suburban street is deserted.

The tarpaulin covering the van with Marshall's body inside is pulled off, the van backs out, Vince runs back to return the key and, at last, with mere seconds to go before the end of the World Cup final, the members of the Firm set off for Purfleet, and Frank Marshall's final resting place.

They haven't even reached the end of the road when the street erupts. Shouts, screams and applause pour from every open window and, within seconds, before they even realise what's happening, the street is full of dancing, celebrating football fans.

Tony is forced to a crawl as a couple of young men in football shirts dance, jumping up and down in a wild embrace, across their path. A gaggle of screaming children emerges from a house just ahead of them, running onto the carriageway, paying no attention to the approaching van. More people arrive, men, women and children hugging and cheering, some even crying.

'We've won the cup! We've won the cup! Ee aye addio, we've won the cup!' chant the euphoric residents of Ruislip at the top of their lungs.

'What the fuck's happening?' demands Gerry angrily from the back.

'I think we won!' shouts Vince.

'No, you idiot! Why ain't we moving?'

'The road's full of people,' explains Tony. 'I can't move.'

Gerry and Cliff jump with fright as someone good-humouredly bangs the roof of the van to the rhythm of the Wembley drum beat, and a young barefoot woman, wearing what appears to be a very skimpy bra and shorts, takes up the beat on the front bonnet.

'Cor!' says Tony. 'Get an eyeful of that!'

'Get moving, you moron!' screams Gerry from the rear.

Tony engages gear again and, hand beeping the horn, he moves off, but no one on the street seems to care. The narrow carriageway is now a dense crowd of happy fans.

'I can't! I'll kill someone!' says Tony desperately.

The vehicle hiccups forward a foot or two and then another.

'Oh shit!' says Vince.

'What?' calls Gerry.

'I think we've hit someone,' replies Vince.

'Keep moving!' orders Gerry.

It's no use. A big man wearing a sleeveless vest bangs angrily on the passenger window.

'Hey! You! You've knocked down my little girl!'

Vince looks wildly from the man to Tony and back again.

'I just glanced her, that's all,' says Tony in a high voice, 'didn't I, Vince? She ain't really hurt.'

A tighter knot of people are now in front of the van, crowding round a little girl who sits on the tarmac holding her hip and howling.

'Open the door!' demands the man, reaching for the door handle.

Tony engages reverse and hits the accelerator. The van lurches backwards but there are people behind it too. The men in the back hear screams and shouts. There is another thump, a more significant collision this time, and the crunch of metal on metal as the van collides with a parked car. The engine stalls. Now there are numerous, repeated blows on the van's roof and sides as angry residents crowd round it.

Vince's nerve is the first to fail. He shoves the passenger door open, manages to get out and starts pushing his way through the crowd. Tony goes next. He is less fortunate, and hands grab him.

'Hold onto him!' someone shouts.

'Call the police!' shouts another.

In the back of the van, unable to see what's happening outside, Cliff is fighting down rising panic. Gerry reaches inside his jacket for his pistol. He looks at Cliff in the semi-darkness.

'Ready?' Cliff nods. 'C'mon, then.'

Gerry kicks open the rear doors. One of the two doors strikes a kid and he goes flying into the air but Gerry is out, surrounded by people, some unaware of what's happened, some angry.

Gerry raises the pistol and fires twice in quick succession. There is an instant of stillness in the crowd — Gerry suddenly imagines himself inside the freeze-frame of Hurst's second, and disputed, goal, the ball hanging motionless above the goal line —followed by pandemonium, screams and explosive movement away from the sound of the shots as people scatter in all directions.

Gerry runs off, back the way the van came, Cliff in close pursuit.

Big Frank remains motionless inside the van, beyond caring.

CHAPTER THIRTY-EIGHT

Charles's footsteps ring on the marble floor of the Great Hall of the Royal Courts of Justice. With almost an hour before the courts sit, there are only a few early birds. Charles goes to the far end of the Hall. There, in an easily unnoticed alcove, he comes to a halt and presses a bell by a thick oak door.

It takes a few moments, but eventually a wicket in the door opens.

'Yes?'

'Counsel to see Stanley Sharpe.'

'The prison van's just pulling in. You can come in and wait.'

He closes the wicket, allows Charles in and leads the way down the stairs to a desk where he takes Charles's details.

'He's our only customer today, sir,' says the gaoler, 'so you can take your pick of cells.'

He shows Charles into a cell. It is bare of all furniture and adornment, and has no natural light. A crypt with bars, and a stone bench set into a wall.

'This'll be fine, thank you,' says Charles.

'I'll get him. I'm afraid I'll have to lock you in.'

'Yes, sure.'

A few moments later, Sharpe appears on the threshold and is propelled gently by the gaoler into the room.

'Bang on the bars or give me a shout when you're done,' he says, and he locks Charles in with his client.

'Would you like to sit down, Mr Sharpe?' says Charles, moving up on the bench.

Sharpe joins him.

'How are you feeling?' asks Charles.

Sharpe smiles wanly. 'Confused. Part of me was glad to wake up. Part of me was not.'

'I don't know what to say,' says Charles. 'I wish I had words of comfort for you. I think Mr Tindall's told you how things went on Friday.'

'Yes.'

'There have been some developments.'

'Oh yes?'

'In the early hours of Saturday morning, I received an anonymous telephone call informing me that Frank Marshall was at an address in Acton, and that he was going to be moved later that morning.'

Sharpe looks up.

'I suspect that the informant was your son, Robin.'

'What would he know about it?'

'This part is not such good news, I'm afraid. It looks as if Robin is in bed with the Krays. They, or their nominees, have control of the garage and there's a suggestion they've been dealing LSD under cover of the car sales. Everyone on the premises was arrested, although I believe they are all now out on bail.'

'What's that got to do with Frank Marshall…? Oh, I see. They needed me out of the way.'

'That's how it appears. At first I was puzzled why the Krays didn't take more … permanent measures. Let's face it, they've done it before. But then, knowing Ronnie Kray as I do, I think I could make a guess.'

'Ronnie Kray likes causing pain.'

'Yes.'

'He has a sort of genius for devising the most painful punishments.'

'Yes.'

'So putting a man of God in prison for something he didn't do, making him appear a hypocrite … that would give him much greater pleasure than simple murder.'

'Exactly. The thing is, although I was able to get the police to take the tip-off seriously, they weren't able to find Marshall or any sign of him.'

'Where does that leave us this morning?'

'Well, if I close our case now, the appeal will be lost. That doesn't mean we can't try again if better evidence is found, but it'd be much more difficult to obtain permission.'

'And the alternative?'

'I try to get the appeal adjourned.'

'What are the chances of that?'

Charles sighs. 'Honestly? Not great. The court will ask for how long, and I've no answer. Saying we hope something will turn up in the next few days won't wash. They'll ask what evidence we expect and when we expect it. Otherwise it just smacks of Micawberism. It might be possible for Robin to give evidence, although I don't think he's actually seen Marshall. He could only give evidence of the conspiracy to hide him away somewhere.'

'No,' says Sharpe firmly. 'I don't want that.'

'You don't want him to give evidence?'

'No.'

'Even if it means the appeal fails?'

'Even then. He'd go to prison, wouldn't he?

'If the Krays don't get him first.'

There's the sound of keys turning in the lock and the gaoler appears.

'I think this gentleman's with you,' he says, and Tindall steps into the cell.

'Thank you. I've got some news!' Tindall says excitedly to Charles and Sharpe.

He waits for the door to be relocked and for the gaoler's footsteps to recede.

'Well?' asks Charles.

'Our enquiry agent has come up with a witness.'

He looks at his notebook and reads. 'A Mr Steve Brokenshire, a PE teacher at Weavers Fields School. He runs the football teams at the school and knows Marshall's two boys, especially the eldest, who has some talent.'

'What does Mr Brokenshire say?'

'He was watching the Under Elevens and saw Mr Marshall standing on the touchline.'

'Doesn't sound much,' comments Charles.

'He's a man of good character and he knows Marshall very well, having spoken to him on a dozen occasions. He had a long face-to-face conversation with him last summer concerning his son's place in the school team. He has no doubt. He's so sure, he's delayed going camping.'

'What, he's here?'

'Yes, upstairs. I've copied his statement and left it with Maria to give to the Crown when they arrive. She's waiting outside court.'

'All right,' says Charles, 'it's better than nothing. Mr Sharpe, my advice would be that you instruct me to apply to call Mr Brokenshire.'

'What have we got to lose?'

'Absolutely nothing. Even if Mr Brokenshire is awful, it'll take up some time.'

'And something might crop up?'

'Frank Marshall, hopefully.'

Charles and Tindall leave Sharpe and head upstairs to the court.

'Hang on a second,' says Charles. 'I'm going to call my friend in the Met, in case there's any news. Go on up. I'll be there in a moment.'

Charles runs to the robing room and asks for an outside line. He has been calling West End central, trying to reach Sloane, every couple of hours since Sloane informed him that Marshall had slipped through their fingers. He now knows the telephone number by heart.

As before, neither Sloane nor Nipper Read can be reached. When he asks directly if anyone can tell him the results of the investigation into Frank Marshall, he is told very firmly that that's police business. He hangs up and races back to court.

Warboys intercepts him as he is walking into the courtroom.

'I've seen this,' he says, brandishing the single sheet of manuscript prepared by Tindall. 'My instructions are to oppose its admission at this late stage.'

'I expected no less,' replies Charles.

The courtroom is as packed as it was on Friday, if anything, more so. Although the story of the disgraced Reverend Sharpe has been pushed off the front pages by the World Cup win, almost every newspaper that morning carried Sharpe's photograph and a report of Friday's proceedings on the inside pages. Charles sees Percy Farrow in the front bench of journalists and recognises one of the TV reporters from the BBC. There is an excited hum of conversation, a wasps' nest stirred with a stick.

Charles just has time to turn to greet Mrs Sharpe and Maria when the judges file in. When the court has settled, Lord Justice Linnard addresses Charles.

'Do you formally close your case, Mr Holborne?'

'No, my Lord. I have an application to call a further witness. I think my Instructing Solicitor has given copies of the witness's proposed evidence to your associate.'

The associate swivels round in her seat and hands up to the judges three copies of the PE teacher's statement. Charles allows them a few moments to read it.

'The court, as you know, has an unfettered discretion to admit further evidence. I appreciate that, of course, in an ideal world it would all be served on the Crown at the same time, but you can see the date upon which Mr Brokenshire was identified and first questioned, namely yesterday. It has been shown to the Crown at the very first opportunity.

'As to your Lordships' discretion to admit, it's an extremely short statement running to little more than two paragraphs, and touches on exactly the same issue as the witnesses you've already heard, namely, a recent sighting of Mr Marshall. It is difficult to see what further instructions Mr Warboys would require — certainly there are no investigations that could be done — and for a man of Mr Warboys's skill and experience, cross-examining a witness on the accuracy of an identification should be child's play.'

'For all we know, Mr Holborne,' intervenes Lord Justice Greenidge, 'Mr Brokenshire might have a criminal record as long as your arm. He might even be a former associate of the prisoner, like Mrs Marshall turned out to be. Or the Crown might be able to prove, for example, that he was nowhere near where he claims to have been at the alleged time of sighting. I can think of numerous further investigations the Crown might wish to make.'

'My Lord, I'm advised that Mr Brokenshire is a man of exemplary character and there is no suggestion of any criminal convictions. And that can be resolved with a single phone call by my learned friend or the officers sitting behind him.'

Mr Justice Davies leans sideways to speak confidentially to Lord Justice Linnard. Linnard listens, pauses, and then nods. He addresses the Great Toad.

'Would Detective Chief Inspector Wheatley be able to make such enquiries within fifteen minutes, Mr Warboys?'

'I expect so,' croaks Warboys.

'Very well. We are prepared to give you fifteen minutes for that phone call to be made, Mr Holborne.'

'All rise!'

Warboys turns and speaks to Wheatley, who promptly leaves court.

Charles desperately wants to try calling West End central again, but is afraid to leave court in case Wheatley returns. In fact, he does return after only ten minutes. He whispers to Warboys. The Great Toad turns slowly in his place and addresses Charles.

'Nothing known,' he says.

'So, a junior school PE teacher who's never been in trouble with the police,' says Charles. 'Are you going to suggest he's been nobbled in some way? And, if so, are you seeking an adjournment to do it?'

'I'm still opposing the admission of this evidence.'

'But on what grounds? It's late, yes, but you've suffered no prejudice by that. But excluding the evidence at this stage simply means I'll be applying for permission to appeal again.'

'Ha!' snorts the Great Toad. 'I'd like to see you try.'

'You may have made a mess of my two earlier witnesses, but we're absolutely convinced that Marshall's still alive. So, in fact, are the police. Did you know they raided an address in Acton on Saturday? They received an anonymous tip-off from a reliable source that Marshall was there, and they acted on it.'

Warboys looks at Charles dispassionately and blinks slowly. His expression gives nothing away. Charles is certain that, had there been a fly on his head, The Great Toad's tongue would've lashed out and captured it.

'If I'm right,' continues Charles, 'new witnesses are going to start popping up all over the place. Next time I could have a dozen, and ones you can't so easily dismiss.'

The man's eyes blink slowly again.

'I'll take instructions,' he says finally.

The associate approaches the barristers' bench. 'Are you ready, gentlemen? The judges are waiting to come in.'

'Yes, thank you,' says Charles.

The judges resume their places. Warboys rises.

'Inquiries have been made, my Lords, and it has been confirmed that this witness is a man of good character and is indeed a teacher at Weavers Fields School. In an effort to bring the appeal to a close, and so it cannot be said that the prosecution prevented admissible evidence being called, the Crown withdraws its objection.'

'Thank you, Mr Warboys,' says Lord Justice Linnard. 'Very well, Mr Holborne. Call your witness.'

'Mr Stephen Brokenshire, please.'

The usher leaves court and returns a moment later with a short compact man of about thirty years, wearing slacks and a sports jacket. The usher takes him to the witness box and administers the oath.

'Mr Stephen Brokenshire?' asks Charles.

'Yes.'

'Please would you give your occupation and professional address to the court?'

'I'm a teacher. My subjects are history and physical education, and I teach both at Weavers Fields School, Mape Street, in the London Borough of Tower Hamlets.' He speaks with a Welsh accent.

'I hope there is a photograph on the witness stand in front of you. Please could you look at it?' says Charles.

Brokenshire picks up the photograph and looks at it. 'Yes. This is Mr Marshall.'

'You know that person?'

'Yes, his name is Frank Marshall and he's the father of two of the boys whom I teach.'

'How well do you know him?' asks Charles.

'Very well. Better than I know most of the parents because Mr Marshall has a particular interest in football, and I coach the Under Nines and Under Elevens at the school.'

'Have you ever spoken to him face-to-face?'

'Yes, on several occasions. Last year we had a long discussion on the school playing field about his older son's football skills.'

'Thank you. Please can you tell the court when you last saw Mr Marshall.'

'It was either four or five weekends ago, at the football pitch on Weavers Fields.'

'Did you speak to Mr Marshall on that occasion?'

'No, I don't think I did. I was coaching the team, including Mr Marshall's elder son, and I saw Mr Marshall on the touchline with several other parents.'

'Do you have any doubt that it was Mr Marshall you saw?'

'No. He's very distinctive.'

'Thank you for taking the trouble to come today, Mr Brokenshire. Please remain there for a moment.'

Warboys rises slowly.

'Are you a footballer?' he asks.

'No. I've never played it professionally, if that's what you mean. Nor on an amateur basis.'

'So you have no connection with the late Mr Marshall, who we understand used to play for West Ham United?'

'No. I played rugby.'

'But you still teach football.'

'I teach all sports, but it's not difficult at that level. The pupils only go up to age eleven.'

'Do you know the prisoner over there, Mr Sharpe?'

'No, I don't think so.'

'Never seen him before?'

Brokenshire shakes his head. 'No.'

'Now, the occasion on which you saw Mr Marshall, was that just a training session or was it a match against another school?'

'It was a match.'

'An important match?'

'Fairly. It was the quarter-finals of the local schools' championship.'

'So you would have been busy shouting instructions to the boys?'

Brokenshire grins. 'I expect so.'

'Running up and down the touchline?'

'Yes.'

'And was the man you saw on your side of the pitch or on the other side?'

'The other side.'

'How many parents were there?'

'I didn't count them, but probably ... twenty or thirty, perhaps.'

'Mostly men?'

'Yes, mostly.'

'So this man was amongst the crowd of other parents, mostly men.'

'That's right.'

'And you were focused on the match.'

'I was.'

'What makes you so sure that the man in this crowd was Mr Marshall?'

'Well, like I said, he is very distinctive. He's very tall, for a start.'

'Tall, yes. Anything else?'

'Very big. In addition to being tall, he is very big.'

'Anything else?'

'Well, he was wearing a hat and had his collar pulled up. It did make me wonder if he was trying to disguise himself.'

'So you saw a big, tall man, who you thought might be trying to disguise himself, on the opposite side of the pitch to you, while you were running up and down encouraging your boys. Have I got that right?'

'Well ... yes, I suppose so.'

'And while you were running up and down in this way, encouraging your boys, no doubt shouting instructions because this was a rather important match, how long do you suppose you actually looked at this man for? The longest period you took your eyes off the match so as to focus on the man on the far side of the pitch?'

'A few seconds, perhaps.'

'A few seconds.'

'Yes.'

'Were you aware that Mr Marshall was supposedly the victim of a murder at the end of last year?'

'I think … I think I heard something about that, yes.'

'It would have been spoken about at the school, surely? Two of your tender pupils deprived of a father in such circumstances? The sort of thing of which staff would be made aware.'

'Yes, I expect so.'

'So when you saw this "dead man" encouraging his boy from the touchline, surely you thought to yourself, "Well, that's funny. He's supposed to be dead. I'd better report that to the police."'

The witness does not answer.

'Mr Brokenshire? Did you do that, sir?'

'Erm, no, actually, I didn't.'

'Why not?'

'I don't know. It didn't occur to me.'

'May I suggest one possible reason, which is, you weren't absolutely sure it *was* Mr Marshall. That big, tall man with his collar up?'

'N-no, perhaps you're right.'

'You're not sure now, are you, now you look back on it, that it *was* Mr Marshall?'

'I *was* sure, but … now you make that point … perhaps I wasn't. Perhaps I'm not.'

'Thank you, Mr Brokenshire.'

The Great Toad resumes his seat, satisfied.

We're sunk.

Charles feels eyes on his back, and he turns. Wheatley is staring at him, a triumphant expression on his thin face. Then, as Charles watches, he sees the expression fade, to be replaced by something else. Charles whirls round.

DS Sean Sloane and DCI Nipper Read have entered the courtroom. Sloane catches Charles's eye and winks at him.

Charles's heart starts to thump and he misses something one of the judges is saying.

'I said, are you now closing your case, Mr Holborne?' repeats Linnard testily.

Charles's attention is still on the two policemen who have just arrived. The Crown's solicitor has made his way along the bench behind Warboys and is in discussion with Read. He scurries back to Warboys and whispers to him.

'Mr Holborne!' shouts Linnard.

'Yes, my Lord, I am very sorry but … I think my learned friend may be in the act of receiving some important information relating to this appeal…'

'Who is that man?' demands Linnard, pointing at Read. 'I won't have proceedings interrupted like this.'

Read looks up.

'My name is Detective Chief Inspector Leonard Read, my Lord, of the Metropolitan Police, stationed at West End Central. I have just informed counsel for the Crown that the body of Mr Frank Marshall has been discovered.'

Like a sudden gust of wind, there is an audible gasp, an intake of breath, from the scores of spectators in the court.

'So he is dead after all?' says Lord Justice Greenidge with the suggestion of a smile.

'He is certainly dead, my Lord.'

'Are you sure of the identification?' asks Linnard.

'We are, my Lord. He has been identified by his fingerprints and by his next of kin.'

'Well, Mr Holborne, that appears to bring your appeal to an end,' says Lord Justice Linnard.

'No, my Lord,' interrupts Read. 'Frank Marshall's body was discovered on Saturday afternoon, shot six times in the chest and head. According to the forensic pathologist who conducted a post-mortem examination yesterday, death occurred no more than twenty-four hours before then.'

DCI Wheatley jumps up. 'That can't be right! That man —' he points dramatically across the court to Sharpe high up in the dock — 'admitted to killing him six months ago!'

'My Lord, there is absolutely no doubt,' says Read. 'I saw the body myself, the condition of which was inconsistent with death more than a few hours earlier. Photographic evidence and statements are being produced as we speak. I can't answer for the alleged confession obtained by my colleague, but I can say with absolute certainty that, until very recently indeed, Mr Marshall was alive.'

The court bristles with the silence that follows. The only sound that can be heard is the scribbling of a score of reporters' pens.

Charles steps into the gap.

'In light of this development, I submit that it's not possible for your Lordships to determine the appeal today. Nor is it possible for my learned friend to decide whether to continue opposing it. May I suggest, my Lords, that the case be adjourned for a period of forty-eight hours to allow the dust to settle, so to speak? Allow the Crown to consider the police evidence that Mr Marshall was, until Saturday, alive and well?'

The three judges lean into a huddle and whisper for a while and then sit upright.

'Mr Warboys,' says Lord Justice Linnard, 'in light of these events, we are disposed to agree with Mr Holborne that a short adjournment would be sensible.'

'With great respect, my Lord, I agree,' croaks Warboys.

'And we will hear Mr Holborne on the issue of bail in the meantime.'

Charles looks across the court to find Sloane grinning at him. Nipper Read, however, has a different expression. Eyes narrowed like a snake's, he is looking towards the back of the court at his corrupt colleague, DCI Wheatley.

CHAPTER THIRTY-NINE

Sally is at last having her housewarming party and her home on Wren Street is full of laughter and conversation. Charles has opened the French windows to the garden and children chase in and out, threading their way between adults' legs.

They have been lucky with the weather. August has been cool and wet, but this weekend the rain has held off, the sun is shining and some of the braver guests are sitting on the grass with their drinks. Others have taken a selection of chairs from various rooms in the house to join them. Although Sally assures Charles that she has barely started on it, the garden looks beautiful, courtesy of her efforts.

Music is playing — The Zombies at that moment — and several guests are dancing and singing along with Colin Blunstone. The live music will start soon. Maria has managed to borrow an electric piano, under which she is presently crawling in an effort to connect it to a guitar amplifier, and she and two of her flatmates, bass and drums, are about to start a short jazz set in the corner of the garden. She was invited as a guest, but her offer to provide some music was enthusiastically accepted by Charles.

Sally worried for weeks about the odd composition of the guest list, but everyone seems to be mixing. Her mum is away, but her two sisters are here with their husbands and children. There are barristers with wives or girlfriends, including Charles's friend Michael Levy, Peter Bateman and Amanda, and some of Sally's closest friends from the clerking community with their other halves. Bateman, known for his easy charm, is getting on famously with Sally's clerking colleagues. Sloane and Irenna arrived late but have now joined the lawyers.

David and Sonia are also there. Millie has come with them. Charles was extremely worried about her presence — what if she made some racist comment to Maria, or some of her Black musician friends? — but he could see no alternative. Mrs Weinstein was unavailable, Millie couldn't be left on her own and he wanted David and Sonia to come. Sonia promised to keep an eye on her.

At this moment Millie is sitting in an armchair in the corner of the lounge, away from the music and chatter of the kitchen. She holds her grandson on her lap and looks vaguely at the people in the room. Sonia hovers close by. She and David have become aware over the last few weeks of another sign of Millie's decline, occasional episodes of incontinence. Sonia has assured Charles that she has taken appropriate precautions.

The speed of Millie's decline terrifies both Charles and David.

Charles and Sally pass briefly in the kitchen, he with a tray now emptied of its bridge rolls, she with a fresh tray of drinks. They pause for a moment, two waiters snatching a kiss.

'How are things upstairs?' asks Sally.

'So far so good. Mum's not speaking much to anyone, but she seems content enough playing with Jonathan.'

'Good. By the way, you look very sexy,' says Sally.

'Still feel a bit uncomfortable, to be honest,' replies Charles, indicating his new flower-patterned shirt and flares. 'Are you enjoying yourself?'

She nods, her eyes sparkling and her face flushed, lit with a smile.

'Me too,' he says. 'I love you, Sal,' he adds softly.

To his surprise, her eyes fill with tears.

'I know you do,' she says. 'I'm very happy.'

'You are?'

'Yes. Completely. And I love you too.'

She lifts her head and this time the kiss continues for longer and is noticed by some of the guests, who cheer and clap good-naturedly.

They disengage and go their separate ways. Charles finds himself face-to-face with his brother in the hall. He makes to go around David but finds a gentle hand on his shoulder.

'What?' asks Charles.

'You're happy,' says David.

'I am,' confirms Charles.

David smiles down at his older brother. 'It shows, Charlie. I'm really pleased for you.'

'Despite…'

'Yes. She's a lovely girl and she adores you.'

'But she's not Jewish.'

'As long as you make one another happy, that's all I care about.'

'Hmm. I wish Mum and Dad were of the same opinion.'

'Give them time,' says David. 'Dad's already coming round.'

'Not Mum, though.'

'You know all this frightens her.' David makes a circling motion with his hand to signify the diversity of the guests. 'Dad ran a business; he dealt with all sorts of people. Mum's life on the other hand was very sheltered. But she likes Sally, and she's incredibly proud of you. It's a start.'

'Yeah?' says Charles doubtfully, and he moves off.

He hears Maria's trio start playing in the garden and, in response, most of the guests move outside to listen. Sean Sloane comes up to him.

'How's your drink?' asks Charles.

'Empty. If it's all the same to you, I'm going to see if there's a beer in the kitchen.'

'If you look in the cupboard above the fridge you'll find a few bottles of Guinness I hid for you, unless they've already been discovered.'

'Grand,' says Sloane. 'By the way, I have some news.'

'Yes?'

'We've had sightings of Robin Sharpe's Jaguar coupé, on the south coast of France, near Nice.'

Charles shakes his head. 'I wish he hadn't run.'

'His choice. Ironically, in the end we probably couldn't have made the charges stick against him. One of the so-called mechanics didn't know one end of a wrench from another, but he knew an awful lot about supplying LSD.'

'You think Robin was an unwitting front for the drugs?'

'Possibly. In any case, we'd have struggled to prove otherwise. After all, he was only an employee by then.'

'I'm sure he ran because he was more afraid of the Krays than your lot. They must have guessed he was the source of the leak re Marshall.'

'If you ever hear from him, Charles, let him know that my boss'd like to talk to him. Off the record.'

'Like he did me?'

'Exactly like that.'

'And Wheatley?' asks Charles.

'Suspended pending investigation. But Read thinks he'll be allowed to take early retirement.'

'Not exactly justice,' comments Charles sourly.

'No,' agrees Sloane, 'but better than nothing.'

'Did I tell you I got a letter last week from Mrs Sharpe, thanking me?' says Charles.

'She should've sent it to me, not you,' jokes Sloane.

'I agree. I spectacularly failed.'

'No, I'm only kidding. You were the cavalry last year on the Greene case, remember? I just returned the favour. And you circled the wagons and held out till we arrived. Anyway, what news of Sharpe senior?'

'He's going to be a missionary in South America. He left last week.'

'Does the C of E do that?'

'You're asking the wrong chap, but I guess so.'

'Well, I'll be damned. It looks like he really did get God.'

'Seems like it.'

They are interrupted by the doorbell. Charles hands Sloane his tray.

'Pop that somewhere in the kitchen on your way down, would you?'

Charles goes to the front door and opens it.

'Good afternoon, Mr Holborne.'

Charles is astonished to see Maria's father on the doorstep.

'Mr Hudson?'

The American diplomat is wearing a jaunty trilby hat, which he takes off respectfully.

'I'm sorry to interrupt you, unannounced again,' he says. 'I'm leaving the country shortly, and I wanted to apologise to you before I left. My behaviour was not what it should have been when we last met, and I am sorry.'

'Thank you,' says Charles. 'I appreciate you were very anxious about Maria.'

'I was. I still am, to be honest.'

'Are you now in touch with her?'

Hudson smiles sadly, twiddling the hat nervously in his hands.

'In a fashion, yes. I still don't know where she's living, but she calls me regularly so I know she's well. Thanks for putting us in touch again.' He pauses. 'I haven't handled that situation very ably, I'm afraid, but at least we have a line of communication. Anyway, I can hear that I have disturbed a celebration of some sort, so I shall be going. Again, please accept my apologies.'

Hudson replaces his hat and turns to go. Charles stands on the threshold, undecided.

'Mr Hudson?' he calls.

Hudson, halfway down the steps, turns.

'Yes?'

'Look, I'm not sure if this is a mistake…'

'What's that?'

Charles chews his lip for a moment, and reaches a decision.

'Maria's here.'

Hudson frowns. 'What, here, at your house, right now?'

Charles nods. 'That's her playing. She's in the middle of a set. But I don't want anything to upset her.'

'I promise you, Mr Holborne, I wouldn't do anything to upset her. Not for the world.'

'No rows? No recriminations? No pressure on her?'

Hudson re-climbs the stairs so that he is standing two steps below Charles.

'You have my absolute assurance, sir. If you are kind enough to invite me into your home after what passed between us on the last occasion, I'd consider it a great favour just to be able to see her, maybe listen to her play for a few minutes.'

Charles looks into the other man's eyes and sees nothing but hope and sincerity. 'Very well. Please come in.'

Charles stands back to let Hudson walk into the hall. The diplomat takes off his hat again and stands nervously.

'Follow me,' says Charles.

He leads the way down into the kitchen. Most of the people from other areas of the house have now congregated there or in the garden, listening to the music. There is a group of small children sitting in a semicircle in front of the musicians.

Charles gently pushes his way through the guests until he reaches the garden doors. He looks behind him. Hudson has dropped back, not wanting to follow. Charles beckons to him but he shakes his head, smiles, and puts up a hand to indicate that he is happy to stay where he is, lost in the crowd.

Charles remains on the threshold, from which position he can see Maria, her trio, and Hudson.

The group finishes the piece, and everyone applauds warmly. Maria leans forward and Charles notices for the first time that she has set up a mic on top of the electric piano.

'Thank you,' she says. 'Now, we're going to try something a bit different.' She pauses, and then announces: 'I'm going to sing!'

Cheers and applause follow the announcement.

'That's very kind, but you'd best save it till you've heard me!'

That produces some laughter.

'I am really only an instrumentalist, but the guys have been on at me to do some vocals, and since you lot can't affect my professional career, you're going to be my guinea pigs.' More laughter. 'Also, now you've all had quite a bit to drink, I'm hoping my reception here will be less critical than on stage. So, at the risk of ruining this wonderful party … here goes.'

She counts the band in and starts. Within the first bar Charles recognises the song, Nat King Cole's "I Love You for Sentimental Reasons". Sally weaves her way through the kitchen and stands beside Charles, sliding her arm around his waist. He puts his arm over her shoulder. They listen together, swaying gently with the song.

'But she has a wonderful voice!' says Sally softly.

'Yes, she does,' he agrees.

'Why hasn't she sung before?'

'I have no idea, but she's got to do it again. Do you think we might be witnessing the birth of a star?'

'In our garden? Wouldn't that be something?'

Sally looks up at him and he kisses her on the nose.

Maria's vocals give way to some improvisation and then she picks up the song again, finishing to genuinely enthusiastic applause.

Someone in the garden cries 'More!' and other voices are raised in support.

'Sorry, no more singing for the moment, but we have one further number before we stop for a while,' says Maria.

The trio start playing an upbeat number unknown to Charles. He turns to see Hudson's reaction to the music, but the man's face is impassive. Charles slips out of Sally's embrace and goes to stand next to Hudson. He lowers his head.

'Are you going to speak to her?' he asks quietly.

'I'd like to, but only if she wants. I'm embarrassed to ask you to become involved but, when she's finished playing, would you tell her I'm here?'

'If you like.'

'I'll wait upstairs, then, by the front door. Whatever's to be said should probably best be said in private.'

'Can I suggest you go to the office on the top floor? There's no one there, and you'll be able to speak to her more comfortably than lurking by the front door.'

'Yes, okay. Thank you.'

Hudson slips out of the kitchen and Charles returns to Sally.

She frowns. 'I didn't know he was here. Did you let him in?'

'Yes. He came to apologise for the last time. He's leaving for the States and he's desperate to see her.'

'How did he know she was here?'

'He didn't. Pure chance. I've sent him up to my study.'

They wait until the music ends, to further applause, and the three musicians get up and head for drinks. Charles intercepts Maria.

'That was wonderful,' he says. 'Thank you so much. I feel really privileged we're the first audience for your singing.'

'Thank you.'

'Listen, Maria. Your father's here.'

'Here?'

'He came to apologise for the way he spoke to us last time. He's leaving for the States. He'd like to talk to you, if you want.'

'I'm not sure I want to.'

'He seems genuinely contrite. He wants to put things right, if he can. And he's promised me there will be no raised voices, no persuasion. It's your choice, but maybe you should give him a chance.'

She falls silent for a while. 'Where is he?'

'Upstairs, in my study.'

She takes a deep breath and nods slowly. 'Okay. Thank you.'

'Would you like one of us to come with you?' asks Sally.

Maria smiles, leans forward and kisses Sally on the cheek.

'You are lovely — both of you! — but no thanks. I'll call if I need help.'

Charles and Sally watch her diminutive form pushing through the partygoers. Sally holds up crossed fingers.

It is almost an hour before they see Maria again. She enters the lounge, her eyes puffy and bloodshot. Sally goes straight to her.

'No, it's okay,' assures Maria. 'I'm just sad. Dad's gone.'

'How did it go?' Sally asks, reaching for Maria's hand.

'Better than I expected. I'm sad because he's going and I won't see him for a while, that's all. But he's given me his blessing, more or less.'

Charles arrives, having heard the last comment. 'More or less? Does that mean he'll help support you?'

'He says he will. An allowance, for the moment, to get me going. Not enough for London rent, though,' she laughs.

'What about your place at Shepherd's Bush?' asks Charles.

'I've got to vacate by the end of next month. Guy — its proper tenant — is returning.'

Charles looks at Sally and she nods immediately.

'Fine. We'd like you to move back here,' he says. 'You can pay what you can afford.'

Maria looks from Charles to Sally and back again, a smile breaking across her face. 'Honestly?'

'Yes!' say Charles and Sally in unison.

'Or you can sing for your supper,' suggests Charles.

Maria does a little skip of joy and pulls Charles and Sally into a three-way hug. 'Thank you! Thank you!' she says, as she starts crying again.

Charles looks over the head of his ex-pupil at the crowd of happy people in his home. Some are dancing, some drinking and chatting in groups. Almost all are smiling. He is surrounded by people he likes — in many cases, loves. He frowns, struggling to identify the emotion he is experiencing.

'What?' asks Sally, looking up, still in his arms.

'I dunno. I'm worried about Mum and Dad of course, but … otherwise … I think this is happiness.'

'Oh, Charles! You twit. Of course it is! This is our motley, patchwork family, and you're home.'

HISTORICAL NOTE

As my regular readers will know, the books in this series are based on actual events and cases, and the criminals, coppers and lawyers I came across during my practice. This one is too, but it is more of a "pick and mix".

Frank Marshall is based quite closely on Frank Mitchell, the "Mad Axeman", who Ronnie and Reggie Kray helped to break out of HM Prison Dartmoor. Mitchell had spent eighteen of his thirty-two years in various forms of detention. He was immensely strong, vain and simple-minded, and idolised Ronnie Kray. Exactly why the Krays decided to spring him from Dartmoor has never been explained, but the theory of John Pearson (*The Profession of Violence*) is that it was a publicity stunt to demonstrate to the underworld how powerful the Krays were. Their problem, having freed him, was what to do with him. At the time, Reggie's pretty wife, Frances, was in hospital following an attempt at suicide and Ronnie was lost in one of his episodes of mental illness, when he saw plots and threats all around him and came up with some of his most bizarre schemes. Providing Mitchell with booze and sex worked for a while, but he was desperate to become Ronnie's right-hand man and best friend, and Ronnie was neither well enough nor interested enough in the Mad Axeman to meet him. In the end they decided to kill him; he had become an embarrassment and an inconvenience.

Ronnie's killing of George Cornell is more or less as I have described it, and was equally irrational. His justification at the time, that Cornell was a member of the rival Richardson gang, does not bear rational analysis. Shortly before the cold-blooded execution of Cornell, there was a shootout involving the Richardsons (in which, to Ronnie's chagrin, the Krays did not feature) and almost all of the gang were in custody, a spent force and no longer a threat to the twins.

By the middle of 1966 Swinging London was in full swing, and England had at last shaken off the grey shadows of the war. I was eleven at that time, just becoming aware of pop music, fashion and youth culture. Allen Ginsberg did come to London for an event at the Royal Albert Hall and offered to read *Howl* at smaller venues without charge. The tour was arranged by Barbara Rubin, and coincided with the showing of her infamous film, which has subsequently become an underground classic. They were friends with the members of the Velvet Underground, who played at just such a London house party as I have invented.

The story of Pickles, the little dog who found the stolen Jules Rimet World Cup Trophy, is exactly as I have told it. He was the most celebrated dog of the age, and was featured for months afterwards in newspapers, and "officiated" at the opening of various events.

As for the legal side of the story, Nipper Read was promoted to detective chief inspector and put in charge of cleaning up Soho ahead of the World Cup. It was only after this success that he was tasked with bringing down the Krays. However, the Krays' policy of corrupting and terrifying those around them was their established MO by then, so I feel justified in joining their story with that of the Sharpe family.

And of course, as everyone knows, on 30 July 1966 England won the World Cup. I hope I have conveyed some of the excitement, felt even by non-football fans, as the tournament progressed and England won a famous victory. I remember even my mother, totally uninterested in football in normal circumstances, jumping out of her armchair and cheering when England's third and fourth goals went in.

These were the principal ingredients I wanted to mix together with Charles's cases and his relationship with Sally, and I have taken a few minor liberties with the timelines and the events to produce a confection of my own. Please don't write to me to say that some of the events are not in the order in which they actually occurred, or that some of the characters are slightly different from their originals. I know. As I say to my friends who insist that all of Charles's flaws are my own, I'm writing fiction. Honest.

A NOTE TO THE READER

Dear Reader,

Nowadays, reviews by knowledgeable readers are essential to authors' success, so if you enjoyed the novel I shall be in your debt if you would spare the few seconds required to post a review on **Amazon** and **Goodreads**. I love hearing from readers, and you can connect with me through my **Facebook page**, via **Twitter** or through my **website**, where you can sign up for my newsletter.

I hope we'll meet again in the pages of the next Charles Holborne adventure.

Simon

www.simonmichael.uk

SAPERE
BOOKS

Printed in Great Britain
by Amazon

18264621R00220